Alexander McCall Smith was born in Zimbabwe and educated there and in Scotland. He is Professor of Medical Law at the University of Edinburgh and is a member of a number of national and international bodies concerned with bioethics. His books include works on medical law, criminal law and philosophy, as well as numerous books for children, collections of short stories, and novels. He has lectured at various universities in Africa, including in Botswana, where he lived for a time. He is married to an Edinburgh doctor, and has two daughters. *The No. 1 Ladies' Detective Agency* has received two Booker Judge's Special Recommendations.

Anthony Minghella and Sydney Pollack's company, Mirage, will be co-producing the *No. 1 Ladies' Detective Agency* TV series with New Africa Media Films.

Also by Alexander McCall Smith
The No. 1 Ladies' Detective Agency
Tears of the Giraffe
Morality for Beautiful Girls
The Kalahari Typing School for Men
The Full Cupboard of Life
The Sunday Philosophy Club

These titles are also available as
Time Warner AudioBooks

The 2½ Pillars of Wisdom

incorporating:

PORTUGUESE IRREGULAR VERBS

THE FINER POINTS OF SAUSAGE DOGS

AT THE VILLA OF REDUCED
CIRCUMSTANCES

ALEXANDER McCALL SMITH

ABACUS

This omnibus edition first published in Great Britain by Abacus in 2004

The 2½ Pillars of Wisdom copyright © Alexander McCall Smith 2004

Previously published separately:
Portuguese Irregular Verbs first published in
Great Britain by Polygon in 2003
Reprinted 2003 (twice)
Text copyright © Alexander McCall Smith 2003
Illustrations copyright © Iain McIntosh

The Finer Points of Sausage Dogs first published in Great Britain
by Polygon in 2003
Text copyright © Alexander McCall Smith 2003
Illustrations copyright © Iain McIntosh

At the Villa of Reduced Circumstances first published in Great Britain
by Polygon in 2003
Text copyright © Alexander McCall Smith 2003
Illustrations copyright © Iain McIntosh

The moral right of the author has been asserted.

A CIP catalogue record for this book
is available from the British Library.

ISBN 0 349 11850 7

Typeset by Palimpsest Book Production Limited, Polmont, Stirlingshire
Printed and bound in Great Britain by Clays Ltd, St Ives plc

Abacus
An imprint of
Time Warner Book Group UK
Brettenham House
Lancaster Place
London WC2E 7EN

www.twbg.co.uk

Von Iglefeld had heard the three of them described as the Three Pillars of Wisdom, but looking at Professor Dr Detlev Amadeus Unterholzer he came to the conclusion that perhaps The 2½ Pillars of Wisdom might be more appropriate. This, he thought, was rather funny.

The 2½ Pillars of Wisdom

Contents

PORTUGUESE
IRREGULAR VERBS

This is for
REINHARD ZIMMERMANN

Contents

The Principles of Tennis

Professor Dr Moritz-Maria Von Igelfeld often reflected on how fortunate he was to be exactly who he was, and nobody else. When one paused to think of who one might have been had the accident of birth not happened precisely as it did, then, well, one could be quite frankly *appalled*. Take his colleague Professor Dr Detlev Amadeus Unterholzer, for instance. Firstly, there was the name: to be called Detlev was a misfortune, but to add that ridiculous Mozartian pretension to it, and then to culminate in Unterholzer was to gild a turnip. But if one then considered Unterholzer's general circumstances, then Pelion was surely piled upon Ossa. Unterholzer had the double misfortune of coming from an obscure potato-growing area somewhere, a place completely without consequence, and of being burdened in this life with a large and inelegant nose. This, of course, was not something for which he could be blamed, but one might certainly criticise him, thought von Igelfeld, for carrying his nose in the way he did. A difficult nose, which can afflict anybody, may be kept in the background by a modest disposition of the head; Unterholzer, by contrast, thrust his nose forward shamelessly, as might an anteater, with the result that it was the first thing one saw when he appeared anywhere. It was exactly the wrong thing to do if one had a nose like that.

The von Igelfeld nose, by contrast, was entirely appropriate. It was not small, but then a small nose is perhaps as much of a misfortune as a large nose, lending the wearer an appearance of pettiness or even irrelevance. Von Igelfeld's nose tended slightly to the aquiline, which was completely becoming for the scion of so distinguished a family. The von Igelfeld name was an honourable one: *Igel* meant hedgehog in German, and von Igelfeld, therefore, was *hedgehogfield*, an irreproachable territorial reference that was reflected in the family coat of arms – a hedgehog recumbent upon a background of vert. Unterholzer, of course, might snigger at the hedgehog, but what could he do but snigger, given that he had no armorial claims, whatever his pretensions in that direction might be.

But even if von Igelfeld was relieved that he was not Unterholzer, then he had to admit to himself that he would have been perfectly happy to have been Professor Dr Dr (*honoris causa*) Florianus Prinzel, another colleague at the Institute of Romance Philology. Prinzel was a fine man and a considerable scholar, whom von Igelfeld had met when they were both students, and whom he had long unconditionally admired. Prinzel was the athlete-poet; von Igelfeld the scholar – well, scholar-scholar one would probably have to say. If von Igelfeld had been asked to stipulate a Platonic von Igelfeld, an ideal template for

6

all von Igelfelds, then he would have chosen Prinzel for this without the slightest hesitation.

Of the three professors, von Igelfeld was undoubtedly the most distinguished. He was the author of a seminal work on Romance philology, *Portuguese Irregular Verbs*, a work of such majesty that it dwarfed all other books in the field. It was a lengthy book of almost twelve hundred pages, and was the result of years of research into the etymology and vagaries of Portuguese verbs. It had been well received – not that there had ever been the slightest doubt about that – and indeed one reviewer had simply written, 'There is nothing more to be said on this subject. Nothing.' Von Igelfeld had taken this compliment in the spirit in which it had been intended, but there was in his view a great deal more to be said, largely by way of exposition of some of the more obscure or controversial points touched upon in the book, and for many years he continued to say it. This was mostly done at conferences, where von Igelfeld's papers on Portuguese irregular verbs were often the highlight of proceedings. Not that this eminence always bore the fruit that might be expected: unfortunately it was Prinzel, not von Igelfeld, who had received the honorary doctorate from the University of Palermo, and many people, including von Igelfeld, thought that this might be a case of mistaken identity. After all, from the viewpoint of the fairly diminutive Sicilian professors who bestowed the honour, three tall Germans might have been difficult to tell apart. These doubts, however, were never aired, as that would have been a breach of civility and a threat to the friendship. But just as the doubts were never mentioned, neither was the honorary doctorate.

At the Annual Congress of Romance Philology in Zürich, the three professors decided to stay in a small village on the edge of the lake. There was an excellent train which took them into the city each morning for the meeting, and in the evening they could even return by the regular boat, which called at the jetty no more than five minutes from the hotel. It was altogether a much more satisfactory arrangement than staying in Zürich itself, surrounded by banks and expensive watch shops. As von Igelfeld remarked to the others: 'Have you noticed how Zürich ticks? *Klummit, klummit, ding!* I could never sleep in such a town.'

The Hotel Carl-Gustav, in which the three professors stayed, was a large old-fashioned establishment, much favoured by families from Zürich who wanted to get away, but not too far away. Anxious bankers, into whose very bones the Swiss work ethic had penetrated, stayed there for their holidays. It was highly convenient for them, as they could tell their wives they were going for a walk in the hotel grounds and then slip off to the railway station and be in their offices in Zürich within twenty minutes. They could then return two hours later, to pretend that they had been in the woods or at the lakeside; whereas in reality they had been accepting deposits and discounting bills of exchange. In this way, certain Zürich financiers had acquired the reputation of never going on holiday at all, which filled their rivals with feelings of dread and guilt.

Prinzel had arrived first, and taken the best room, the one with the uninterrupted view of the lake. He had felt slightly uneasy about this, as it was a room which should really have gone to von Igelfeld, who always got the best of everything on the strength of *Portuguese Irregular Verbs*. For this reason Prinzel was careful not to mention the view and contrived to keep von Igelfeld out of his room so he could not see it for himself. Unterholzer, who always got the worst of what was on offer, had a slightly gloomy room at the side of the hotel, above the dining room, and his view was that of the hotel tennis court.

'I look out onto the tennis court,' he announced one evening as the three gathered for a glass of mineral water on the hotel terrace.

'Ah!' said von Igelfeld. 'And have you seen people playing on this tennis court?'

'I saw four Italian guests using it,' said Prinzel. 'They played a very energetic game until one of them appeared to have a heart attack and they stopped.'

The three professors contemplated this remarkable story for a few moments. Even here, in these perfect surroundings, where everything was so safe, so assured, mortality could not be kept at bay. The Swiss could guarantee everything, could co-ordinate anything – but ultimately mortality was no respecter of timetables.

Then Prinzel had an idea. Tennis did not look too difficult; the long summer evening stretched out before them, and the court, since the sudden departure of the Italians, was empty.

'We could, perhaps, have a game of tennis ourselves,' he suggested.

The others looked at him.

'I've never played,' said von Igelfeld.

'Nor I,' said Unterholzer. 'Chess, yes. Tennis, no.'

'But that's no reason not to play,' von Igelfeld added quickly. 'Tennis, like any activity, can be mastered if one knows the principles behind it. In that respect it must be like language. The understanding of simple rules produces an understanding of a language. What could be simpler?'

Unterholzer and Prinzel agreed, and Prinzel was despatched to speak to the manager of the hotel to find out whether tennis equipment, and a book of the rules of tennis, could be borrowed. The manager was somewhat surprised at the request for the book, but in an old hotel most things can be found and he eventually came up with an ancient dog-eared handbook from the games cupboard. This was *The Rules of Lawn Tennis* by Captain Geoffrey Pembleton BA (Cantab.), tennis Blue, sometime county champion of Cambridgeshire; and published in 1923, *before the tie-breaker was invented*.

Armed with Pembleton's treatise, described by von Igelfeld, to the amusement of the others, as 'this great work of Cambridge scholarship', the three professors strode confidently onto the court. Captain Pembleton had thoughtfully included several chapters describing tennis technique, and here all the major strokes were illustrated with little dotted diagrams showing the movement of the arms and the disposition of the body.

It took no more than ten minutes for von Igelfeld and Prinzel to feel sufficiently confident to begin a game. Unterholzer sat on a chair at the end of the net, and declared himself the umpire. The first service, naturally, was taken by von Igelfeld, who raised his racquet in the air as recommended by Captain Pembleton, and hit the ball in the direction of Prinzel.

The tennis service is not a simple matter, and unfortunately von Igelfeld did not manage to get any of his serves over the net. Everything was a double fault.

'Love 15; Love 30; Love 40; Game to Professor Dr Prinzel!' called out Unterholzer. 'Professor Dr Prinzel to serve!'

Prinzel, who had been waiting patiently to return von Igelfeld's serve, his feet positioned in exactly the way advised by Captain Pembleton, now quickly consulted the book to refresh his memory. Then, throwing the tennis ball high into the air, he brought his racquet down with convincing force and drove the ball into the net.

11

Undeterred, he tried again, and again after that, but the score remained obstinately one-sided.

'Love 15; Love 30; Love 40; Game to Professor Dr von Igelfeld!' Unterholzer intoned. 'Professor Dr von Igelfeld to serve!'

And so it continued, as the number of games mounted up. Neither player ever succeeded in winning a game other than by the default of the server. At several points the ball managed to get across the net, and on one or two occasions it was even returned; but this was never enough to result in the server's winning a game. Unterholzer continued to call out the score and attracted an occasional sharp glance from von Igelfeld, who eventually suggested that the *Rules of Tennis* be consulted to see who should win in such circumstances.

Unfortunately there appeared to be no answer. Captain Pembleton merely said that after six games had been won by one player this was a victory – provided that such a player was at least two games ahead of his opponent. If he was not in such a position, then the match must continue until such a lead was established. *The problem with this, though, was that van Igelfeld and Prinzel, never winning a service, could never be more than one game ahead of each other.*

This awkward, seemingly irresoluble difficulty seemed to all of them to be a gross flaw in the theoretical structure of the game.

'This is quite ridiculous,' snorted von Igelfeld. 'A game must have a winner – everybody knows that – and yet this . . . this *stupid* book makes no provision for *moderate* players like ourselves!'

'I agree,' said Prinzel, tossing down his racquet. 'Unterholzer, what about you?'

'I'm not interested in playing such a flawed game,' said Unterholzer, with a dismissive gesture towards *The Rules of Lawn Tennis*. 'So much for Cambridge!'

They trooped off the tennis court, not noticing the faces draw back rapidly from the windows. Rarely had the Hotel Carl-Gustav provided such entertainment for its guests.

'Well,' said Prinzel. 'I'm rather hot after all that sport. I could do with a swim.'

'A good idea,' said von Igelfeld. 'Perhaps we should do that.'

'Do you swim?' asked Unterholzer, rather surprised by the sudden burst of physical activity.

'Not in practice,' said von Igelfeld. 'But it has never looked difficult to me. One merely extends the arms in the appropriate motion and then retracts them, thereby propelling the body through the water.'

'That's quite correct,' said Prinzel. 'I've seen it done many times. In fact, this morning some of the other guests were doing it from the hotel jetty. We could borrow swimming costumes from the manager.'

'Then let's all go and swim,' said von Igelfeld, enthusiastically. 'Dinner's not for another hour or so, and it would refresh us all,' adding, with a glance at Unterholzer, 'players and otherwise.'

The waters were cool and inviting. Out on the lake, the elegant white yachts dipped their tall sails in the breeze from the mountains. From where they stood on the jetty, the three professors could, by craning their necks, see the point where Jung in his study had pondered our collective dreams. As von Igelfeld had pointed out, swimming was simple, in theory.

Inside the Hotel Carl-Gustav, the watching guests waited, breathless in their anticipation.

Duels, and How to Fight Them

Heidelberg and youth! *Ach, die Jugendzeit*! When he was a student, von Igelfeld lodged in Heidelberg with Frau Ilse Krantzenhauf, a landlady of the old school. Her precise age was a matter of speculation among generations of students, but she showed no signs of retiring, and on their graduation from the university her lodgers frequently promised to send their own sons to her when the next generation's time came. For her part, Frau Krantzenhauf solemnly promised to reserve a room for twenty or so years hence. In many cases this promise was called upon, and a fresh-faced boy from a Gymnasium in Hanover, or Hamburg, or Regensburg would find himself received by his father's old landlady and led to the very room which his father had occupied, to sit at the same desk and look out at the same view.

Three other students lodged with Frau Krantzenhauf during von Igelfeld's days in Heidelberg. Two of these were regarded by von Igelfeld as being of no interest, and only barely to be tolerated. Dorflinger was a tall, bony youth from a farm near Munich, while Giesbach, his ponderous friend, was as rotund as Dorflinger was thin. They both studied engineering, knew next to no Latin, and spent every evening in a beer hall. Von Igelfeld exchanged a few words with them and then retreated into silence. There was nothing more to say to people like that – nothing.

Far more congenial in von Igelfeld's view was a young student of philology from Freiburg, Florianus Prinzel. Prinzel was tall, had dark wavy hair, and invariably fixed those to whom he spoke with a direct, honest look. Von Igelfeld, whose notions of friendship were those of nineteenth-century romanticism, in which young men aspired to noble friendships, thought that here, at last, was one whose qualities he could respect. He, von Igelfeld, the aesthete-scholar, could befriend the athlete-hero, Prinzel. He could see it already; Prinzel streaking past his hopelessly outclassed competitors, leaping over hurdles, his brow high in the wind; Prinzel's manly chest breasting the finishing tape; Prinzel receiving the fencing trophy and handing it over to von Igelfeld to hold while he removed his gauntlets. It was to be the sort of friendship which had been commonplace fifty years before, in military academies and such places, but which had been irretrievably ruined by the reductionist insights of Vienna.

Unfortunately, von Igelfeld's vision of the relationship was fatally flawed. Although Prinzel was tall and strong, and perhaps should have been an athlete, he had not the slightest interest in athletic matters. Prinzel was, in fact, every bit as intellectual and bookish as was von Igelfeld, and not at all capable of being a hero on, or indeed off, the field. He could not run very fast; he had no interest in rowing; and he regarded ball games as absurd.

16

Undeterred, von Igelfeld decided that even if Prinzel were to prove slow to realise his natural prowess, he could be made to appreciate just how fundamentally he had mistaken his destiny. Von Igelfeld began to tell others of Prinzel's sporting instincts and abilities.

'My friend, Prinzel,' he would say, 'is very good at games. I'm not really so accomplished at that sort of thing myself, but you should see him. A consummate athlete!'

Others believed this, and soon Prinzel had a reputation of being a great sportsman. And if anybody thought it strange that they should never have seen Prinzel on the field, then they reasoned that this must be because he did not deign to do much with the very inferior competition which he found in Heidelberg.

'Is it true that Prinzel represented Germany somewhere at something or other?' von Igelfeld was asked from time to time.

'Yes, it's quite true,' he answered, not deliberately seeking to tell a lie, but replying in this way because he had persuaded himself that Prinzel must indeed be the holder of records of which he was silent. Or, if he were not the holder, then the records could certainly be his for the asking if only he would bother to win them.

It may all have remained at the level of fantasy, harmless enough, even if somewhat irritating for Prinzel, had it not been for von Igelfeld's sudden conviction that Prinzel could be a fine swordsman, were he to try the sport. Unprotected fencing amongst students was then strongly discouraged, even if there had been a time when it had flourished greatly in Heidelberg. In spite of this twentieth-century squeamishness, a small group of students obstinately adhered to the view that the possession of a small duelling scar on the cheek made an important statement about one's values, and was also of incidental value in later advancement in one's career. It was widely suspected that a man with a scar would always give a job to another man with a scar, even if there was a stronger, unscarred candidate. Of course, this mock duelling was carried out in a spirit of fun, and nobody was meant to be seriously hurt, but the flashing of swords and the graceful thrusts and parries of those unencumbered by clumsy protective jackets was much appreciated by the more reactionary students. These students were unexcited by the heady messages from Paris that made German universities in the nineteen-sixties and -seventies such hotbeds of radicalism and ferment.

The students who believed in fencing were naturally attracted to von Igelfeld. Not only was it his name that appealed to them, being redolent of an earlier era and lost territories, it was the knowledge of the estate in Austria and the close connection which von Igelfeld enjoyed with noble Bavarian families. For these reasons, von Igelfeld had been invited to take a glass of wine with the fencing faction.

The members of this group immediately realised that von Igelfeld, for all his background, was an unredeemed intellectual and therefore quite unsuited to any further involvement with their own, rather dark, social activities. At the same time, his background deserved respect and so they listened attentively to him as he spoke to them about his interest in the arid wastes of medieval Latin verse.

'And this Prinzel character,' one of them said. 'We see you about with him a great deal. Tell us something about him.'

'Prinzel's an amazing athlete,' von Igelfeld said. 'He's

one of those people who's just naturally good at sports.'

This remark was met with silence. Several glances were exchanged.

'Is he a swordsman?' asked a rather heavily scarred young man, casually.

'He's a fine swordsman,' said von Igelfeld enthusiastically. 'In fact, I'm sure he'd be honoured to meet any of you gentlemen. At any time!'

Further glances were exchanged, unnoticed by von Igelfeld, who, draining his third glass of wine, was becoming slightly drunk.

'I'm most interested to hear that,' said the bearer of the scars. 'Could you tell him that I shall meet him next Friday evening at a place to be notified? Just for a bit of fun.'

'Of course,' said von Igelfeld, expansively. 'In fact, I can accept on his behalf, right now. We'll be there!'

Glasses were raised in a toast, and the conversation then moved on to the arrival in Heidelberg of two girls from Berlin whose interests were much to the taste of the group and whose company was being sought that Friday night, after the duel.

Prinzel was dismayed.

'You had no right to do that!' he protested, his voice raised in uncharacteristic anger. 'You had no right at all!'

Von Igelfeld gazed at his friend. So complete was his admiration for Prinzel, so utter his belief in the nobility of Prinzel's character, that he could not entertain the thought that the other might object to what was being proposed for him. It was as if he did not hear him.

'But it's all arranged,' went on von Igelfeld. 'And I shall

be your second.' He added: 'That's the person who stands by, you know. He carries the towel.'

'For the blood?' snapped Prinzel. 'To mop up the blood?'

Von Igelfeld laughed dismissively. 'There's no need for blood,' he said. 'Blood hardly comes into it. You're not going to kill one another – this is merely a bit of sport!'

Prinzel waved his hands about in exasperation. 'I simply can't understand you,' he shouted. 'You seem to have a completely false notion of my character. I'm a scholar, do you understand? *I am not an athlete. I am not a hero.* I have absolutely no interest in fencing, none at all! I've never done it.'

Von Igelfeld appeared momentarily nonplussed.

'Never?' he said.

'Never!' cried Prinzel. 'Let me repeat myself. I am a scholar!'

Von Igelfeld now seemed to recover his composure.

'Scholars sometimes engage in martial pursuits,' he asserted. 'There are many precedents for this. And swordmanship is a traditional matter of honour at universities. We all know that. Why set your face against our heritage?'

Prinzel shook his head. For a few moments he was silent, as if at a loss for words. Then he spoke, in a voice which was weak with defeat.

'Who are these types?' he asked. 'How did you meet them?'

Noting his friend's tone of acceptance, von Igelfeld laid a hand on his shoulder, already the reassuring second.

'They are a group of very agreeable characters,' he said. 'They have some sort of *Korps*, in which they drink wine and talk about various matters. They asked to meet me because they thought I was old-fashioned.'

20

Von Igelfeld laughed at the absurdity of the notion. They would see next Friday just what sort of friends he had! Old-fashioned indeed!

Prinzel sighed.

'I suppose I have no alternative,' he said. 'You seem to have committed me.'

Von Igelfeld patted his friend's shoulder again.

'Don't you worry,' he said. 'It'll be a very exciting evening. You'll see.' The place chosen for the match was a field which lay behind an inn on the outskirts of the city. The field was ringed by trees, which gave it a privacy which had been much appreciated by those who over the years had used it for clandestine purposes of one sort or another. When von Igelfeld and Prinzel arrived, they thought at first that there was nobody there, and for a brief joyous moment Prinzel imagined that the whole idea had been a joke played on von Igelfeld. This made him smile with relief, a reaction which von Igelfeld interpreted as one of confidence.

'Of course you're going to win,' he said excitedly. 'And afterwards we shall all have a grand celebration at the inn.'

Then, from out of the shadows, there stepped four members of the *Korps*. They looked perfectly sinister, clad in capes of some sort, with long suitcases in which the swords were concealed.

'Look, there they are!' shouted von Igelfeld excitedly. 'Hallo there, everybody! Here we are!'

Prinzel froze. Had von Igelfeld had the eyes to see, he would have been presented with a picture of a man facing a firing squad. Prinzel's face was white, his eyes wide with horror, his brow glistening with beads of sweat.

The scarred student stepped forward and shook von Igelfeld's hand. Then he crossed to Prinzel, bowed and introduced himself.

'This is a fine evening for sport,' he said. Gesturing to the weapons, he invited Prinzel to make his choice.

'We shall have six rounds of three minutes each,' said one of the *Korps*. 'When a gentleman draws blood, the contest shall stop.'

Von Igelfeld nodded eagerly.

'That's correct,' he said. 'That's how we do it.'

Prinzel glanced at his friend.

'How do you know?' he hissed angrily. 'If you know so much about this, why don't you fight instead of me?'

'I fight?' said von Igelfeld, astonished. 'That's quite out of the question. I would lose, I'm afraid.'

Prinzel muttered something which von Igelfeld did not hear. It was too late now, anyway, as his opponent had now taken his position and everybody else was looking expectantly at Prinzel.

There was a flash of swords. Prinzel thrust forward and parried his opponent's strike. Then his own sword shot forward and steel met steel with a sharp metallic sound. Von Igelfeld gave a start.

Then it was stand-off again. Prinzel watched warily as his opponent began to move around him, sword raised almost to the lips, as if in salute. Then, so rapidly and daintily, as if to be invisible, the other's sword cut through the air with a whistling sound and, with almost surgical grace, sliced off the very tip of Prinzel's nose.

Prinzel stood quite still. Then, with a low moan, he dropped his sword and went down onto his hands and knees, as if searching for his severed flesh. For a few moments von Igelfeld was paralysed, unable to believe what he had seen. But then, remembering his duties as second, he shot forward, picked up the tip of the nose, a tiny, crumpled thing, and pressed it against his friend's face, as if to stick it back on.

Slowly Prinzel rose to his feet. There was not much blood – at least there was not as much as one might have expected – and he was able to maintain an aloof dignity.

'Take me to the hospital,' he said out of the corner of his mouth. 'And keep your hand where it is.'

Prinzel's opponent watched impassively.

'Well fought!' he said. 'You almost had me at the beginning.' Then, almost as an afterthought: 'Don't worry about that nick. It always seems so much worse than it really is. Imagine what a distinguished scar you will have! Bang in the middle of your face – can't be missed!'

The landlord of the inn called an ambulance, complaining all the while about the inconvenience to which students put him.

'They're always up to no good,' he grumbled, peering at Prinzel. 'I see you've been fencing. Would you believe it? This is the Federal Republic of Germany, you know, not Weimar. And we're meant to be in the second half of the twentieth century.'

Von Igelfeld looked at him scornfully.

'You don't even know what this is all about,' he said. 'It's a student matter; nothing to do with you. Nothing at all.'

It was Prinzel's misfortune to be attended at the hospital by a doctor who was drunk. Von Igelfeld thought that he could smell the fumes of whisky emanating from behind the surgical mask, but said nothing, reckoning it might be ether, or it might indeed be whisky, but used for medicinal purposes. Prinzel by now had closed his eyes, and was determined to hear, see and smell nothing. He felt von Igelfeld release the pressure on his face, and he felt the doctor's fumbling fingers. He felt a cold swab on his exposed arm, and then the prick of an injection. And after that, there was only numbness.

The drunken doctor examined the severed tip and realised that all that was required were several well-placed stitches. These he inserted rapidly. Then he stood back, admired his handiwork, and asked a nurse to apply a dressing. It had been a simple procedure, and there was no doubt but that the nose would heal up well within a few weeks. There would be a scar, of course, but that's what these young men wanted after all.

'You've made a very good recovery,' von Igelfeld said to Prinzel a fortnight later. 'You can hardly see the scar.'

Prinzel gazed at himself in the mirror. It was all very well for von Igelfeld to congratulate him on his recovery, but there was still something wrong. His nose looked different, somehow, although he could not decide exactly why this should be so.

Von Igelfeld had also studied Prinzel's nose and had come to a dreadful conclusion. The drunken doctor had sewn the tip on *upside down*. Of course he could not tell Prinzel that, as such knowledge could be devastating – to anyone.

'I shall remain silent,' thought von Igelfeld. 'In time he'll become accustomed to it, and that'll be the end of the matter.'

For Prinzel there was one consolation. Von Igelfeld no longer talked about his sporting prowess, and whenever references were made by others to such matters as fencing, or even noses, von Igelfeld immediately changed the subject.

Early Irish Pornography

In the final years of his doctoral studies it had been von Igelfeld's dream to be invited to serve as assistant to one of the world's greatest authorities on Early Irish. This language, so complicated and arcane that there was considerable doubt as to whether anyone ever actually spoke it, had attracted the attention of German philologists from the late-nineteenth century onwards. The great Professor Siegfried Ehrenwalt of Berlin, founder of the *Review of Celtic Philology*, had devoted his life to the reconstruction of the syntactical rules of the language, and he had been followed by a long line of philologists, the latest of whom was Professor Dr Dr Dr Dieter Vogelsang. It was with Vogelsang that von Igelfeld wished to work, and when the call at last came, he was overjoyed.

'I couldn't have hoped for a better start to my career,' he confided in Prinzel. 'Vogelsang knows more about past anterior verbs in Early Irish than anybody else in the world.'

'More than anyone in Ireland?' asked Prinzel dubiously.

'Surely they have their own institutes in Dublin?'

Von Igelfeld shook his head. 'Nobody in Ireland knows anything about Early Irish. This is a well-established fact.'

Prinzel was not convinced, but did not allow his doubt to diminish his friend's delight in his first post. He himself was still waiting. He had written to several institutes in Germany and Switzerland, but had received few encouraging replies. He could continue to study, of course, and complete another doctorate after the one on which he was currently engaged, but there would come a point at which without an assistant-ship he would seriously have to reconsider his academic career.

The post as assistant to Professor Dr Vogelsang involved a move to Munich. Von Igelfeld acquired lodgings in the house of Frau Elvira Hugendubel, the widow of the retired lawyer and dachshund breeder, Aloys Hugendubel. Dr Hugendubel had been the author of *Einführung in die Grundlagen des Bayerischen Bienenrechtes*, and Frau Hugendubel felt, as a result, that she was a part of the greater intellectual life. The presence of an academic lodger provided reassurance of this, as well as providing the widow with something to do.

Von Igelfeld settled happily into his new life. Each morning he would walk the three miles to Vogelsang's institute, arriving at exactly nine-fifteen and leaving in the evening at six o'clock. The hours in between were spent checking Vogelsang's references, searching out articles in the dustier corners of the library, and preparing tables of adjectives. It was the lowest form of work in the academic hierarchy, made all the more difficult by the tendency of Professor Vogelsang to publish papers based almost entirely on von Igelfeld's work, but under the Vogelsang name and with

27

no mention made of von Igelfeld's contribution. In one case – which eventually prompted von Igelfeld to protest (in the gentlest, most indirect terms) – Vogelsang took a paper which von Igelfeld asked him to read and immediately published it under his *own name*. So brazen was this conduct that von Igelfeld felt moved to draw his superior's attention to the fact that he had been hoping to submit the paper to a learned journal himself.

'I can't see why you are objecting,' said Vogelsang haughtily. 'The paper will achieve a far wider readership under my name than under the name of an unknown. Surely these scholarly considerations are more important than mere personal vanity?'

As he often did, Vogelsang had managed to shift the grounds of argument to make von Igelfeld feel guilty for making a perfectly reasonable point. It was a technique which von Igelfeld had himself used on many occasions, but which he was to perfect in the year of his assistantship with Professor Vogelsang.

Frau Hugendubel, of course, provided copious amounts of sympathy.

'Young scholars have a difficult time,' she mused. 'Herr Dr Hugendubel never treated his young assistants with anything but the greatest courtesy. Herr Dr Hugendubel gave them books and encouraged them in every way. He was a very kind man.'

There were, of course, some benefits to which von Igelfeld was able to look forward. At the beginning of his assistantship, Vogelsang had alluded to a field trip to Ireland at some future date, and had implied that von Igelfeld could expect to accompany him. For some months, nothing more was said of this until the day when Vogelsang announced that they would be leaving in a fortnight's time and told von Igelfeld to arrange the tickets.

Frau Hugendubel insisted on packing von Igelfeld's suitcase herself. She starched his collars particularly carefully, folded his night-shirts and ironed the creases. A pile of freshly laundered handkerchiefs was tucked into a corner of the case and beside these she put a small jar of Bavarian honey for her lodger's breakfast toast.

They travelled by train to St Malo, where they caught the night steamer to Cork. Vogelsang and von Igelfeld had been allocated a shared cabin, an arrangement over which Vogelsang protested vociferously until von Igelfeld offered to sit up all night on the deck. By the time the coast of Ireland hove into sight through the morning mist, von Igelfeld was yawning and bleary-eyed; Vogelsang, fresh from his comfortable berth, greeted him cheerfully but berated him over his lack of enthusiasm for the sight of the Irish coast.

'Look,' he said. 'There, before us, is the blessed coast of Ireland, the island of saints. Can you not manage more than a yawn?'

They docked, and the German party made its way down the gangway of the steamer, into the welcoming arms of Dr Patrick Fitzcarron O'Leary, formerly of the Advanced Technical College, Limerick, and now Reader in Irish in the University College of Cork. He and Vogelsang knew one another well, and addressed one another as old friends. Then, turning to von Igelfeld, Vogelsang introduced his assistant.

'My assistant – Dr Moritz-Maria von Igelfeld.'

'Good heavens!' said Patrick Fitzcarron O'Leary

opaquely, seizing von Igelfeld's hand. 'How are you then, Maria old chap?'

Von Igelfeld blanched. Maria? What a strange way to address somebody whom one had only just met. Did the Irish use the second Christian name in such circumstances? If that indeed was the custom, then how should he address O'Leary? Would it be rude to call him Dr O'Leary, which seemed the most correct thing to do?

For a few moments, von Igelfeld was utterly perplexed. So concerned was he to follow correct usage at all times, and in all places (even in Ireland), that it seemed appalling to him that he should run the risk of committing a social solecism virtually the moment he set foot on Irish soil. He looked to Vogelsang for assistance, but his superior just stared back at him blandly, and then looked pointedly at the suit-cases, which he was clearly expecting von Igelfeld to carry.

'Very well,' mumbled von Igelfeld. Adding, in his confusion, 'Not bad, in fact.'

'Good fellow,' said O'Leary. 'Absolutely. Good for you.'

O'Leary now seized both suitcases and led the visitors off to a somewhat battered car which he had parked up against the edge of the quay. Then, with von Igelfeld in the back seat and Vogelsang sitting beside the Irishman, they drove off erratically in the direction of the red-brick guest house in which the two visitors were to spend their first night in Ireland. It was all very strange to von Igelfeld, who had never before been further than France and Italy. Everything was so *here and there*; so well loved and used; so lived-in. There were men with caps, standing on the street corners, doing nothing; there were women with jugs propped up in their doorways; there were orange cats prowling on the top of walls; churches with red walls and white marble lintels, and white religious statuary.

The next two days were spent largely in the company of O'Leary. He showed his visitors the university; he took them to lunch in hotels where the proprietors greeted him by name and appeared to make a great fuss of him; and he spent long hours locked in his study with Vogelsang – meetings to which von Igelfeld was not admitted. On these occasions, von Igelfeld walked through the streets of Cork, marvelling at the softness of the light on the warm brick buildings, sniffing at the heavy, languid air, savouring the feel of Ireland. Occasionally, small groups of boys followed him on these walks, calling out to the tall German in a language which von Igelfeld did not understand, but which he assumed to be the local dialect of English. Once, on a bridge, a woman threw a stone at him, and then crossed herself vigorously, but this occurrence did not trouble von Igelfeld in the slightest, as the stone missed, making a satisfactory plop in the water below.

That evening, O'Leary forsook Vogelsang, who wanted to retire early, and took von Igelfeld to a bar. It was a splendid, mirrored room, in which men in dark, shapeless suits leaned against the counter drinking black stout.

The barman greeted O'Leary with the same warmth that seemed to herald his every appearance in Cork.

'Now then, Paddy,' said the white-aproned tender. 'What is it this evening for you and your Teutonic friend over there.'

Paddy! thought von Igelfeld. That must be the name to use, and he replied to O'Leary's offer of a drink: 'A beer, if you don't mind, Paddy!'

The drinks poured, O'Leary guided von Igelfeld towards a section of the bar, where two of the men in dark suits were standing.

'Fitz, my friend,' said one of the men, slapping O'Leary on the back. 'Sure it's yourself, so it is!'

Fitz! thought von Igelfeld. Perhaps this was an alternative name which close friends used, just as his childhood friends had called him Morri, until they had put behind them the childish things. If that were the case, then he should avoid it, as its use would claim an intimacy which did not exist and the Irishman would think him rude. But just as this was resolved, the other man said:

'Pat, if it isn't you, then who is it?'

Von Igelfeld frowned. Here was another name – obviously a contraction of Patrick. That was plain enough, but what puzzled him was the choice of names. Was it an entirely free one? Could Pat become Paddy if one felt like it? Or could Fitzcarron become Fitz if a change seemed desirable? And what about O'Leary – was that ever used? He gazed down upon the white head to the glass of dark beer and wondered whether it was wise to leave the certainties of home. He had read that to travel is to expose oneself to all sorts of vulnerabilities, and surely this was true.

'Now then, von,' said O'Leary cheerfully. 'Tell me about yourself. You seem a fairly tall sort of person.'

The drinking companions nodded their heads in agreement, looking up at von Igelfeld with a mixture of awe and amusement.

'He is that,' said one, gravely. 'You're right there, O.'

Von Igelfeld put down his glass. O? Was that yet another

contraction? Really, there was something very strange – and unsettling – about Ireland.

The two days in Cork ended with a trip to the railway station in O'Leary's old car and prolonged, emotional farewells on the platform. O'Leary slapped von Igelfeld on the back several times, to his considerable discomfort, while Vogelsang, with whom he had only shaken hands, looked on in undisguised amusement. Then their train drew out and they passed from the warm warren of red brick into the lush greenness of the countryside. Hedgerow-lined fields, low, folding hills; stone houses, white-washed, red-doored; lanes that wandered off into tight valleys; a blue curtain of sky that would without warning turn white, releasing sifting veils of rain; a sudden sight of children on a wall, tousle-haired, bare-legged, waving at the train; thus were they drawn deep into Ireland.

And then, in the distance, the hills appeared. The soft slopes merged into blue expanses, and the skies opened to wide canvases of cloud. The houses shrank, transformed themselves into clusters of tiny stone dwellings; and beyond was the sea, silver-blue, stretching out towards the pale, glowing horizon, and America.

'This is where Irish is spoken,' pronounced Vogelsang sacramentally. 'In these farmhouses, the verbs, the nouns, the differentiated adjectives – they're all still there.'

Von Igelfeld looked out of the window. Little droplets of rain coursed across the glass and made the countryside quiver. He had been thinking of how landscape moulds a language. It was impossible to imagine these hills giving forth anything but the soft syllables of Irish, just as only certain forms of German could be spoken on the high crags of Europe; or

Dutch in the muddy, guttural, phlegmish lowlands. How sad it was that the language had been so largely lost; that it should survive only in these small pockets of the countryside. This was happening everywhere. The crudities of the modern world were simplifying or even destroying linguistic subtleties. Irregular verbs were becoming regular, the imperfect subjunctive was becoming the present subjunctive or, more frequently, disappearing altogether. Where previously there might have been four adjectives to describe a favoured hill, or the scent of new-mown hay, or the action of threading the warp of a loom, now there would only be one, or none. And as we lost the words, von Igelfeld thought, we lost the texture of the world that went with them.

It was at this moment, as the train drew into the small, apparently deserted station at which the two passengers were due to alight, that von Igelfeld realised what his life's work would be. He would do everything in his power to stop the process of linguistic debasement, and he would pick, as his target, the irregular verb. This moment, then, was the germ of that great work, *Portuguese Irregular Verbs*.

The station was not deserted. An ancient station master, surprised at the arrival of passengers, emerged from a green wooden building and agreed to take them to the small hotel which was to be found at the nearby loughside. There they settled in, the only guests, and ate a meal, while a succession of people passed by the dining room window, affecting nonchalance, and then staring in hard at the two Germans.

The next day was the first working day of the field trip. Vogelsang had been told of the existence of an extremely old man who lived on a nearby hillside and who spoke a version of Irish which was considered by all to be exceptionally

34

archaic. If there were to be any vestiges of Old Irish extant, then in the words used by this old man might such linguistic remnants be found.

'You can certainly call on old Sean,' said the hotel proprietor. 'But I can't guarantee your reception. He may speak interesting Irish, but he's an extremely unpleasant, smelly old man. Not even the priest dares go up there, and that's saying something in these parts.'

Undaunted, Vogelsang led the way up the narrow, unused track that led to Sean's cottage. At last they reached it and, carefully negotiating the ramble of surrounding pigsties, they approached the front door.

Vogelsang knocked loudly, and then called out (in Old Irish): 'We are here, Sean. I am Professor Vogelsang from Germany. And this young man is my assistant.'

There was silence from within the cottage. Vogelsang knocked again, louder now, and this time elicited a response. A frowning, weather-beaten face, caked with dirt, appeared at the window and gesticulated in an unfriendly fashion. Vogelsang bent down and put his face close to the window so that his nose was barely a few inches from Sean, but separated by a pane of clouded glass.

'Good morning, Sean,' said Vogelsang. 'We have come to talk to you.'

Sean appeared enraged. Shouting now, he hurled words out at the visiting philologists, shaking both fists in Vogelsang's face.

'Quick,' said Vogelsang, momentarily turning to von Igelfeld. 'Transcribe everything he says. Do it phonetically.'

As Sean continued to hurl abuse at Vogelsang, von Igelfeld's pencil moved swiftly over the paper, noting everything that the cantankerous and malodorous farmer said. Vogelsang nodded all the while, hoping to encourage the Irishman to open the door, but only succeeding in further annoying him. At last, after almost three quarters of an hour, Vogelsang observed that the visit might come to an end, and with the echoing shouts of Sean following them down the hill, they returned to the hotel.

A further attempt to visit Sean was made the next day, and the day after that, but the visitors were never admitted. They did, however, collect a full volume of transcribed notes on what he shouted at them through the door, and this was analysed each evening by a delighted Vogelsang.

'There is some very rare material here,' he said, poring over von Igelfeld's phonetic notations. 'Look, that verb over there, which is used only when addressing a pig, was thought to have disappeared centuries ago.'

'And he used it when addressing us?' said von Igelfeld wryly.

'Of course,' snapped Vogelsang. 'Everything he says to us is, in fact, obscene. Everything you have recorded here is a swear word of the most vulgar nature. But very old. Very, very old!'

They spent a final day in the hotel, this time not attempting to visit Sean, but each engaging in whatever pursuit he wished. Von Igelfeld chose to explore the paths that wound around the lough. He took with him a sandwich lunch prepared for him by the hotel, and spent a contented day looking at the hills and watching the flights of water birds that rose out of the reeds on his approach. He met nobody until, at the very end of the day, he encountered Vogelsang coming in the

yēz: (n) "
gä"hn
-êlé púg̱ !
...-ee

opposite direction. Vogelsang looked furtive, as if he had been caught doing something illicit, and greeted von Igelfeld curtly and correctly, as one might greet a slight acquaintance on the street of a busy town. Von Igelfeld began to tell him of the wild swans he had seen: 'Four and twenty were there,' he began; but Vogelsang ignored him and he stopped.

The next day they returned to the railway station and boarded the train back to Cork. The mountains were now behind them, shrinking into a haze of blue. Von Igelfeld looked back wistfully, knowing, somehow, that he would never return. In Cork they only had a few hours to pass before the steamer sailed. These hours were filled by Patrick Fitzcarron O'Leary, who materialised from the railway station bar and was soon locked in earnest discussion with Vogelsang over the lists of words which had been obtained.

It was dark by the time they boarded the steamer. After they had been shown their cabins (to von Igelfeld's relief he had been allocated a berth) they both stood at the railings and looked down on the quay. It was raining, but only with that light, warm drizzle that seems always to embrace Ireland, and it did not deter them from standing bare-headed in the dampness. O'Leary had taken up position under the shelter of a crane, and he waved to them as the boat edged out from the quay. He continued to wave until they were out of the harbour, when he extracted a torch from his pocket and waved that. That was the last they saw of Ireland, a tiny pin-prick of light moving in the darkness, winking at them.

Back in Munich, von Igelfeld was greeted warmly by Frau Hugendubel and shown up to his spotlessly clean room. When she withdrew, he unpacked his suitcase, noticing the jar of honey, which he had not touched. This he put on a shelf for future use. Then he sat down and spread out on his desk the lists of words which he had transcribed during their encounters with Sean. Vogelsang wanted them arranged alphabetically and tabulated, with approximate German translations written opposite. Von Igelfeld began his task.

After an hour of work, von Igelfeld felt the desire to go out and have a cup of coffee in his favourite café nearby. He would buy a newspaper, read the Munich news, and then get back to his desk for further work. It would be a way of returning to Germany; his head, he feared, was still full of Ireland. He slipped out and walked briskly to the café.

A short time later, his half-read newspaper under his arm, he returned to the house and made his way upstairs. His door was open, and Frau Hugendubel stood in his room, be-aproned, clutching a feather duster.

'Dr von Igelfeld,' she said, her voice shaking with emotion. 'I must ask you to leave this house immediately.'

Von Igelfeld was astonished.

'To leave?' he stuttered. 'Do you mean to move out?'

Frau Hugendubel nodded.

'I would never have known you to be a . . .' she paused. 'A pornographer!'

Von Igelfeld saw her throw a frightened glance towards his desk and he knew at once what it was all about.

'Oh that!' he laughed. 'Those words . . .'

Frau Hugendubel cut him short.

'I do not wish to exchange one more word with you,' she said, her voice firmer now. 'I shall not ask you for the rent you owe me, but I shall be grateful if you vacate the room within two hours.'

She cast a further disappointed glance into the room, this time at the jar of unopened honey, and then, shuddering her way past her deeply wronged lodger, she disappeared down the stairs.

When he heard the next day of the misunderstanding and of von Igelfeld's plight, Vogelsang declined to intervene.

'It's most unfortunate,' he said. 'But there's nothing I can do. You should not have left obscene words on your desk.'

Von Igelfeld stared at Vogelsang. He knew now that Irish philology was a mistake and that it was time to move on. He would find another professor who would take him on as assistant, and his career would be launched afresh. Enquiries were made and letters were written, leading, at last, to an invitation from Professor Walter Schoeffer-Henschel to join him as his second assistant at the University of Wiesbaden. This was exactly what von Igelfeld wanted, and he accepted with alacrity. The air was filled with the scent of new possibilities.

Italian Matters

Ten years passed – just like that – pouf! By the time he was thirty-five, after a long period in the service of Schoeffer-Henschel, von Igelfeld had received a call to a chair and was safely established in the Institute. In the years that followed, and particularly after the publication of that great work, *Portuguese Irregular Verbs*, honour upon honour fell upon von Igelfeld's shoulders. These brought the rewards of recognition – the sense of *value* of one's work and the knowledge of pre-eminence in the subject. And it also brought frequent invitations to conferences, all of which seemed to be held in most agreeable places, often, to von Igelfeld's great pleasure, in Italy.

It had been a tedious day at the Comparative Philology Conference in Siena. Professor Alberto Morati, the host, had given his paper on Etruscan pronouns – for the fourth time. Many of the delegates were familiar with it: von Igelfeld had heard it before in Messina five years previously. He had then heard it again in Rome the following year, and had caught the very end of its final section in Montpelier. Prinzel had heard it too, in his case in Buenos Aires, and had found the pace of the argument and its ponderous conclusions quite soporific, even in such an exotic location.

But even if Morati were not enough, the chairman of the conference had called on that legend of the international philology network, Professor J. G. K. L. Singh, of Chandighar. As the great Indian philologist (author of *Terms of Ritual Abuse in the Creditor/Debtor Relationship in Village India*) ascended the platform, there emanated from the audience a strange sound; an inspiration of breath or a spontaneous communal sigh – it was difficult to tell which. Those delegates nearest the door were able to creep out without too much disturbance; those closer to the platform were trapped. Amongst the escapees was von Igelfeld, who spent the next two hours in the Cathedral Museum, admiring the illuminated manuscripts. Von Igelfeld then had time to take a cup of scalding, strong coffee in a nearby bar, read the front two pages of *Corriere della Sera*, and post three letters at the post office before returning to face the last five minutes of Professor J. G. K. L. Singh.

'Do not underestimate the extent of the problem,' Singh warned the delegates. 'The usage of the verb prefix "ur-rachi" (sometimes represented as "ur-rasti" is not necessarily indicative of a close relationship between addressor and addressee. *In fact, quite the opposite may be the case.* Just as a Frenchman might say to one who assumes excessive familiarity in modes of address: "Don't you *tutoyer* me", so too might one who wishes to maintain his distance say: "Don't you 'ur-rachi' me, if you ('ur-rachi') please!" In so doing, however, he might himself use the "ur-rachi" form, thus loading his own prohibition with deep irony, even sarcasm.'

Professor J. G. K. L. Singh continued in this fashion for a short time further and then, to enthusiastic applause from his relieved audience, left the platform. This was the signal for von Igelfeld to ask his question. It was the same question which he had asked Professor J. G. K. L. Singh before, but von Igelfeld could think of no other, and the delegates relied on him to save them all the embarrassment of nothing being said.

'Is it the case, Professor J. G. K. L. Singh,' asked von Igelfeld, 'that the imperfect subjunctive has no insulting connotations in India?'

'Not at all!' said J. G. K. L. Singh, indignantly. 'I can't imagine who told you that! It is quite possible to give an imperfect subjunctive insult in Hindi. There are countless examples.'

So the debate continued. Professor Hurgert Hilpur of Finland delivered his paper, and was replied to by Professor Verloren van Themaat (Amsterdam); Professor Verloren van Themaat then gave his own paper, and was replied to by Professor Hurgert Hilpur. Professor Dr Dr Florianus Prinzel asked a question, which was answered by Professor Alberto Morati, who was contradicted, with some force, by Dr Domenico Palumbieri (Naples). There were many treats.

At the final session of the conference, von Igelfeld announced to Prinzel and Unterholzer that he proposed to visit Montalcino, a village in the Sienese hills, renowned for its Brunello wine and for the subtle beauty of the surrounding countryside. His suggestion enthused the other two, but as they were committed on the Friday and the Saturday, they would be able to join him there only on Sunday afternoon.

'I shall go first then,' said von Igelfeld. 'By the time you arrive on Sunday I shall have identified all the principal sights and shall be able to conduct you to them personally.'

Prinzel and Unterholzer thought this a good idea, and so late on the Friday morning they escorted von Igelfeld to the bus station near the Church of Santa Caterina and duly despatched him. In little more than an hour, von Igelfeld's blue-grey bus was climbing up the steep, winding road that led to Montalcino. At the small Church of Santa Maria he disembarked, glanced over the low wall at the countryside so far below, and walked the few yards to the Albergo Basilio, of which he had read in his guide to the hotels of Tuscany. The guide said very little, but ended its entry with the curious remark: *Caution advised, if you are German.*

The Albergo Basilio was a small, intimate country inn, of the sort which has so largely died out in all but the most remote corners of Europe. It had no more than ten beds, in plain, white-washed rooms; a parlour with a few chairs and a glass-topped table; and a dining room that gave off the kitchen. Its charm undoubtedly lay in its simplicity. There were no telephones, no artificial comforts; nothing, in fact, which would not be found in a modest farmhouse.

The owner was Signora Margarita Cossi, the widow of a raisin merchant from Grosseto. She had bought the hotel cheaply from her husband's cousin, and had made a moderate success of the enterprise. The hotel was well placed to do considerably better than that, of course; Montalcino drew many wine pilgrims, and one might have expected the hotel to be full all the time. Unfortunately, this was not the case, and many visitors avoided staying there for more than one night and even went so far as to warn their friends against it. And the reason for this, beyond doubt, was the rudeness of Signora Cossi, who was an incorrigible xenophobe. She disliked people from Rome; she detested Venetians; she despised anybody from the South, and her views on the other nations of Europe were cussedly uncomplimentary. About every nation she had a deep-rooted prejudice, and when it came to the Germans this took the form of the conviction that they ate better, and in larger quantities, than any other people in Europe.

The source of this prejudice was a magazine article which Signora Cossi had read in an old issue of *Casa Moderna*, in which the author had disclosed to the readers that the average German was fifteen pounds overweight. Signora Cossi was so horrified by this figure, that it was but a short step to the conclusion that the quantities of food which they must have eaten to achieve this impressive obesity could only have been obtained at the expense of less gluttonous nations, particularly the Italians. On this basis, Signora Cossi took to making disparaging remarks about her German guests and making them feel unwelcome.

Von Igelfeld had no inkling of what lay ahead when he signed the register and handed over his passport to Signora Cossi that morning.

'I hope that you are comfortable here,' she said, glancing at his passport, 'Signor von Whatever. I know you people like your physical comfort.'

Von Igelfeld laughed. 'I'm sure that I shall be well looked after,' he assured her. 'This hotel seems delightful.'

'You've hardly seen it,' said Signora Cossi dismissively. 'Do you always make your mind up so quickly?'

Von Igelfeld gave a polite, if somewhat forced smile.

'Yes,' he said. 'When a place is so clearly delightful as this is, I see no point in prevarication.'

Signora Cossi looked at him suspiciously, but said nothing more. Silently she handed him his key and pointed to the stairway that led to the bedrooms. Von Igelfeld took the proffered key, bowed slightly, and went off up the stairs with his suitcase. He was unsure whether he had inadvertently said something offensive and whether Signora Cossi had the right to be so short with him. Had he used an unusually familiar term? He thought of Professor J. G. K. L. Singh and his 'ur-rachis'. Had he unwittingly 'ur-rachied' this disagreeable woman?

Although he did not yet realise it, von Igelfeld had been allocated the worst room in the hotel. There was no furniture in it at all apart from a single bed, covered with a threadbare cotton cover. This bed had been bought second-hand from the house of a deceased dwarf in Sant'Amato, and was therefore very short. Von Igelfeld gazed at it in disbelief and then, putting down his suitcase, tried to lie down on the bed. He put his head on the pillow and then hoisted his legs up, but the bed was a good thirty inches too short and his calves, ankles and feet hung down over the edge. It would be impossible to sleep in such a position.

After a few minutes of uncomfortable meditation, von Igelfeld made his way downstairs again. Signora Cossi was still at her desk, and she watched him with narrowed eyes as he came down into the hall.

'Is everything all right?' she asked. Her tone was not solicitous.

'The room itself is charming,' said von Igelfeld

courteously. 'But I'm afraid that I find the bed somewhat short for my needs.'

Signora Cossi's eyes flashed.

'And what might these needs be?' she challenged. 'What are you proposing to do in that bed?'

Von Igelfeld gasped.

'Nothing,' he said. 'Nothing at all. It is just that my legs do not fit. The bed is too short for me to lie down upon. That's all.'

Signora Cossi was not to be so easily placated.

'It's a perfectly good Italian bed,' she snapped. 'Are you suggesting that Italians are shorter than . . . than others?'

Von Igelfeld held up his hands in a gesture of horrified denial.

'Of course not,' he said quickly. 'I suggest no such thing. I'm sure I shall sleep very well after all.'

Signora Cossi appeared to subside somewhat.

'Dinner,' she said grudgingly, 'will be served at seven o'clock. Sharp.'

Von Igelfeld thanked her, handed over his key, and set off for his afternoon walk. There were many paths to be explored; paths that went up and down the hillside, through olive groves, vineyards, and forests of cypress. There was much to be seen before Prinzel and Unterholzer arrived, and he was determined to be as familiar as possible with the surroundings before Sunday. In that way he would have a psychological advantage over them which could last for the rest of the Italian trip, and even beyond.

Outside, the air was pleasantly cool. Von Igelfeld thought of how hot it would be in Siena, and how uncomfortable Prinzel and Unterholzer would be feeling. The thought set him in good humour for his walk, although the problem of his bed remained niggling in the back of his mind. It was not true what Signora Cossi had said: Italian beds were by no means all that size. His bed in the Hotel del Palio in Siena had been of generous proportions, and he had encountered no difficulty in sleeping very well in it. Of course, it might be that people in hill towns were naturally shorter – there were such places, particularly in Sicily, where sheer, grinding poverty over the generations had stunted people, but surely not in Tuscany.

Von Igelfeld looked about him for confirmation. There were not many people out in the narrow street that led to the Pineta, but those who were about seemed to be of average height. There was a stout priest, sitting on a stone bench, reading a sporting newspaper; there was a woman standing in her doorway peeling potatoes; there were several boys in the small piazza at the end of the road, taunting and throwing stones at the goldfish in the ornamental pond. If this were a representative selection of the population, there was nothing unusually small about them.

Von Igelfeld was puzzled. There was definitely something abnormal about the bed, and he decided to take it up with the hotel on his return. He began to suspect that it might be some sort of calculated insult. He had experienced this once before at a conference in Hamburg, when a socialist waiter, who no doubt harboured a bone-deep resentment of all *vons*, had deliberately placed his thumb (with its dirt-blackened nail) in his soup.

He reached the Pineta, the small municipal park on the edge of the town. He admired the pines and then struck off along the road that led to Sant'Angelo in Colle. Soon he was in the deep countryside, making his way along a dusty white track that led off to the west. Classical Tuscan vistas now opened up on both sides of him; hills, valleys, red-roofed farmhouses, oaks, somnolent groves. He passed a farmyard with its large, stuccoed barn and a cluster of trees under which rested an ancient wooden-wheeled cart. A man came out of the house, waved a greeting to von Igelfeld, and then disappeared into the barn. A few moments later he re-emerged, herding before him two great white oxen with floppy ears and giant horns. Von Igelfeld smiled to himself. This was the real Italy, unchanged since the days of Virgil. This might be Horace's farm; the farmer himself a pensioned poet, like Horace, perhaps, tired of the high culture of the city, now seeking the solace of rustic life.

Von Igelfeld's walk continued for some miles more. Then, as evening approached, he turned and made his way back to Montalcino. By the time he reached the Albergo Basilio it was already dusk, and the lights were on in the streets and in the piazza. He retrieved his key, ventured under the shower in the small bathroom off his room (he was unable to persuade the hot tap to work) and then, refreshed and more formally dressed, he made his way downstairs for dinner.

There were three other guests in the dining room, and all three responded courteously to von Igelfeld's murmured greeting. Von Igelfeld sat down at a table near the window, and picked up the small hand-written menu. There was not a great deal of choice: soup or mozzarella; pasta; lamb cutlet or stew; ice cream or cake. Von Igelfeld pondered: rural soups could be strong and rich – perhaps that was the delicious smell he had noticed as he came downstairs. He would start, then, with soup and proceed to the lamb cutlets by way of a bowl of pasta. He had walked a considerable distance that day, and he felt justifiably hungry. He would also order half a bottle of Brunello, which may well have come from one of the vineyards he had seen on his walk.

It was a full ten minutes before Signora Cossi appeared and stood before von Igelfeld, pencil poised to take his order for dinner.

'The cooking smells delicious,' said von Igelfeld politely. 'I am looking forward to my meal.'

'Oh yes, I'm sure you are,' said Signora Cossi. 'You Germans certainly enjoy your meals. You polish off most of Europe's food anyway.'

Von Igelfeld's mouth dropped open in surprise. He was utterly flabbergasted by the accusation and for a few moments he was quite unable to reply.

'Not that I blame you,' went on Signora Cossi, staring pointedly out of the window. 'If you can afford it, eat it, I always say. And that's certainly what you people do, even if it means short rations for the rest of us.'

Von Igelfeld looked away. Really, this woman was impossible! He had never been so profoundly insulted in his life, and he was tempted to rise to his feet and walk out without further ceremony. But something stopped him. No. That would just play into her hands. Instead, he would show her.

'You are quite wrong,' he said. 'In fact, I was just about to ask you whether you had something lighter – a salad perhaps.'

Signora Cossi curled a lip, clearly annoyed.

'Is that all?' she asked abruptly.

'Yes, please,' said von Igelfeld. 'A small mixed salad is all I require.'

'And to drink?' said Signora Cossi. 'A bottle of Brunello?'

'No thank you,' said von Igelfeld, through pursed lips. 'Water, please.'

'With gas?' Signora Cossi's pencil hovered above her pad.

'No,' said von Igelfeld firmly. He would deny himself even that. He would show her. 'Without.'

That night passed in agony. Hungry and uncomfortable, von Igelfeld tried every possible way of arranging his frame on the tiny bed, but was unable to prevent his legs from hanging painfully over the edge. Eventually, by placing a chair at the end and putting his pillow on it, he managed to create an extension to the bed. Although his head and neck were now uncomfortable, he at last dropped off to sleep.

The night was plagued with bad dreams. In one, he was walking through the Pineta, admiring the pine trees, when he suddenly came upon Professor J.G.K.L. Singh. The Indian philologist was delighted to see him, and insisted on raising a hopelessly abstruse point. Von Igelfeld awoke, sweating, cramped and uncomfortable. After a time he drifted off to sleep again, but only to encounter Signora Cossi in his dreams. She looked at him balefully, as if accusing him of some unspoken wrong, and again he awoke, feeling unsettled and vaguely guilty.

The next morning, von Igelfeld went down for breakfast and found a single, frugal roll on his plate. Signora Cossi arrived to give him coffee and asked him whether he would like another roll. Von Igelfeld was about to order three, when he remembered his resolve of the previous evening and checked himself. Signora Cossi, looking somewhat disappointed, walked away to deal with another guest.

After breakfast, von Igelfeld walked out into the village. He bought *La Nazione* from the small paper shop and began to walk down the street, glancing at the headlines. Everything in Italy was coming apart, the newspaper said. The Government was tottering, the currency unsteady. The judiciary and the courts were being held to ransom by organised criminals from Naples and Palermo; there were daily kidnaps and every sort of atrocity. And now, as if to confirm the country's humiliation, the Japanese were buying up all of Italy's small-denomination coins and taking them off to Japan to make into buttons! It was infamous. He would read about all this in the piazza, and then set off to inspect the Church of Saint Joseph the Epistulist, to be found in a neighbouring hamlet.

He turned a corner in the street and found himself outside a small grocer's shop. In the window were loaves of bread, cakes, and thick bars of chocolate. The Italian State might be crumbling, but it would not stop the Italians enjoying pastries and chocolate. Von Igelfeld stopped, and stared at the food. Several cups of coffee had taken the edge off his appetite, but his hunger was still there in the background. And later it would be worse, after his walk, and he would never be able to order a decent meal from the dreadful Signora Cossi.

Von Igelfeld entered the shop. He was the only customer, and the woman who owned the shop appeared to be talking on the telephone in a back room. Von Igelfeld looked at the shelves, which were packed with household provisions of every sort. His eye fell on a packet of almond biscuits and then on a large fruit tart; both of these would do well. He could eat the fruit tart while sitting in the Pineta, and the almond biscuits would do for the walk itself.

The woman put down the telephone and emerged, smiling, into the shop. At that moment, the door from the street opened and in came Signora Cossi.

'*Buongiorno dottore*,' said the shopkeeper to von Igelfeld. 'What can I do for you this morning?'

Von Igelfeld froze, aware of the penetrating stare of Signora Cossi behind him.

'Do you have a pair of black shoe-laces?' he asked.

The shopkeeper reached for a box behind her and von Igelfeld bought the laces. Signora Cossi said nothing, but nodded curtly to him as he left the shop. Once outside, von Igelfeld bit his lip in anger.

'I shall not be intimidated by that frightful woman,' he muttered to himself. 'I shall make her eat her words.'

He strode off, tossing the shoe-laces into a rubbish bin. Ahead of him lay a long walk, fuelled only by hunger. He thought of Prinzel and Unterholzer. They would no doubt be sitting in some outdoor café in Siena, enjoying coffee and cakes. Unterholzer, in particular, had a weakness for cakes; von Igelfeld had seen him on one occasion eat four at one sitting. That was the sort of gluttony which gave Germany a bad name. It was Unterholzer's fault.

That evening, von Igelfeld again returned from the walk shortly before dinner. The menu was unchanged, and the smell of the soup was as delicious as before. But again, he ordered a small helping of salad and two slices of thin bread. This time, Signora Cossi tried to tempt him by listing the attractions of the lamb cutlets.

'Thank you, but no,' said von Igelfeld airily. 'I do not eat a great deal, you know. There is far too much emphasis on food in Italy, I find.'

He tossed the comment off lightly, as one would throw in a pleasantry, but it found its target. Signora Cossi glared at him, before turning on her heels and marching back into the kitchen. Von Igelfeld's salad, when it arrived twenty-five minutes later, was smaller than last night, being composed of one tomato, four small lettuce leaves, two slices of cucumber and a shaving of green pepper. The bread, too, was so thinly sliced that through it von Igelfeld was able to read the inscription *Albergo Basilio* on the plate.

Another night of physical agony passed. At least this evening there were no dreams of Professor J. G. K. L. Singh, but as he lay on his sleepless and uncomfortable couch, von Igelfeld thought of what he could say to Signora Cossi when he at last left on Monday morning. Prinzel and Unterholzer were due to arrive at three the following afternoon, and to spend a night in the hotel before they all left for Florence. He would tell them about her insults, and they might be able to suggest suitable retorts. It would be easier, perhaps, when they outnumbered her.

The next day, Sunday, von Igelfeld refused his roll at breakfast and merely drank three cups of coffee. This will show her, he thought grimly; even if she failed to abandon her prejudice after this, she could surely take no pleasure in it. There must, after all, be a limit to the extent of self-deception which people can practise.

He left the hotel at half past ten and set off along the route he had followed on his first walk. By noon he found himself approaching the farm which had so entranced him before, and he saw, to his pleasure, that the farmer was busy unyoking the two large oxen from his cart. Von Igelfeld left the road and offered to help with the harnesses. His offer was gratefully received, and afterwards the farmer, pleased to discover that von Igelfeld spoke Italian, introduced himself and invited von Igelfeld to take a glass of wine with him and his wife.

They sat at a table under one of the oak trees, a flask of home-produced wine before them. Toasts were exchanged, and von Igelfeld closed his eyes with pleasure as the delicious red liquid ran down his parched throat. Glasses were refilled, and it was when these had been emptied that the farmer's wife invited von Igelfeld to stay for lunch.

'My wife is one of the best cooks in Tuscany,' said the farmer, bright-eyed. 'That's why I married her.'

'I should not wish to impose,' said von Igelfeld, hardly daring to believe his good fortune.

'It would be no imposition at all,' he was reassured by the farmer's wife. 'We have so much food here, and only two mouths to eat it now that our children have gone to Milan. You would be doing us a favour, truly you would.'

The meal was served at the table under the tree. To

begin with they ate *zuppa crema di piselli*, rich and de-licious. This was followed by bowls of *tagliatelle alla paesana*, heavy with garlic. Finally, an immense casserole dish of *capretto al vino bianco* was brought out, and of this everybody had three helpings.

Von Igelfeld sat back, quite replete. During the meal, conversation had been somewhat inhibited by the amount of food which required to be consumed, but now it picked up again.

'You must be a happy man,' observed von Igelfeld. 'How lucky you are to live here, in this charming place. It's so utterly peaceful.'

The farmer nodded.

'I know,' he said. 'I've never been to Rome. I've never even set foot in Florence, if it comes to that.'

'Nor Siena,' interjected his wife. 'In fact, you've never been anywhere at all.'

The farmer nodded. 'I don't mind: enough happens here to keep us busy.'

'Oh it does,' agreed his wife. 'Tell the *professore* about the angels.'

The farmer glanced at von Igelfeld.

'We have seen angels here,' he said quietly. 'On several occasions. Once, indeed, while we were sitting under this very tree. Two of them passed more or less overhead and then vanished behind those hills over there.'

Von Igelfeld looked up into the echoing, empty sky. It seemed quite possible that angels might be encountered in such a setting. It was against such landscapes, after all, that Italian artists had painted heavenly flights; it seemed quite natural.

56

'I can well believe it,' he said.

'The priest didn't,' snapped the farmer's wife. 'What did he say to you? Accused you of superstition, or something like that.'

'He said that angels weren't meant to be taken seriously,' said the farmer slowly. 'He said that they were symbols. Can you believe that? A priest saying that?'

'Astonishing,' said von Igelfeld. 'Angels are very important.'

'I'm glad to hear you say that,' said the farmer. 'The angels are really our only hope.'

They were silent for a moment, and von Igelfeld thought of angels. He would never see one, he was sure. Visions were reserved for the worthy, for people like this farmer who uncomplainingly spent his entire life on this little corner of land. Visions were a matter of desert.

'And then,' said the farmer. 'We had a major incident during the war – on that very hillside.'

Von Igelfeld looked at the hillside. It was quite unexceptional, with its innocent olive groves and its scattered oaks. What could have happened there? A terrible ambush perhaps?

'I was only eight then,' said the farmer. 'I was standing in the farmyard with my father and two of my uncles. All the trouble had passed us by, and so we were not worried when we saw the large American transport plane fly low overhead. We watched it, wondering where it was going, and then suddenly we saw a door in its side open and several parachutists jumped out. They floated down gently, coming to land on the hillside. Then the plane headed off over Montalcino and disappeared.

'We ran over to where the men had landed and greeted

them. They smiled at us and said: "We're Americans and we've come to free you."'

'Well, we told them that we'd already been freed and that there was really nothing for them to do. So they looked a bit disappointed, but they came and had dinner with us. Then, after dinner, they went off to sleep in the barn, using their parachutes for bedding, and one of them went into the village. He never came back. He met a girl in the village and married her. The others were very cross and debated about going into the village to find him and shoot him, but they decided against it and instead went away on some bicycles they had requisitioned. My mother made shirts and underpants out of the parachutes. They lasted indefinitely, and I still occasionally wear them. That was it. That was the war. We've never forgotten it. It was so exciting.'

Von Igelfeld eventually bade a late and emotional farewell to his hosts and began the walk back to Montalcino. The pangs of hunger were a dim memory of the past; he would need to eat nothing that evening – that would show Signora Cossi! He entered the hotel, and hung his hat on one of the hat pegs. He was late, and dinner had already started. Then he remembered. Prinzel and Unterholzer had already arrived – he had totally forgotten about them – and there they were, at the table, tucking into the largest helpings of pasta which von Igelfeld had ever seen.

Von Igelfeld's heart sank. Look at them eat! It was enough to confirm Signora Cossi's views one hundred times over. And indeed it did, for as von Igelfeld stared in dismay at his companions, Signora Cossi swept out of the kitchen carrying two large plates, piled high with lamb cutlets.

'For your friends!' she said triumphantly, as she passed her speechless guest.

Prinzel and Unterholzer could not understand von Igelfeld's bad mood. Nor did they understand his expression of dismay when, after they had settled their bills, a smirking Signora Cossi handed von Igelfeld a small package.

'I saw you throw these away,' she said, giving him his laces. 'You must surely have done so by mistake.'

Her expression was one of utter, unassailable triumph, and von Igelfeld was to remember it well after he had forgotten his walks through that timeless landscape, that marvellous meal under the farmer's oak tree, and the vision, so generously shared, of angels.

Portuguese Irregular Verbs

They took up residence in Regensburg one by one – von Igelfeld first, then Unterholzer and finally Prinzel. Prinzel's new wife, Ophelia, had been reluctant to leave Wiesbaden, where she acted as secretary to her father in the Wiesbaden Project on Puccini. This project, which had been running for fourteen years, was set to run for at least a further decade, or more, and absorbed almost all the energies of both herself and her father. A move was quite out of the question.

At the time when Unterholzer moved to Regensburg, von Igelfeld was himself involved in his own difficulties over publication. Studia Litteraria Verlag, the publishers of his renowned and monumental work *Portuguese Irregular Verbs*, had written to him informing him that they had managed to sell only two hundred copies of the book. There was no doubt about the book's status: it was to be found in all the relevant libraries of Europe and North America, and was established as a classic in its field; but the problem was that the field was extremely

small. Indeed, almost the entire field met every year at the annual conference and fitted comfortably into one small conference hall, usually with twenty or thirty seats left over.

The publishers pointed out that although two hundred copies had been sold, there still remained seven hundred and thirty-seven in a warehouse in Frankfurt. Over the previous two years, only six copies had been sold, and it occurred to them that at this rate they could expect to have to store the stock until well into the twenty-second century. Von Igelfeld personally saw nothing unacceptable about this, and was outraged when he read the proposal of Studia Litteraria's manager.

'We have received an offer from a firm of interior decorators,' he read. 'They decorate the apartments of wealthy people in a style which indicates good taste and education. They are keen to purchase our entire stock of *Portuguese Irregular Verbs*, which, as you know, has a very fine binding. They will then, *at their own expense and at no cost to*

yourself, change the embossed spine title to *Portuguese Irrigated Herbs* and use them as book furniture for the bookshelves they install in the houses of their customers. I am sure you will agree that this is an excellent idea, and I look forward to receiving your views on the proposition.'

It was no use, thought von Igelfeld, to attempt to use the arguments of scholarship and value when dealing with commercial men, such as the proprietors of Studia Litteraria undoubtedly were: they only understood the market. It would be far better, then, to ask them to wait for a while and see whether the sales of *Portuguese Irregular Verbs* picked up. From the commercial point of view, it would surely be more profitable to sell the book as a book, rather than as – what was the insulting expression they had used? – *furniture*.

Yet it was difficult to imagine sales picking up. There was no event, no anniversary, on the horizon to suggest that *Portuguese Irregular Verbs* might suddenly become more topical. Nor was von Igelfeld's own fame, though unquestioned in the field, likely to become markedly greater. No, any sudden increase in interest in the book would have to be the result of von Igelfeld's own efforts to persuade those who did not currently own a copy to buy one.

As an experiment, von Igelfeld wrote to his mother's cousin in Klagenfurt, Freiherr Willi-Maximilian Guntel, asking him whether the library in his country house contained a copy of the work. A prompt reply was received.

'*My dear Moritz-Maria,*' the letter ran. '*My failing health makes me something of a recluse these days, and it is therefore such a great pleasure to receive mail, especially from the family. How kind of you to offer to give me a copy of your book. I must admit that my library has little about Portugal in it. In fact, it contains nothing at all about Portugal. Your kind gift would therefore be most appreciated.*

Now, on another matter, do you remember cousin Armand, the thin one, who used to mutter so? Well, it really is the most extraordinary story . . .'

Von Igelfeld was, of course, trapped, and in due course the order department of Studia Litteraria was surprised to receive an order for a copy of *Portuguese Irregular Verbs*, with an accompanying cheque drawn on the account of the author, Professor Dr Moritz-Maria von Igelfeld. Clearly, caution would have to be shown in soliciting purchases, or it could become an expensive business.

Von Igelfeld thought again. What he should try to do is to find out by more indirect means who owned a copy and who did not. Unterholzer, for example: did he own a copy, or did he merely make free use of library copies?

'Unterholzer,' von Igelfeld said one day as the two philologists sat in the Café Schubert, drinking coffee. 'I've been thinking recently about updating *Portuguese Irregular Verbs*. What do you think?'

63

Unterholzer looked surprised. 'Does it need it?' he asked. 'Have the verbs changed recently? Becoming more regular?'

Von Igelfeld reacted crossly to what he thought was an unnecessarily flippant remark.

'Of course not,' he snapped. 'But scholarship always marches on. There have been several very important developments since the last edition.'

Unterholzer was apologetic. 'Of course, of course.'

Von Igelfeld glanced sideways at his friend. Now, perhaps, was the time to strike.

'But I wonder if people would want to buy a new edition . . .' He paused, raising the coffee cup to his lips. 'Especially if they already have a copy.'

'They might,' said Unterholzer. 'Who knows?'

Von Igelfeld lowered his cup. 'Take somebody like you, for example. Would you buy a new edition?'

Von Igelfeld felt his heart pounding within him. He was astonished at his own sheer bravery in asking the question. Surely he had Unterholzer cornered now.

Unterholzer smiled. 'I should hope for a review copy from the *Zeitschrift*,' he said lightly.

Von Igelfeld was silent. Unterholzer had given nothing away. Could his remark have meant that he had received a review copy of the first edition? And if so, then where was the review? Von Igelfeld had not seen it. Or had Unterholzer really bought a copy of the first edition and was now hoping to be spared the cost of a second? That was conceivable, but how could one possibly tell?

As days passed, von Igelfeld's chagrin increased over the inconclusive nature of his discussion with Unterholzer. He realised that if he did not know whether or not even a close colleague like Unterholzer had a copy of *Portuguese Irregular Verbs*, then there would be little chance of encouraging sales. He could hardly tout the book on an indiscriminate basis; the only way would be by the subtle, individual approach.

It would have been simple, of course, if Unterholzer had kept his books in the Institute. Had that been the case, then all von Igelfeld would have had to do would be to cast an eye over his colleague's bookshelves on his next visit to his room. Unfortunately, Unterholzer was the only person in the Institute whose room was virtually devoid of books. He largely worked in the library, and his own collection, he had explained to everyone, was kept in his study at home.

Von Igelfeld pondered. He knew where Unterholzer lived, but he had never been in his flat. They had walked past it one day, and Unterholzer had pointed up at his windows and balcony, but no invitation had been extended to drop in for a cup of coffee. By contrast, Unterholzer had been invited to von Igelfeld's house five or six times; he had attended the party which von Igelfeld had thrown for Florianus and Ophelia Prinzel, and he had certainly been present at the stylish reception which von Igelfeld had held in honour of Professor Dr Dr (*h.c.*) (*mult.*) Reinhard Zimmermann. There was no doubt but that by any criteria of reciprocity of hospitality, Unterholzer should have invited von Igelfeld into his home.

Von Igelfeld decided to act. If Unterholzer was not going to invite him, then he must commit the solecism of arriving at the doorstep one day, uninvited. Unterholzer could hardly turn him away, particularly if it was raining, and in this way he would be able to inspect his bookshelves and settle once and for all the issue of whether he was an owner of *Portuguese Irregular Verbs*. All that was required was a rainy Saturday afternoon. Unterholzer would be in; von Igelfeld knew that he never went out, other than to go off on one of his solitary walks by the river; and not surprising, reflected von Igelfeld wryly – if he never issues any invitations then it's quite right that he should get none in return. In fact, the more he thought about it, the more unacceptable appeared Unterholzer's behaviour.

A suitably overcast Saturday afternoon arrived. Von Igelfeld made his way to the building in which Unterholzer lived. Standing outside, he looked up at the balcony which Unterholzer had pointed out and he noted with satisfaction that there was a light on inside. Good, he thought. Unterholzer was too mean to leave lights burning if he was not in.

Von Igelfeld peered at the plate above the bell and drew in his breath sharply. *Professor Dr Dr D-A. von Unterholzer.* What extraordinary, bare-faced cheek! It was little short of an outrage, on *three* counts, no less. Firstly, Unterholzer did not have two doctorates; there was no doubt about that. Secondly, what was all this nonsense about the hyphen between Detlev and Amadeus? Amadeus was his second name, as the whole world knew, not part of his first. And finally, and perhaps most seriously of all, there was the *von*. Von Igelfeld felt the anger surge up within him. If people got away with adding *vons* to their names whenever the mood took them, then that immeasurably reduced the significance of the real *vons*. So this was why Unterholzer had never invited him to his flat; it was simply because he knew that his pretensions would be exposed. But then, if nobody was ever invited, then who was there to be impressed by the bogus credentials? The postman? Or was it some bizarre, private fantasy on Unterholzer's part, designed to give him some inexplicable, solitary pleasure?

Von Igelfeld gave the bell an imperious, righteous push, in the way in which a policeman might ring a bell when he knew that a long-elusive quarry was hiding within. He heard the bell sounding and then, after a few moments, the door opened and Unterholzer stood before him.

'Good afternoon, Herr Unterholzer,' said von Igelfeld, throwing a glance in the direction of the name plate. 'I was walking past and the sky looked a bit threatening. I wondered if I might take shelter here for a while.'

Unterholzer frowned. 'The sky looked fine to me, when I last saw it.'

'It changes so quickly, though,' retorted von Igelfeld. 'The rain is definitely coming on.'

Unterholzer still looked unwilling to admit von Igelfeld.

'I'm also rather thirsty,' went on von Igelfeld. 'A glass of fruit juice would be most welcome.'

Unterholzer looked regretful. 'I'm afraid I have no fruit juice at the moment. There is, however, a small café round the corner.'

'Water would do quite well,' countered von Igelfeld. 'I take it that you haven't run out of that.'

It seemed to von Igelfeld that Unterholzer now had no alternative.

'Do come in,' the latter said. He suddenly became the genial host, as he ushered his guest into the hall and closed the front door behind him. 'Why don't we sit in my study?'

Von Igelfeld followed Unterholzer along a short corridor

and into a large well-lit room. Two of the walls were covered with bookshelves, all of which were filled with books. There was a desk, on which sundry papers were scattered, a couch, and several armchairs. It was a pleasant enough room, if somewhat spartan in its tone. It did not give the air of being well used: none of the armchairs looked as if they had ever been sat in, and on those shelves on which small ornaments were placed, these had been positioned strictly according to size.

Unterholzer gestured to the sofa while he himself sat in one of the armchairs.

'I can't remember when you were last here,' he said to von Igelfeld, fixing him with a challenging stare.

Von Igelfeld pretended to search his memory. 'I can't remember either. It must have been a long time ago.'

He looked about the room, noting the cheap and unattractive framed views of the Rhine. It was not the sort of thing to which he would give wall space. It was almost kitsch in fact.

'I have a very good housekeeper,' said Unterholzer. 'Frau Kapicinska comes every morning. She keeps everything very clean.'

'That is very good,' said von Igelfeld. 'Is she Polish, by any chance?'

Unterholzer nodded. 'Yes. Polish.'

'Ah,' said von Igelfeld. 'I see.'

There was silence. Unterholzer looked up at the ceiling while von Igelfeld's gaze returned to the views of the Rhine. Really, they were terrible. They were coloured engravings – coloured well after the original had been printed. And there, facing these ill-depicted views of the Rhine, was a large framed photograph of a sausage dog. This was even worse. Could Unterholzer be one of those people who liked those unfortunate dogs? Von Igelfeld was aware of their popularity, but had always been irritated by what he considered to be the ridiculous appearance of the dachshund, with its absurd little legs and its long, sausage-like body. The von Igelfelds had always had large dogs, suitable for hunting on the plains of their now confiscated estates. They would never have owned a sausage dog. It was most irritating, really, to see these clichéd views of the Rhine and a sausage dog in such proximity.

'Do you have a dog, Herr Unterholzer?' asked von Igelfeld, looking about the room for signs of canine occupation.

Unterholzer smiled. 'Yes,' he said, proudly. 'I have a very fine dachshund. He is called Walter.'

Von Igelfeld raised an eyebrow. Walter? 'And does this dog live here, in this apartment?' he asked.

'He does,' said Unterholzer. 'He is sleeping now and we should not wake him up. But one day I will introduce you to him.'

'That would be very kind,' said von Igelfeld. He wanted to laugh, though, at the thought: Unterholzer saying to his ridiculous sausage dog, 'And this is Professor von Igelfeld' and von Igelfeld shaking the dog's proffered paw and saying, 'Good morning, Herr Unterholzer!' – because what else could he call the dog? He could hardly call him Walter on first meeting, and so it would have to be Herr Unterholzer. That, of course, would make it difficult to distinguish whether he was talking to Unterholzer or his dog, and could lead to confusion.

'Would you care for coffee?' Unterholzer asked suddenly. 'I could make some in the kitchen.'

Von Igelfeld accepted rapidly. He wanted to get Unterholzer out of the room for a few minutes so that he could check the bookshelves. It would not take long, but he could hardly do it while his host was present. And the moment that Unterholzer left, von Igelfeld was on his feet, his eye running rapidly over each shelf in turn. Not that one, nor that one; not there; no; *undsoweiter* until he had searched every shelf and reached the terrible, damning conclusion: Unterholzer did not own a copy of *Portuguese Irregular Verbs*.

When Unterholzer returned, he found von Igelfeld sitting in a different chair. He paid no attention to this; he had assumed that his guest would probably try to go through his papers in his absence. Well, there was nothing for him to find there; he was just wasting his time.

Von Igelfeld sipped at the coffee which Unterholzer had given him – not very good coffee, he noted. Was there anything to be said in Unterholzer's defence – anything at all? Could it be argued that he had suffered in some way, and that his suffering deserved sympathy? No. Unterholzer was not a refugee from the East or anything like that. Nor had he suffered at the hands of a cruel or bullying step-parent; von Igelfeld understood his father to be a perfectly reasonable retired bank manager. So there was no doubt but that Unterholzer was answerable for the various wrongs which had been so quickly and damningly chalked up against him.

As he thought this, von Igelfeld saw something else on the wall. It was a framed coat of arms, and underneath, in Gothic script, he made out: 'The arms of von Unterholzer'. Well, really! That was even worse than the views of the Rhine, which appeared to be in good taste by comparison.

Von Igelfeld bit his lip. Then he could remain silent no longer.

'I must say that I can't understand what you see in those views of the Rhine,' he said. 'Did some student give them to you?'

Unterholzer looked at the pictures and then looked at von Igelfeld.

'You mean you don't like them?' he asked.

'Yes,' said von Igelfeld icily. 'That's what I do mean. I think they're terribly, terribly vulgar.'

Unterholzer's jaw sagged open.

'Vulgar?' His voice was the voice of a broken man, but von Igelfeld pressed on.

'Kitsch, Herr Unterholzer,' he said. 'Kitsch. I gather that it's becoming fashionable again, but I didn't expect to find you, of all people, living in a . . . in a palace of kitsch!'

Unterholzer said nothing, as he looked about his study. Then, almost absent-mindedly, he offered von Igelfeld more coffee from his china coffee-pot with its curious chinoiserie pattern. Was that kitsch too, he wondered?

'Look out,' said von Igelfeld. 'You've splashed it on my shirt.'

With shaking hands, Unterholzer put down the coffee-pot.

'I'm terribly sorry,' he said. 'Do let me fetch a cloth.'

'No thank you,' said von Igelfeld coldly. 'Just you direct me to the bathroom and I'll attend to it myself.'

Von Igelfeld left Unterholzer in the study and walked angrily down the corridor to the bathroom. There he sponged off the two small coffee splashes and adjusted his tie. He closed the bathroom door behind him and started off down the corridor. There was a large bookshelf on his right, and from ancient habit he stooped to look at the contents. There, on the bottom shelf, standing out with their excellent bindings, stood not one, but two copies of *Portuguese Irregular Verbs*.

Von Igelfeld stood stock still. Then, cautiously, drew out the first copy and paged through it. It was well used and had been annotated here and there in Unterholzer's characteristic script. *Precisely* read one comment; *confirmed by Zimmermann* said another.

He put the book back in its place and took out the second copy. This was in pristine condition, and had clearly been little used. He looked at the flyleaf to see if Unterholzer had stuck in his book plate, which he had not. Instead, in Unterholzer's writing again, there was the following inscription: *To my dear friend and colleague, in gratitude: the author, Moritz-Maria von Igelfeld.*

For a moment Von Igelfeld did not know what to think. Of course he had never given Unterholzer a copy; it had never occurred to him. But why should he then have decided to write his own inscription, as if a presentation had been made?

Von Igelfeld replaced the book on the shelf, straightened his tie again, and went back into the study. As he entered the room, he paused, looked at the views of the Rhine again, and stroked his chin pensively.

'You do know I was just joking a few minutes ago,' he said. 'Those really are very attractive pictures.'

Unterholzer looked up sharply, his eyes bright with pleasure. 'You don't think them kitsch?'

'Good heavens!' exclaimed von Igelfeld. 'Can't you take

a joke, Herr Unterholzer? Kitsch! If those are kitsch, then I don't know what good taste is.'

Unterholzer beamed up at his guest.

'I have a cake in the kitchen,' he said eagerly. 'It's a cake cooked by Frau Kapicinska. Should I bring it through?'

Von Igelfeld nodded. 'That would be very nice,' he said warmly. 'A piece of cake is just what's required.'

While Unterholzer was out of the room, von Igelfeld put down his cup of coffee and moved over to examine the alleged crest of the von Unterholzers, and he was standing there when Unterholzer returned.

'It's a funny thing, Herr Unterholzer,' said von Igelfeld. 'But I've always thought that you might be *von* Unterholzer.'

Unterholzer laughed. 'It's not absolutely established,' he said. 'So I don't really use the *von* in public.'

'Of course not,' said von Igelfeld. 'But it's good to know you're entitled to it, isn't it?'

Unterholzer did not reply. He was busy cutting a large piece of cake. Frau Kapicinska had baked it five weeks ago and he hoped that it would still be fresh; he had no idea how long cakes could be expected to last.

Von Igelfeld's teeth sank into the cake. It was heavy and stale, but he would eat every crumb of it, he decided, and thank Unterholzer for it at the end. Indeed, he would ask for another piece.

Holy Man

Auden had called such places 'weeds from Catholic Europe', and this is how Professor Dr Moritz-Maria von Igelfeld thought of them too; as usual, Auden's imagery struck him as so rich, so laden with associations, and when he received the letter from Goa, with its unfamiliar, faded stamp, the haunting metaphor crossed his mind again.

It was a thin, dejected-looking envelope, much tattered by its journey. Indeed, in one corner it appeared that some animal, possibly a dog, had bitten it, leaving small tooth holes. In another corner, the paper had split, revealing a single sheet of greying parchment within. Von Igelfeld turned it over and saw the address of the sender, typed erratically across the back flap: Professor J. G. K. L. Singh. The name made his heart sink: J. G. K. L. Singh of Chandighar, author of *Dravidian Verb Shifts*.

Impulsively, von Igelfeld tossed the letter into his wastepaper bin. It had clearly met with near disaster on its trip to Germany, von Igelfeld thought; had the dog swallowed it, then it would never have arrived at all. If he threw it away now, then he was merely fulfilling its manifest destiny.

Von Igelfeld turned away and picked up the next letter, a quiet, reassuring letter, with a solid, familiar, German stamp, and the name of the sender neatly typed in the right hand corner: Professor Dr Dr (*h.c.*) Florianus Prinzel. This was Prinzel's monthly letter, in which he would bring von Igelfeld up to date on developments in the Institute in Wiesbaden. At the end, penned in the slightly unsettling violet ink she habitually used, would be a small postscript from Ophelia Prinzel, with heart-warming domestic news of a trivial sort. This was exactly the sort of letter which von Igelfeld liked to receive, but even as he opened it and smoothed out the pages, his gaze turned guiltily to the poor, abandoned Indian letter, with its sad stamp and its flimsy paper.

Von Igelfeld wondered whether there was a moral obligation to read a letter. Surely the moral principles involved were the same as those which applied when somebody addressed a remark to one. One does not have to answer; but inevitably does. Yet, why should one have to answer: was there anything intrinsically wrong about ignoring somebody who said something to you if you hadn't asked them to say something in the first place? Von Igelfeld wondered what view Immanuel Kant had expressed on this subject. Would Kant have thrown Professor J. G. K. L. Singh's letter into his wastepaper basket? Von Igelfeld doubted it: the matter was clearly embraced by the Categorical Imperative. That settled that, but then the disturbing thought occurred: what would Jean-Paul Sartre have done if he had received a letter from J. G. K. L. Singh? Von Igelfeld suspected that

Sartre might have had little compunction in doing as von Igelfeld had done, provided it made him feel authentic, but then, *and here was the crucial difference*, he would not have worried about it. Or would he?

Von Igelfeld laid aside the epistle from Prinzel and retrieved the letter from the bin. Slitting open the remains of the flap, he took out the grey sheet within and unfolded it.

'*Dear Professor von Igelfeld*,' he read. '*Greetings from Goa, and from your colleague, Janiwandillannah Krishnamurti Singh! I am down in this part of the world making arrangements for the All-India Union Congress of Philological Studies. We are meeting here in four months time and I wonder whether you will come to read a paper. All arrangements will be made, with despatch, by myself, and it will be very good to have some of you German fellows down in these parts again. The programme will be first class, and we shall have many excellent chin-wags. Please let me know . . .*'

Von Igelfeld sighed. Now that he had opened the letter, his questions about obligation seemed utterly answered. He would have to go: he was sure that Kant would agree.

The organising committee of the All-India Union Congress of Philology had made a booking for von Igelfeld in the old wing of the Hotel Lisboa. It was a large, rambling hotel, surrounded by shady verandahs. The gardens of the hotel were filled with bougainvilleas, frangipanis, palms, and there were winding paths that led to small, secluded summerhouses. Von Igelfeld was delighted. The air was scented with blossom; the sky was of an echoing emptiness; Europe and all its frenzy was far beyond any conceivable horizon. He sat in the wicker chair that occupied most of the minute balcony outside his room and looked out over the tops of the gently swaying palms. What a relief it was that Kantian ethics had pressed him into coming!

There had as yet been no sign of Professor J. G. K. L. Singh. One of the other committee members, Professor Rasi Henderson Paliwalar, had been detailed to meet von Igelfeld and to make sure that he was well settled in his hotel. Professor Rasi Henderson Paliwalar appeared to have an intimate knowledge of the timetables of the Indian State Railways and explained that Professor J. G. K. L. Singh was on his way to Goa, but was travelling by train and could not be expected to arrive for another thirty-six hours. This news had been conveyed to von Igelfeld apologetically, but it had in fact gladdened the recipient's heart. The Congress was not due to start for another three days, and of those three days at least one and a half could be enjoyed without any fear of encountering the author of *Dravidian Verb Shifts*.

Professor Rasi Henderson Paliwalar was much taken up with arrangements for the Congress and was relieved when von Igelfeld indicated that he could easily take care of himself until the opening session.

'I should like to look about Goa,' explained von Igelfeld. 'There is so much interesting architecture to see.'

'Indeed,' said Professor Rasi Henderson Paliwalar, sounding somewhat doubtful. 'Much of it is falling down, I'm afraid to say. In fact, all of India is falling down, all the time. Soon we shall have nothing but a fallen down country, all over. I am telling you. These people here appreciate none of the finer things of life.'

As he made these disparaging remarks, the professor pointed dismissively at the manager of hotel, who beamed

77

encouragingly and made a small bow. Von Igelfeld looked up at the ceiling of the Hotel Lisboa. There was an elaborate cornice, but several parts were missing, having fallen down.

That evening, after he had taken a refreshing drink of mango juice on the main verandah, von Igelfeld ventured out onto the road outside the hotel. Within a few seconds he had been surrounded by several men in red tunics, who started to quarrel over him until a villainous-looking man with a moustache appeared to win the argument and led von Igelfeld over to his cycle-driven rickshaw.

'I shall show you this fine town,' he said to von Igelfeld as the philologist eased himself into the small, cracked leather seat. 'What do you wish to see? The prison? The library? The grave of the last Portuguese governor?'

Von Igelfeld chose the library, which seemed the least disturbing of the options, and soon they were bowling down the road, overtaking pedestrians and slower rickshaws, the sinister rickshaw man ringing his bell energetically at every possible hazard.

The library was, of course, closed, but this did not deter the rickshaw man. Beckoning for von Igelfeld to follow him, he took him through the library gardens and walked up to the back door. Glancing about him, the rickshaw man took out a small bunch of implements, and started to try each in the lock. Von Igelfeld watched in amazement as his guide picked the lock; he knew he should have protested, but, faced with such effrontery, words completely failed him. Then, when the door swung open, equally passively he followed the rickshaw driver into the cool interior of the Goa State Library.

The building smelled of damp and mildew; the characteristic odour of books which have been allowed to rot.

'Here we are,' said the rickshaw man. 'These books are very, very old, and contain a great deal of Portuguese knowledge. The Portuguese brought them and now they have gone away and left their books behind.'

Von Igelfeld moved over to a shelf to examine the contents. He picked up a large, leather-bound tome, and turned the pages. The paper was yellowed and rotting, but he could make out the title quite clearly: *A Jesuit in Portuguese Goa* by Father Goncavles Persquites SJ. He laid it down and picked up the next one: *The Lives of the Portuguese Sailors* by Luis Valatar. This was in an even worse condition, and the binding fell away in his hands as he attempted to open the book.

'It is time to go now,' said the rickshaw man suddenly. 'I shall take you to the prison. There is more to see there.'

Von Igelfeld left the library sadly, imagining the desolation of the deserted, decaying books. Could Father Persquites have envisaged that Goa would come to this, and that his book would lie rotting and undisturbed until a chance hand should pick it up for a few moments? Could Valatar have envisaged his covers coming off at the hands of a casual visitor, who had effectively broken into the library to view its utter abandonment, in an era when the Portuguese navigators meant nothing any more?

The prison was just around the corner, an imposing fort of a building. Von Igelfeld wondered whether his guide would repeat his key-picking trick, but they rode past the front gate and turned round the corner. Here the rickshaw man dismounted and indicated to von Igelfeld that he should follow him to a small window in the outer wall of the prison.

'Look through there,' he said, gesturing to the window.

Von Igelfeld peered through the tiny opening. On the other side, through the thickness of the fortress wall, was the very heart of the prison, a vast hall topped by great barred skylights. Around the edges of the hall, men sat at tables and benches, quietly absorbed in their work of sewing pieces of cloth together.

'It is the tailoring workshop,' whispered the rickshaw man in von Igelfeld's ear. 'They are trying to make these no-good characters into good tailors, but they are wasting their time.'

Von Igelfeld found himself fascinated by the scene within. He watched intently as a stout man walked into the hall from the other end, accompanied by a warder. The prisoners momentarily stopped sewing and looked expectantly at their visitor.

'That is one of the governors of the prison,' whispered his guide. 'He is called Mr Majipondi and he is very rich because he sells all these suits these bad fellows make to merchants in the town. He is also a well-known murderer.'

Von Igelfeld stared as several of the prisoners approached the governor with their work. The governor nodded, and suits were given to the warder. Then he turned on his heels and left the room.

'Whom did he murder?' asked von Igelfeld.

The rickshaw man looked about him. 'He murdered his wife's brother's second wife's son,' he said in a surprised tone, as if that was something that von Igelfeld should have known. 'The Portuguese would have shot him. Now that they've gone, there's nobody to shoot people any more.' For a few moments he looked saddened, as if bereft. Then he added brightly: 'And now, would you like to see the municipal park?'

Von Igelfeld had had enough, and asked to be taken back to the Hotel Lisboa. The unorthodox approach of his guide was somewhat disturbing, and he could not imagine what strange angle he might present on the municipal park. It was safer, he thought, to return to the hotel and its restful gardens. He would have a mango juice, write a brief note to Prinzel and Unterholzer, and then retire early to bed. There would be time enough for the municipal park tomorrow.

The rickshaw driver was somewhat unwilling to bring the tour to an end, but eventually reluctantly agreed to return to the hotel.

'There are many interesting things happening in the municipal park,' he said sulkily. 'They should not be missed.'

'I'm sure that's true,' said von Igelfeld. 'But I have letters to write,' adding, for effect, 'Many letters.'

This appeared to impress the driver, who immediately nodded his compliance and began to cycle back with considerably more energy than before. Von Igelfeld sat back in the cracked red leather seat and reflected on what he had seen. He wondered whether anybody ever used the library, and who looked after it. He wondered about the prisoners in their hall: what crimes had they committed, what weight of guilt pressed upon their shoulders? And as for Mr Majipondi: how had his murder remained unpunished if everybody, including the rickshaw drivers of the town, knew about it? Then, what transpired in the municipal park – what dealings, what trysts, what tragedies? Was that, perhaps, where Mr Majipondi had murdered his wife's brother's second wife's son? He sighed. These were all such difficult questions, and they remained obstinately un-resolved in von Igelfeld's mind for the rest of the journey and well into the hot, sleepless hours of the night.

Von Igelfeld awoke early the next morning and took his breakfast on the main verandah. The morning sky was white and brilliant; the trees were filled with chattering birds; and there were two fresh hibiscus flowers in a vase on his table. All of this effectively dispelled the anxieties of the night and put von Igelfeld in a good mood for the day's exploring. He was determined to resist any imprecations from rick-shaw drivers and he would see what he wanted to see on foot. There were interesting old buildings all around the hotel, and these would suffice for the moment.

Von Igelfeld had noticed that there was a back entrance to the hotel gardens, used by the staff and for deliveries. He decided to leave by this route rather than by the front, as in this way he would be able to avoid the rickshaw driv-ers. Adjusting his broad-brimmed white hat, he walked briskly out of the back gate into the undistinguished serv-ice road that lay outside.

Not far along this road he came upon a building which seemed to invite inspection. It was an extraordinary edifice, three storeys high, and built in that curious, heavy style which the Portuguese so admire. There were scrolls above each window, a top-heavy neoclassical portico, and a courtyard which appeared to be harbour-ing an uncontrolled jungle. Von Igelfeld stepped back and looked at the building. Many of the windows were broken, and there was a general air of desertion about the place. He was struck by the feeling of melancholy which seemed to hang about the building, as if the very stones felt the loss of pride.

Von Igelfeld ventured through the portico. There was a bench directly to the right, and a doorway boarded up. Another door was slightly ajar, but the room within seemed sunk in darkness. Von Igelfeld moved on and peered into the courtyard.

It was not quite as much a jungle as it had appeared from outside. Certainly there was a profusion of plants, but they had been cut back here and there, revealing odd pieces of broken statuary. There was a stone urn in the Roman style, a figure of a boy caught in mid-leap, both arms broken off, and a toppled stone vase which had been covered in creepers.

It was then that von Igelfeld saw the Holy Man. He was sitting on the ground, at the side of the courtyard, a small bag at his side and a staff propped up against the wall behind. He was watching von Igelfeld, and when the philologist gave a start of surprise, the Holy Man raised an arm in salute.

'Do not be afraid of me,' he called out. 'I am just sitting here.'

Von Igelfeld was at a loss as to what to do. He was an intruder, and felt almost guilty, but the friendly salute and the reassuring message had set him at his ease. He walked across to where the Holy Man was sitting and reached out to shake his hand.

'I am sorry to disturb you,' he said. 'I was merely admiring this beautiful old building.'

The Holy Man lifted his eyes and cast a glance around the courtyard.

'Is this beauty?' he said. He seemed to reflect for a moment, then: 'Yes, perhaps it is. There is beauty in everything, even an old building that is now just a home for rats and mice.'

'That is true,' said von Igelfeld. He thought of Germany, where there were no rats or mice any more. 'Sometimes it's difficult to find beauty in my own country. Even the very earth is sick there.'

The Holy Man shook his head sadly. 'Man is very destructive. That is why he can never be like God.'

'That is very true,' agreed von Igelfeld. 'If only God would show us.'

The Holy Man closed his eyes. 'He does show us, sir. Oh yes, he does show us. If only we are prepared to see.'

Von Igelfeld was silent. His suspicion that this was a Holy Man was being proved correct. But how should he address him? Should he call him guru, as he had read one might do in such circumstances? Was he a real guru, though, or was he of some lower, or even higher, rank in the gradations of holiness? The situation was distinctly difficult.

'You are quite right, O guru,' he ventured hesitantly. 'If only we would see.'

The Holy Man did not appear to object to being called guru, and this put von Igelfeld at his ease. He was beginning to feel excited about the encounter. This was the real East, and he felt as if he was being vouchsafed a glimpse of something denied to so many casual visitors who presumably saw nothing more than the library or the prison. He imagined, with pleasure, the envy which Prinzel and Unterholzer would feel when he came to tell them about his meeting with the Holy Man. It would be quite outside their experience, and they would really have nothing at all to say. They would have no alternative but to listen.

'May I sit down, guru?' he asked, pointing to the ground next to the Holy Man.

The Holy Man smiled, and patted the earth affectionately. 'This is the earth on which we may all sit down,' he said. 'Even the poorest, most miserable man may sit down on the earth. It is your friend. Yes, sit down; your friend is beckoning you.'

Von Igelfeld sat down, next to the small bag, and waited for the Holy Man to say something. For a few minutes there was silence, but not an awkward one. The Holy Man seemed to be concentrating on something in the middle distance, but after a while he turned and looked at his guest.

'I have a gift of seeing things in the lives of people,' he said suddenly. 'God has entrusted me with this power.'

'I see,' said von Igelfeld, adding, rather lamely, 'Most of us cannot see very far, I suppose.'

The Holy Man nodded. 'God has been very good to me. I have nothing in this life other than my stick here and this small bag. But I have great riches otherwise.'

Von Igelfeld made a mental note to remember this sentiment: it was exactly what a Holy Man should say. He would repeat it to Prinzel and Unterholzer, and they would, he hoped, feel humbled.

'Yes,' said the Holy Man. 'And I can see some things about your life. Would you like to hear them?'

Von Igelfeld felt his heart racing. Did he want to receive a message, whatever it might turn out to be, from this Holy Man? It could be something disturbing, of course, something quite discouraging; but when would another chance like this present itself? He would have to seize the opportunity.

'You are very kind,' he said. 'I should like to hear.'

The Holy Man closed his eyes. For a few moments he mumbled a chant of some sort, and then he spoke.

'There is one thing which is close, and one thing which is far,' he began. 'The close thing is a man who is coming here to meet you, in this place. I see water, and I see the water all about the man. He is from the North. That is all I see of that.' He paused. What on earth could that be, thought von Igelfeld? It made no sense at all.

'Then,' went on the Holy Man. 'There is the far thing. That is a plot. There are people plotting against you in a distant land. They are plotting something terrible. You must go back as soon as you can and deal with these wicked people and their plot. That is all I see in that department now.'

Von Igelfeld drew in his breath. This was a clear, unequivocal warning, of the sort that one could not ignore.

Suddenly, Goa seemed threatening. Suddenly, the sense of optimism he had felt at the breakfast table departed and he felt only foreboding. How stupid to have asked the Holy Man for his visions. He had been as foolish as Faust: only torment lay that way.

The Holy Man now stood up and picked up his bag.

'I must continue with my search,' he said. 'There are many paths and it is late.'

Von Igelfeld rose to his feet, and fished in his pocket for a bank note. This he pressed into the Holy Man's hand.

'These are alms for you,' he said. 'They are to assist you on your way.'

The Holy Man did not look at the money, but quickly slipped it into his dhoti.

'You are a good, kind man,' he said to von Igelfeld. 'God will illumine your path. Most surely he will.'

Then, without further words, he strode away, leaving von Igelfeld alone in the courtyard with the broken statues and the sound of the rats creeping around in the undergrowth.

Back at the Hotel Lisboa, von Igelfeld was handed a large, cream-coloured envelope on which his name had been written in an ornate script. He thought it might be a letter from Professor Rasi Henderson Paliwalar, with some news of the next day's conference proceedings, but it was not. It was, in fact, a letter from the President of the Portuguese Chamber of Commerce, inviting von Igelfeld to be the guest of honour, and speaker, at that evening's dinner of the Chamber. Von Igelfeld was astonished at the brevity of the notice, but assumed that this must be quite normal in Goa, where things appeared to be ordered differently from the way in which they were ordered in Germany, or anywhere else for that matter.

He spent the rest of the day reading and preparing a short talk for the meeting. He had decided that he would explain to the businessmen what philology was all about, and in particular draw their attention to recent developments in Portuguese philology. He was pleased with the talk, when he had finished it: it was not too simple, so he could not be accused of talking down to his audience; yet it assumed only the barest acquaintance with linguistic and philological terms. It would be ideal for such an audience.

The Portuguese Chamber of Commerce turned out to be one of the best buildings in Goa. The home of a seventeenth-century merchant, it had subsequently been converted into a banking hall, and when the bank failed, the merchants had taken it over as a club. Von Igelfeld was shown the Members' Room, a marvellous saloon with leather armchairs and mahogany writing tables, and then, when the members had assembled in the dining room, he was accompanied in by the President and seated at the top table.

The meal was delicious, and the conversation of the President most entertaining. He was an exporter of sultanas, as his father and grandfather had been before him. The world of sultanas, he informed von Igelfeld, was full of intrigue, and he revealed a few of the juicier details over the soup.

After the meal, while they were waiting for coffee, and before his speech, von Igelfeld ran his eye about the room. There were about eighty guests, all men, all dressed in formal attire. Von Igelfeld looked at the physical types represented: the fat, prosperous merchants; the thin, nervous-looking accountants; the sly bankers; and then he stopped. There, halfway down the third table, was the prison governor, Mr Majipondi. Von Igelfeld was astonished. Surely it was inappropriate for a prison governor, even if he did have dealings with the town's merchants, to mix socially with those who corrupted him? And what about the murder? Did the members of the Chamber of Commerce know all about that? Was a blind eye turned here, as apparently it was everywhere else?

These perplexing questions in his mind, von Igelfeld heard the applause that followed his introduction and rose to his feet. As he spoke, he tried not to look at the table at which Mr Majipondi was sitting, but he felt the eyes of the prison governor upon him, weighing him up, imagining him in a prison suit, or peeling potatoes perhaps?

There was prolonged applause when von Igelfeld finished his talk. Several of the members, who were clearly moved by what had been said, banged their spoons on the table, until quietened by a gesture from the President. Then the President stood up, thanked von Igelfeld profusely, and invited questions from the members.

There was complete silence. The candle flames guttered in the breeze; a waiter, standing against a wall, coughed slightly. Then a member from the top table stood up and said:

'That was most interesting, Professor von Igelfeld. It is always enlightening to hear of the work of others, and you have told us all about this philology of yours. Now, tell me please: is that all you do?'

The silence returned. All the members looked expectantly at von Igelfeld, who, completely taken aback by the question, merely nodded his head.

'He says: yes,' said the President. 'Now, if there are no

89

more questions, members may adjourn to the saloon.'

As he accompanied the President into the rather dowdy, high-ceilinged room which served as the saloon, von Igelfeld turned over in his mind the events of the past hour. He had been surprised that there were no further questions, but he thought that perhaps the merchants would wish to ask him these in the relative informality of the saloon. He was sure that there must have been something which he had said which would have given rise to doubts that would need to be resolved. Had his point about pronouns been entirely understood?

The President steered von Igelfeld to a place near the large, discoloured fireplace and placed a glass of port in his hand. Then, beckoning to a small group of members standing nearby, he drew them over and introduced them one by one to von Igelfeld.

'And this,' said the President, 'is Mr Majipondi.'

Von Igelfeld, who had been bowing slightly to each member, looked up. He had taken the proffered hand in mid-bow and only now did he see the beaming face of the prison governor before him.

'I am most honoured to meet you,' said Mr Majipondi in a low, unctuous voice. 'Your talk was most informative. Indeed,' and here he turned to the President for confirmation, 'it was the most learned talk we have ever enjoyed in this Chamber.'

The President nodded his ready agreement.

Von Igelfeld tried to shrug off the compliment. He felt distinctly uneasy in the presence of Mr Majipondi, and his only wish was to get away. But the prison governor had moved closer and had reached out to touch the lapel of his suit with a heavy, ring-encrusted hand. He held the material between his fingers, as if assessing its quality, and then, reluctantly letting go, he returned his gaze to von Igelfeld's face.

'I am the governor of our little prison here,' he said. 'We are very concerned about rehabilitation. We are making silk purses out of sows' ears – that is my business!'

He laughed, challenging von Igelfeld to do the same. But von Igelfeld felt only repulsion, and he pointedly ignored the invitation.

'And what about murderers?' he suddenly found himself asking. 'Do you make them better too?'

Mr Majipondi gave a slight start (or did he? von Igelfeld asked himself). He was looking closely at von Igelfeld, his eyes tiny points of cunning in his fleshy face.

'We do not have many of those,' he said. 'In fact, if you listen to what people say, you'd think I'm the only one around.'

Von Igelfeld battled to conceal his utter astonishment. Was this Mr Majipondi confessing, or was he suggesting that the rumours were just that – rumours?

It was a situation quite beyond von Igelfeld's experience. Nobody in Germany would make such a remark – even an incorrigible murderer. Von Igelfeld believed that such people tended to look for excuses, and that they usually blamed their crimes on somebody else or on some abnormal mental state. Nobody accepted blame these days, and yet here in Goa, it was perhaps different, and a murderer could cheerfully confess to his crime with no sense of shame. Was it something to do with Eastern attitudes of acceptance? Could it be that if you were a murderer, then that was your lot in life, and it should be borne uncomplainingly? Was it something to do with karma? He looked at Mr Majipondi again, who returned his gaze with undisturbed equanimity.

'Do you mean that people accuse you, the prison governor, of being a murderer?' asked von Igelfeld at last, trying to sound astonished at the suggestion.

Mr Majipondi laughed. 'What people say about others is of no consequence,' he answered. 'The important thing is how you feel inside.'

It was the sort of answer which the Holy Man would have given, and it rather took von Igelfeld by surprise. As he pondered its significance, the President exchanged a glance with Mr Majipondi, who suddenly bowed and withdrew from the group. It was now the chance of Mr Verenyai Butterchayra to speak to von Igelfeld, and while this successful cutlery manufacturer engaged the visiting scholar in conversation, von Igelfeld was able from time to time to get a glimpse of Mr Majipondi again, holding forth elsewhere to the evident pleasure of his fellow guests.

The following day was the first day of the conference. Von Igelfeld listened courteously to every paper, skilfully concealing the intense boredom he felt as speaker after speaker made his trite or eccentric contribution to the debate. One paper stood out as excellent, though, and this, in von Igelfeld's mind, made the whole thing worthwhile. This was Professor Richimantry Gupta's report on Urdu subjunctives – a masterpiece which von Igelfeld resolved to attempt to secure for publication in the *Zeitschrift* – if it had not already been published.

Then, at four o'clock, the day's proceedings came to an end. Von Igelfeld slipped out of the hall as quickly as he could, hoping to be able to get some fresh air before the sun went down. He was not quick enough, though, to avoid the attention of the day's chairman, who seized his elbow and asked him his view of the day's proceedings.

Von Igelfeld was tactful. 'It's such a pity that Professor J. G. K. L. Singh has been delayed,' he said. 'How he would have enjoyed Professor Gupta's contribution.'

The chairman nodded his agreement. 'So sad,' he said. 'I do hope that he makes a quick recovery.'

'A recovery?' asked von Igelfeld. 'I was under the impression that he was merely delayed, not ill.'

The chairman shook his head. 'Oh my dear Professor von Igelfeld,' he said, his voice lowered. 'I thought that you knew. Professor J. G. K. L. Singh's train fell off a railway bridge and into a river. Our dear colleague was spared drowning, but was seriously inconvenienced by a crocodile.'

Von Igelfeld's dismay greatly impressed the chairman.

'I can see that you were fond of him,' he said. 'I am sorry to be the bearer of such ill tidings.'

Von Igelfeld nodded distractedly. The words of the Holy Man's prophecy were coming back to him quite clearly. *There is one thing which is close and one thing which is far. The close thing is a man who is coming here to meet you, in this place. I see water, and I see the water all about the man. He is from the North.*

Could it be that at the very moment that the prophecy was being delivered, the girders of the bridge had given way and the ill-fated train had plunged down into the river? It was very sad for Professor J. G. K. L. Singh, of course, but what about the second part of the prophecy? The first part had been shown to be true, and this meant that somebody, somewhere, was plotting against von Igelfeld. Who could this be, and where? Were the plotters in Germany? If they were, then it would be night-time there and they would be asleep in their shameless beds. But as the day began, then the plotters would presumably resume their nefarious activities. The thought chilled von Igelfeld, and a feeling of foreboding remained with him throughout the rest of the night and was still there in the morning.

The second day of the conference was worse than the first. Von Igelfeld delivered his own paper, and was immediately thereafter assaulted by a barrage of irrelevant and unhelpful questions. He was in a bad mood at lunch, and spoke to nobody, and in the afternoon his mind was too exercised with the prophecy and its implications to pay any attention to the proceedings. At the end of the afternoon, when the conference came to its end, he avoided the final reception and slipped off to the hotel to pack his bags. Then, settling his account and bidding farewell to the manager of the hotel, he drove out to the airport in an old, cream-coloured taxi and waited for the first available seat on a plane to Europe.

India, with all its colours, confusions and heartbreak, slipped below him in a smudge of brown. Von Igelfeld sat at his window seat and looked out over the silver wing of steel. It had been a mistake to visit Goa, he concluded. It might be that some achieved spiritual solace in India, but this had been denied him. His one encounter with a Holy Man – perhaps the only such encounter he would be vouchsafed in his life – had turned into a nightmare. There was no peace in that – only horrible, gnawing doubt. And at the back of his mind, too, was the image of

Professor J. G. K. L. Singh in the muddy waters of the river and of the great jaws of the crocodile poised to close upon the helpless philologist. It was an awful, haunting image, and it brought home to von Igelfeld his great lack of charity in relation to Professor J. G. K. L. Singh. He would make up for it, he determined. He would send a letter to Chandighar with an invitation to the Institute in Regensburg, which could be taken up once Professor J. G. K. L. Singh got better. He would make it clear, though, that the invitation was only for one week; that was very important.

Dear, friendly, safe, comfortable Germany! Von Igelfeld could have kissed the ground on his arrival, but wasted no time in rushing home. His house was in order, and Frau Gunter, who housekept for him, assured him that nothing untoward had happened. For a moment von Igelfeld wondered whether she was a plotter, but he rapidly dismissed the unworthy thought from his mind.

He took a bath, dressed in an appropriate suit, and made his way hurriedly to the Institute. There he attended to his mail, none of which was in the slightest bit threatening, and then sat at his desk and looked out of the window. Perhaps there was nothing in it after all. Certainly the clear, rational light of Germany made it all seem less threatening: a Holy Man made no sense here.

Von Igelfeld decided to visit the Institute library to glance at the latest journals. He put away his letters, picked up his briefcase, and sauntered down the corridor to the library.

'Professor Dr von Igelfeld!' said the Librarian in hushed

tones. 'We thought you would be away for another three days.'

'I have come back early,' said von Igelfeld. 'The conference was not very successful.'

He looked about him. Something was happening in the library. Two of the junior librarians were taking books out of the shelves in the entrance hall and placing them on a trolley.

'What's happening here?' asked von Igelfeld. Librarians were always busy rearranging and recataloguing; von Igelfeld thought that it was all that stood between them and complete boredom.

The Librarian looked at his assistants.

'Oh, a little reorganisation. A few books in here are being taken into the back room.'

Von Igelfeld said nothing for a moment. His eye had fallen on the trolley and on one book in particular placed there and destined for the obscurity of the back room. *Portuguese Irregular Verbs*!

Slowly he recovered his speech. 'Who suggested this reorganisation?' he asked, his voice steady in spite of the turbulent emotions within him.

The Librarian smiled. 'It wasn't my idea,' he said brightly. 'Professor Dr Unterholzer and one of our visiting professors suggested it. I was happy to comply.'

Von Igelfeld's breathing was regular, but deep. It was all clear now, oh so clear!

'And who was this visiting professor?' he asked icily.

'Professor Dr Dr Prinzel,' answered the Librarian. He looked curiously at von Igelfeld. 'If you disapprove, of course . . .'

Von Igelfeld stepped forward and retrieved the copy of *Portuguese Irregular Verbs* from the trolley. The Librarian gasped.

'Of course . . .' he stuttered. 'I had no idea that that work was involved.' He snatched the tome from von Igelfeld and replaced it on the shelf. 'It will, of course, remain exactly where it was. I should never have agreed to its being put in the back room, had I known.'

Von Igelfeld walked home. He was tired now, as the journey had begun to catch up on him. But he knew that he would be able to sleep well, now that he had identified the terrible plot which had been made against him. He would take no action against Prinzel and Unterholzer, who would just see that *Portuguese Irregular Verbs* remained in its accustomed place of prominence. He would not even say anything to them about it – he would rise quite above the whole matter.

It was a course of action of which the Holy Man would undoubtedly have approved.

Dental Pain

Professor Dr Moritz-Maria Von Igelfeld had excellent teeth. As a boy, he had been taken to the dentist every year, but treatment had rarely been necessary and the dentist had dismissed him.

'Only come if you have toothache,' he said to von Igelfeld. 'These teeth of yours will last you your life.'

Von Igelfeld followed this questionable advice, and never thought thereafter of consulting a dentist. Then, shortly after his return from the French Philological Forum in Lyons, he felt a sudden, gnawing pain at the back of his lower jaw. He looked at his mouth in a mirror, but saw nothing other than a gleaming row of apparently healthy teeth. There were no mouth ulcers and there was no swelling, but the pain made him feel as if a long, heated needle was being driven into his bone.

He put up with it for a full morning, and then, after lunch, when it seemed as if his mouth would explode in searing agony, he walked to a dental studio which he had noticed round the corner from the Institute. A reception-ist met him and took his history with compassion.

'You're obviously in great pain,' she said. 'Dr von Brautheim will take you next. She will finish with her patient in a few minutes.'

Von Igelfeld sat down in the reception room and picked up the first magazine he saw on the table before him. He paged through it, noticing the pictures of food and clothes. How strange, he thought – what sort of *Zeitschrift* is this? Do people really read about these matters? He turned a page and began to read something called the *Timely Help* column. Readers wrote in and asked advice over their prob-lems. Von Igelfeld's eyes opened wide. Did people discuss such things in open print? How could anybody talk about things like that? He read a letter from a woman in Hamburg which quite took his breath away. Why did she marry him in the first place, if she knew that was what he was like? Such men should be in prison, thought von Igelfeld, although that was not what the readers' adviser suggested. She said that the woman should try to talk to her husband and persuade him to change his ways. Well! thought von Igelfeld. If I wrote that column I would give very differ-ent advice. In fact, I should pass such letters over to the police without delay.

The door of the surgery opened and a miserable-looking man walked out. He put on his coat, massaged his jaw, and nodded to the receptionist. Then von Igelfeld was invited in, and found himself sitting in the dental chair of Dr Lisbetta von Brautheim. It was a new experience for him; the only dentist he had ever consulted had been a man. But there was nothing wrong with a woman dentist, he thought; in fact, she was likely to be much more sympathetic and gentle than a man.

Dr von Brautheim was a petite woman in her mid-thirties. She had a gentle, attractive face, and von Igelfeld found it very easy to look at her as she peered into his mouth. Her hands were careful as she prodded about in the angry area of his mouth, and even when her pick touched the very source of the pain, von Igelfeld found that he could bear the agony.

'An impacted supernumerary,' said Dr von Brautheim. 'I'm afraid the only thing I can do is remove it. That should give you the relief you need.'

Von Igelfeld nodded his agreement. He was utterly won over by Dr von Brautheim and would have consented to any suggestion she made. He opened his mouth again, felt the prick of the anaesthetic needle, and then a marvellous feeling of relief flooded over him. Dr von Brautheim worked quickly and efficiently, and within minutes the offending tooth was laid on a tray and the gap had been plugged with dressing.

'That is all, Professor Dr von Igelfeld,' she said quietly, as her instruments were whisked away into the steriliser. 'You should come back and see me the day after tomorrow and we shall see how things have settled down.'

Von Igelfeld arose from the couch and smiled at his saviour.

'The pain has gone,' he said. 'I thought it would kill me, but now it has gone.'

'Those teeth can be quite nasty when they impact,' said Dr von Brautheim. 'But otherwise your mouth looks very healthy.'

Von Igelfeld beamed with pleasure. To receive such a compliment from the attractive Dr von Brautheim gave him a considerable thrill, and as he walked down the stairs he reflected on his good fortune in being able to see her again so soon. He would bring her a present to thank her for her help – a bunch of flowers perhaps. Was she married, he wondered? What a marvellous wife she would make for somebody.

There was no more pain that night, nor the next morning. Von Igelfeld dutifully swallowed the pills which Dr von Brautheim had given him and at the Institute that day he regaled everybody with the story of the remarkable cure which had been effected. The others then told their own dental stories: the Librarian related how his elderly aunt had lost several teeth some years before but was now, happily, fully recovered; the Deputy Librarian had an entire row of fillings, following upon a childhood indulged with sweets; and the Administrative Director revealed that he had in fact no teeth at all but found his false teeth very comfortable indeed.

That afternoon, von Igelfeld sat in his room, the proofs of the next issue of the *Zeitschrift* on his desk before him. He was wrestling with a particularly difficult paper, and was finding it almost impossible to edit in the way which he felt it needed to be edited. 'Spanish loan words,' wrote the author, 'appear to be profuse in Brazilian dialects, particularly those used by river-men. But are they really loan words, or are they Brazilian misunderstandings of Portuguese originals . . .'

Von Igelfeld looked up from the paper and stared out of his window. No matter how hard he tried to concentrate, his mind was distracted. What were these river-men like? He tried to picture them; tough-looking men, no doubt, with slouch hats; characters from a Conrad story, perhaps. But the image faded and his thoughts returned to the memory of his trip to the dental studio and of the sweet face of Dr von Brautheim above him. What did she think of her patients, and of their suffering? He imagined her as a ministering angel, gently bringing relief to those in pain. Von Igelfeld recalled the touch of her hands and the delicious smell of the soap, a reassuring, almost-nursery smell. To be looked after by such a being must be paradise indeed. Just imagine it!

He got up from his desk and walked about his room. Why was it that he kept thinking of her, when he should have been thinking of the *Zeitschrift*? This had only happened to him once or twice before, and he distrusted the feeling. It had happened once when he was nineteen, and he had met, for a mere afternoon, the daughter of his Uncle Ludwig's neighbour. She had been at the conservatory in Berlin and had played her viola for him. He had seen her once or twice after that and then she had gone to America and never come back. He imagined a crude fate for her in the United States – living in a characterless apartment block with urban ugliness all about and a husband who growled and talked through his nose.

Von Igelfeld left his room and walked down the corridor to Unterholzer's small study. Unterholzer was in, leafing through his share of the *Zeitschrift* proofs, shaking his head disapprovingly.

'These printers,' he said to von Igelfeld. 'They must be illiterate. Here's a page with the diacritical marks all in the wrong place. They'll have to reset the whole thing.'

Von Igelfeld nodded absent-mindedly.

'I went to the dentist yesterday,' he announced. 'I was in great pain.'

Unterholzer looked up, concerned.

'I'm sorry to hear that. Did he fix everything up?'

'She,' said von Igelfeld, smiling. 'It was a lady dentist. And she made everything much better.'

'Oh,' said Unterholzer, his eyes returning to the proofs. 'I'm happy to hear that you're no longer in pain.'

Von Igelfeld crossed Unterholzer's room and looked disapprovingly out of the window: in contrast to the view from his own room, Unterholzer had a very unedifying view of the Institute car park. Perhaps it was good enough for him; poor Unterholzer.

'Yes,' he said. 'She was a very charming dentist indeed. Very charming. In fact, I certainly would not mind pursuing her acquaintance.'

'Is that so?' said Unterholzer, still looking at the proofs. 'Perhaps I should go and have my teeth checked. Where is her studio?'

'Just round the corner,' said von Igelfeld. 'And it's a good idea to go to the dentist regularly, you know. When did you last go?'

'About a year or two ago,' said Unterholzer vaguely.

Von Igelfeld tut-tutted. 'That's not frequently enough,' he said. 'Dr von Brautheim recommends a visit once every six months.'

'Don't worry,' said Unterholzer. 'I'll make an appointment soon.'

Von Igelfeld gave up. He had hoped to be able to tell Unterholzer a little bit more about Dr von Brautheim, but he was clearly not going to be at all receptive. That was the trouble with Unterholzer, he thought – he was too literal. He had very little imagination.

On the appointed day, von Igelfeld dressed with care for his visit to the dental studio. He put on the bright red tie he had bought in Rome, and he took especial care in choosing his shirt. Then, with at least half an hour in hand, he made his way to the dental studio, carrying with him the present he had decided to give Dr von Brautheim. It was not a present which he usually gave to people, as it was not at all inexpensive. But Dr von Brautheim was different, and he had carefully wrapped it in soft purple paper he had acquired from a gift shop near his house.

He intended to do more than give her a present, though. He had decided that he would enquire discreetly of the receptionist whether her employer was single, and if that was the case – Oh bliss! – then he would ask her to join him for lunch some weekend. He would set up a lunch party – perhaps Zimmermann might come – and that would be a good setting in which to get to know her better.

The receptionist did not appear surprised by the question.

'Dr von Brautheim is unmarried,' she said. 'She lives with her elderly parents. Her father was Professor of Dentistry in Cologne.'

Von Igelfeld was delighted with this information. What a perfect background for such a person! Dentistry might not be the most prestigious career, but it was an honourable calling and people were wrong to look down upon it. And undoubtedly the von Brautheim family had once done something better, as the name suggested distinction of some sort.

He was admitted into the studio and, blushing slightly, took his place in the chair.

Dr von Brautheim took no more than a few minutes to attend to his mouth.

'It's healing nicely,' she said. 'And I see no complications. You may rinse your mouth out now.'

Disappointed at the brevity of the treatment, von Igelfeld became flustered. He had intended to raise the subject of the lunch party at this stage, but there was something about the situation which suggested that it would be inappropriate. There was still the present, though, and as he stood at the doorway he thrust it into her hands.

'This is a small token of my appreciation,' he said formally. 'You've been so kind.'

The dentist smiled, a warm, melting smile that made von Igelfeld feel weak at the knees.

'How kind of you Professor Dr von Igelfeld,' she said. 'How unnecessary, but how kind. May I open it now?'

'Of course,' said von Igelfeld. 'I should be delighted.'

Dr von Brautheim unwrapped the soft purple paper and there it was, in her hands, *Portuguese Irregular Verbs*!

'How kind!' she repeated. 'Such a large book too!'

Over the next week, von Igelfeld thought of little else. He had decided that he would leave it about ten days before he sent the note inviting her to the lunch, which would be held a month after that. This would mean that it would be unlikely that she would have another commitment and would therefore accept. In due course the letter was written, and a prompt reply received. Yes, she would be delighted to attend his lunch party on the stated date.

Meanwhile, Unterholzer announced that he had himself consulted Dr von Brautheim, who had suggested two fillings and a new crown. He was delighted with her treatment, and told von Igelfeld that for the first time in his life he found himself looking forward to being in the dentist's chair. Von Igelfeld found this rather presumptuous, but said nothing.

A few days before the lunch party was due to take place, von Igelfeld decided that he could properly call on Dr von Brautheim again to give her directions as to how to reach his house. It was not strictly speaking necessary, as she would undoubtedly have a map of the town, but it would give him an opportunity to see her again.

He made his way up to the dental studio, his heart hammering with excitement. The receptionist greeted him

warmly and asked him whether he was experiencing further trouble with his teeth. Von Igelfeld explained his mission, and was disappointed when the receptionist told him that it was Dr von Brautheim's afternoon off and that she would not be in until tomorrow.

'You may leave her a note, though,' she said.

Von Igelfeld glanced towards the studio, the door of which was open. There was the drill apparatus, the couch, the chest of instruments, and there, on the floor beside the chair was *Portuguese Irregular Verbs*. For a moment he said nothing. Then a wave of emotion flooded through him. She was reading his book in between patients! What a marvellous, wonderful thing!

'That book,' he said to the receptionist. 'Is Dr von Brautheim reading it at present?'

The receptionist glanced in the direction of the studio and smiled. 'That? Oh no. You know that Dr von Brautheim isn't very tall, and she's found that standing on that book brings her up to just the right height for when the chair's reclined.'

Von Igelfeld left a brief note, confirming the time and place of the lunch. Then he went out into the street, his mind in turmoil. No, he should not take offence, he told himself. It was quite touching really. It was unfair to expect everybody to be interested in philology, and at least she had found a use for the book. Perhaps she even used it because it reminded her of him! Yes, that was it. If he looked at it that way, then the ignominious fate of *Portuguese Irregular Verbs* was nothing to worry over.

He made his way into the Institute and settled down to the work that had piled up over the last few weeks of distraction. There was a great deal to do, and when six o'clock came he had made little impression on it. Most of the staff of the Institute had left, and von Igelfeld was surprised when Unterholzer knocked at his door.

'What's keeping you in, Unterholzer?' von Igelfeld asked.

Unterholzer stood in the doorway, beaming with pleasure.

'I'm in because I've been out,' he said. 'I took the afternoon off and now I've come in to do what I wanted to do during the afternoon.'

'Oh yes,' said von Igelfeld, with a distinct lack of interest. 'What did you do?'

Unterholzer stepped forward into the room.

'I went out . . .' he began, halting in his excitement. 'I went out with my new fiancée. We went to buy a ring.'

Von Igelfeld dropped his pen in amazement.

'Your new fiancée!' he exclaimed. 'Unterholzer, what dramatic news! Who is she?'

'My dentist!' crowed Unterholzer. 'The delightful Dr von Brautheim. I have been seeing her regularly and we have fallen in love with one another. At lunchtime she agreed to become my wife. I shall be calling on her father tomorrow. Do you know that he had the Chair of Dentistry in Cologne?'

Von Igelfeld stayed in the Institute until half past eleven, alone with his papers. Then he walked home, following his usual route, reflecting on the sadnesses of life – visions unrealised, love unfulfilled, dental pain.

Death in Venice

The wedding of Professor Dr Detlev Amadeus Unterholzer and Dr Lisbetta von Brautheim was a particularly trying occasion for the author of *Portuguese Irregular Verbs*. Von Igelfeld tried to rise above the feelings of resentment he experienced on finding that Unterholzer, of all people, had succeeded in securing the affections of the woman he had been planning to marry, but it was difficult. If only he had not waited; if only he had invited her to lunch immediately, rather than a full five weeks later, then matters would have turned out differently. And, of course, if he had not been so foolish as to recommend that Unterholzer have his teeth seen to, then the couple would never have met and it would have been him, rather than Unterholzer, standing beside Lisbetta at the altar.

Such thoughts, of course, led nowhere. Von Igelfeld put on as brave a face as he could, and tried to show pleasure in the evident happiness of the bride and groom. At the wedding itself, a large occasion attended by over two hundred people, he sat next to Florianus and Ophelia Prinzel, and this helped to take his mind off the thought of what might have been. Ophelia Prinzel found weddings extremely moving occasions and wept voluminously, with Prinzel and von Igelfeld taking it in turns to comfort her.

Later, though, von Igelfeld confessed to Ophelia what had happened, and she was aghast at the story.

'What awful, awful bad luck,' she said sympathetically. 'You would have made a much better husband for her, Moritz-Maria. Unterholzer's all very well, but . . .'

Von Igelfeld nodded. 'I know,' he said. 'But it's too late now, and I suppose we must wish them every happiness.'

Ophelia Prinzel agreed that this was the charitable thing to do, but she was secretly thinking of what it would be like to share a bed with Unterholzer and the notion did not appeal. In fact, she closed her eyes and shuddered.

'However,' she said, 'there's no point in thinking of what might have been. The important thing is: how do you feel?'

For a moment von Igelfeld said nothing, then he turned to her and said, 'Terrible! I feel all washed up and finished. I feel as if there's no point to life any more, even to my work. What's the use? Where does it all lead?'

Ophelia laid a comforting hand on his shoulder.

'You need to get away,' she said. 'You must come with us to Venice, mustn't he, Florianus?'

Prinzel quickly agreed with his wife. 'We're going to go in two months time. We shall spend a month there in September, when the worst of the crowds have gone. You'd be very welcome, you know.'

Von Igelfeld thought for a moment. He usually went to Switzerland in the late summer, but it was a good three years since he had been to Venice and perhaps it was just what he needed. In Switzerland he always walked and climbed – it was really no holiday – whereas in Venice he could take things very easily, read, and enjoy good Italian meals. Yes, it was an excellent idea altogether. The Prinzels travelled down to Venice first, motoring in a leisurely way through the hills of Austria. Von Igelfeld followed by train, and when his carriage eventually drew into Venice station, there was Prinzel to meet him. They boarded a *vaporetto* and were soon heading out across the lagoon, through that waterscape of legend, past the proud liners at anchor, past the tether posts, past the cypress-crowned islands. Von Igelfeld watched as the city retreated and the Lido drew near, and then they were ashore, and a liveried porter of the Grand Hôtel des Bains was struggling with the von Igelfeld cabin trunks, the very same trunks which his grandfather had himself brought to the beguiling city.

Established in his room overlooking the hotel gardens and the beach, von Igelfeld changed out of his suit and donned a white linen jacket and lightweight trousers. Then, with his Panama hat in hand, he made his way down to the main terrace where Prinzel and Ophelia were waiting for him. They sat and drank lemon tea, chatting for over an hour, and then von Igelfeld returned to his room for a siesta. He was already beginning to feel relaxed, and he knew that Ophelia's advice had been sound. How pointless in such surroundings to worry about lost chances and the petty irritations of life! Here all that mattered was art and beauty.

He slept deeply, awaking shortly after six o'clock. Drawing his curtains, he noticed that the sun was setting over the city, a great red ball sinking behind the distant domes, setting fire to the pale blue water. He stood for a few minutes, quite entranced, and then he left his room and went down to the terrace again. They had all agreed to meet for dinner at eight, and until then, von Igelfeld sat on the terrace, reading the copy of *I Promessi Sposi* which he had extracted from one of his cabin trunks. It was a perfect evening, and the hours before dinner went rather too quickly for von Igelfeld. He could have sat there forever, he thought, looking at his fellow guests and the bobbing lights upon the sea.

They dined in the main dining room. Ophelia chose all the courses, and every one of them was approved of by von Igelfeld. The conversation was light and entertaining: neither Unterholzer nor Dr von Brautheim was mentioned once, although the occasional painful memory momentarily crossed von Igelfeld's mind. After dinner, they returned to the terrace to drink small cups of strong, scalding coffee.

'This is perfect,' said von Igelfeld. 'I could stay here indefinitely, I'm sure.'

Prinzel laughed. 'You think you could,' he said. 'But remember, we're only visitors. The reality of Venice might be rather different when one's exposed to it all the time. This city has other moods, remember.'

'Oh?' said von Igelfeld. 'What do you mean by that?'

Prinzel paused before answering. 'It's corrupt. Some say that it's dying. Can't you smell it? The decay?'

Von Igelfeld thought about this for some time, and later on, in the small hours of the morning, he was troubled by a dreadful nightmare. He was alone in a small Venetian street, a street that appeared to lead nowhere. At every corner there were mocking figures wearing elaborate Venetian masks, laughing at him, ridiculing him. He sat up in bed and shivered. He had left the window slightly open, and a breeze was moving the curtains. He turned on a light, looked at his watch, and took a long draught of mineral water. What was wrong? Why had Prinzel said that Venice was dying? What had he meant?

The next morning, with the sun streaming in through his window, von Igelfeld was able to put the terrors of the night well behind him. He showered, once again donned his light linen jacket, and went downstairs for breakfast. They had agreed to pursue their own activities and interests during the day and to meet each evening for dinner – a good arrangement, von Igelfeld thought, as they didn't want to be too much on top of one another.

Sitting at the starched white cloth of his table, von Igelfeld smiled as he addressed his breakfast. He looked at the twenty or so other guests who were making an early start to the day. There was a young couple, absorbed in each other, with eyes for nobody else; there was an elderly woman with purple-rinsed hair, American, thought von Igelfeld, and lonely; there was a clergyman of some sort, probably English, von Igelfeld decided; and then there was a large family, of mother, governess and four children. Von Igelfeld watched the family. They were elegantly and expensively dressed, three girls and a boy. The girls wore light blue dresses and ribbons in their hair – almost a family uniform – and the boy, who was about fifteen or sixteen, wore a sailor suit.

Von Igelfeld's eye passed to the mother. What a beautiful woman she was, he thought, and she was so clearly used to admiration and respect, as she sat with an air of almost palpable authority, speaking to each of her children in turn, occasionally saying something to the governess. 'Where is father?'

he wondered. Was he still working in some distant city, supporting this expensive family in luxury, or had something terrible happened to him? Certainly the mother did not look like a widow; she was vivacious and carefree, whereas widows, in von Igelfeld's experience, *pace* Franz Lehar, never were.

Von Igelfeld buttered a further roll and allowed honey to drip all over it. Then he took another sip of coffee and glanced over at the family's table again. As he did so, the boy turned his head and looked directly at him. Von Igelfeld dropped his gaze, but he felt that the boy was still staring at him. He concentrated on his roll. Had the honey been evenly spread, or was it too concentrated at the one end? He looked up again and the flaxen-haired boy was still staring in his direction with wide blue, inquisitive eyes. Von Igelfeld fingered at the knot in his tie and turned away. He was accustomed to being stared at, being so tall, but it always made him feel uneasy. The mother should teach him not to stare, he thought; but parents appeared to teach their children nothing these days.

After he had finished his roll, von Igelfeld poured himself another large cup of strong, milky coffee, and drained it with pleasure. The family had arisen from the table now, and was trooping out of the dining room. The boy was the last to go, and as he left he turned and glanced at von Igelfeld, tossing his hair back as he did so. Von Igelfeld frowned, and looked down at his tie. Was there something odd in his dress that made the boy look at him? Did his shoes match? Of course they did.

He walked out onto the terrace and felt the morning sun on his face. It was going to be a marvellous day, although it could well become a little warm at noon. He would go to the *Accademia* this morning, he told himself, and then afterwards he would seek out the peace of one of the quieter churches. He had always liked the church of San Giovanni Cristostomo, and perhaps he would spend an hour or so there looking at Bellini's *St Jerome with St Christopher and St Augustine*. That would keep him busy until lunchtime, which he would spend in a small restaurant that he always visited when he was in Venice and where he was known to the proprietor. After lunch he could return to the hotel, sleep, and then meet the Prinzels for dinner. It would be a most satisfactory day.

The *Accademia* was surprisingly quiet. Von Igelfeld wandered from room to room, feasting his eyes on the great, brooding paintings. By mid-morning he was in Room Seven, standing before Lotto's *Portrait of a Young Man in his Study*. Von Igelfeld gazed at the great canvas, his eye moving over the objects which made up the young man's world – the mandolin, silent, but a reminder of the carefree pleasure of youth (he thought of Heidelberg, and of the easy fellowship of student years, never, never recaptured); the hunting horn (*Als ich ein Junge war*, muttered von Igelfeld); and there, on the ground, the painter had painted the fallen rose petals – his final statement on the transience of life. Von Igelfeld walked away, throwing a glance over his shoulder at the picture. Suddenly, for no reason at all, he thought of the boy in the hotel. *He* could play the mandolin, no doubt, and blow the hunting horn too, for that matter. But would he come back, thirty, forty years from now and look at this picture, just as von Igelfeld was now doing? Perhaps he would.

In San Giovanni Cristotomo von Igelfeld was virtually by himself. He sat on a chair near a confessional, gazing up at the ceiling, letting the stress of the city drain out of his limbs. The sun filtered in through a high window, a dusty yellow shaft, the colour of butter. Von Igelfeld closed his eyes and thought: I'm in a house of God, but who is he? Where is he, this person he had always addressed as God but who had never spoken back to him, ever. He was not sure about the existence of God, but he had always been convinced that if he did exist, he would be the God of Mediterranean Christianity, not the cold, hard God of the Northern churches. But that, perhaps, was to draw too much comfort; he might even turn out to be the God of the quantum physicists, a final point implosion, or perhaps just a single particle, a tiny event. That would be terribly disappointing – if God were to prove to be an electron.

He opened his eyes. A group had entered the church and was making its way across the nave. It was a family, and von Igelfeld noticed with a sudden shock that it was the family from the hotel. He watched cautiously as the mother pointed towards the altar. One of the girls asked a question and the mother handed her a guidebook. Then the boy in the sailor suit stepped forward and tapped at his mother's elbow. She listened to him for a moment, and then laughed. Sulking, he moved away, walking towards von Igelfeld. Now he was in the shaft of sunlight, and for a moment he appeared to be an angel, from Giorgione's studio, perhaps, clothed in the softness of the light, glowing with gold.

Suddenly the boy looked in von Igelfeld's direction. When he saw the professor, he gave a slight start, but then smiled, and again, as at the breakfast table, he stared. Von Igelfeld did not know what to do. Should he acknowledge the youth, or should he ignore him? He could hardly

116

pretend not to have seen him, and yet he had no desire to do anything which would concede to the boy that he had any right to intrude on his privacy as he was so clearly doing. What did this boy want of him after all? The whole situation was peculiar; familiar in a curious, inexplicable way; redolent of something he had read somewhere; but where?

The mother came to von Igelfeld's rescue.

'Tadseuz!' she called. 'Viens ici! Nous allons voir quelque chose de grand interêt . . .'

Tadseuz! thought von Igelfeld. So they are Polish. How very interesting! Perhaps Polish boys are particularly given to staring at people. The Poles were definitely very strange about certain things, and this might be one of them. He rose to his feet and slipped out of the church before the boy could bother him any further. His restaurant was just round the corner, and there, at least he would be safe from the unwelcome attentions of Polish boys.

'*Caro* Dottor von Igelfeld!' exclaimed the proprietor of the restaurant. 'Here you are again! We turn our back for two or three years, and, *Caspita*, there you are again!'

He led von Igelfeld to a table in a quiet corner and summoned a waiter. Von Igelfeld felt a warm rush of satisfaction; he knew that to the proprietor he was no more than a client whose name had happened to lodge in the mind, but he felt as if he was amongst friends.

A bottle of chilled wine from the hills was produced and the proprietor filled a glass for himself as well as for von Igelfeld.

'We are so glad to see you,' he said, raising his glass in toast. 'There are fewer people coming these days. This summer there were virtually no Germans in Italy. It was terrible!'

'No Germans!' Von Igelfeld was astonished at the hyperbole, but the proprietor seemed serious.

'They are keeping away from Venice for some reason,' he went on. 'They say it is something to do with the sea.'

'Is there anything wrong with the sea?' von Igelfeld asked, thinking of the beach at the Grand Hôtel des Bains. There had been people on it, hadn't there?

The proprietor shook his head vigorously. 'No! No! The sea is still there. The sea is fine. No, there is no reason for the Germans not to come.'

Von Igelfeld was puzzled and would have continued the discussion, but the proprietor clearly wanted to change the subject and he drew von Igelfeld's attentions to certain items on the menu.

'These are very good,' he said enthusiastically, drawing attention to the scallops. '*Scallopini alla Marie Curie*. I shall supervise their cooking personally. You will not be disappointed.'

After lunch, which lasted for over two hours, von Igelfeld walked back slowly towards the landing stage where he could board a *vaporetto* for the Lido. The back streets were quiet, and his footsteps rang out against the walls of the houses. Somewhere above him, in one of the windows, a woman was singing – a snatch of song, an aria that he had heard before but could not quite place. He stopped and listened. The singing continued for a few minutes and then it faded. Now a cat called somewhere in a doorway and there was the sound of a lock being turned.

Von Igelfeld went on. At the end of the street, the pavement took a turn and ran for a few yards to a small bridge across the canal. As he reached this point, von Igelfeld noticed two men clad in white crouching down beside the water. The men were unaware of his presence and he watched them as they dipped a container of some sort into the canal. Then they took it up and decanted a small quantity of water into a bottle. One of the men shook his head, while the other wrote something in a notebook. Then they stood up, and came face to face with von Igelfeld.

'*Scusi*,' said one of the men, and the two then bustled off. Von Igelfeld noticed that the white clothes were a uniform of some sort, and that one of them had a small two-way radio with him, which crackled into life as they walked away.

He paused, standing at the edge of the canal, and looked down into the water. It was green and murky, and if one fell in, he thought, well, what then? He remembered reading about a film producer in Rome who had fallen off a houseboat into the Tiber and who had died the next day from swallowing water. Would that happen in Venice? Was the whole city surrounded by poison? And then what was it that the proprietor of the restaurant had said about the sea? Was that poisonous too?

He walked on, but the image of the two men in white stayed in his mind, and he resolved to ask the manager of the hotel all about it if he had the opportunity that evening. Then he could warn the Prinzels about swimming, if need be.

No opportunity presented itself to talk to any of the hotel staff before dinner, so the topic did not come up at the table. The Prinzels had had an exhausting day, with a trip to Murano and several circumnavigations of the city on *vaporetti*. Ophelia had insisted upon a gondola ride, which Prinzel had eventually agreed to, but it had not been a success as the gondolier had apparently deliberately splashed Prinzel with water, or so Prinzel alleged.

'Did it get in your mouth?' von Igelfeld asked anxiously, but Prinzel assured him that it had merely covered his jacket.

'But why do you think it was deliberate?' von Igelfeld asked.

Prinzel's reply came quickly. 'Because he said to me, "Why are you Germans so scared of the water these days?" and then, before I had the chance to ask him what he meant, he splashed me. It was deliberate all right!'

Von Igelfeld caught his breath. This was consistent with what the restaurant proprietor had said to him about the Germans not coming. But why should they be afraid of the water? Nobody had said anything about the sea being dangerous in any way. There were no notices; there was nothing in the newspapers. Certainly the Grand Hôtel des Bains continued to offer its guests beach towels and bathing cabins. If the sea were perilous, then surely no responsible hotel would do that.

Von Igelfeld felt uneasy, but he did not wish to alarm the Prinzels unnecessarily. The following day he was to visit his one friend in Venice, Dottore Reggio Malvestiti, Librarian of the Biblioteca Filologica of the University of Venice. He knew that he could ask him about it and expect an honest answer. And at least Prinzel had not swallowed any water, so they were still safe.

Dottore Reggio Malvestiti, alerted by von Igelfeld's telephone call from the Grand Hôtel des Bains, was waiting for his visitor on the steps of the Biblioteca Filologica, a handsome sixteenth-century palazzo on the Rio dei Santi Apostoli.

'Dear Igelfeld,' he said, moving forward to embrace the great philologist. 'You must come to see us more often. We miss you so!'

Von Igelfeld, always slightly taken aback by Italian emotionalism, searched for an appropriate response, but found none. He need not have worried, however; Malvestiti immediately drew him into the entrance hall of the library and launched into an impassioned address on the subject of Morati's behaviour at the Siena Conference. Von Igelfeld listened as best he could, nodding agreement from time to time, but unable to make his way through the labyrinths of internecine Italian academic politics. Malevestiti appeared to be reaching the conclusion that Morati had at last lost his reason, and von Igelfeld signalled here his warm assent. He had always found a somewhat manic aspect to Morati's conduct. In the past he had put this down to his being Italian, but perhaps there was more to it than that. Perhaps Malvestiti was right.

They progressed through the entrance hall and made their way along a narrow corridor to Malvestiti's office. There Malvestiti pushed von Igelfeld into a chair (somewhat rudely, von Igelfeld thought) and continued his diatribe against Morati. Von Igelfeld, waiting for a pause, at last managed to interject his question.

'Is there something wrong with Venice?' he asked. 'Please give me a direct answer. That is all I want.'

Malvestiti, about to reveal a further perfidy on Morati's part, was stopped in his tracks.

'Venice?' he asked. 'Something wrong?'

Von Igelfeld nodded. 'Yes, Venice. I have seen men in white coats peering into the canal and taking samples of the water.'

For a few moments Malvestiti appeared to be thinking about this and said nothing. Then he sighed.

'Alas, you are right,' he said quietly. 'There is a great deal wrong with Venice. The water is rising. The city is sinking. Soon we shall all be gone. Even this library . . .' He stopped, and spread the palms of his hands in a gesture of despair. Then he continued: 'We have already lost an entire floor of this library – our entire Slavonic collection. It is now completely underwater.'

Von Igelfeld drew in his breath sharply. Surely the books themselves could not be submerged. Malvestiti, as if anticipating his question, smiled ruefully.

'Yes,' he said. 'It may seem ridiculous, but we just didn't have the time to save them. Come, let me show you.'

They made their way down further corridors, lit only with weak, bare bulbs. Then, faced with a small panelled door, Malvestiti pushed it open. There was a staircase immediately beyond the door, and this descended sharply into water some two or three feet below.

'There,' said Malvestiti sadly. 'Look at that.'

Von Igelfeld stared down at the water. Malvestiti had taken a torch from the wall and was shining it onto the surface of the water, just below which he could make out the beginnings of a bookshelf and the spines of books.

'I can hardly believe it,' he said. 'Were you unable to do anything to save the books?'

Malvestiti looked down at the water, as if willing it to retreat.

'It happened without our realising it,' he said. 'Very few people ask for those books, and months, even years can go by with nobody going downstairs. Then, suddenly, an Archimandrite working in the library asked for a work on Church Slavonic, and there we were . . . Now, if you see the mark *s.a* on a book's catalogue card, you know it means that it is *sub aqua*. It is very sad.'

That evening von Igelfeld sat on the terrace of the Grand Hôtel des Bains in sombre mood. His mind was on his meeting with Malvestiti – normally such a warm occasion – this year an encounter which left him filled with nothing but feelings of foreboding. He had realised that his friend had not in fact provided the answers to the real question which he had asked. Everybody knew that Venice was sinking – that was not the point. The real question was what was wrong with the water?

He gazed out at the sea, now becoming dark with the setting of the sun. It looked so beautiful, so maternal, and yet there must be something very wrong with it. Von Igelfeld sipped on his drink, a cold glass of beer, noticing with satisfaction that the label on the bottle said 'Brewed in Belgium'. That must be safe; there was nothing threatening about Belgium. Ineffably dull, perhaps; but not threatening.

Taking a further sip of his beer, von Igelfeld glanced down the terrace. There was hardly a soul about yet, although the terrace would fill up as the evening wore on. People were in their rooms now, showering or bathing; preparing for the civilised delights of the Venetian evening. In a short while, the Prinzels would appear, and they would discuss the events of the day. The prospect made von Igelfeld feel considerably more cheerful. Ophelia, in particular, could always be counted upon to raise the dullest of spirits.

He looked at the tubs of bright flowers, perched on the parapet. How good the Italians were with colours; how bold the reds, how deep the purples, and . . . what was that? Somebody had left something on one of the chairs near the parapet. It looked rather like a camera.

Von Igelfeld looked about to see if there was a waiter whose attention could be drawn to the lost item, but nobody was there. So he got up, strode across to the chair, and lifted up the small instrument. It was a very curious camera, he thought, and very heavy.

The weight made him suspicious, and so his examination continued further. He thought perhaps it was a light meter, as there was a dial across the face of the instrument, and a small hand piece that was presumably pointed in the direction of the light source. But then he saw it, neatly printed beneath the dial: Geiger Counter: Made in Switzerland.

For a moment von Igelfeld stood quite still, his thoughts in turmoil. He was no scientist, but he was well enough informed to know Geiger counters were designed to measure radiation. Who could have left it there, and why? He remembered seeing men in white coats around the hotel just before he came out on the terrace. He had assumed that they were collecting samples of water, but was this what they were doing? The thought appalled him.

Von Igelfeld returned to his table, cradling the Geiger counter in his arms, as if it might explode if he dropped it. He saw that there was an on/off switch and with his heart thumping wildly within him, he turned the switch to the on position. Nothing happened. A light glowed behind the dial, but the needle stayed quite still.

He picked up the hand piece and pointed it down at the ground. Nothing. Then he moved it towards his shoes, and for a moment the needle gave a slight twitch and von Igelfeld thought he heard a click. But the needle went back, and he breathed again. Then, hardly daring to look, he moved the hand piece up over his trouser legs and towards his stomach. Nothing. Nothing except the wild thumping of the heart. Further up, over the breast, face, hair. Nothing.

Von Igelfeld put down the instrument and heaved a sigh of relief. It was ridiculous, he thought. He was imagining the whole thing. People used Geiger counters for all sorts of purposes, he thought, such as . . . He stopped. Was there any other reason to have a Geiger counter?

'Moritz-Maria! So here you are!'

Ophelia, standing above him, bent down and kissed his brow.

'Well,' said Prinzel, from behind her. 'What sort of day have you had?'

Von Igelfeld smiled as his guests sat down – Ophelia

opposite him, Prinzel right next to him. And as Prinzel sat down, the Geiger counter beside him emitted a loud clicking sound.

'What was that?' asked Prinzel. 'Did you want to say something?'

Von Igelfeld was too shocked to speak. Mutely, he pointed at the Geiger counter.

'What's that?' asked Prinzel. 'Is that some sort of radio?'

'A Geiger counter,' von Igelfeld stuttered.

'Ah,' said Prinzel. 'How useful! Let me test myself!'

With an awful sense of his own inability to prevent the occurrence of a tragedy, von Igelfeld watched as Prinzel turned the hand piece towards himself and ran it down his body. Once again the instrument clicked, and the needle jerked on the dial.

'Mmm,' said Prinzel, peering at the dial. 'A bit of a reaction. Not too bad.'

Von Igelfeld gasped. 'You mean . . .'

'Yes,' said Prinzel calmly. 'I seem to have picked something up. Probably something I ate.'

Von Igelfeld protested lamely. 'But that's awful,' he said. 'Radioactivity is terribly dangerous.'

'Yes,' agreed Prinzel. 'I think I had probably better go and seek treatment at home. They'll give me iodine pills or something.' He looked across the table at Ophelia, who was smiling benignly. She clearly knew little about radioactivity.

'I shan't be upset to be going home early,' she said. 'Venice is still so hot . . .'

For von Igelfeld, an early departure could not be early enough. He had found out what was wrong with the city, and he was horrified. It was worse than plague; it

was worse than cholera. It was almost too awful to contemplate.

They finished their drinks quietly, and then processed into the great dining hall. Von Igelfeld took the Geiger counter with him, determined to run it over each course before they ate it, and this he did discreetly, hoping not to attract the attention of the waiters. The paté was quite all right, as was the salad, but the fish sent the needle shooting to the top of the scale, and it was dispatched back to the kitchen, with no explanation.

Then the band struck up, playing one of those infectiously gay Italian country tunes. Couples began to dance, and Prinzel and Ophelia, with von Igelfeld's blessing, left the table, and were soon out on the dance floor. Von Igelfeld stayed where he was, and was sitting with the Geiger counter on his lap as the Polish boy, in a fresh white sailor suit, glowing with health, walked slowly past him, and threw him a glance as he did so.

Von Igelfeld's puzzled irritation was matched only by his surprise. As the boy walked past, the Geiger counter clicked hysterically and the needle shot up to the very reddest part of the scale. Von Igelfeld's mouth opened in an astonishment that was quickly followed by dismay. He must have been swimming. That was it! Poor youth!

He looked about him. The boy had now joined his mother and sisters at their table and their meal was being ordered. Oh what tragedy! thought von Igelfeld. And so young too! It was as if the very floor of the Grand Hôtel des Bains was littered with fallen rose petals and abandoned mandolins.

For a few minutes he wrestled with conflicting emotions. He assumed that there was nothing he could really do at this stage to help the unfortunate youth. It was none of his business, really, or was it? Was he his neighbour's keeper, even when his neighbour was a rather strange Polish boy who kept looking at him in a disconcerting fashion? Yes, he was, he decided. He must warn the mother – that's what he must do.

Von Igelfeld arose from his table, straightened his tie, and walked over to the Polish family's table. As he approached, the mother raised her eyes, and smiled at him.

'*Excusez-moi, Madame,*' said von Igelfeld. '*Permettez-moi de vous dire que votre fils, votre très agréable Tadseuz, est devenu un peu radio-actif.*'

The mother listened, and inclined her head gravely at the information.

'*Merci, monsieur,*' she said after a short pause. '*Vous êtes très gentil de me donner ces informations. Je vous remercie bien. J'ai des convictions bien intensives au sujet de la radio-activité parmi les enfants.*'

Von Igelfeld waited for something further to be said, but it was not, and so he bowed, and returned to his table, where the Prinzels were now waiting. They passed the Geiger counter over their coffee, to negative results, and enjoyed the rest of the evening as one might enjoy an evening which was to be one's last in Venice, ever.

It might have been a melancholy departure the next day, but as they made their farewells to the manager, who expressed great regret on their premature departure, a telegram arrived addressed to von Igelfeld. He opened it with all the sense of foreboding with which one opens telegrams when away from home, but his face lit up as he read the message.

MEDAL AWARDED BY PORTUGUESE GOVERNMENT,

the telegram ran.

QUITE DELIGHTED. BEST WISHES, UNTERHOLZER.

Von Igelfeld thrust the telegram into Ophelia's hands and turned to Prinzel.

'Prinzel,' he said, the dignity in his voice overlaying the emotion. 'I have been honoured by the Portuguese Government – at last!'

They left in the hotel's motor launch, riding over the lagoon to the fatal, exquisite, doomed city, and then on to the mainland. Thereafter they made their way slowly through the mountains and into Austria. Throughout the journey von Igelfeld was in a state of complete euphoria. What would his medal look like? By whom would it be awarded, and what would be said at the ceremony? There were so many questions to be answered.

Then, as they passed through a tiny village, with a minute, whitewashed church, Prinzel suddenly turned round and made an observation.

'That telegram,' he said. 'It's just occurred to me that Unterholzer didn't say they'd awarded the medal to you. The wording suggests that it was really to him.'

'What do you mean?' said von Igelfeld angrily. 'He said quite clearly: Medal awarded by Portuguese Government. Quite delighted . . .' He broke off, becoming silent; could it be . . . ?

They had passed out of the village now, and there was a long, steep mountain pass ahead. Von Igelfeld sat in silence, unable to speak. *Oh!* he thought. And then, *Oh!* again. *Why have I had such bad luck in this life? Why? All I want is love, and a tiny bit of recognition from the Portuguese, and I get neither. And soon it will be too late; nobody will read my book any more, and there will be nobody to remember me.*

He brought himself to order. There was no point in self-pity, which was something he invariably disliked in others. No; he would not allow himself to be discouraged. He had much to be proud of in this life; much for which he should be grateful. He was, after all, Professor Dr Moritz-Maria von Igelfeld. That, on its own, would have been quite enough; but there was more: he was the author of *Portuguese Irregular Verbs*, and that was something that would forever be associated with his name, just as when people thought of Thomas Mann they thought of . . .

Von Igelfeld stopped. And then he laughed, which made Prinzel swerve the car slightly before he righted it and they continued their journey back to Germany, where they belonged.

THE FINER POINTS
OF SAUSAGE DOGS

Contents

The Finer Points of Sausage Dogs

Professor Dr Moritz-Maria Von Igelfeld, author of that great triumph of Germanic scholarship, *Portuguese Irregular Verbs*, had never set foot on American shores. It is true that he had corresponded from time to time with a number of noted American philologists – Professor Giles Reid of Cornell, for example, and Professor Paul Lafouche III of Tulane – and it is also true that they had often pressed him to attend the annual meeting of the American Modern Languages Association, but he had never been in a position to accept. Or so von Igelfeld said: the reality was he had never wanted to go and had inevitably come up with some excuse to turn down the invitations.

'I have absolutely no interest in the New World,' von Igelfeld said dismissively to Professor Dr Dr Florianus Prinzel. 'Is there anything there that we can't find in Germany? Anything at all? Can you name one thing?'

Prinzel thought for a moment. Cowboys? He was a secret admirer of cowboy films but he could never mention this to von Igelfeld, who, as far as he knew, had never watched a film in his life, let alone one featuring cowboys. Prinzel rather liked the idea of America, and would have been delighted to be invited there, preferably to somewhere in the West.

Then, one morning, Prinzel's invitation arrived – and from no less an institution than the ideally situated University of San Antonio. This was a city redolent of cowboys and the Mexican border, and Prinzel immediately telephoned von Igelfeld to tell him the good news.

Von Igelfeld congratulated him warmly, but when he replaced the receiver his expression had hardened. It was quite unacceptable that Prinzel should go to America before he did. After all, the Americans might think that Prinzel, rather than he, von Igelfeld, represented German philology, and this, frankly, would never do. Quite apart from that, if Prinzel went first, they would never hear the end of it.

'I have no alternative but to go there,' he said to himself. 'And I shall have to make sure that I go before Prinzel. It's simply a matter of duty.'

Von Igelfeld found himself in a difficult position. He could hardly approach any of his American friends and solicit an invitation, particularly after he had so consistently turned them down in the past. And yet the chance that an invitation would arrive of its own accord was extremely slender.

Over coffee at the Institute the next day, he directed a casual question at Professor Dr Detlev Amadeus Unterholzer.

'Tell me, Herr Unterholzer,' he said. 'If you were to want to go to America to give a lecture, how would you

. . . well, how would you get yourself invited, so to speak?' Quickly adding: 'Not that I would ever be in such a position myself, but you yourself could be, could you not?'

Unterholzer had an immediate answer.

'I should contact the *Deutscher Akademischer Austauschdienst*,' he said. 'I should tell them who I was and I should ask them to arrange a lecture somewhere in America. That is what they are paid to do.'

'I see,' said von Igelfeld. 'That would no doubt save embarrassment.'

'Of course,' said Unterholzer. 'They are experts in finding places for German academics to go and lecture to other people, whether or not they want to hear them. They are very persuasive people. That is how I went to Buenos Aires and gave my lecture there. It really works.'

And indeed it did. The local director of the *Deutscher Akademischer Austauschdienst* was delighted to hear from von Igelfeld the following day and assured him that a scholar of his eminence would be snapped up should he deign to leave Germany. It was only a question of finding the right institution and making the detailed arrangements.

'Rest assured that you will be invited within days,' von Igelfeld was assured. 'Just leave it all in our capable hands.'

* * *

Thus von Igelfeld found himself arriving in Fayetteville, Arkansas, a charming college town nestling in the Ozark Mountains, seat of the University of Arkansas, or at least of that part not located in the minor campus at Little Rock. When the whole idea was conceived, he had not envisaged going to Arkansas. He had imagined that his destination might be California, or New York, perhaps, but one American state was very much the same as another – at least in von Igelfeld's view, and it really made no difference. The important thing was that he was going to America, and a good two weeks ahead of Prinzel.

Von Igelfeld's host greeted him warmly. They had insisted that he stay with them, rather than in a hotel, and so von Igelfeld found himself installed in the sleeping porch of a traditional Ozark farmhouse on the edge of the town, the home of Professor R. B. Leflar. After he had unpacked, he and von Igelfeld sat down on the swingseat on the front verandah and discussed his programme. There would be visits to the surrounding area the next day, promised Professor Leflar, and the day after that a set-piece lecture had been planned before an open audience.

That night, after dinner, von Igelfeld retired to his bed and looked out through the gauze-covered porch windows. The house was surrounded by mixed forest, oak trees and sycamores, and their shapes, dark silhouettes, swayed in the breeze. And there, he thought, there's the moon, rising slowly over the trees like a giant lantern. What were they planning for him tomorrow? Would they show him their libraries? Were there manuscripts? What about Leflar's maternal grandfather, the adventurer, Charles Finger? He had been in South America and may have come across

140

some Portuguese manuscripts of note, which could well be in the attic above his very head. Arkansas, it seemed, was rich in possibilities for the philologist.

The next morning he ate a hearty breakfast with Professor and Mrs Leflar before they set off.

'We're heading north,' said his host. 'We'll show you a typical hog operation.'

'Most intriguing,' said von Igelfeld. 'I am always interested in . . .' He paused. What was he interested in? Philology? Portuguese verbs? 'I am always interested in everything.'

They drove out of town, following a road that wound up into the hills. It was a gentle landscape – limestone hills which had been softened by the action of the rain; meandering valleys dotted with farmhouses under shady oak trees. Von Igelfeld had not thought of America as being at all like this; there were no dry plains, no glittering Dallas in the distance, no leafy suburbia with neat white houses. This could have been Bavaria, or even Austria.

Suddenly Leflar turned off the road and followed a dusty track leading towards a large, unpainted barn.

'Here we are,' he said. 'They're expecting us.'

The farmer came out and shook von Igelfeld's hand. Von Igelfeld sniffed the air; it was distinctly malodorous.

'This way,' said the farmer. 'The hogs are in here.'

The farmer opened a door in the side of the barn and ushered von Igelfeld inside. For the next half hour, they wandered between rows of large sties, each surmounted by a large sun lamp and each filled with a squealing mass of pigs. The farmer demonstrated the automatic feeding system and showed von Igelfeld the blood-sampling equipment.

'We're mighty careful about viruses here,' he said. 'You'd know all about that.'

Von Igelfeld looked at the farmer. Did pigs get colds, he wondered?

'You have to be careful about viruses,' he agreed. 'I myself always use vitamin C during the winter . . .'

He did not finish. 'You're right,' said the farmer. 'Each pig gets sixty IU vitamin C every morning with its food. And then we give them a shot of B group when they're seven weeks old. Some people are trying a short course of potassium a week before market. What do you think?'

Von Igelfeld shook his head. 'You have to be careful,' he said. 'I would never use potassium myself.'

The farmer listened intently. 'You hear that, Professor Leflar? No potassium. I'm inclined to agree with our visitor. You tell those folks down in Little Rock, no potassium – the Germans recommend against it.'

Leflar nodded. 'Could be,' he said.

An hour later they set off again. After a brief lunch, they made their way to a chicken farm, where von Igelfeld was shown the latest methods of production by a farmer who spoke in such a way that he could understand not one word. Then there was a call at some sort of animal laboratory, which interested von Igelfeld very little. Then home to dinner.

That night, in the silence of his sleeping porch, von Igelfeld reflected on his day. It had been interesting, in its way, but he wondered why they had chosen to show him all those farms and animals. Animals were all very well; indeed he had once written a small paper on the nature of collective nouns used for groups of animals, but that was about as

142

far as his interest went. Still, this was America, and he assumed that this was what they laid on for all their visitors.

The lecture was to be at six thirty, following a short reception. When von Igelfeld arrived with Leflar the audience was largely assembled, milling about the ante-room of the lecture theatre. Glasses of wine had been provided, and plates of snacks were being circulated by waitresses dressed in black and white.

Everybody seemed keen to talk to von Igelfeld.

'We've all heard about your work,' said one man in a light-weight blue suit. 'In fact, I've got an off-print here which I thought you might care to sign.'

'I'd be happy to do so,' said von Igelfeld. And what about *Portuguese Irregular Verbs?* he reflected. Were there copies even here in Fayetteville, amongst these charming hills?

The man in the blue suit produced a pamphlet from his pocket.

'I was sent this by a colleague in Germany,' he said. 'He thought that I might find it useful. And I sure did.'

Von Igelfeld took the pamphlet. The cover was unfamiliar; all his off-prints from the *Zeitschrift* were bound in a plain white cover. This one was blue.

He adjusted his reading glasses and looked at the title page. *Further Studies of Canine Pulmonary Efficiency*, he read. And then: *by Professor Martin Igelfold, University of Münster*.

Von Igelfeld stared at the page for a moment, his heart a cold stone within him. It was immediately clear to him what had happened. They thought that he was Professor Igelfold, Dean of Veterinary Medicine at Münster. Von Igelfeld knew of Igelfold's existence, as he had seen the

143

remarkably similar name in the newspaper during an anthrax scare. But he had never dreamed that there would be confusion on such a heroic scale! Those foolish, bumbling people at the *Deutscher Akademischer Austauschdienst* had mixed them up and sent him off to lecture on veterinary medicine in Arkansas! It was a situation of such terrible embarrassment that for a moment he hardly dared contemplate it. And the lecture was about to begin, before all these people – these expectant scientists, veterinarians and dog breeders – and he had proposed to talk about modal verbs in the writings of Fernando Pessoa.

Almost without thinking, he signed the pamphlet and returned it to the other man.

'We're so honoured to have you here in Fayetteville,' said the man. 'We understand that you are the world authority on the sausage dog. We are looking forward to what you have to say to us tonight. Sausage dogs are quite popular here. German settlers brought them with them in the late eighteen nineties and have bred them ever since.'

Von Igelfeld stared at him in horror. Sausage dogs! He was expected to talk about sausage dogs, a subject on which he knew absolutely nothing. It was a nightmare; like one of those dreams where you imagine that you are about to take the lead part in a Greek play or where you are sitting down to write an examination in advanced calculus. But he was awake, and it was really happening.

Leflar was at his side now.

'Almost time,' he said. 'Should I ask people to move into the hall?'

'Not yet,' said von Igelfeld, looking about him desperately. 'I have so many colleagues yet to meet.'

144

He detached himself from Leflar and made his way over to a knot of people standing near the door. This proved to be a group of veterinary surgeons who welcomed him to their circle and refilled his glass from a bottle of wine which one of them was holding.

It was in this group that one of the guests drew him aside and engaged him in distinctly unsettling conversation.

'I was sorry to read about your death,' said the guest.

Von Igelfeld looked at him in astonishment.

'My death?'

'Yes,' said the guest. 'There was a small item in the *International Veterinary Review* this week reporting the very recent death of Professor Igelfold. There was a glowing obituary.'

Von Igelfeld stared glassily at the man before him, who was surveying him over his drink.

'I did not read it,' he said weakly.

'Not surprising,' said the man. 'One rarely has the pleasure of reading one's own obituary.'

Von Igelfeld laughed, mopping his brow with his handkerchief.

'Very amusing,' he said. 'And you are so right!'

'So this *is* a posthumous lecture,' said the man.

'Well,' said von Igelfeld. 'It would appear to be something of that sort.'

The man looked pensive. 'I must say that you don't look at all like your photograph. They published one with the obituary, you know.'

Von Igelfeld gripped at the stem of his glass. 'The camera is often deceptive, I find.'

'You were a smaller man in the photograph,' went on the other. 'Not nearly so tall.'

'I see,' said von Igelfeld icily. 'A smaller photograph, perhaps? Anyway, do you not know that in Germany we sometimes publish obituaries *before* a person's demise. It happens quite often. This is because we Germans are so efficient. An early obituary means that there is never a backlog. That, I suspect, is the explanation.'

There was a silence. Then von Igelfeld spoke again.

'You must excuse me,' he said. 'I am feeling rather tired.'

'Quite understandable,' muttered the man. 'In the circumstances.'

But von Igelfeld did not hear him. He had moved away and was looking about him. The simplest solution was to escape, to vanish entirely. If he managed to get out of the hall he could summon a taxi, go back to the Leflar house, creep in through the back and reclaim his belongings. Then he could make his way to the airport and await the first flight out of town, wherever it happened to be going.

The front door was impossible. Everybody would see him leaving and somebody was bound to come after him to enquire where he was going. But there was another door at the side of the room, a door out of which it looked much easier to sneak. He moved over towards it, smiling at people as he walked past, nodding his head in acknowledgement of their greetings. Then, having reached the door, he discreetly turned the handle and pushed against it.

'Oh, there you are,' said Leflar. 'Is everything all right?'

'I am very well,' said von Igelfeld. 'I was just trying . . .' His voice faded away.

Leflar glanced anxiously at his watch . . .

'We don't have much time,' he said. 'The hall has to be used for another purpose in twenty-five minutes.'

'Please don't hurry,' said von Igelfeld. 'The real point of these meetings is that there should be personal contact and I am making sure that this happens by talking to all these excellent people.'

A few minutes later, von Igelfeld looked out over the faces of his audience. They had enjoyed the reception, and the supply of wine had been liberal. He, too, had taken several glasses and had recovered after the shock of discovering that he was dead. Now it now seemed to him that to talk for – what time remained? – ten minutes at the most about sausage dogs would not be an impossible task. And by now he had remembered that Zimmermann himself had been in such a situation some years before, when he had been mistaken for another Zimmermann and had been obliged to deliver a lecture on developments in exhaust systems, a subject of which he was completely ignorant. And yet had he not done so, and with distinction? With such distinction, indeed, that the resulting paper had been published in the *Karlsruher Forum für Moderne Auspuffkonstruktion*? If Zimmermann could do it, then surely he could do so too.

'The sausage dog,' he began, 'is a remarkable dog. It differs from other dogs in respect of its shape, which is similar to that of a sausage. It belongs to that genus of dogs marked out by their proximity to the ground. In most cases this is because of the shortness of the legs. If a dog has short legs, we have found that the body is almost invariably close to the ground. Yet this does not prevent the sausage dog from making its way about its business with considerable despatch.'

He glanced at his watch. One minute had passed, leaving nine minutes to go. There would be one minute, or perhaps two, for thanks at the end, which meant that he now had to speak for no more than seven minutes. But what more was there to say about sausage dogs? Were they good hunting dogs? He believed they were. Perhaps he could say something about the role of the sausage dog in the rural economy, how they had their place and how unwise it was to introduce new, untested breeds.

This went down well with the audience, and there were murmurs of agreement from corners of the room. Emboldened, von Igelfeld moved on to the topic of whether there should be restrictions on the free movement of sausage dogs. Should sausage dog breeders not be allowed to export animals with as few restrictions as possible? Again the audience agreed with von Igelfeld when he said that this was a good idea.

There were several other points before it was time to stop. After thanking Leflar and the University of Arkansas, von Igelfeld sat down, to thunderous applause.

p = proximity

Leflar leaned over to von Igelfeld as the sound of clapping filled the room.

'Well done,' he said. 'That went down very well. Guest speakers are sometimes far too technical for an open lecture like this. You hit just the right note.'

Von Igelfeld nodded gravely.

'I hope I lived up to expectations,' he said modestly.

'Oh you did,' said Leflar. 'It was a resounding success. Even if you were somewhat brief.'

From his seat on the aeroplane, von Igelfeld looked down at the Ozarks as they became smaller and smaller beneath him. It was a good place, America, and Arkansas was a good state. He had been invited to return, but how could he, particularly when the news of Professor Igelfold's death became widespread? Besides, he reflected, he had nothing further to say about sausage dogs; indeed he had already said more than enough.

A Leg to Stand On

Arkansas had been a welcome diversion for von Igelfeld. He had felt quite exhausted before embarking on the trip but had returned entirely refreshed, ready to face the pressing burdens of daily life at the Institute for Romance Philology in Regensburg.

The reason for von Igelfeld's fatigue before his departure was the effort that he had been obliged to expend – at very short notice – on the writing of a radio talk on Portuguese orthography. He had taken great care with this talk, and the programme had eventually been broadcast by German State Radio at five o'clock on a particularly wet Thursday evening.

Von Igelfeld had been pleased with his talk, which he felt had achieved the requisite delicate balance between the rival theories on the issue. Some weeks later he had telephoned the producer to establish whether there had been any reaction to what he had said.

The producer had sounded evasive.

'It's rather difficult to gauge reaction,' he had said. 'That's a tricky slot on Thursday evening. Many people are still on their way home from work.'

'I know that,' snapped von Igelfeld. 'But there are still plenty of people at home. They could have listened.'

'Well . . .' said the producer. 'It's a difficult time. And the audience research reports . . .'

'Is that some sort of survey?' interrupted von Igelfeld. 'Does it show how many people listened?'

'Well,' said the producer, hesitantly. 'I'm afraid it was not all that encouraging. In fact, we had a negative result. Apparently nobody tuned in at all. Nobody heard you.'

There was a silence at the other end of the line.

'Nobody?'

'Of course, these things are often unreliable.'

'I should think they are,' said von Igelfeld. 'I, for one, listened. And then there's my colleague, Professor Dr Unterholzer. He listened, I can assure you.'

'There you are,' said the producer. 'That's something.'

In fact, unbeknown to von Igelfeld, Unterholzer had not listened. He had fully intended to do so, having been reminded by von Igelfeld on four separate occasions of the time of the broadcast, but had become so absorbed in a musical concert that he had forgotten to switch stations. So, as far as anybody knew, von Igelfeld was the only person in Germany to hear his own talk.

But the radio broadcast seemed distant now, and other challenges were on the horizon. There was the Berlin meeting on Celtic philology – always a major date in von Igelfeld's calendar – and there was a lecture to prepare for Salzburg. And then there was, of course, the work which had to be done on *The Portuguese Pluperfect*, the book on which von Igelfeld had been working for the last few years and which, in the opinion of all those who had glimpsed the manuscript, was sure to become a worthy successor to *Portuguese Irregular Verbs* itself.

When the letter arrived from Professor R. B. Leflar, von Igelfeld opened it almost absentmindedly. He was aware of the fact that it bore an American stamp; American stamps, he had observed, always showed people *doing* things, whereas German stamps were designed not to excite people too much and were somehow more appropriate. He was reflecting on this when he noticed the fateful postmark: *Fayetteville, Arkansas*. Had he seen that, he would have known at once the authorship of the letter.

'*Dear Professor von Igelfeld*,' the letter began. '*I would never have imagined, when we said farewell to one another in Arkansas barely nine months ago, that I should be seeing you so soon. But I now find myself having to come to Germany and I should therefore like to take you up on your kind invitation to visit Regensburg . . .*'

Von Igelfeld smiled as he read the letter. He had enjoyed Professor Leflar's company and the thought of showing him around Regensburg was an attractive one. He would take him down to the river and, if the weather was fine, perhaps they could . . . He stopped. The awful thought had occurred that as far as Leflar was concerned, von Igelfeld was still a professor of veterinary medicine and the world's leading authority on the sausage dog. He had not disabused him of this misconception, although he should perhaps have done this right at the outset. But once he had allowed matters to persist and had delivered the lecture on sausage dogs, then it had been too late. Now it was impossible to confess that he had enjoyed the hospitality of his hosts in Fayetteville under entirely false pretences.

That would not have been too troubling had it not been for the fact of Leflar's impending arrival. It would be impossible to maintain the pretence of being a professor of veterinary medicine right here in Regensburg, where everybody knew that he was a Romance philologist. But did he have any alternative? It would be simply too embarrassing to tell the truth now, to confess to an utter ignorance of sausage dogs; he would simply have to brazen it out and pretend for the two days of Leflar's visit that he was, indeed, what he so patently was not. It was not an appealing prospect.

'I shall not be coming into the Institute next week,' he said to Unterholzer. 'I shall be . . .'

Unterholzer looked at him expectantly.

'In Berlin?' he asked, a note of jealousy creeping into his voice. 'Has somebody asked you to go to Berlin?'

Von Igelfeld shook his head. It was typical of Unterholzer to be immoderately inquisitive. How von Igelfeld spent his time had nothing to do with him and there was no call for him to reveal such vulgar curiosity.

Unterholzer persisted. 'Munich?' he pressed. 'Wiesbaden?'

Von Igelfeld felt the irritation well up within him. 'I shall be right here in Regensburg,' he snapped. 'I shall just not be coming into the Institute. That is all.'

Unterholzer was silent. He knew that von Igelfeld was concealing something, but short of following him about, which he clearly could not do, there was little chance of his discovering what it was. For von Igelfeld's part, he realised that silence might have been more advisable: if he had simply said nothing, then Unterholzer may never even have noticed his absence. As it was, he would have to make sure that their paths did not cross during Leflar's visit. Unterholzer was noted for his insecurity. He would surely interpret the presence of a mysterious stranger in von Igelfeld's company as some sort of threat to himself and could be counted on to try to find out his identity.

The essential difficulty was that life was unfair, and Unterholzer was one of those who was destined to play second fiddle, or worse. He had the worst office in the Institute; his book was all but ignored by everybody in the field; and he rarely received invitations to lecture anywhere of the remotest interest. His Buenos Aires invitation had come merely because they could get nobody else to attend the conference, although von Igelfeld had generously refrained from telling him that. He had hinted it, though, but Unterholzer, with typical lack of insight, had failed to read his meaning. Poor Unterholzer! reflected von Igelfeld. What it must be to be such a failure and to have so little . . .

Von Igelfeld's reveries came to an abrupt end. To have so little in this life and yet to have received – oh, the sheer injustice of it – a medal from the Portuguese Government! A medal which must have been intended for himself, von Igelfeld, not for the hopelessly obscure Unterholzer. All he had ever done for the Lusophile world had been to pen a badly received volume on the Portuguese imperfect subjunctive. This was a book which was barely fit to rest on the same shelf as *Portuguese Irregular Verbs*, and yet some misguided official in Lisbon has recommended the award of a medal! It was quite clear to von Igelfeld that the medals of this world were pinned on quite the wrong chests, just as were the metaphorical barriers inevitably placed in quite the wrong place.

Leflar arrived on a Tuesday. It was a wonderful spring day and the air was sharp and invigorating.

'A peach of a day!' the American visitor remarked as von Igelfeld met him at the railway station. 'The sort of day that in Arkansas makes us go hippety-hop!'

'Hippety-hop?' said von Igelfeld, slightly taken aback. 'Oh yes. We Germans like to go hippety-hop too on days like this.'

They travelled by taxi to the Hotel Angst, where von Igelfeld had booked Leflar in for the two nights of his stay.

'I am sure that you'll be very comfortable here,' he explained. 'The Institute always uses this hotel for its visitors. We put Professor Hutmann here last time. He is an old friend of mine from student days in Heidelberg.'

Leflar looked surprised. 'Heidelberg? I didn't realise they taught veterinary medicine at Heidelberg.'

Von Igelfeld froze. Leflar had scarcely arrived and he had already made a bad mistake.

'Heidelberg?' he said quickly. 'Who said anything about Heidelberg?'

'You did,' said Leflar. 'You referred to being a student at Heidelberg. You said you studied at Heidelberg.'

'I did not,' said von Igelfeld. 'You must have misheard me. I said that Professor Hutmann was an old friend, in Heidelberg, from student days. That is, we were friends, in student days, but now he is in Heidelberg.'

155

'So,' he went on quickly. 'I shall leave you here for a while, but I shall be back soon to take you out to lunch. In the afternoon, I can show you round the town.'

They bade farewell and von Igelfeld made his way home, deep in thought. If matters were difficult at this stage, then how much more complicated they would become when it came to taking Leflar to the Veterinary Institute tomorrow, as he had requested.

Tuesday afternoon was a considerable success. Leflar enjoyed a walk in the hills above the town and they both ate a hearty meal in a small inn on the river. But von Igelfeld's pleasure at his friend's delight in the beauty of Regensburg was tinged with apprehension. The moment was fast approaching when he would have to present himself at the Veterinary Institute and join Leflar in the tour which had been arranged for him. That, at least, had been easy. He had simply informed the Director of the Institute that a personal friend, a prominent American expert in animal health, was visiting and that he would like to show him the

Institute. The Director had promised to conduct the tour himself and had invited von Igelfeld to join them. What would happen if the Director made some remark which indicated that von Igelfeld was an outsider from a totally different part of the university? And would Leflar expect von Igelfeld to join in any debate engaged in by himself and the Director? If that happened, there would be no alternative but to claim an urgent appointment elsewhere.

By the time they arrived at the Institute, von Igelfeld was already beginning to feel a cold chill of dread. But when the Director, a charming man wearing a neat bow-tie, welcomed them both, his fear dissipated somewhat. The Director addressed all his technical remarks to Leflar and all that von Igelfeld had to do was to nod in agreement.

'We're engaged in a major programme of research on the genetics of degenerative disease in turkeys,' said the Director, and von Igelfeld nodded, as if to convey that he, too, was heavily involved.

'It's an important topic,' said Leflar.

'Yes,' agreed von Igelfeld. 'Very important. From the . . . from the . . . turkey point of view.'

The Director threw him a glance. Now they moved on to the laboratories, where humming centrifuges and bubbling flasks attested to a high level of research activity.

'$Mg_2 H_2O + HgSO_4$,' explained the Director, pointing to a vat of curiously coloured powder.

'H_2?' asked Leflar.

'$MgCO_2$,' responded the Director.

'O,' said von Igelfeld. 'H.'

'O?' asked Leflar.

Von Igelfeld stroked his chin. 'Perhaps.'

'Definitely,' interjected the Director. '$H_2O + NaCl_3$.'

They moved on to the physiology laboratory, where Leflar found a great deal to interest him. Von Igelfeld felt relaxed now; there seemed to be no reason why Leflar should suspect anything and all that remained was to join the Director for a social cup of coffee in his office. That, it transpired, was even easier, as the conversation was restricted to small talk and a discussion of the relative merits of Fayetteville and Regensburg. Then the Director took his leave, as he had a meeting to attend, leaving von Igelfeld to escort Leflar towards the front door. And it was at this point that the movement of the planets brought about what, for von Igelfeld, was a thoroughly disagreeable concatenation of events.

Nemesis took the form of a young man, evidently a student, who suddenly dashed out of a door and seized von Igelfeld's arm.

'Herr Professor,' he said. 'You must come in immediately. We've had a casualty brought in to the clinic. I can't find Dr Steenbock and the staff in the lab said that I should ask you.'

Von Igelfeld found himself being ushered into a small room, the stark white walls of which were lit by a large overhead light. There was a high table with a stainless steel top and stretched out on that, connected by a tube to a cylinder of gas, was the anaesthetised form of a sausage dog.

'He was brought in a few minutes ago,' said the young man. 'One of his legs has been crushed by a car. I've just developed the X-rays.'

He flicked the switch of a light box, illuminating a ghostly picture of bones and tissue.

'The trouble is,' went on the young man. 'I'm only a third year student. Dr Steenbock would normally supervise me. I'm not allowed to do unsupervised surgery yet.'

Von Igelfeld looked about him wildly. This was worse – far worse – than his ordeal in Arkansas. He was utterly cornered. But he would cope with the situation, just as he had coped with everything that had gone before. This was no time for defeat.

'Well, I'll just stand back and let you get on with it,' said Leflar helpfully. 'I do very little small animal surgery. I'll just watch.'

'You do it,' said von Igelfeld to the student. 'I'm sure that you'll be fine.'

'But what shall I do?' asked the student.

Von Igelfeld craned his neck to examine the X-ray.

'The leg is broken,' he said. 'Look at this.'

'Yes,' said the student. 'It's a badly impacted fracture.'

'Then we shall have to amputate it,' said von Igelfeld. 'Cut it off.'

The student nodded. Then, opening a drawer below the table he extracted a scalpel and a large, terrifying instrument that looked to all intents and purposes like a pair of garden secateurs.

'Go ahead,' said von Igelfeld.

The student took the rear leg of the dog in his hand and made an incision. Bright canine blood appeared like a line of tiny flowers, but that was only the beginning. Soon the deeper structures were exposed and then, with a firm snip, the bone was cut neatly by the secateurs. It did not take long for the wound to be sewn up and there, in a metal dish, lay a small, detached leg.

'Good,' said von Igelfeld. 'Well done.'

The student leaned forward to peer at the X-ray. Suddenly he groaned.

'Oh no, Herr Professor! That was the wrong leg!'

Von Igelfeld looked at the plate. The broken leg was on the right, as was the leg which had been removed, but now, looking more closely, it was clearly in the front.

'Take the right one off,' he said sharply. 'You have been very careless.'

The student reached again for his instruments and began the process of cutting into the injured leg. Again there was a bloodflow, quickly stemmed with a smouldering cauteriser, and soon another leg joined the one already in the dish.

'Good,' said von Igelfeld, emboldened. 'I shall now assist you, in order to give you more confidence.'

He reached forward and took the scalpel from the student's shaking hand. But as he did so, he slipped, and the sharp blade plunged deep into the remaining back leg. There was a fountain of blood and the student gave a shout.

'You've severed an artery, Herr Professor!'

'Take the leg off then,' said von Igelfeld. 'Hurry.'

Again the amputation procedure went ahead, leaving the poor sausage dog with a sole leg, in the front. Leflar, who had been watching intently, had been silent, save for a sharp intake of breath at the more dramatic events.

'Poor dog,' he said at last. 'He's not going to be able to get around very well with only one leg.'

Von Igelfeld looked at the sadly diminished sausage dog.

'He can roll,' he pronounced. 'He will be able to get around by rolling.'

In the meantime, the student who had gone outside to sterilise the instruments had returned.

'The owner is waiting outside, Herr Professor,' he said. 'Could you explain to him what has happened?'

Von Igelfeld nodded. 'I shall tell him that it has been necessary to perform extensive surgery,' he said. 'Bring him in and I shall tell him what we have done.'

The student retreated and returned a few moments later with the anxious owner.

It was Unterholzer.

On the Couch

Relations between Professor Dr Moritz-Maria von Igelfeld, author of *Portuguese Irregular Verbs*, and Professor Dr Detlev Amadeus Unterholzer, author of a considerably less well-regarded work on the Portuguese imperfect subjunctive, were somewhat strained. Nothing was said, of course, but it was clear to von Igelfeld that Unterholzer continued to harbour a grudge against him over the unfortunate incident involving his dog. It was von Igelfeld's view that he was entirely blameless in this affair, and that if anyone bore any responsibility for it, then Unterholzer himself might be the most appropriate candidate. After all, it was his own failure to supervise the dog adequately that had left it free to run out into the road and collide with a passing motorist. Unterholzer should feel ashamed of this; if people failed to take adequate care of their sausage dogs, then accidents were only to be expected. And anyway, von Igelfeld reflected, the outcome could have been infinitely worse. It was true that the dog had lost three legs in the incident, but the Veterinary

Institute had gone out of its way to fit it with a prosthetic appliance that appeared to be working very well. An elaborate harness was secured round the dog's body and attached to this were three small wheels. By using its remaining leg as a paddle, the dog could propel itself on its wheels and get anywhere it wished to get. Only very occasionally did the system not work, as had happened once or twice on a hill, when the dog had got out of control and careered down the pavement on its tiny wheels, unable to stop itself, and had ended up on a lawn or in a bush. But these were minor inconveniences, and it was quite wrong for Unterholzer to maintain a coldness in his dealings with his senior colleague; Romance philology was too small a field to allow for animosity, at least with regard to personal disputes. Academic questions were another matter, of course; the issues there were real and it was sometimes inevitable that one had to be direct in one's criticisms of a colleague's misconceptions.

'I trust that all is going well, Herr Unterholzer,' remarked von Igelfeld one morning, in an attempt to break the ice.

'In part,' replied Unterholzer. 'Some matters are progressing well, but there are others which are not so satisfactory.'

There was silence for a few moments, as Unterholzer awaited von Igelfeld's response to the challenge. But none came.

'What I mean,' went on Unterholzer, 'is that it takes a toll to be looking after a handicapped dog. There are so many things to worry about. Such a dog might become stuck in the mud, for example, if one's dog happens to have wheels, that is. Only yesterday I had to oil him. One does not usually have to oil a dog, I think.'

Von Igelfeld bit his lip. It really was too much, this stream of unspoken accusations.

'Indeed,' he said, in a steely tone. 'Supervising a dog is very demanding. One would not want one's dog, while unsupervised, or negligently supervised perhaps, to run out into the traffic, would one, Herr Unterholzer?'

Unterholzer said nothing, but turned away and busied himself with some task. Von Igelfeld, for his part, was pleased with the way he had managed to turn the encounter to his advantage. Unterholzer would think twice now before he raised the question of the sausage dog again.

There was no further word from Unterholzer for two weeks. They passed one another in the corridor, and uttered courteous greetings, but no pleasantries were exchanged. Von Igelfeld was content to leave matters as they stood: if Unterholzer wished to smoulder, let him do so. He would only make himself look ridiculous in the eyes of a world which, if it were ever to discover the true background to the affair, would certainly side with von Igelfeld.

When Unterholzer eventually struck, it was with a suddenness that took von Igelfeld entirely by surprise. The *Zeitschrift*, which had previously been edited by von Igelfeld, but which was now edited from Frankfurt, arrived on the first day of every third month. Von Igelfeld had a personal subscription and enjoyed nothing more than taking his copy home on the day of its arrival and settling down to read it in his study over a glass of Madeira wine. It was, in many respects, the highlight of his existence: to savour the unadulterated pleasure of at least four articles on Romance philology, together with at least ten pages of book reviews, and several pages of *Notes and Queries*. Usually he finished his first reading of the journal that evening, and would return to it over the following days, after he had mulled over the contents.

On this occasion, he sat down with the Madeira and the review, and fixed his eye upon the Contents page. There was an article by Professor Dr Dr Mannhein on particles. (*A treat!* thought von Igelfeld.) There was a review essay on an important new etymological dictionary of Spanish, and . . . He faltered, the glass of Madeira toppling dangerously to one side.

It was there in black and white, the letters imprinted on the page with all the awful finality of names inscribed in some awful monument to an atrocity: *Irregular Verbs: Flaws in the von Igelfeld Hypothesis.* Von Igelfeld gasped, and gasped again when he saw what followed: by Professor Dr Dr Detlev Amadeus Unterholzer (Regensburg).

With fumbling hands he turned to the first page of the article and began to read.

'*Since the publication of the controversial* Portuguese Irregular Verbs *by Professor Dr Moritz-Maria von Igelfeld, scholars of Romance philology have been questioning some of the basic assumptions as to the behaviour of the indicative in its irregular manifestations. The growing band of those who are unconvinced by the tentative hypothesis advanced by von Igelfeld have begun to suggest that third person mutations happened later than von Igelfeld naïvely assumes . . .*'

It was almost too much for von Igelfeld to bear. With his heart hammering within him, he struggled to the end of the article, reeling at the subtle digs which virtually every sentence seemed to contain. Not only was he, according

165

to Unterholzer, 'naïve' (page 34), but he was also 'misguided' (page 36), 'misinformed' (page 37) and 'potentially meretricious' (page 39).

He finished the article and laid the *Zeitschrift* down on the table beside his chair, next to the untouched glass of Madeira. He had never before – not once – been attacked in print. The reviews of *Portuguese Irregular Verbs* had been unanimously favourable; at conferences, colleagues had tripped over one another in the race to compliment him on his papers; and Zimmermann himself had never – not on one single occasion – uttered anything but praise of his work. And now here was Unterholzer – Unterholzer! – daring to question his theories, clothing himself, it would seem, in the support of a so-called 'growing band' of those unconvinced of his hypothesis. Who was in this 'growing band' on whose behalf Unterholzer purported to speak? Was Prinzel involved? Von Igelfeld had spoken to him only three weeks ago and there had been no indication of doubts as to the hypothesis. No, it was more likely that Unterholzer spoke for nobody but himself and had merely invented the support of others, in the same way as those who are unsure of themselves may use the first person plural when they express a view.

For the rest of the evening, von Igelfeld considered his response. One possibility was to confront Unterholzer and to ask him to explain himself. Another was to appear so wounded by the remarks that he would induce in Unterholzer a feeling of guilt for his appalling betrayal. And finally, he could just ignore the article altogether and pretend that he had not noticed the attack. The first and the second options were fraught with risks. He was unwilling to engage with Unterholzer in a point for point refutation of the criticisms he had made – to do that would be to lend to them a gravity that they patently did not deserve. And if he appeared wounded, then Unterholzer would have the satisfaction of knowing that the ridiculous barbs had struck home, which was presumably what he wanted. This left him the option of dignified silence, which he knew he was capable of managing. He had often shown a dignified silence in the past when faced with Unterholzer and his doings, and so all that he would have do would be rather more dignified and silent than usual.

Over the next few days, whenever von Igelfeld saw Unterholzer in the Institute, he merely nodded gravely in his direction and passed on. Unterholzer tried to speak to him on one occasion, but von Igelfeld pretended to be deep in thought and not to notice him. He thought, but could not be certain, that Unterholzer looked worried, and this gave him considerable pleasure. He could continue to keep his distance – for years if necessary – until Unterholzer knocked on his door with an unconditional apology. And even then, it might take some time before an apology could be accepted, so grave was the offence which Unterholzer had committed.

Yet as the days passed, von Igelfeld found himself increasingly puzzled by Unterholzer's apparent ability to endure the Coventry to which he had been consigned. Unterholzer was seen laughing and joking with some of the junior assistants and was, in von Igelfeld's hearing, described by the Librarian as being 'in remarkably good spirits'. It seemed to von Igelfeld that his colleague had acquired an extraordinary new confidence. Not only had he shown the temerity to criticise *Portuguese Irregular Verbs* in the columns of the *Zeitschrift*, but he seemed to have overcome his previous hesitance and inadequacy in his everyday dealings with his colleagues. This was disturbing; if Unterholzer were to start throwing his weight around, then the Institute would become a distinctly less attractive place. Nobody wanted Unterholzer's opinions on anything, and it was highly undesirable that he should see fit to give them.

Von Igelfeld decided to take the matter up with the Librarian, who had always enjoyed a close relationship with Unterholzer.

'Professor Unterholzer seems in very good form these days,' he remarked. 'He's rather more confident than before, would you not say?'

'Dear Professor Unterholzer!' said the Librarian. 'He's certainly more forthcoming than he used to be. But then that's psychoanalysis for you!'

Von Igelfeld narrowed his eyes. 'Psychoanalysis?' he said. 'Do you mean that Professor Unterholzer is undergoing analysis?'

'Yes,' said the Librarian. 'In fact, I can take some of the credit for it. I recommended it to him and arranged for him to meet Dr Hubertoffel. He's a very good analyst – one of the best, I believe.'

Von Igelfeld made a noncommittal sound and brought the discussion to an end. Stalking off to his office, he began to ponder the implications of what he had been told. *Confidence! Psychoanalysis! Dr Hubertoffel!* It was all profoundly unsettling. He was used to the order of things as they were, and the thought of a liberated Unterholzer, free of the manifold inadequacies which up to now had made his company just bearable, was extremely disturbing. He would have to find out more about this Dr Hubertoffel and see whether there was any way of restraining the baneful influence which he seemed to be having on Unterholzer's life. If this involved a visit to Dr Hubertoffel himself, then von Igelfeld was prepared to do even that. He had always harboured the gravest mistrust of both Freudians and Freemasons, whom he regarded as being inextricably linked, but the task ahead of him had now acquired an urgency which could not be ignored: the reputation of the Institute, and that of *Portuguese Irregular Verbs* itself, could depend on bringing Unterholzer to heel before even more damaging attacks could be made. To this end, he was even prepared to wander into the Freudian cage itself and deal with whatever lion figures may be found within.

Dr Max Augustus Hubertoffel of the *Hubertoffel Klinik für Neurosen und Psychopathologie* looked every inch a man who was suited to his calling. He was a slight, dapper man, with slickly parted hair, a Viennese bow-tie, and carefully polished

black patent-leather shoes. His consulting rooms, discreetly tucked away in a quiet street in Regensburg's professional quarter, were reached by a winding stair that culminated in a dark green door. Onto this door had been screwed Dr Hubertoffel's brass plate into which von Igelfeld, recovering his breath from the stairs, now peered and saw his own face staring back.

Once admitted to the analyst's sanctum, von Igelfeld found the doctor looking at him politely over his desk. Von Igelfeld was asked a few questions and his answers were noted down by Dr Hubertoffel in a large black notebook. Then the latter gestured to a green baize-covered couch and invited von Igelfeld to lie down.

The author of *Portuguese Irregular Verbs* settled himself on the couch. It was comfortable, but not so comfortable as to be soporific.

You may close your eyes, if you wish,' said Dr Hubertoffel. 'Some analysands prefer to do that, although there is always the danger of sleep if you do.'

Von Igelfeld found himself wondering if Unterholzer closed his eyes during analysis, or whether he gazed up at Dr Hubertoffel's ceiling and plotted. Indeed, it was quite possible that the idea of attacking *Portuguese Irregular Verbs* had been conceived on this very couch – oh hateful, hateful thought!

'You will have heard of free association,' said Dr Hubertoffel. 'I find it a useful tool in the discovery of what is troubling a patient. Then, on the basis of this knowledge, I know what I should look out for during the process of analysis. The mind, you see, is full of dark furniture.'

Von Igelfeld gave a start. Dark furniture? Was his own

mind full of such a thing? Perhaps it was unwise to under-take analysis, even for the purpose of equipping himself to deal with Unterholzer. If the furniture of the mind was dark, then perhaps it would be best to leave it where it was – in the shadows.

'So,' said Dr Hubertoffel. '*The sea.*'

'The sea?' asked von Igelfeld.

'Yes. I say *the sea* and you tell me what comes into your mind.'

'The sea,' said von Igelfeld.

'No,' said Dr Hubertoffel, patiently. 'I said *the sea*. You tell me what you envisaged.'

'I thought of the sea,' said von Igelfeld. 'That's why I replied the sea when you said the sea.'

Dr Hubertoffel tapped his pencil on the edge of his notebook. 'You must think of something else,' he said. 'Don't be too literal. I'll try again. *Father.*'

'Whiskers,' said von Igelfeld.

'Good,' said Dr Hubertoffel. 'That's a very good reply. Your father had whiskers, I take it.'

'No,' said von Igelfeld. 'But other boys' fathers had them.'

'*Oedipus,*' went on Dr Hubertoffel.

'Mother. No, uncle.'

The psychoanalyst nodded. 'Excellent. Now: *Scissors.*'

'The Suck-a-Thumb Man,' said von Igelfeld. 'You'll remember him from *The Struwelpeter*. He's the man who came to cut off the thumbs of the children who sucked them. I was very frightened of him.'

'And still are, perhaps?' ventured Dr Hubertoffel. 'The shades of the nursery are apt to linger. But let us move on. *Id.*'

171

'Darkness. Inner me.'

'Excellent. *Sausage*.'

'Dog.'

'*Dog*?'

'Sausage.'

'*Sausage dog.*'

'When I was a boy,' said von Igelfeld, a little later, 'we used to live in Austria, where my grandfather had an estate near Graz. I lived there from the age of six until I was fifteen. Then I was sent to a military academy in Germany. I was very sad to leave Austria and I remember leaning out of the window to catch a last glimpse of my parents and my Uncle Oedipus as they stood on the platform waving to the train. I saw my father raise his hand and then lower it to place it on my mother's shoulder as if to comfort her.'

'Or possibly to reassert ownership,' interjected Dr Hubertoffel.

'My mother turned away and walked back towards our car and I put my head back in the carriage. I was only fifteen, you see, and I had never been away from home. Now I was on my way to the military academy and had no idea of what to expect. I had read *The Young Torless*, of course, and I feared that this was what I was in for. So

I sat in my seat and stared dumbly out of the window.

'When I arrived at the school, I was shown to my place in the dormitory. There were forty other boys, all living in the same long room, all engaged in various initiation rituals, whipping one another with wet towels or exchanging blood-brotherhood vows. Several were cutting into one another's hands with blades, in order to mingle blood.

'I was at a loss. There seemed something strange about the dormitory. There were forty boys, but only twenty beds. We had to share, you see.

'I turned to the boy with whom I had been detailed to share. He was sitting at the end of the bed, gazing glumly at his boots.

'I asked him if he had a nurse at home, and he said that he had just left her. She was a girl called Hysteria, who came from a Bavarian farm, but who was a very good nurse. They had only one bed in the nursery, and he had shared with her. Now he had to share with me, and he was desolate.'

Dr Hubertoffel was listening avidly. 'This is extremely interesting material,' he said, scribbling furiously. 'I am fascinated by this. It is all very pathological.'

Von Igelfeld closed his eyes. It was easier to make up stories with one's eyes closed, he found.

'I survived that first night, although the sobbing of my bed companion largely prevented me from getting any sleep. Then, the next morning, after we had all been forced to take a cold shower, which we shared, our lessons began. The school was very interested in the Franco-Prussian War and devoted many lessons to it. Apart from that, we were taught very little.'

'And were the masters cruel?' asked Dr Hubertoffel.

'Immensely cruel,' said von Igelfeld. 'They used to take great pleasure in devising fresh tortures for the boys, and some of the boys simply could not stand it. Those were the ones who ran away. Sometimes they were returned, and punished all the more. Sometimes they got away and we never heard of them again. I longed to be one of them. But I did not have the courage to leave and, besides, one of the larger boys had cut the soles off my boots to affix to his. I could not have got very far with boots without soles. But there was another reason, too. I was protecting a boy who was being ruthlessly bullied. I had rescued him from his tormentors, but now he relied on me to look after him. If I deserted him, it would be like throwing him to the wolves.'

'Tell me about this boy,' said Dr Hubertoffel.

'He was called Unterholzer,' said von Igelfeld. 'Detlev Amadeus Unterholzer. At least, I think that was his name.'

Von Igelfeld could see that what he had just said had had a marked effect on Dr Hubertoffel.

'Unterholzer?' asked the doctor. 'You protected this . . . this Unterholzer?'

'Yes,' said von Igelfeld. 'He was a very unhappy boy. He had been sent to the military academy by his parents, who hoped that the discipline of such a place would cure him of his dreadful lies. But it did not work, and he continued to be unable to tell truth from falsehood. The other boys did not like this – we had this strict code of honour, you see – and they responded by bullying him. I was the only one to defend him.'

Dr Hubertoffel stared at von Igelfeld.

'So he lied all the time?' he said, eventually.

'Everything he said was untrue,' said von Igelfeld. 'And

I suspect it is just the same today. Such people do not really change, do they?'

Dr Hubertoffel thought for a moment. 'Usually not,' he said, gravely. 'Such behaviour indicates a fundamental personality disorder and there is very little we can do about that. Even psychoanalysis is of little help.'

'That's very sad,' said von Igelfeld. 'It must be a great disappointment to you to have patients of that sort.' Adding hurriedly: 'That is, if you do have any like that.'

He left the consulting room shortly afterwards, feeling immensely pleased with himself. He was sure that he had completely derailed Unterholzer's analysis; Dr Hubertoffel had become virtually silent after he had mentioned Unterholzer. He was probably seething with anger that Unterholzer had misled him during the analysis; to sit there and write down all the lies – just as a judge has to do in court – must be a difficult experience.

He walked out into the street. It was a fine evening and he had decided to walk home. Analysis was extraordinary, he reflected. He had gone in feeling somewhat gloomy and had come out feeling quite optimistic. He looked up at the cloudless evening sky and smiled with satisfaction. Unterholzer's little plans would be spiked now; Dr Hubertoffel may have given him the confidence to launch an attack on *Portuguese Irregular Verbs*, but where would that confidence be once he had lost the support of the psychoanalyst?

He walked past a bookshop window and glanced in. There was a display of new academic titles. *The Economy of the Sudanese Uplands* – extremely dull, he thought. *The Upanishads Reviewed* – more promising. Then: *Truth: a Philosophical Defence*.

He paused. Truth. He was on the side of truth, and always had been: it would need no defending while he was around. And was not the motto of the von Igelfelds *Truth Always*? His gaze shifted from the book to his own reflection in the glass of the window, and at that moment an awful pang of guilt shook him. He was looking at the face of a liar!

Von Igelfeld stood stock still. He had done a terrible, dreadful thing. He had walked into the consulting rooms of that poor Freudian and had told him a whole pack of lies. There never was a military academy. He had never had an Uncle Oedipus. It was all nonsense, of the sort that these misguided Freudians like to hear. And as for the accusations against Unterholzer – even if Unterholzer had behaved appallingly in criticising his hypothesis, that was no excuse for him, a von Igelfeld, to stoop to that level. He remembered his scorn for Unterholzer when Unterholzer had claimed to be von Unterholzer. Now he, a real von, was behaving just as badly.

He stood stock still for a moment, consumed by misery. Then, his head lowered in shame, he continued his walk home, his mind a turmoil. Should he rush back and apologise to Dr Hubertoffel? Should he write him a letter and try to explain? Whatever he did, he would look ridiculous.

He paused. His route had taken him past a small Catholic church, set back from the street. And there on the notice board was a sign which read: *Sinned? Confessions are heard in this House of God from 6 pm to 8 pm each Wednesday and Saturday evening. Inside, there is one who listens.* And today, von Igelfeld recalled, was Wednesday, and it was undoubtedly evening.

The inside of the church was half-lit. A woman was kneeling at the altar rail of a small side-chapel, but apart from her the church seemed deserted. Von Igelfeld went forward hesitantly, glancing at the pictures that hung on one wall. The Virgin herself looked down on him, a smile of compassion on her lips. And there was Saint Francis, his hands extended towards the birds, and another saint whom he did not recognise, a finger raised in silent admonition, as if of von Igelfeld himself.

He spotted the confessional and moved towards it. He was not a Catholic – the von Igelfelds had always been Lutheran – but he was familiar with the procedure. You went in and sat on a small bench and spoke to the priest behind the grille. It did not matter whether you were a member of the Church; the priest was there for all manner and conditions of men – mendacious philologists not excepted.

He moved the curtain aside and slipped into the box. There was indeed a small grille and a sound behind it, a rustling of a cassock perhaps, told him that the priest was in.

'Good evening,' whispered von Igelfeld.

'Hello,' said a disembodied voice from behind the grille. 'How are you this evening?'

'Not very well,' said von Igelfeld. 'In fact, I am feeling very bad about a terrible thing that I have done.'

The priest was silent for a moment, as if digesting the information. Then he spoke: 'Terrible? How terrible, my son? Have you killed a man?'

Von Igelfeld gasped. 'Oh no! Nothing that bad.'

'Well then,' said the priest. 'Most other things can be undone, can't they? Tell me what this terrible thing is.'

Von Igelfeld drew a deep breath. 'I lied,' he said.

'Lied?' said the priest. 'Lied to the police? To your wife?'

'To a psychoanalyst,' said von Igelfeld.

There was a strange sound from behind the grille, a sound which was rather difficult to interpret, but which sounded rather like disapproval.

'That is *very* bad,' said the priest. 'Psychoanalysts are there to help us. If we lie to them, then we are lying to ourselves. It is a terrible thing.'

'I know,' said von Igelfeld. 'I told him all sorts of lies about my past. And I even made up words in the free association.'

'Both of those things are sins,' said the priest firmly. 'Free association is there to help the psychoanalyst unlock the secrets of the mind. If you mislead in that respect, then the analysis is distorted.'

'But worse than that,' went on von Igelfeld. 'I told lies about my colleague, Unterholzer. He had published an attack on my book and I wanted to ruin his analysis.'

'I see,' said the priest. 'And now you are feeling guilty?'

'Yes,' said von Igelfeld.

'Guilt is natural,' said the priest quietly. 'It is a way in which the Super-ego asserts itself in the face of the primitive, anarchic urges of the Id. Guilt acts as a way of establishing psychic balance between the various parts of the personality. But we should not let it consume us.'

'No?' asked von Igelfeld.

'No,' said the priest. 'Guilt fuels neurosis. A small measure of guilt is healthy – it affirms the intuitive sense of what is right or wrong. But if you become too focused on what you have done wrong, then you can become an obsessive neurotic.'

'I'm sorry,' said von Igelfeld. 'I truly am sorry for what I have done. Please forgive me.'

'Oh, you're absolved,' said the priest. 'That goes almost without saying. God is very forgiving these days. He's moved on. He forgives everything, in fact. What you have to do now is to repair the damage that you have caused. You must go and see this Unterholzer and say to him that you are sorry that you have lied about him. You must ask his forgiveness. Then you must write to Dr Hubertoffel – I assume that you're talking about him, by the way, and tell him what you told him about the military academy was untrue. I went to a military academy, incidentally.'

Sinned?

'Oh?' said von Igelfeld. 'Were you unhappy there?'

'Terribly,' said the priest. 'We were crammed together in dormitories, sharing everything, and they made us take cold showers all the time. I still shudder when I take a cold shower.'

'You still take them?' asked von Igelfeld.

'Yes,' said the priest. 'I must confess that I do. I suppose that it's ritualistic. But it may also be that it invokes memories of the military academy and I suspect that there's part of me that wants to remember that.'

'You should forget,' said von Igelfeld. 'You should try to move on.'

'Oh, I try,' said the priest. 'But it's not always easy.'

'But if we may return to my case,' said von Igelfeld, hesitantly. 'Am I truly forgiven?'

'Of course,' said the priest. 'In the name of the Father, the Son and the Holy Ghost. ✠ Forgiven entirely.'

Von Igelfeld returned home in high spirits. He had taken to this agreeable priest and had decided that he might well return to listen to some of his sermons. They would surely be very entertaining, unlike the Lutheran dirges he recalled from his boyhood. Filled with the spirit of forgiveness, he wrote an immediate letter of apology to Dr Hubertoffel and went out into the street to post it. Then, retiring to bed, he fell into the first sound sleep that he had had since the awful article had first appeared in the *Zeitschrift*.

Unterholzer looked at him suspiciously when he went into his office the following morning.

'Good morning, Herr Unterholzer,' von Igelfeld said brightly. 'I have come to apologise.'

Unterholzer gave a start. This was not what he had expected.

'Yes,' von Igelfeld continued. 'I have done you several great wrongs.'

'Several?' stuttered Unterholzer.

Von Igelfeld looked up at the ceiling. He had not expected it to be easy, and indeed it was not.

'There was the matter of your poor sausage dog,' he said. 'That was most regrettable. I can only assure you that I had not intended that to happen.'

'Of course not,' said Unterholzer. 'I never said that. . . .'

Von Igelfeld cut him short. 'And then I went off to Dr Hubertoffel and tried to ruin your analysis. I told him all sorts of lies.'

Unterholzer's jaw dropped. 'You told him lies about me?'

'Yes,' said von Igelfeld. 'I had intended that he should form a bad impression of you and that your analysis should come to an end.'

For a moment Unterholzer stared mutely at von Igelfeld. Then he began to smile. 'But that's very convenient,' he said. 'I've been looking for a way out of all that without offending Dr Hubertoffel. Now he will be pleased if I no longer go. Frankly, I found it all an expensive waste of time. I've already paid him thousands, you know.'

'So you're pleased?' asked von Igelfeld lamely.

'Absolutely,' said Unterholzer, beaming even more. 'He kept trying to make me something I was not. I don't like to be an assertive, gregarious person. That's not my nature.'

'You're right,' said von Igelfeld. 'Well, I must say that I'm glad that I have been able to help you.'

Unterholzer had sunk back in his chair and the smile

181

had disappeared. 'But I have something for which to apologise,' he muttered. 'I wrote a very spiteful piece about *Portuguese Irregular Verbs*. I did it because of my sausage dog, but now I really regret it. Did you see it?'

'No,' said von Igelfeld. *Truth Always*. 'Well, perhaps I glanced at it. But it was nothing.'

'I shall do all that lies in my power to correct it,' said Unterholzer. 'I can assure you of that.'

'You are very kind, Herr Unterholzer,' said von Igelfeld. 'Let us now put all this behind us and get on with the important work of the moment.'

And that is exactly what happened. The life of the Institute returned to normal. In the next issue of the *Zeitschrift* there appeared a prominent piece by Unterholzer, entitled *Further Thoughts on von Igelfeld's Portuguese Irregular Verbs*. It amounted to a complete recantation of the earlier piece, which was described as having been intended only to engender debate, written by one who had cast himself, unwillingly, in the role of *Avocatus Diaboli*.

It was a thoroughly satisfactory outcome. Only the Librarian had appeared to regret how things had turned out.

'Poor Herr Unterholzer seems to have lost his new drive,' he commented to von Igelfeld. 'I wonder why?'

'No idea,' began von Igelfeld, but then corrected himself. *Truth Always*. 'At least I think I know, but these matters are confidential and I'm very sorry but I simply cannot tell you.'

The Bones of Father Christmas

Italy beckoned, and this was a call which Professor Moritz-Maria von Igelfeld always found very difficult to resist. He felt at home in Italy, especially in Siena, where he had once spent several idyllic months in the Istituto di Filologia Comparata. That was at the very time at which he was putting the finishing touches to his great work, and indeed many of the streets of that noble town were inextricably linked in his mind with insights he experienced during that creative period of his life. It had been walking along the Banco di Sopra, for example, that he had realised why it was that in Brazilian Portuguese there was a persistent desire to replace the imperative tense with the present indicative. Was it not linked with the tendency to confuse *tu* and *voce*, since the singular of the indicative had the same form as the imperative singular *at least for the second person*? It was: there could be no other explanation. And had he not rushed back to the Istituto, oblivious to the bemused stares of passers-by? Had he not stumbled briefly on the stairs as he mentally composed the paragraph which would encapsulate this insight, a stumble which had caused the prying concierge to whisper to his friend in the newsagent next door, 'That German professor, the tall one, came back from lunch yesterday *drunk*! Yes, I saw it with my own eyes. Fell downstairs, at least two flights, head over heels.'

And then there was the idea which had come to him one morning while he took a walk past the Monte di Paschi bank and had seen the bill-poster slapping a notice on the wall. The poster had been one of those announcements that the Italians like to put on walls; the death of a local baker's mother. *E morta!* the poster had proclaimed in heavy, Bodoni type, and below that, simply, *Mama!* Von Igelfeld had stopped and read the still gluey text. How remarkable that private pain could be so publicly shared, which meant, of course, its dilution. For we are all members of one another, are we not, and the baker's loss was the loss, in a tiny way, of all those fellow citizens who might know him only slightly, but who would have read his cry of sorrow. And like Proust's tiny madeleine cakes dipped into tea, the sight of one of these posters could evoke in von Igelfeld's mind the moment when, after passing on from that melancholy sign, he had suddenly realised how the system of regular vocalic alternations had developed in the verb *poder*.

But Siena was more for him than those heady days of composition; he cherished, too, a great affection for the Sienese hills. He liked to go to the hills in spring, when the air was laden with the scent of wild flowers. His good friend, Professor Roberto Guerini, was always pleased to entertain him on his small wine estate outside Montalcino, where von Igelfeld had become well known to the proprietors of surrounding estates and was much in demand at dinner parties in the region. One of these dinner parties was still talked about in Italy. That was the occasion when the current proprietor of the neighbouring estate, the Conte Vittorio Fantozzi, known locally as *il Grasso* (the fat one), had conducted a lengthy dinner-table conversation with von Igelfeld in which both participants spoke old Tuscan dialects now almost completely lost to all but a small band of linguistic enthusiasts. In recognition of his guest's skill, the count had bottled a wine which he named after the distinguished visitor. The label showed a picture of a hedgehog in a field, an allusion to the literal translation of von Igelfeld's name (hedgehog-field, in English, *campo del porcospino* in Italian). Thereafter, von Igelfeld was referred to in Sienese society as 'our dear friend from Germany, *il Professore Porcospino*'.

It would have been good to get back to Tuscany – perhaps even to Montalcino itself – but when the call arrived, it was of a rather different nature.

'Florianus and I are going to Rome,' said Ophelia Prinzel when she encountered von Igelfeld in the small park near his house. 'Would you care to accompany us?'

Von Igelfeld remembered with pleasure the trip to Venice which he had made with the Prinzels a few years earlier. It was true that the holiday had been cut short, when Prinzel discovered that he had been rendered slightly radioactive as a result of contact with polluted canal water, but that had soon been dealt with and was not allowed to place too much of a pall over the trip. Von Igelfeld might have been more pleased had the offer been to go to Venice again, or even to Naples or Palermo, but Rome in the agreeable company of his two old friends was still an attractive prospect, and he accepted readily.

'As it happens,' he said, 'I have some work I've been meaning to do in Rome. I shall be able to spend the days in the Vatican Library and then devote the evenings to leisurely pursuits.'

'So wise,' said Ophelia. 'A break is what you need. You push yourself too hard, Moritz-Maria. I'm quite happy to leave the Puccini project for weeks at a stretch.'

Von Igelfeld was not surprised to hear this, and was tempted to say: *That's why you'll never finish it*, but did not. He had grave doubts whether Puccini's correspondence would ever be published, at least in the lifetime of any of them, but loyalty to his friend forbade any comment.

They set off at the end of April, winding their way down to the plains of Lombardy. They had decided to break the journey, spending a few days in Siena before making the final assault on Rome. From their hotel, perched on the top of the city walls, they had a fine view of the surrounding countryside and its warm, red buildings. Von Igelfeld sat on the terrace and gazed out over the terracotta-tiled rooftops down below him, reflecting on how everything in Italy seemed to be so utterly in harmony with its surroundings. Even the modern works of man, buildings which in any other country would be an imposition on the landscape, here in Italy seemed to have a grace and fluidity that moulded them into the natural flow and form of the countryside. And the people too – they occupied their surroundings as if they were meant to be there; unlike Germany, where everybody seemed to be . . . well, they seemed to be so *cross* for some reason or another.

If life were different – if instead of being the author of *Portuguese Irregular Verbs*, with all that this entailed, he were a man of independent means, able to spend his time as he wished, then he could live in Italy, in some renovated Tuscan farmhouse. He would rise late, attend to his vines, and then take a leisurely drive into the nearby village to buy his newspaper and collect his mail. Perhaps he would even get married and his wife keep him company and play Schubert on the piano for him in the evening. That would be heaven indeed, but there was no point in dreaming; he *was* the author of *Portuguese Irregular Verbs*, he had no house in Italy, and such domestic comfort as he enjoyed was at second hand, crumbs from the table of the Prinzels. If only Unterholzer had not stolen – yes, *stolen* – from him the charming dentist, Dr Lisbetta von Brautheim who should, if there were any justice, have married von Igelfeld himself. And now he had even overheard Unterholzer talking about buying a small house in Italy! What use would that be to him, thought von Igelfeld bitterly. How could Unterholzer even begin to understand the subtle pleasures of the Italian landscape? How could Unterholzer begin to savour the scent of thyme in dusty summer air, with that great big nose of his? More of a lump than a nose, really, if one came to think about it. If Unterholzer were ever to contemplate a scene of hills and cypresses, all he would be able to see would be his own nose, and perhaps a blur beyond it. Italy, with all its visual treats, would be utterly wasted on Unterholzer, who would do far better to stay in Germany, where people like that were somehow less conspicuous.

But what could one expect? thought von Igelfeld. What could one really expect? There was nothing that could be done about Unterholzer. He should have been something else altogether. Perhaps the Burgermeister of a small town somewhere in Bavaria. Instead of which he had poked his large, unsuitable nose into philology, where it had no business to be. Really, it was most vexing.

He sighed. It was not easy maintaining one's position as the author of *Portuguese Irregular Verbs*. Not only was there Unterholzer (and all that tiresome business with his dog), but von Igelfeld also had to cope with the distinct unhelpfulness of the Librarian and with the unmitigated philistinism of his publishers. Then there was the awkward attitude of the university authorities, who recently had shown the temerity to ask him to deliver a series of lectures to undergraduate students. This had almost been the last straw for von Igelfeld, who had been obliged to remind them of just who he was. That had caused them to climb down, and the Rector had even sent a personal letter of apology, but von

Igelfeld felt that the damage was done. If German professors could be asked to lecture, as if they were mere *instructors*, then the future of German scholarship looked perilous. He had heard that one of his colleagues had even been asked whether he proposed to write another book, when he had already written one some ten years previously! And the alarming thing was that people were taking this lying down and not protesting at the outrageous breach of academic freedom which it unquestionably was. What would Immanuel Kant have made of it? What would have happened if the University of Koenigsberg had asked Kant whether he proposed to write another *Kritik der reinen Vernunft*? Kant would have treated such a question with the contempt it deserved.

It was the old problem of the poets and the legislators. The poets were not legislators, and the legislators were not poets. The wrong people were at the top, in positions where the people at the bottom might do very much better. Look at the sort of people who became Chancellor of Germany! Who were they? Von Igelfeld paused to address his own question. Who were they indeed? He had very little idea, but they were certainly very dull people, who were, on balance, best ignored. Sooner or later they went away, he found.

'Oh dear!' said von Igelfeld, out loud. '*Il nostro mondo! Che tedio!*'

'My goodness,' said a rich, rather plummy voice behind him. 'What a sentiment!'

Von Igelfeld turned sharply. Somebody had addressed him from behind.

'My dear sir,' said the man standing behind him. 'I did not mean to make you start! It's just that I, too, was admiring this view and reflecting on the state of the world, but was reaching an optimistic conclusion when you expressed yourself.'

Von Igelfeld rose to his feet and bowed slightly to the stranger.

'I am von Igelfeld,' he said.

The stranger smiled. 'And I'm the Duke of Johannesburg,' he said warmly, reaching out to shake hands.

Von Igelfeld looked at the Duke. He was a tall man, seemingly in his mid-forties, almost as tall as von Igelfeld himself, but more heavily-built. He had a fine, aquiline nose, rather reddened, von Igelfeld noted, a large moustache, and a crop of dark hair, neatly brushed back in the manner of a 'thirties dancing instructor. He was wearing a lightweight linen suit, but in place of a tie there was a red bandana tied loosely about his neck.

They engaged in light talk about the view from the terrace. The Duke was not staying at the hotel, he explained. He had a house of his own several streets away, but unfortunately it had no terrace. So he sometimes came down to the hotel in the evenings to take an aperitif and look out over the hills.

'So that's why I'm here,' he said simply.

They discussed Siena. The Duke explained that he had been spending several months a year there for some time, pursuing his researches. Then, when von Igelfeld mentioned Professor Guerini, they discovered a mutual acquaintance. The Duke, it transpired, had also known Guerini for years and had visited his estate several times. This information broke the ice further, and by the time that the Duke had finished his martini von Igelfeld had been invited back to join the Duke for dinner.

'Not a large party,' said the Duke. 'Just one or two people who are passing through and, of course, my research assistant.'

Von Igelfeld was delighted to accept. He was pleased to hear about the research assistant, too, as this confirmed that the Duke himself was a serious scholar. All in all, it seemed a most agreeable prospect and, after the Duke had gone, he rushed off to inform the Prinzels that he would not be joining them for dinner in the hotel that night. As it happened, this suited his companions well. Ophelia Prinzel had a slight headache and was proposing to have an early night and the heat had destroyed Prinzel's appetite. It was agreed that they would meet for breakfast and then spend the earlier part of the morning in the Cathedral Library, admiring the illuminated manuscripts before hordes of schoolchildren and parties of chattering Japanese tourists began to flock in. Von Igelfeld found Japanese tourists particularly trying. They were often fascinated by tall Germans, and he found it most disconcerting to be photographed by them. It was sobering to contemplate how many photograph albums in Tokyo or Kyoto contained his image, frozen in time, quite out of context, pored over and pointed out to interested relatives of the travellers. Why should they want to photograph him? Had they not seen a German professor before? It was another vexing thought, and so he put it out of his mind in favour of the contemplation of dinner at the Duke's house and the warm prospect of edifying conversation and a good table. The Duke's nose was a good portent. Its colour at the end suggested that a considerable quantity of fine Chianti had suffused upwards, by some process of osmosis. This implied the existence of a good cellar, and a generous hand. Let the

Prinzels call room service and gnaw at some inedible little morsel; finer things were in store for him.

The Duke's house was in a narrow street off the Piazza del Risorgimento. An inconspicuous door led off the street into a courtyard dominated by a small fountain. Stunted fig trees grew in terracotta pots against the walls and a large black cat sat on a stone bench, grooming its fur. The cat looked up and stared at von Igelfeld for a moment or two before returning to its task.

The main door of the house, on the other side of the courtyard, was ajar and von Igelfeld found no bell to ring. He entered somewhat cautiously, finding himself in a large, well-lit entrance hall. The floor, of black and white marble, was clearly an architectural reference to the famous striped cathedral tower which dominated the skyline a few winding streets away. On the walls, framed on either side by gilt sconces, were paintings of Tuscan scenes, one of a cypress-crossed hillside, another of a young man in the Renaissance style, a notary perhaps, seated at his desk before an open window. The window framed a hillside on which deer grazed and improbable birds strutted.

A door opened at the other end of the hall and a young woman – of nineteen at the most, little more than a girl – emerged into the hall. It was a moment or two before she saw von Igelfeld, and when she did, she gave a start.

She raised a hand to her mouth as if to stifle a gasp. Then she spoke, in foreign-accented but correct Italian. 'You gave me a fright. I was not expecting to find anybody in here.'

Von Igelfeld made a self-deprecating gesture.

'There was no bell,' he said apologetically. 'I should have

rung had I found a bell. I do not like to walk into the houses of other people without giving them notice.'

The girl laughed. 'Johannesburg doesn't mind,' she said. 'All sorts of people walk in here. He's always happy to see them.'

'I am glad,' said von Igelfeld. Then, after a short pause, he introduced himself and explained that he had been invited for dinner.

'Oh,' she said. 'So you are the German professor he met earlier today when he slipped out for his martini. He told me about you. He said you were very . . .'

She broke off suddenly, the hand going to the mouth. Von Igelfeld frowned. Very what? he wondered.

'Anyway,' said the girl, quickly recovering her composure. 'You must be wondering who I am. I am Beatrice. I'm the Duke's research assistant.'

Von Igelfeld had been wondering who she was and he was pleased that the research assistant was so refreshingly attractive. His research assistants had been uniformly plain and he had always envied colleagues who seemed to have assistants who were glamorous and vivacious. Indeed, he had once raised the matter with Prinzel, drawing attention to the strikingly beautiful young Russian recently recruited by Professor Vochsenkuhn. She had turned every head at the last Romance Philology Congress and had been utterly charming in spite of her linguistic limitations. She spoke only Russian, which von Igelfeld thought must have restricted her ability to conduct research in Romance philology, particularly since Professor Vochsenkuhn himself was not known to speak any Russian.

Prinzel had laughed. 'The reason why other people have

attractive research assistants, Moritz-Maria, is because they don't recruit them on academic ability. In fact, academic ability is probably the last criterion for selection.'

Von Igelfeld had found himself at a loss to understand.

'But if they have no academic ability,' he had objected, 'why recruit them as research assistants?'

Again Prinzel had laughed.

'Because research assistants often have talents which go beyond pure research,' he had said. 'That is widely known. They provide . . . *inspiration* for the professors who employ them. Inspiration is very important.'

Von Igelfeld was not convinced. 'I still cannot see the justification,' he had said. But Prinzel had merely shaken his head and changed the subject. Now here, clearly, was one of those attractive young research assistants who provided inspiration. Prinzel was evidently right.

Beatrice gestured towards the door from which she had emerged.

'They're in the salon,' she said. 'We should join them.'

She led von Igelfeld through a corridor and into a large room at the rear of the building. One of the walls was entirely covered with bookshelves; the others were hung with paintings of the sort von Igelfeld had already encountered in the hall. At the far end, standing before the gaping mouth of a high marble fireplace, stood the Duke, glass in hand; in a chair to his left sat a grey-bearded man dressed in the long black cassock of an Orthodox priest.

'My dear Professor von Igelfeld,' said the Duke, putting down his glass and advancing towards his guest. 'You are most welcome to this house.'

Von Igelfeld bowed slightly to the Duke and then turned

towards the priest, who had risen to his feet and had extended a ring-encrusted hand. For a moment von Igelfeld was uncertain whether he was expected to kiss one of the rings, but the gesture very quickly made itself apparent as a handshake.

'And this,' said the Duke genially. 'This is my old friend, Angelos Evangelis, Patriarch of Alexandria and All Africa Down as Far as Somalia.'

Von Igelfeld shook hands with the Patriarch, who smiled and inclined his head slightly.

'We are a very small party tonight,' the Duke went on. 'But, in a way, that is always preferable.'

'Very much better,' agreed von Igelfeld. 'I cannot abide large parties.'

'Then you should not come to this house too often,' said Beatrice. 'Johannesburg gives large parties every other night, more or less.'

Von Igelfeld felt a flush of embarrassment. He had been unwise to condemn large parties; it was obvious that somebody like the Duke of Johannesburg would entertain on a splendid scale.

'Of course, I like large parties too,' he said quickly. 'It's just that I can't abide them when I'm in the mood for a small party. It all depends, you see.'

'Of course,' said the Duke. 'I know in my bones when I get up whether it's going to be a large party day or a small party day.'

As this conversation was unfolding, Beatrice had busied herself in obtaining a drink for von Igelfeld and in filling up the glasses of the Patriarch and the Duke. There was then a brief silence, during which the Patriarch stared at von Igelfeld and the Duke adjusted the blue cravat which he had donned for the evening.

In an attempt to stimulate conversation, von Igelfeld turned to the Patriarch and asked him where he lived.

The Patriarch looked at von Igelfeld with mournful eyes.

'I live in many places,' he said. 'I live here. I live there. It is given to me to move a great deal. At present I am in Rome, but last year I was in Beirut. Where shall I be next year? That is uncertain. Perhaps you can tell me.'

'Well,' said von Igelfeld. 'I'm not sure . . .' He tailed off.

'I must explain that the Patriarch is currently afflicted with schisms,' interjected the Duke. 'He has been so afflicted for some years.'

Von Igelfeld was about to express his sympathy, but Beatrice now intervened.

'The Patriarch is a very brave man,' she said. 'If I had schisms I would not know where to turn. Is there a cure?'

The Duke took a sip of his wine. He was smiling.

'Dear Beatrice,' he said. 'Your question is so utterly pertinent, but, alas, one thousand years of Coptic history cannot be so easily resolved. I suggest, therefore, that we go to table. Signora Tagliatti has prepared some wild boar for us and my uncorked wines will rapidly lose their impact if we keep them waiting much longer. Shall we go through?'

In the Duke's dining room, von Igelfeld sat flanked by Beatrice and the Patriarch, with the Duke, a beaming host, at the head of the table. The Duke spoke of his researches – an investigation of the concept of empathy in Hume and compassion in Schopenhauer.

196

'Much the same thing, don't you think?' he asked von Igelfeld.

Von Igelfeld was not sure. He remembered reading that Hume believed that our minds vibrated in sympathy, and that this ability – to vibrate in unison with one another – was the origin of the ethical impulse. And Schopenhauer's moral theory was about feeling, was it not; so perhaps they were one and the same phenomenon. But he could hardly pronounce on the matter with any authority, having not read Schopenhauer since boyhood, and he looked to Beatrice for support.

'Schopenhauer!' she murmured dreamily.

'You must know a lot about him,' encouraged von Igelfeld.

'Hardly,' she said.

Von Igelfeld was silent for a moment. Was it her role, then, merely to *inspire*? He looked at the Patriarch, who stared back at him with melancholy, rheumy eyes.

'I have known many who have lacked compassion,' the Patriarch said suddenly. 'The pretender to the Bishopric of Khartoum, for example. And the Syrian Ordinary at Constantinople.'

'Especially him,' agreed the Duke.

Von Igelfeld was surprised at the bitterness with which the Patriarch spoke – a bitterness which seemed to find a ready echo in the Duke's response.

'Your schisms,' von Igelfeld began. 'They are clearly very deep. But what are they actually *about*?'

'A variety of important matters,' said the Duke. 'For example, there is a serious dispute as to whether a saint's halo goes out when he dies or whether it remains lit up.'

'It does not go out,' said the Patriarch, in the tone

of one pronouncing on the self-evident.

'Then there's the question of miracles,' went on the Duke. 'There is a major schism on the issue of miracles. Are they possible? Does God choose to show himself through the miraculous? That sort of schism.'

'But of course miracles exist,' said Beatrice. 'Miracles occur every day. We all know that. You yourself said that it was a miracle when you and I . . .'

The Duke cut her off, rather sharply, von Igelfeld thought.

'Be that as it may,' he said. 'But it is not really the personal miracles that are at issue. It's the miracles of ecclesiastical significance that are the real substance of the debate. The Miracle of the Holy House, for example. Did angels carry the Virgin Mary's house all the way to Italy from the Holy Land, as is claimed?'

'Of course they did,' said the Patriarch. 'No sensible person doubts that.'

Von Igelfeld looked down at his plate. Had five fish appeared on it at that moment, it seemed that nobody would have been in the slightest bit surprised. But, for his part, he had always found the story of the Holy House rather too far-fetched to believe. How would the house have withstood the flight, even in the care of angels? It seemed to him highly improbable.

Over breakfast the next morning, von Igelfeld reflected on the experiences of the evening. He had enjoyed himself at the Duke's dinner party, but had come away moderately perplexed. Who was Beatrice, and why did she know so little about Schopenhauer? Who was the Patriarch, and who was behind the schisms which seemed to cause him

The Duke of Johannesburg

such distress? If he were the Patriarch, then could he not unilaterally put an end to schism simply by expelling schismatics? That is what von Igelfeld himself would have done. Unterholzer, after all, was a sort of schismatic, and von Igelfeld had found no difficulty in dealing with him decisively. Presumably patriarchs had at their disposal a variety of ecclesiastical remedies that put fear into the heart of any dissident. Inverted candles – snuffed out; that was the ritual which von Igelfeld associated with such matters and that would surely silence all but the most headstrong of rebels. And then there was the mystery of the Duke himself. Von Igelfeld did not purport to know anything about the non-German aristocracy – which he considered to be a pale imitation of its German equivalent – and he had never been aware of a Dukedom of Johannesburg. But the British were peculiar – it was well known – and they used extraordinary titles. Was there not a Scottish nobleman simply called The MacGregor, as if he were a whisky? And the Irish were not much better, when one came to think about it. There was a man who went under the title of The McGillicuddy of the Reeks, and somebody actually called the Green Knight. The Green Knight was now defunct, he had heard, which was not at all surprising. What were these people thinking of when they assumed these ridiculous names? At least in Germany people used simple territorial designations which let you know exactly where you stood.

The Duke appeared to be a man of substance. The house was in every respect suitable for aristocratic inhabitation, with its rich furnishings and its air of solid age. But there had been one very peculiar experience which had made von Igelfeld wonder whether all was how it seemed. As he was leaving, he had passed too close to one of the paintings in the hall and had tilted it slightly. He had stopped to straighten the heavy gilt frame, and as he had done so his finger had inadvertently come into contact with the canvas. It was a painting of a sixteenth-century papal coronation, presumably by an artist of the time, and von Igelfeld had touched the lower corner, which showed a crowd amassed outside the gates of the Vatican. This was unexceptional, but what was quite astonishing was the fact that the paint had not quite dried! He had been too surprised to investigate further and anyway the Duke of Johannesburg had appeared at this point and it would have been rude to be seen testing the dryness of one's host's oil paintings. Indeed it would be tantamount to a suggestion of *nouvelle arrivisme*.

The German party breakfasted together on the terrace.

Ophelia Prinzel had quite recovered from her headache and was looking forward to a day of wandering about Siena. Prinzel himself had acquired an appetite overnight and tucked into three large almond rolls with apparent gusto, washing them down with at least four cups of steaming milky coffee.

'Wonderful!' Prinzel exclaimed at the end of breakfast. 'Now to the Cathedral before the hordes arrive. Then a browse in the antique shops followed by lunch and a long siesta. What a marvellous day lies ahead of us!'

They walked together to the Cathedral, which had just opened its doors for the day. A taciturn attendant admitted them to the Cathedral Library, where the great illuminated manuscripts lay in their glass cases, displaying their medieval delights to the eyes of moderns, most of whom were now as virtually incapable of using a pen as was the *profanum vulgus* of those distant years. Von Igelfeld concentrated on the finer points of medieval Latin grammar as displayed in the text, while Prinzel and Ophelia discussed the use of colour in the elaborately ornamented capitals or on the bestiary upon which the monks based their parables.

'Look,' said Ophelia, pointing at a page of intricately illuminated text. 'A hedgehog. Moritz-Maria, come and look at this hedgehog.'

Von Igelfeld crossed the room. His family crest contained a hedgehog, as one might expect, and he always felt a tug of affection towards hedgehogs in all their manifestations. It was a noble creature, he thought, every bit as impressive as more conventional heraldic creatures, such as the eagle. Germany, it was true, used the eagle as its symbol, but von Igelfeld had often thought that a hedgehog would be more suitable. It was not impossible to imagine the Prussian flag with a hedgehog rampant rather than its severe eagle.

'Dear little hedgehog,' said Ophelia, pointing at the tiny creature monastically caught in a scurry across the bottom of a page of the Psalms. 'Look how timid he is. Minding nobody's business but his own. Compare him with that boastful unicorn.'

'The hedgehog is not timid,' said von Igelfeld sharply. 'In iconography, I must point out, he represents sagacity.'

'No,' said Prinzel. 'That's the owl.'

'Not only the owl, Herr Prinzel,' snapped von Igelfeld. 'The hedgehog has always been admired for its wisdom. You will be familiar, I assume, with what Pliny the Elder thought about hedgehogs? Or what the *Physiologus* says of their virtues?'

'This hedgehog doesn't look very wise,' said Ophelia. 'Perhaps the monk used as his model a hedgehog which happened not to be very bright. Aristotle made the same mistake about moles when he said that all moles were blind. It's just that the mole he examined was blind.'

Prinzel now joined in. 'And then there's St Basil,' he said. 'Did he not say that hedgehogs were unclean?'

Von Igelfeld glared at his friends. He had not come to this holy and learned place to be insulted, and he thought it best to withdraw to the other side of the room and leave the Prinzels to engage in whatever misguided discussion of symbolism they wished. He had found an interesting example of the ablative absolute in the transcription of a psalm and he wished to ponder it further.

It was while he was studying this text that the doors suddenly opened and the attendant wearily admitted a large group of Japanese visitors. There was a collective intake of breath as they saw the painted ceiling. Several dozen cameras were immediately produced and flashes of light followed hard upon one another. Then the leader of the group gave a cry when he noticed von Igelfeld and called out some command in Japanese. This was the signal for a large group, cameras at the ready, to advance upon von Igelfeld.

'Tall sir,' said the leader as he approached. 'Be so kind as to stand with me in this photograph.'

Without waiting for an answer, the leader positioned himself next to von Igelfeld and looked up at him in admiration.

'You would be a living monument in Japan,' he said politely. 'Japanese people like very tall people and very tall trees.'

Von Igelfeld stood tight-lipped as the photographs were taken. Really, the whole morning was proving to be quite insupportable. Firstly there had been the tactlessness of the Prinzels, and now there was this Japanese imposition. It was all too much, and as soon as the Japanese had departed he announced to the Prinzels that he had decided to leave and that he would meet them at lunch. It transpired that they, too, were beginning to find the library oppressive and would welcome some fresh air. So the German party left and soon found itself seated in a pleasant pavement café, with the soft morning sun warm upon their brows and the flags waving in a balmy breeze. There was no more talk of hedgehogs and von Igelfeld decided that he would overlook the earlier, ill-advised remarks of his friends. One did not come to Italy to argue; one came to Italy to allow the soul to bask in the sheer beauty of art and its ennobling possibilities.

* * *

Von Igelfeld enjoyed his siesta that day. It had been an exhausting morning in one way or another, and when they returned to the hotel after lunch he felt disinclined to do anything but sleep. He woke up shortly after four and read for three hours or so before venturing out for a short walk. He was due to meet the Prinzels for dinner at eight, in a restaurant which had been recommended to them by the hotel manager, and he decided to spend the hour until then wandering about the back alleys of the town. This was a time when people were quite lively, preparing for their evening meal, gossiping with one another, performing the final chores of the day.

He was walking up a narrow street – too narrow for cars, but wide enough for the occasional hurtling moped – when he felt a tug at his sleeve. He turned round sharply and saw the Patriarch standing behind him.

'Professor von Igelfeld,' said the priest. 'I hoped that it was you.'

Von Igelfeld greeted him courteously. Was he enjoying the evening? he asked. And how was the Duke? Had he seen him?

'Yes, yes, yes,' said the Patriarch quickly. 'Wonderful evening. The Duke is in good spirits. I saw him this morning.'

Von Igelfeld waited for something more to be said, but the Patriarch merely looked over his shoulder furtively. Then he turned round and tugged at von Igelfeld's sleeve again.

'Could we please talk for a moment?' he asked. 'There is a little courtyard here on the right. It is always deserted.'

Intrigued, von Igelfeld followed as the Patriarch led him into the dusty, disused courtyard. The Patriarch still seemed anxious and only when they had crossed to the farther side of the courtyard did he begin to talk.

'Professor von Igelfeld,' he began. 'I should like to ask a favour of you. I need your help. Indeed, the whole Church needs your help.'

For a moment, von Igelfeld was at a loss as to what to say. 'But I don't see how I can help the Church . . .'

The Patriarch brushed aside the objection. 'You can help in a way which is small, but which is also big. Small and big.'

The Patriarch had something tucked under his cassock, which he now took out and held before him. Von Igelfeld saw a small, candy-striped box, with a domed-top, the corners of which were lined with brass fittings.

'This reliquary,' said the Patriarch, 'contains relics of the very greatest significance for the Church. Inside this box there rest the bones of St Nicholas of Myra. They are the object of the most particular reverence in the Coptic Church.'

Von Igelfeld looked at the box in astonishment. He knew that St Nicholas, the bishop of Myra in Turkey in the fourth century, was the original model for none other than the Saint Nicholas, or Santa Claus, of popular legend. These, then, were the bones of Father Christmas.

The Patriarch now held the box out towards von Igelfeld.

'I want you to look after these for me,' he said. 'There are schismatics in the Church who would dearly love to seize them and use them to sow dissension. While they are with me, they are in danger. If you take them, I can recover them from you at some time in the future. It will not be long. You said you were going to Rome for a month. I could get them back from you while you are there. By then, the danger will have passed.'

Von Igelfeld felt the box being thrust into his hands. 'But why have you chosen me?' he stuttered. 'We have only met once.'

The Patriarch looked up at him and gave a rare smile. 'I can tell that you are a man of integrity. I can entrust these to you in the confident expectation that you will not let me down.'

Von Igelfeld looked at the box again.

'You may open it, if you wish,' said the Patriarch. 'But please don't lose the bones. Without them, my Church is bereft and my own position is considerably weakened.'

'I shall do my best,' said von Igelfeld.

'Thank you,' said the Patriarch. 'Now I must tell you where I shall be in Rome and you tell me where you shall be. But please do not attempt to contact me. Nor, if you come across me in public, must you appear to recognise me. *Rome has ten thousand eyes* and there are many there who would wish to weaken our cause.' He paused, fixing von Igelfeld with that disconcerting, mournful stare. 'Do I have your agreement?'

It seemed to von Igelfeld as if there was no alternative. There was an air of such sadness about the Patriarch that it would have been churlish to decline to help him. And besides, it was a small thing to look after a reliquary. It could be tucked into his suitcase and left there until reclaimed. That was very little to ask when so much was at stake.

'I shall do my best,' he whispered, unconsciously mimicking the Patriarch's conspiratorial air. 'The bones will be safe with me.'

The Patriarch bowed his head. 'You are a good man, Professor von Igelfeld,' he said. 'May the protection of

Saint Nicholas himself be with you now and in the days to come.'

And with that he slipped away, leaving von Igelfeld standing in the tiny, dark courtyard with the holy striped box nestling in his hands and a hammering within his breast. There were still so many questions to be asked, but there would be time enough for that in the future. Von Igelfeld's immediate task was to stride back to the hotel through the streets of Siena, the box tucked under his jacket. If there were schismatics abroad, even in the heart of Siena, then it would be advisable to have the box safely locked up in his hotel room, away from prying eyes.

They left Siena early the following day, following an indirect, winding route down towards Rome. Von Igelfeld had not mentioned the encounter with the Patriarch, nor had he revealed to the Prinzels the contents of the small overnight bag which he had placed on the seat beside him. Prinzel had attempted to load the bag with the rest of the luggage, but von Igelfeld had resisted.

'That would be safer beside me,' he had said.

Prinzel gave his colleague a sideways look. 'Are you carrying a fortune with you?' he had joked. 'Gold bars perhaps?'

Von Igelfeld had ignored the cheap dig. It gave him some pleasure to imagine that he could offer the Prinzels a prize of any amount – thousands and thousands – to guess the contents of his bag and they would never arrive at the truth. It was, quite simply, an unguessable secret.

And when they stopped for lunch, as they did in a small village at the foot of a hill, von Igelfeld took the bag with him from the car and tucked it away carefully under his chair. Seeing him place it there, the waiter had come forward and sought to take it from him.

'Allow me to put this in the cloakroom, signore,' said the waiter. 'It will be quite safe there.'

'No thank you,' said von Igelfeld firmly. 'I would prefer to have it with me.'

'As signore wishes,' said the waiter sulkily, looking suspiciously at the bag. 'I was only trying to help.'

'Thank you,' said von Igelfeld. 'There are important contents in that bag. That is all.'

'Important contents?' said Prinzel. 'What have you got in there, Herr von Igelfeld? You weren't so protective of it when we left Germany.'

'No,' said Ophelia. 'And I couldn't help but notice how light it was when we left. Now it is quite a bit heavier. You must have acquired something in Siena.'

Von Igelfeld glared at Ophelia. It was none of her business what he put in his bags. Did he ask her what she had in her luggage? It was a very intrusive thing to do and he was surprised that the Prinzels knew no better.

'Well?' said Prinzel, as he looked at the menu. 'Well?'

'There is something of purely personal value,' said von Igelfeld. 'Something I do not wish to discuss.'

'Oh,' said Ophelia. 'I'm sorry. We have been very tactless. It just seems so strange that you should be so protective of that bag and not tell us what is in it. After all, if I had an important bag I should not be so unkind as to make everybody wonder what was in it.'

'No,' said Prinzel. 'She would not. And nor would I. If you came up to me and said: "What's in your bag?" I

208

would give a civil reply. I would not play some ridiculous game of cat and mouse. I would come straight out and tell you.'

Von Igelfeld stared at the menu. He was again being subjected to intolerable pressure, just as he had been in the museum when they had argued about the significance of hedgehogs. It was as if they were setting out to goad him.

He took a deep breath. It was important not to lose one's calm in circumstances of this sort.

'There is a secret in this bag,' he said quietly. 'You would never imagine – not even in your wildest dreams – how important are the contents of my bag. I have given my word that what is in this bag will not be revealed to others. So please allow me to keep to that undertaking.'

'Oh,' said Ophelia. 'So what is in the bag does not belong to you. You must be carrying it for somebody else.'

'Yes,' said von Igelfeld coldly. 'You could say that.'

The waiter, who had been standing behind von Igelfeld's chair during this exchange, now joined in.

'I wonder if it's anything illegal,' he said. 'If it's so secret, it could be contraband. Are you sure that you aren't being used as some sort of courier? For a terrorist group, perhaps? In which case, I would look out if I were you. The Carabinieri are always prowling around, looking in other people's bags. It would be best if you told us what was in it and we could advise you.'

'Yes,' said Prinzel. 'That would be far better.'

Von Igelfeld twisted in his seat to fix the waiter with his most discouraging stare.

'I am surprised that you should think it your business

209

to enquire as to what your guests have in their bags,' he said icily.

The waiter pouted. 'I was only trying to help,' he said. 'You Germans think you can carry all sorts of bags around in Italy. Well you can't.'

Prinzel now rose to von Igelfeld's defence. 'It's none of your business,' he said abruptly. 'What is in this bag is between our colleague here and ourselves. It does not concern you in the slightest.'

'You brought the subject up,' said the waiter. 'If this tall gentleman gets himself arrested, then don't say that I didn't try to help.'

'Well we don't want your help,' said Prinzel.

'Then in that case who's going to bring you your lunch?' shouted the waiter.

'Clearly not you,' said Prinzel. 'And there are plenty of other restaurants.'

'Not around here,' said the waiter. 'You're going to go hungry.'

'Oh really,' said von Igelfeld. 'This is all a fuss about nothing.'

'Then why won't you tell us what's in your bag?' crowed the waiter. 'Put an end to the dispute.'

There was a silence. All eyes were turned to von Igelfeld, who looked fixedly ahead.

'I suggest we leave,' said Ophelia, after a moment. 'Our lunch is spoiled.'

They rose to their feet and returned to the car. Not a word was said for at least ten minutes as they continued their journey south. Then Ophelia turned to face von Igelfeld in the back seat.

'Did you remember your bag?' she enquired.

Von Igelfeld sat bolt upright.

'Stop!' he cried. 'Please turn round immediately.'

The waiter was expecting them.

'Hah!' he said. 'Did we forget something? Did we forget a little black bag?'

'Please give it to me this very moment,' said von Igelfeld.

The waiter turned to retrieve the bag from behind the reception desk. Smirking, he handed it over to von Igelfeld.

'So it's bones,' he said. 'What a fuss over a few old bones.'

'You looked!' said von Igelfeld. 'You looked in my bag!'

'Well,' said the waiter calmly. 'It was my patriotic duty. If you had been carrying contraband, I should have had to report you to the Carabinieri. I had to satisfy myself that you were not carrying something illegal.'

'You are an extremely insolent man,' said von Igelfeld. 'I am very surprised that anybody comes to this appalling restaurant.'

'Very few do,' said the waiter.

Von Igelfeld stormed out, followed by Prinzel, who had come in to help retrieve the bag.

'Bones,' mused Prinzel, as they made their way to the car. 'Very strange, Herr von Igelfeld. Bones.'

Von Igelfeld sighed. He had no alternative now but to let the Prinzels in on the secret. It was a relief, in a way, as the responsibility for the relics had begun to weigh on him, and he was appalled with his own carelessness in leaving the bag in the restaurant. How could he have faced the Patriarch with the information that he had abandoned his precious charge in a restaurant, where the box was at the mercy of a prying, self-opinionated waiter? Perhaps once the Prinzels knew what was in the bag they would help him guard the reliquary.

The Prinzels listened carefully.

'What an extraordinary story!' said Prinzel, once von Igelfeld had finished his account. 'We shall have to be very careful.'

Ophelia shuddered. 'I feel quite concerned,' she said. 'I can just imagine those schismatics! Moritz-Maria, you are a very brave man!'

Von Igelfeld nodded, acknowledging the compliment.

'We must be vigilant,' he said. '*Rome has ten thousand eyes.*'

The Prinzels said nothing. They were busy digesting this last comment, which made the innocent Italian landscape, normally so benign in its aspect, seem so strangely threatening. Ahead lay Rome, with its great weight of history and intrigue. What had been intended to be an entirely ordinary month of quiet work in the cool depths of the Vatican Library now threatened to be a month of furtive watchfulness. Von Igelfeld was not sure if he relished the prospect, but he had undertaken to perform a duty on behalf of the Coptic Church and he would carry it out to the letter. The bones would be guarded carefully, and it was only when the Patriarch came to claim them that the candy-striped box would be handed over to its owner. That, at least, was the plan.

The Pensione Garibaldi was one of the quietest and most respectable pensions in Rome. It had been established in the nineteen twenties by a retired civil servant who had secured a lucrative contract for the accommodating of other middle-ranking civil servants visiting Rome from the provinces. These were people who could not afford to stay in the hotels de luxe, but who expected a standard of comfort in keeping with their position. After all, if you were the Deputy Head of the customs office in Bari, in Rome for a three-day meeting on preferential tariffs, you would be entitled to expect a reasonable view and your own table in the dining room. You would also expect a desk clerk who would address you properly as *Ragionere* and take any telephone calls without asking for your name to be spelled out letter by letter. The Garibaldi provided all this, and more, and when the civil servants went elsewhere they were easily replaced by German scholars in Rome to avail themselves of the city's libraries and galleries. It was in the Pensione Garibaldi that the art historian, Gustave Hochler, stayed while writing his *Life of Caravaggio*, and it was at the much sought-after table in the window of the pension's small library that Professor Edmond Winterberg penned his devastating critique of Humperdinck, suggesting that it was Wagner who wrote passages of Humperdinck rather than the other way round!

Prinzel had been the first to discover the Garibaldi and had in due course recommended it to von Igelfeld.

'Rome is so noisy,' he had said. 'It's almost as bad as Naples in that respect. The Garibaldi is a haven of quiet.'

Von Igelfeld had spent two weeks there while visiting *la Sapienza* and had fully endorsed Prinzel's views. Now the three of them were back again, and there was the same man at the desk who greeted them all as if they had never been away. Von Igelfeld was given the room he had occupied last time, and the Prinzels were given a room at the back, overlooking the carefully cultivated garden with its white marble figure of Augustus and its lily-covered pond.

Von Igelfeld lost no time in ensuring that the reliquary was safely stored in his wardrobe. This was a large mahogany cupboard with a sturdy lock, and it was clear that nobody would be able to gain entry to it without the exertion of considerable force. In an establishment like the Garibaldi, with its well-ordered atmosphere, the prospect of that happening was slight.

The bones secured, von Igelfeld went out and took a coffee in the small coffee bar at the end of the street. He felt a strange sense of exhilaration: not only had he a month of stimulating work ahead of him but he could also look forward to enjoyable architectural rambles with his friends the Prinzels. In every respect, it promised to be a most rewarding time. Not even the newspaper, which he read over his coffee, could dampen his mood. It reported that the Government had fallen – which was nothing unusual, thought von Igelfeld – and one of the judges of the Supreme Court of Italy had shot a fellow judge in the course of an argument. Again, there was nothing surprising in that, reflected von Igelfeld. Fortunately the judge had survived and had taken a remarkably tolerant view of his brother justice's action.

'We are all human,' he had said from his hospital bed. '*Nihil humanum mihi alienum est.* The work of the court must go on.'

The following day, while the Prinzels went off to the nearby Villa Borghese Gardens, von Igelfeld made his way to the Vatican Library. He had secured advance permission to work in the Library, which he had used before. He was interested, in particular, in the manuscript sources, including several volumes of bound correspondence from early

Jesuit missionaries in Goa. Although they wrote their formal reports to the Vatican in Latin, a number of them had appended notes in Portuguese, and one or two of them had actually commented on the reception of Portuguese terms in the East. This was a topic of considerable interest to von Igelfeld, who had once written a paper on the origin of the word *alfandica*. An *alfandica* was a customs house for foreign merchants in India, and was obviously derived from the Portuguese *alfandega*. But was this really based on the Arabic, *al-funduk*, which signified an inn? If the Italian term was *fundaco*, this might not be expected to have a Moorish connection, or might it? There were many similar examples.

It was one of von Igelfeld's favourite libraries. The real pleasure of working there lay in the knowledge of the great and beautiful things with which the Library was filled. Here were the very earliest books, the purest texts of the classics, the finest products of Renaissance Humanism. Here was a sheer accumulation of cultural treasures that outshone that of any other library in any other country. And it was all at his fingertips, ready to be brought to him, on his request, by one of the obliging library staff.

Because of his status, von Igelfeld was allowed to use a special reading room beyond the main public section of the Library. This was a room with an airy, open aspect, decorated with sixteenth-century frescoes. There were six or seven large tables in this room, each equipped with several book rests on which large volumes could be safely placed. The chairs in this room were commodious, and well padded – a fact which had somnolent results for some of the more elderly scholars who frequented this part of the Library. One cardinal in particular was known to retreat

215

to the Library for long hours at a stretch, thereby avoiding duties in his office and enjoying, under the pretence of scholarship, an undisturbed siesta.

Von Igelfeld established himself at a table in the middle of the room, spread out his papers, and called for the first volume of letters to be brought to him. This was a volume which he had not examined before, and he found it to contain a substantial amount of dross. But there were one or two letters which would repay closer study, and these he prepared to transcribe.

The first day of work went well. That evening, he had dinner with the Prinzels in a restaurant near the Garibaldi, and then took an evening walk with them through a pleasant neighbouring part of the city. The next day, he was back at the Vatican Library shortly after it opened, and spent a satisfactory day wading through his manuscripts. He dined alone that night – the Prinzels were at a concert – and retired early to bed, his head still full of the whirls and cursives of the Jesuit script which he had spent the day deciphering.

On the third day, uncomfortably hot outside, but cool in the scholarly inner sanctum of the Vatican Library, von Igelfeld's concentration on his task was considerably interrupted by one of the other readers. This reader, who was at the table next to his, had arrived with one or two other people, and had set himself down to browse through a large folio volume which the Prefect of the Library himself, an ascetic-looking Monsignor, had brought and placed on the table before the reader. Then the Prefect had retired, but there had followed a succession of other visitors who had come up to the table to whisper to the reader or to pass him notes.

Von Igelfeld felt his annoyance growing. Any scholar of standing knew that the Library rule of silence had to be respected, even at the cost of considerable personal inconvenience. If this person wished to talk to his friends, then he should go out to do so under the Library portico. It was very distracting for everybody else if conversations were carried out in the Library, even if they were *sotto voce*. Von Igelfeld gave a loud sigh, hoping that his fellow reader would notice his displeasure, but the offender merely looked briefly in his direction and met his gaze – rather impudently, thought von Igelfeld. Then, a few minutes later, a cleric came in, approached the other table, and proceeded to have a five-minute conversation, neither of them bothering to lower their voices to any extent. This, in von Igelfeld's view, was the last straw and when the cleric had gone he rose to his feet and approached the offending reader at his table.

'Excuse me,' he began. 'Since you came in this morning you've done nothing but chat to your friends and create a general disturbance. I would have you know that there are serious scholars working in this library and we find it very difficult if people like you don't respect the basic rules.'

The reader looked at him in astonishment. It was obvious to von Igelfeld that he was barefacedly unrepentant. Well! Let him think about what had been said and he would, if necessary, make an official complaint to the Prefect of the Library if matters did not improve.

Turning on his heel, von Igelfeld returned to his seat and took up his work again. He was pleased to see that the Prefect must have noticed what was happening, as he had gone across to the other reader and was having a whispered conversation with him. He was presumably telling him off, thought von

Igelfeld. As well he might! He noticed that the reader shook his head briefly – denying it! thought von Igelfeld – and the Prefect went back to his office. A few minutes later, the noisy reader decided that he had finished his researches – some researches thought von Igelfeld – and left the library.

As von Igelfeld was preparing to leave the Library that evening, the Prefect, who had been hovering around all afternoon, beckoned him over to his office.

'Professor von Igelfeld,' he said, his voice lowered. 'I understand you had some difficulty this morning.'

'I did,' said von Igelfeld. 'There was an extremely noisy reader. People kept coming in to see him and he kept talking. It was thoroughly inconsiderate behaviour on his part. So I told him to keep quiet – in no uncertain terms!'

The Prefect shook his head. 'Most unfortunate,' he said. 'Most regrettable.'

'Unfortunate that I told him off?' said von Igelfeld indignantly. 'That sort of person needs to be reminded of Library rules. It was not the slightest bit unfortunate.'

'Well,' said the Prefect quietly. 'That was the Pope.'

For a few minutes von Igelfeld was unable to say anything. He stood there, rocking slightly on the balls of his feet, as he contemplated the enormity of what he had done. He had told the Pope to keep quiet in his own library. It was a solecism of quite monumental proportions; something that, if it were ever to be related, would simply not be believed. There was nothing – *nothing* – with which it could be compared.

He closed his eyes and then reopened them. He was still in the Vatican Library, standing before the Prefect of the Library, who was looking at him reproachfully over his half-moon spectacles.

'I didn't realise,' von Igelfeld began, his voice thin and reedy. 'I had no idea . . .'

'Evidently not,' said the Prefect dryly. 'In past times, that would have been a most serious offence – it probably still is, for all I know. His Holiness is an absolute monarch, you know, and his writ clearly runs to this library.'

Von Igelfeld nodded miserably. He had never before felt so utterly wretched. If an earthquake had struck and swallowed him up it would have been a complete relief. But there was no earthquake, not even a tremor; the walls of the Library continued their same solid witness to his terrible mistake.

'I should like to apologise to His Holiness,' he said weakly. 'Would that be possible?'

The Prefect shrugged his shoulders. 'It's not all that simple to get an audience,' he said. 'There are people who work in this building for years and years and never see him.'

'But could you not ask?' pleaded von Igelfeld. 'On a matter like this – a personal matter – it may be possible.'

With an air of great weariness, the Prefect leaned forward and picked up a telephone. A number was dialled and a brief conversation was had with a thin, tinny voice at the other end.

'You may go tomorrow morning to the Office of Holy Affairs,' said the Prefect. 'There is a Monsignor Albinoni there who will speak to you at ten o'clock. He may be able to help.'

Von Igelfeld thanked the Prefect and made his way out of the Library like a man leaving the scene of his crime. He took a taxi back to the Garibaldi, gazing steadfastly down at the floor of the vehicle rather than look out, as he normally would, on the streets and piazzas.

'Are you all right?' asked the taxi driver solicitously at the end of the journey. 'You seem very sad.'

Von Igelfeld shook his head.

'You are kind to ask,' he said. 'I am all right. Thank you for your concern.'

'Nothing is that terrible,' said the driver quietly. 'Remember, there is no despair so total that it shuts out all the light.'

Von Igelfeld thanked him again for his advice, paid the fare, and made his way into the pension. Ophelia, who was in the entrance hall studying a map, saw him enter and greeted him enthusiastically.

'We found the most wonderful antiquarian book-dealer, Moritz-Maria,' she began. 'All sorts of things . . .' She tailed off, noticing her friend's crestfallen expression.

'Has something happened?' she asked, taking hold of von Igelfeld's arm.

'Yes,' he said. 'I've done something absolutely unforgivable.'

Ophelia gasped. 'You've mislaid the reliquary again?'

'No,' said von Igelfeld. 'Worse than that. I told the Pope to keep quiet in his own Vatican Library.'

Ophelia gasped again. By this time, Prinzel had wandered into the hall and was told by his wife what had happened. Together they led von Igelfeld to a chair and listened while he explained what had happened.

'But you weren't to know,' said Prinzel soothingly. 'Presumably he was sitting there like any other reader. If he does that, then he can't expect not to be

220

mistaken for an ordinary person from time to time.'

'Perhaps,' said von Igelfeld. 'But that makes me feel no better.'

'I'm not surprised,' said Ophelia. 'I can imagine just how you feel.'

The Prinzels did their best to ease von Igelfeld's burden of guilt and embarrassment, but by the time that he set off for his appointment at the Vatican the following morning he felt every bit as bad – possibly worse – than he had felt before. Nor did the atmosphere of the Office of Holy Affairs do anything to help his mood. This was an austere suite of rooms located at the end of a winding corridor; a place without light. Von Igelfeld had been given a small pass to give him access, and the motif at the top of this looked remarkably like a prison portcullis. The Office of Holy Affairs, it would seem, had some sort of disciplinary role.

Monsignor Albinoni was waiting for him. He sat impassively behind his desk while von Igelfeld narrated the circumstances of the previous day's encounter with the Pope and his only indication of a response was a slight intake of breath when von Igelfeld repeated the words he had used in his scolding of the Pope. Then, when von Igelfeld finished, he uttered his response.

'There is no precedent for this,' he pronounced. 'I feel, therefore, that I should refer you to my immediate superior, Cardinal Ponthez de Cuera. I will speak to him immediately.'

The Cardinal, it transpired, would see von Igelfeld without delay. A young priest was summoned and he led an increasingly miserable von Igelfeld out of the Office of

Holy Affairs, back down the corridor, and up a rather intimidating set of marble stairs. At the head of the stairs he knocked at a large set of double doors, which were shortly opened to admit von Igelfeld to a large, airy room with a view over St Peter's Square.

The Cardinal was reading a book when von Igelfeld was admitted. He rose to his feet graciously, straightened his scarlet cassock, and shook hands politely with his visitor.

'I am so sorry to disturb you, Your Eminence,' began von Igelfeld in Portuguese. 'I am Professor von Igelfeld from Regensburg.'

The Cardinal beamed. 'Professor Moritz-Maria von Igelfeld, author of *Portuguese Irregular Verbs*? The very same?'

For the first time that day, von Igelfeld felt the cloud of depression that had hung over him lift slightly. He acknowledged his identity and the Cardinal clapped his hands together with satisfaction.

'But I have long admired that book,' he exclaimed. 'My principal academic interest, you see, is the philology of the Romance languages. And there is nobody who understands the history of our dear Portuguese language better than yourself, dear Professor von Igelfeld.'

Von Igelfeld could hardly believe his good fortune. From the role of criminal, he had been transformed into his proper status, that of the author of *Portuguese Irregular Verbs*. The relief was overwhelming.

'And see!' said the Cardinal, pointing to a large, glass-fronted bookcase. 'There is your book. In pride of place.'

Von Igelfeld glanced at the bookshelf and smiled. There indeed was *Portuguese Irregular Verbs*.

'But my dear Professor,' went on the Cardinal. 'What brings you to the Vatican, and to my fortunate door?'

Von Igelfeld described the events of the previous day and the Cardinal listened intently.

'So I should like somehow to apologise to His Holiness,' finished von Igelfeld.

The Cardinal nodded. 'Of course,' he said. 'A very good idea. I'm sure that the Holy Father will not hold it against you. But it would be nice to be able to say sorry in person.' He paused, looking down at his watch. 'Why don't we try to get him now while he has his coffee?'

Von Igelfeld was astonished. 'You mean . . . now. In person? I had not thought of seeing him; I merely wanted to write a note.'

'But I'm sure he would appreciate a visit,' said the Cardinal. 'Look, you wait here while I nip through and check. He's only a few doors down the corridor.'

Von Igelfeld spent a few nervous minutes before the Cardinal returned and announced that the Pope would receive him for coffee.

'I'm afraid it will just have to be the two of you,' the Cardinal explained. 'I am terribly behind on some correspondence and must get it done. But perhaps you and I could meet for lunch afterwards? We've got a terribly good Italian restaurant downstairs.'

A Swiss Guard escorted von Igelfeld from the Cardinal's office. They walked down a corridor and through another set of high double doors. Now they were in an ante-room of some sort, at the end of which was a further set of double doors surmounted by the keys of St Peter. Two further guards, standing outside these doors, now moved smartly aside to allow von Igelfeld to pass and to enter the room beyond.

The Pope was sitting at a small coffee table, reading a copy of the *Corriere della Sera*. When he saw von Igelfeld enter, he rose to his feet and waved.

'Come over here, Professor von Igelfeld,' he said. 'The coffee is still warm.'

Von Igelfeld moved over to the table and reached out to take the Pope's hand. Then, still holding the papal hand, he bowed slightly.

'Good morning,' said the Pope warmly. 'Good morning, and blessings. Please sit down and I'll pour the coffee.'

Von Igelfeld sat down.

'I've come to say how sorry I am about that regrettable incident yesterday,' he said. 'I had no idea it was Your Holiness.'

The Pope laughed. 'Oh that! Think no more of that. It's good of you to come and apologise. You know, there are so many who expect us to apologise to them. They ask us to apologise for the Inquisition, to apologise for the over-enthusiasms of missionaries of the past, to apologise for all sorts of terrible things that happened a long time ago. And nobody ever comes to apologise to me! Except you. It's really quite refreshing.'

'Well,' said von Igelfeld. 'I am very sorry indeed.'

'No need to say any more,' said the Pope. 'It's very good to have the chance to chat to you. I have a wretchedly boring time for the most part. You've got no idea what a tedious life it is being Pope. I'm totally isolated from the rest of humanity. You saw me yesterday on one of my rare busy days. Do you know how many social invitations I received last year? No? Well, I shall tell you. None. Not one. Nobody dares to invite the Pope to anything. They all assume that I would never be able to come, or that it would be presumptuous to invite me. So I get none. And I sit here most days and play solitaire. That's what I do.'

The Pope pointed to a table at the side of the room and von Igelfeld saw that it was covered with cards in a solitaire pattern.

'Do you play solitaire yourself?' asked the Pope.

'No,' said von Igelfeld. 'I used to. But not any more.'

The Pope nodded, looking slightly despondent. He took a sip of his coffee and stared out of the window. For a few minutes nothing was said and the only sound in the room was that of ticking from a long-case clock behind the Pope's chair. Then the Pope sighed.

'I look out of my window and see the Vatican gardens,' he said. 'The trees. The greenery. The paths where I take my walks. The fountains. And I remember a field behind my house in my native village. And I remember the river beyond it where we used to swim as boys. We had a rope tied onto the branch of a tree and we used to swing out over the water. And I've never had any greater pleasure since then. Never. And I've never had any better friends than I had then. Never.'

'We all have a land of lost content,' said von Igelfeld. 'I used to go and stay on my grandfather's estate near Graz. I liked that. Then, a bit later, when I was a student, my friend Prinzel and I used to go walking down the river and drink a glass of beer in a riverside inn. That's what we used to do.'

The Pope said nothing. But, after a moment, he spoke

in a quiet voice: 'Now I have my solitaire. I suppose that is something.'

The clock chimed. 'Heavens,' said the Pope. 'That's the end of the coffee break. I must get back to my solitaire. Could you possibly show yourself out? The Swiss Guards will direct you.'

The Pope rose to his feet and ushered von Igelfeld to the door.

'Goodbye, dear Professor von Igelfeld,' he said. 'Good bye. We shall not meet again in this life, I fear, but I have enjoyed our brief meeting. Please remember me.'

And with that he turned and went back to his solitaire table, leaving von Igelfeld in the care of the guards.

The Prinzels insisted on being told every detail of von Igelfeld's remarkable day. Ophelia quizzed him closely as to the decoration of the Pope's private apartment and as to the precise exchange of views which had taken place between them. Prinzel was more interested in the geography of the Vatican and in the mechanism of obtaining an audience; it had seemed so easy for von Igelfeld, but surely it could not be that easy for others. Perhaps all one had to do was to insult the Pope first – if one had the chance – and then insist on an audience of apology

But there had been more to von Igelfeld's day. After he had left the Pope's apartment he had returned to the Vatican Library for some time before the Cardinal had come to collect him for lunch. Then they had gone downstairs to a remark-able restaurant, patronised only by clerics and their guests, where a magnificent Roman meal of six courses had been served. He and the Cardinal had got on extremely well, discussing a variety of philological matters, and von Igelfeld had enjoyed himself immensely. But just as the last dish was being cleared from their table and coffee and liqueurs were about to be served, von Igelfeld had seen a familiar figure enter the restaurant. It was the Duke of Johannesburg. The Duke, who was in the company of an elegantly attired monsignor, had not seen him, and von Igelfeld had been able to make a discreet enquiry of his host.

The Cardinal had turned his head discreetly and glanced at the ducal table.

'The cleric,' he said, 'is none other than Monsignor Ernesto Pricolo. He is the head of an office here which deals with relations with our dear misguided Orthodox brethren. Personally, I find his activities to be distasteful.'

Von Igelfeld shivered. 'Distasteful?'

'Yes,' said the Cardinal. 'He involves himself in their schisms. In fact, I believe he is currently attempting to destabilise the Patriarchy of Alexandria.'

'The Patriarch Angelos Evangelis?' asked von Igelfeld. 'A tall Patriarch with a beard?'

'They all look like that,' said the Cardinal. 'I can never tell them apart. But, yes, that's the one. He has terrible schism problems and our friend Pricolo does nothing to help. Personally, I can't see what possible advantage there is for Rome in it all, but there we are. We are, I suppose, a state and we must do all the things that states do.'

Von Igelfeld succeeded in leaving the restaurant without being seen by the Duke of Johannesburg, but he felt that a cloud had come over the day. If the Duke of Johannesburg was on the side of the schismatics, then he must have deceived the Patriarch into thinking he was really a supporter of his. And if that were the case, then the Duke probably knew, or suspected at least, that the Patriarch had given the reliquary to him, and the schismatics would themselves know that. Which meant that even as he and the Prinzels went about their innocent business in Rome, they could be being observed by the scheming schismatics who would, he assumed, stop at little to retrieve the bones of Father Christmas.

The Prinzels listened carefully to von Igelfeld's account of the lunch.

'This is very serious,' said Prinzel at last. 'We shall have to redouble our vigilance.'

'I suggest that we transfer the reliquary to my cupboard,' said Ophelia. 'They may know that Moritz-Maria has the bones, but they might not suspect us. After all, the Duke of Johannesburg never saw you or myself, did he, Florianus?'

It was agreed that the reliquary would be transferred to the Prinzels' room and hidden in a locked suitcase within their locked wardrobe. This was done, and the evening came to a close. Never had von Igelfeld experienced a more dramatic day: he had met the Pope and over lunch he had witnessed high-level ecclesiastical plotting taking place before his very eyes. In a curious way he was beginning to acquire a taste for this. He imagined that the life of a diplomat, or even a schismatic if it came to it, could be almost as fulfilling as life as a professor of Romance philology. Almost, but not quite.

For the next two weeks, von Igelfeld worked every day at the Vatican Library, only taking off the occasional afternoon to spend with the Prinzels in their architectural explorations.

They had intended to visit, and annotate, every important Baroque church in Rome, allowing several days for the study of each church. It was a major undertaking, and already their notebooks were bulging with observations.

Von Igelfeld's own work progressed well. He had unearthed several previously unknown manuscripts thanks to the efforts of the Prefect, who had obviously been informed by the Pope that von Igelfeld was to receive special consideration. And indeed the Pope occasionally sent down a messenger with a small present for von Igelfeld, usually an Italian delicacy – *panforte di Siena* or *amarettini di Sarona* to eat with his morning coffee.

Then, one evening after von Igelfeld had returned to the Garibaldi, he had found a telegram awaiting him. He opened it with some foreboding, as one does with any telegram received while away from home, and saw that the message came from the Patriarch. He was, he explained, in a monastery in the Apennines. For various reasons he was unable to come to Rome to collect the relics, and he wondered if von Igelfeld would be kind enough to come to the monastery to deliver them to him. The relics would be safe there, he assured him.

Von Igelfeld showed the telegram to the Prinzels, who immediately consulted their road atlas and found the town from which it had been sent. The telegram had emanated from Camaldoli, a small town in the mountains, some four hours from Rome.

'If we leave after breakfast tomorrow,' said Prinzel, 'we shall arrive by noon. According to our guidebook there is an inn there. We can stay there and complete our mission the following day.'

The plans laid, they booked themselves out of the Garibaldi, on the understanding that should they wish to return after a day or two there would be no difficulty in finding them rooms. In fact, they were all ready to leave Rome. Von Igelfeld had effectively come to the end of his work in the Vatican Library and the Prinzels were running out of Baroque churches. It was time for a change of surroundings.

The journey to Camaldoli took them high into the mountains of Umbria. From a landscape of rolling hills and comfortable villas they ventured onto mountain roads and broad views of valleys and pine forests. Although it was still sunny, the air now had a sharp edge to it and the streams which cascaded boyishly down the hillsides were icy cold. The inn was exactly as one might expect an old-fashioned Apennine inn to be; wood-panelled, with open fire-places in which the evening log fire had been laid. Each room, which was simply furnished, had a view either of the mountain rising above or the valley falling away below on the other side.

The monastery, they were told, was about an hour's walk away. It could not be reached by car, as it was tucked away on the mountainside above the town. It was too late to go there that afternoon, but they were told that unless an unexpected mist descended the following morning they could easily make the journey up and down before lunch. That night von Igelfeld slept with the reliquary under his mattress. He did not sleep well. From time to time he awoke to some sound and froze, thinking that there were schematics outside the door. But the switching on of his light dispelled such terrors, and he would eventually drift back into an uneasy sleep.

At breakfast the next day there was another message.

The Patriarch had heard of their arrival and had sent a note with a boy who was making his way down the mountain-side to collect bread for the monks. In the note, he explained that he would be down in the town the next day and that they should do nothing until then. 'Please do not leave the hotel,' he warned. 'Even at this late stage, there may be dangers.'

They read and re-read the note, each more frightened than could be publicly admitted. It was decided that they would interpret the Patriarch's warning liberally. As long as one of them was in the hotel at any one time, the others should feel free to wander about the small town or go for a slightly longer walk along the river.

Prinzel and Ophelia went for such a walk after break-fast, leaving von Igelfeld in the hotel. He was sitting in the cramped living room, paging through old Italian maga-zines and listening to the chatter of the kitchen staff, when the new guests arrived. He looked up to see who they were. Germans perhaps? They were. It was Unterholzer and his wife, and, following closely behind them, their unfortunate dog, with its prosthetic wheels.

There was a great deal of mutual surprise.

'I thought you were all in Rome,' said Unterholzer, pump-ing von Igelfeld's hand enthusiastically. We had no idea we would meet up with you. What a marvellous coincidence!'

'Yes,' said von Igelfeld reluctantly. 'The Prinzels are here too. They have gone for a walk along the river.'

'Wonderful idea,' said Unterholzer. 'We'll just get every-thing sorted out and then perhaps you could come for a short walk with us.'

They went off to sign the register and to receive their

keys. Then, closely followed by the dog, they went up to their bedroom to unpack.

The Prinzels were late coming back but von Igelfeld decided to risk leaving the hotel before they returned. Since he was with the Unterholzers, he thought, he could hardly be in any danger. So they wandered off along a path that led into the forest, from which, at various points, they would be afforded a fine view of the valley below.

The walk was most enjoyable, and when they returned the Prinzels were already awaiting them. They were extremely surprised to see the Unterholzers but if they felt any dismay they succeeded in hiding it effectively. Then it was time for lunch, and it was at this point that von Igelfeld made the dreadful discovery.

He went into his room to change the collar of his shirt. At first he saw nothing untoward but after a moment his eye fell on an object on the floor beside his bed. For a moment his heart stopped: it was the reliquary – and it was empty.

He fell to his knees with a cry, seizing the box and lifting it up. The mattress had been disturbed and the reliquary had been pulled from underneath it. He examined it closely: there were strange marks on it, marks which looked, to all intents and purposes, as if they were teeth marks! Some creature had come into the room, smelled out the reliquary, and gnawed it.

He rushed to the door and looked out into the corridor. As he did so, there came a bark from the next door room. Unterholzer's sausage dog! Without wasting a moment, von Igelfeld ran to the open door of the Unterholzers' room and looked inside. Frau Professor Dr

Unterholzer was standing in the middle of the rug, wagging a finger in admonition at the dog.

'You are a naughty, naughty creature,' she said severely. 'Where did you get those bones? Now you've eaten them you will have no appetite for your lunch!'

Von Igelfeld stood where he was, his heart a cold stone within him. Unterholzer's dog had achieved, in several quick mouthfuls, what an entire faction of schismatics had so singularly failed to do.

They all spent a bleak and sleepless night. Von Igelfeld felt even worse than he had done when he had told the Pope to keep quiet. At least that was something that could be remedied; there was no possible means of sorting out this dreadful situation with the bones. He had no idea what he would say to the Patriarch when he arrived.

He would have to tell him the truth, of course, but that would be such an awful blow to him that he could hardly bring himself to do it.

When the Patriarch eventually arrived the next morning, he immediately sensed that something was wrong.

'The schismatics,' he said. 'They have the bones . . .'

Von Igelfeld shook his head. 'It's even worse than that,' he said. 'I'm terribly sorry to have to tell you this, but Professor Unterholzer's sausage dog ate them yesterday.'

The Patriarch stared at von Igelfeld for a moment as if he did not believe what he had heard. Then he emitted a strange cry – a wail which was redolent of centuries of Coptic sorrow and suffering. Ophelia tried to comfort him, but he was inconsolable, his great frame heaving with sobs.

Unterholzer, who had said nothing during the harrowing encounter, suddenly whispered something to his wife, who nodded her assent.

'Your Holiness,' he said, placing a hand on the Patriarch's shoulder. 'I have the solution. You may have my dog.'

The Patriarch stopped sobbing and turned a tear-stained face to Unterholzer.

'I do not wish to punish it,' he said. 'It's a dumb creature. It cannot be held to account.'

'But that was not what I had in mind,' said Unterholzer. 'I was merely reflecting on the fact that if my dog has eaten those old bones, they become part of him, do they not? He must absorb something.'

The Patriarch nodded. 'He absorbs part of Saint Nicholas. He . . .' He stopped. For a moment he frowned, as if wrestling with some abstruse theological point. Then he broke into a rare smile.

'I see what you are suggesting!' he cried. 'This dog can become an object of veneration during his life. Then, when he eventually dies, we can put his bones in a reliquary too as they will be, in a sense, the bones of Saint Nicholas!'

'Indeed,' said Unterholzer. 'I take it that he will be well looked after?'

'Of course,' said the Patriarch. 'And the schismatics will never suspect that this innocent little dog is the custodian of our most holy relic!'

'A brilliant scheme' said von Igelfeld, feeling extremely relieved. 'A highly satisfactory outcome from all angles.'

Unterholzer's sausage dog was handed over at a touching little ceremony the following day. Then, the whole affair settled, the now enlarged German party settled down to a thoroughly enjoyable celebratory dinner with the Patriarch. Von Igelfeld took the opportunity to warn the Patriarch about the Duke of Johannesburg, but it transpired that the Patriarch had known all along.

'I knew which side he was on,' he explained. 'But I never gave him the impression that I knew. He therefore did not know that I knew.'

'But why is he a schismatic?' asked von Igelfeld. 'What drives him?'

'A desire to find a point for his life,' said the Patriarch. 'The feeling that he is being useful to somebody, even if only schismatics.'

'And that young research assistant of his, Beatrice?' asked von Igelfeld. 'What about her?'

'She's actually working for my side,' said the Patriarch. 'She files regular reports for us.'

'Oh,' said von Igelfeld, rather lamely.

'But I'm withdrawing her from active service,' said the Patriarch. 'She has done enough.'

'Will she need a job?' asked von Igelfeld. 'Have you anything for her to do.'

'No,' said the Patriarch. 'But I have just this moment fixed her up with a new post. I spoke to your colleague Professor Unterholzer about her and gave him a full description of her talents. He very kindly agreed to take her on with immediate effect.'

Von Igelfeld was silent. *Unterholzer!* How utterly transparent! He began to shake at the thought of the injustice of it, and was still shaking half an hour later when the party had broken up and he found himself lying in bed in his darkened room, gazing out of his window at the moonlit mountainside. Oh, the injustice of it! Why should Unterholzer, who deserved nothing, get everything? It was so, so unfair.

He took a deep breath. He would rise above this, as he had risen above all the other injustices that blighted his life After all, he was Professor Moritz-Maria von Igelfeld, author of *Portuguese Irregular Verbs*, friend of cardinals and popes. That was something to think about.

He stopped. Should he say friend of cardinals and popes when he knew only one of each, or should he say friend of a cardinal and a pope, or even friend of a cardinal and the Pope?

Puzzling on this difficult point, von Igelfeld eventually fell asleep, and dreamed that he was playing solitaire in a remote field, a long time ago, while at the edge of the field the Pope swung out on a rope over a river that ran silently and very fast. And he was happy again, as was the Pope.

The Perfect Imperfect

It was clear to everybody at morning coffee that something was tickling Professor Moritz-Maria von Igelfeld. Morning coffee at the Institute was normally a relatively uneventful affair: the Librarian might expound for some time on the difficulties of finding sufficiently conscientious nurses to attend to the needs of his aunt; Unterholzer might comment on the doings of the infinitely wearying local politicians in whose affairs he seemed to take such an inordinate interest; and Prinzel would sit and fiddle with the ink reservoir of his pen, which was always giving him trouble. Von Igelfeld had given up pointing out to him the folly of buying French pens when there were German alternatives to be had, but Prinzel refused to listen. Well, thought von Igelfeld, here we have the consequences – pens that never work and which cover his fingers in ink. *We get the pen we deserve in this life*, he said to himself. It was an impressive-sounding adage, and he was quite pleased to have coined it, but then he began to wonder about its meaning. Do we, in fact, get the pen

237

we deserve? His own pen worked well – and that was possibly a matter of desert – but then Unterholzer had a particularly satisfactory pen, which never went wrong, and which had served his father well too. Unterholzer did not *deserve* a good pen – there could be no doubt about that – and so the theory was immediately disproved. On the other hand, perhaps Unterholzer's father had deserved a good pen and Unterholzer was merely enjoying his father's moral capital. That was quite possible; so perhaps the adage was correct after all.

That morning, when von Igelfeld entered the coffee room with a smile on his lips, Prinzel had removed the barrel of his pen and was attempting to insert a straightened paper clip into the reservoir. Unterholzer was snorting over an item in the local paper and pointing indignantly at the photograph of a politician, while the Librarian browsed through a leaflet published by a private nursing company.

'Something amusing?' asked Prinzel, now attempting to work out how to remove the paper clip from the pen's innards.

'Mildly,' said von Igelfeld.

The Librarian looked at him.

'Do tell me,' he said. 'My poor aunt needs cheering up and I find there's so little positive news I can bring from the Institute.'

'I received a very amusing letter,' said von Igelfeld, extracting a folded sheet of paper from his jacket pocket. He paused, watching the effect of his words on his colleagues.

'Well,' said the Librarian. 'Do tell us about it.'

'It's from a shipping company,' von Igelfeld said. 'They

run cruises which go from Hamburg to the Aegean, and they have lectures on these cruises. They have invited me to be one of the lecturers.'

'Oh,' said the Librarian. 'And will you go?'

'Of course not,' said von Igelfeld. 'I am a philologist, not an entertainer. It's an outrageous suggestion.'

'Good,' said Unterholzer quickly. 'In that case, may I write to them and offer my services in your place? I would love to go on one of those lecture cruises. So would my wife. The lecturers can take their wives for nothing, I gather. That is, if one has one, of course, which you don't.'

'I'd very readily go too,' interjected Prinzel. 'I can think of nothing more enjoyable. Sitting on the deck, watching the sea go past! Occasionally having to sing for your supper, but not too often! What a wonderful way of spending a few weeks.'

Von Igelfeld was quite taken aback. He had assumed that his colleagues would have shared his disdain for the whole idea, instead of which they seemed anxious to take his place. This was troubling. Perhaps he had been too quick to turn the company down. In fact, he probably had a duty to do it now, as this would be the only way he could prevent Unterholzer from going in his stead and subjecting all those poor passengers to some terribly dull set of lectures on the subjunctive. It would quite ruin their holidays. No, he would have to re-examine his decision.

'On the other hand,' he said quickly. 'It is perhaps our duty to impart knowledge to the public from time to time. Perhaps I have been too selfish; perhaps I should go after all.'

'But you said that you wouldn't,' protested Unterholzer.

'If your heart isn't in it there is no point in your going. It's not fair to the company or to the passengers. I, by contrast, would be very enthusiastic.'

Von Igelfeld ignored this. 'I think I must go after all,' he said firmly, adding: 'It would be a pity to disappoint the organisers. I'm sure that you would do it very well, Herr Unterholzer, but the organisers did ask for me and not for you. If they had wanted to get you, then they would have written to you rather than to me. Perhaps next time, after I have done it, they might ask for you personally. One never knows.'

Unterholzer muttered something and returned to his newspaper. Prinzel, however, was beginning to warm to the theme.

'You know,' he said, 'I've heard about these lecture cruises. They usually get art historians or archaeologists to talk about the places that the ship visits. They have lectures on Minoan civilisation and the like. Or even talks on Byzantine history.'

'My aunt went on a cruise,' said the Librarian. 'They had a famous psychologist who lectured on relationships. My aunt wasn't much interested in that. But they also had a man who told them all about sea trade in the early Mediterranean. She enjoyed that very much, and still talks a lot about it. And I've even heard that they've had Marcel Reich-Ranicki and famous people like that.'

Von Igelfeld beamed. He was pleased to discover that instead of being insulting, the invitation was something of an honour. They must have taken soundings, he thought; they must have asked people for recommendations before they came to me. In fact, it was quite the opposite. The entertainments officer of the cruise company had chosen von Igelfeld's name from a list of German writers on Portugal. Since the cruise was calling in at both Oporto and Lisbon, before steaming on to the Mediterranean, it had been decided that some of the lectures should reflect this fact. They had tried to get the services of an authority on port wine, who was known to give extremely interesting lectures on the history of the trade, but he was being treated in a clinic and could not oblige. So they had picked von Igelfeld more or less at random, noting that he had 'written a well-known book on the Portuguese language'.

'He'll be able to talk about amusing Portuguese folk tales and the like,' said the entertainments officer. 'With a name like that he could hardly be anything but entertaining.'

'I hope so,' said the manager. 'Let's give him a try.'

'And you never know,' speculated the entertainments officer. 'He might be a success.'

The cruise left Hamburg on a warm June evening. It was a large ship, and the voyage was fully subscribed. They would sail down through the English Channel and out into the Bay of Biscay. Their first port of call was Oporto, and after this they would make their way to Lisbon and Gibraltar before entering the Mediterranean. Von Igelfeld's lectures would start after they arrived at Oporto and continue until they docked at Naples. Thereafter, unencumbered by duties, he would be free to enjoy the remaining ten days of the voyage that would take them all the way to Piraeus.

Von Igelfeld had been allocated a cabin on the port side. He was shown the way by a steward, who then left him standing in the doorway, contemplating his home for the next eighteen days. It was not very large; in fact, it was one of the smaller cabins, and von Igelfeld was very doubtful as to whether the length of the bed would be adequate. And although there was a small table, it was hardly large enough to write upon. Opening a cupboard, he noticed that there were only four coat hangers and a shoe rack with space for two pairs of shoes at the most, and small shoes at that.

For a few minutes he was uncertain what to do. He had only been on a ship once before when, as a research assistant he had accompanied Professor Dr Dr Dr Dieter Vogelsang to Ireland. That was many years ago and he had very little recollection of the accommodation. But the situation was quite different now: far from being the young scholar, happy to make do with what was offered him, he was now Professor Dr Moritz-Maria von Igelfeld, author of *Portuguese Irregular Verbs*. The thought of this spurred him on. If the shipping company thought that they could put the author of *Portuguese Irregular Verbs* in cramped accommodation like this, then they should be promptly disabused of that notion. The thought crossed his mind: *You get the cabin you deserve in this life.* Well, if that were the case he should get something very much larger and more suitable.

Leaving his bags in the corridor, von Igelfeld made his way back to the central reception hall, where the purser and his staff were engaged in the myriad of tasks which accompanied the settling-in of passengers.

'I regret to say, but I think there has been a mistake,' said von Igelfeld, to a smartly dressed officer. 'I need a larger cabin.'

The officer looked him up and down.

'I'm very sorry, sir,' he said. 'The ship is full. We can't really change people around at this stage.'

'In that case, I demand to see the Captain,' said von Igelfeld.

'He's busy,' said the officer. 'The ship is about to leave port.'

'I am busy too,' said von Igelfeld. 'There is a paper which I must complete on this voyage. I must see the Captain.'

A small group of passengers, sensing that something was wrong, had gathered by von Igelfeld's side.

'Why can't he see the Captain?' said one elderly woman. 'Is there something wrong with the Captain?'

'Is the Captain ill?' asked another slightly worried-looking passenger.

The officer sensed that the situation was getting out of control. Ships were breeding-grounds for rumour and, if the passengers got it into their minds that the Captain was ill, or evading them, the whole vessel would be awash with panicky rumours by the following morning.

'Please calm down,' said the officer. 'I shall take you to see the Captain.'

The officer escorted von Igelfeld up a steep flight of stairs and onto the bridge. The Captain, dressed in his formal uniform, was standing over a chart, talking to another officer, while several others were engaged in various tasks. The officer who had escorted von Igelfeld up spoke briefly to the Captain, who glanced in the professor's direction and frowned.

'I really must insist on something more appropriate,' said von Igelfeld. 'If nothing is available, then I must ask you to release me from my obligation to lecture.'

The Captain sighed. If von Igelfeld withdrew, the lecture programme would be thrown into disarray and there would be complaints, which were always troublesome. They only had three lecturers on board as it was, and that was cutting matters somewhat fine.

'Have you nothing else?' he asked the junior officer.

'No, sir. Everything's occupied.'

'Oh, very well,' said the Captain. 'Professor von Igelfeld, you may have my cabin. I'm sure that I shall be comfortable enough in yours.'

Von Igelfeld smiled. 'That's very generous, Herr Kapitan! I had not intended to inconvenience you, but I am sure that this arrangement will work very well. Thank you.'

Before the ship put to sea, von Igelfeld was transferred from his inadequate, cramped cabin to the Captain's gracious quarters behind the observation deck. Not only did he receive a larger sleeping cabin, but he also had a substantial sitting room, with a bureau. This suited von Igelfeld extremely well, and he had soon unpacked his clothes into the copious wardrobe and spread his papers about the bureau. His earlier ill-humour had deserted him and to celebrate the beginning of the voyage he decided to go down to the bar and take a small sherry.

They put to sea in the evening, with the ship sounding its horn and the lights of the pilot boat weaving about in the half-darkness. Von Igelfeld returned to his cabin an spent an hour at work before dinner. In the dining room, he discovered that he had been given a table with several other passengers but a firm complaint to the steward resulted in his being moved to a solitary table near the door. This suited him very much better, and he enjoyed a good meal before retiring to his cabin for the night.

It was three days before they reached Oporto and the first lecture was to be delivered. The company liked to give the passengers a choice, and so at the time that von Igelfeld was to deliver his introductory talk, *Early Portuguese*, one of the other two lecturers, the popular novelist, Hans-Dieter Dietermann, author of a slew of relentlessly contemporary detective novels, was scheduled to deliver his own introductory talk, *The Modern Sleuth*. Von Igelfeld had met Dietermann briefly at a reception given by the Captain, but had exchanged only a few words with him. He had no idea why the company should engage such a person to lecture to their passengers, and he only assumed that it was to cater for those passengers who found it difficult to concentrate or who would be out of their depth in listening to a real lecture. Poor Dietermann, thought von Igelfeld: a perfectly decent man, no doubt, but not one who should be attempting to lecture to anybody.

The lectures were due to take place at ten o'clock in the morning, while the ship was still five hours out of Oporto. There was an announcement on the ship's public address system as von Igelfeld made his way to the room in which his lecture was to be given. Chairs had been placed in rows, and at the head of the room there was a table with a jug of water and a lectern.

Von Igelfeld walked up to the table and placed his notes on the lectern. Before him, dotted about the room, was his audience of seven passengers. He glanced at his watch. It was five minutes after the advertised time. He was to be introduced by one of the purser's staff, who now glanced at him sympathetically.

'I'm terribly sorry about the turn-out,' whispered the officer. 'Perhaps people are doing something else.'

'Perhaps they are,' said von Igelfeld coldly. 'Perhaps my lecture was not sufficiently well advertised.'

'But it was!' protested the officer. 'There were posters all over the place. And there was a big notice in the ship's newspaper.'

Von Igelfeld ignored this. 'Let us begin, anyway,' he said. 'There are at least some intellectually curious passengers on this ship.'

The lecture began. After fifteen minutes, two of the passengers seated near the back slipped out. Three of the others, all elderly ladies, now nodded off, while the remaining two, sitting together at the front, took copious notes. After an hour, von Igelfeld stopped, and thanked his audience for their attention. The two passengers at the front laid down their notebooks and applauded enthusiastically. The three who had been sleeping awoke with a start and joined in the applause. Von Igelfeld nodded in the direction of the two in the front and walked out of the room.

On his way back to his cabin, he found the corridors blocked by passengers streaming out of one of the other rooms. Like most of the passengers on the ship, they were almost all middle-aged women, and they all seemed to be in an exceptionally good mood. Pressed against the wall to allow them to pass, von Igelfeld heard snippets of conversation.

'So amusing . . . I haven't read him I confess, but I shall certainly do so now . . . Do you think that the ship's bookshop has his books? . . . Oh they do, I saw a whole pile of them . . . Very interesting . . . I can't wait for his next lecture . . .'

Von Igelfeld strove to catch more, but the comments merged in the general hubbub. One thing was clear, though: this was the crowd on its way from listening to that poor man, Hans-Dieter Dietermann. He must have had an audience of at least three or four hundred, and they all seemed to have enjoyed themselves. How misguided can people be!

He sat alone at his table over lunch, reflecting on the morning's humiliation. He had never before had so small an audience. Even in America, where he had been obliged, through a misunderstanding, to deliver a lecture on sausage dogs, there had been a larger and distinctly more enthusiastic audience. It was obviously the company's fault – possibly the fault of the Captain himself, and there was no doubt in his mind that the Captain should do something about it.

'I am most displeased,' he told the Captain, when he confronted him on the bridge immediately after lunch. 'Not enough has been done to ensure support for my lectures.'

The Captain smiled. 'But I heard that there had been a very large crowd this morning,' he said. 'I understand that it was a great success.'

'That was the other lecturer, Herr Kapitan,' interjected one of the junior officers. 'That was Herr Dietermann.'

Von Igelfeld turned and glared at the junior officer, but refrained from saying anything.

'Oh,' said the Captain. 'I see. Everyone went to the other one and not to yours.'

'Yes,' said von Igelfeld. 'And I would like something done about it.'

'Well, we can't change the programme,' said the Captain. 'That just confuses everybody.' He thought for a moment. 'I could get some of the crew to go. That might swell the audience for the next one.'

Von Igelfeld nodded. 'I am sure that they would find it very interesting.'

The Captain nodded. 'I'm sorry I won't be able to come myself,' he said. 'Somebody has to stay up here. By the way, is my cabin comfortable enough for you?'

'It is quite adequate,' said von Igelfeld. 'I hope that you are comfortable in . . . in that other cabin.'

'I don't notice these things,' said the Captain politely. 'I'm usually so busy I don't get much time to sleep.'

'Most unfortunate,' said von Igelfeld. 'Sleep is very important.'

He left feeling quite mollified by the Captain's sympathetic view of the situation. He had great confidence in the Captain, and indeed at the next lecture, which took place after they had left Oporto, some twenty members of the crew, acting under Captain's orders and all neatly attired in their white uniforms, sat in two solid rows, listening to von Igelfeld's remarks on the development of the gerundive in Portuguese. Their expression, von Igelfeld thought, tended to the somewhat glassy, but they were probably tired, like the Captain.

The next day, von Igelfeld received a visit from the officer who ran the ship's newspaper. She was planning a short interview with all three lecturers, so that she could publish a profile for the passengers to read over their breakfast. She spoke to von Igelfeld about his work and about his interests, noting his replies down in a small notebook. She seemed particularly interested in *Portuguese Irregular Verbs*, and von Igelfeld spent some time explaining the research which lay behind this great work of scholarship. Then she got on to the personal side of his life.

'Now tell me, Herr Professor,' she asked, 'does your wife mind your going off on these lecture cruises?'

'I am unmarried,' said von Igelfeld. 'I was almost married once, but that did not work out.' *Unterholzer*! he thought bitterly. Had Unterholzer not outflanked him in the courtship of Lisbetta von Brautheim then history would have been very different.

'So you would like to get married one day?' she asked.

'Indeed,' said von Igelfeld. 'It is simply a question of finding the right person. You could say, I suppose, that I am ready to propose marriage should the right lady present herself.'

'Ah!' said the journalist. 'You are a professor in search of a wife.'

Von Igelfeld smiled. 'You might say that,' he said. 'However, my heavy workload prevents my being too active in that respect most of the time.'

'But one might have time on a cruise, might one not?' said the journalist playfully.

Von Igelfeld allowed himself a slight laugh. 'One never knows,' he said. 'Life is full of surprises, is it not?'

The profiles of the three lecturers appeared in the ship's newspaper the next morning. There was a fairly long description of Hans-Dieter Dietermann and a summary of his recent novel. He, it was revealed, was married to a Munich kindergarten teacher and they had three young children. The other lecturer was accompanied by his wife, and there was a photograph of the two of them standing at a ship's railing, looking out to sea. Then there was the feature on von Igelfeld, with a word-for-word account of the discussion about being single and looking for a wife. Von Igelfeld read this with a certain amount of embarrassment, but he was pleased enough with the lengthy discussion of *Portuguese Irregular Verbs*.

This book, the article said, *is generally regarded as one of the most important books to be published in Germany this century. As a work of scholarship, it is said by many to be without parallel and is known throughout the world. It is clearly a book that we all should read, if we ever had the time. The Company is honoured to have one of the most distinguished*

scholars in the world lecturing to its passengers – another exam-
ple of the high standards of excellence which the Hamburg and
North Germany Cruise Line has long maintained.

Von Igelfeld re-read this passage several times. He resolved to drop a note to the officer who wrote it and thank her for her perceptive and accurate remarks. He might send a copy to the Librarian at the Institute – just for record purposes, of course, and Prinzel and Unterholzer would probably like to see it as well, now that one came to think of it.

He arose from his breakfast table, folded the newspaper carefully, and walked out of the dining room. As he did so, some sixty pairs of eyes, all belonging to the middle-aged widows and divorcees who formed the overwhelming bulk of the cruise passengers, followed his progress from the room. These same eyes had just finished reading the profile in the paper, skipping over the paragraph about *Portuguese Irregular Verbs* but dwelling with considerable interest on the passage about von Igelfeld's single status. That was a matter of great significance to them, as it was undoubtedly the case that of the three hundred widows on the ship, at least two hundred and ninety of them harboured a secret wish in her heart that she might meet a future husband on the cruise. Unfortunately, for complex reasons of dem- ography, von Igelfeld *was the only unmarried man on the boat*, apart from the younger members of the crew, who were too young and who were anyway under strict instruc- tions not to socialise with the passengers; and the two hair- dressers, who were not suitable, for quite other reasons.

'What a nice, *tall* man,' whispered Frau Krutzner to her friend, Frau Jens. 'Such a distinguished bearing.'

251

'So scholarly!' said Frau Jens, dreamily. 'And such a waste! I do hope that he meets a suitable lady soon. In fact, I'm sure that I could look after our dear Professor von Igelfeld myself.'

'Frau Jens!' said Frau Krutzner. 'You have many talents, my dear, but I fear realism may not be one of them. Poor Professor von Igelfeld will be looking for somebody a bit younger than you.'

'Such as you?' retorted Frau Jens.

'I was not going to suggest that,' said Frau Krutzner. 'But since you yourself have raised the possibility, well, who can tell?'

There were many similar conversations amongst friends, the general gist of which was to discuss the prospects of snaring von Igelfeld before the voyage was out. Strategies were laid; outfits which had been brought 'just in case' were retrieved from trunks and pressed into service. The two hairdressers, busy at the best of times, were inundated with requests for appointments and there was a serious danger that supplies of hair dye would be exhausted before there was time to replenish stores at Marseilles.

Von Igelfeld himself was quite unaware of all the excitement amongst the passengers. That afternoon, there were due to be two more lectures: *Portuguese: a Deviant Spanish?* from him, and *Romantic Heroes* from Hans-Dieter Dietermann. Von Igelfeld was reconciled to an audience of twenty-five – composed of obedient crew members and the hard core of his own attenders – with the result that he was astonished when he went into the room and found that it was so packed with people as to allow standing room only for late-comers. For a few moments he thought that he had come to the wrong room; that he had wandered, by mistake, into the auditorium in which Hans-Dieter Dietermann was due to speak. But the officer who was accompanying him assured him that they had come to the right place and that the audience was expecting him to lecture.

For the next hour, von Igelfeld lectured to an enraptured audience, composed, with the exception of the crew members, entirely of ladies. Everything that von Igelfeld said, every move and gesture, was followed with rapt attention by the excited ladies, and after the lecture, when von Igelfeld tried to leave, he was mobbed by eager questioners.

'Tell me, Herr Professor,' said one matron. 'Is Portuguese *all* that different from Spanish? I've been dying to know the answer to that question. And my name, by the way, is Frau Libmann. I am from Munich. Do you know Munich well? My late husband had a large printing works there.'

And: 'Dear Professor von Igelfeld! What a marvellous lecture. I hung on every word – every word! I am Frau Baum from Regensburg. Yes, Regensburg too! Do you know Professor Zimmermann? I have known him for many years. Will you perhaps come and have dinner with Professor Zimmermann and myself some day?'

And: 'Herr Professor! I can't wait to read your book! I am trying to read Herr Dietermann's at the moment, but I am sure that your own book is far more interesting. Do they stock it in the ship's book shop, I wonder? Could you perhaps come and help me find it there?'

Von Igelfeld tried valiantly to deal with all these questions, but eventually, after an hour and a half, when it was apparent that the tenacity of his audience knew no bounds, he was rescued by one of the officers and escorted back to his cabin. On the way they passed the bar where, had they looked, they might have seen a disconsolate Hans-Dieter Dietermann sitting on a stool, wondering why it was that his audience had dwindled to eight.

'You were a real hit back there,' said the officer. 'They loved everything you said. It was quite surprising.'

'Oh?' said von Igelfeld. 'Why should it be surprising? Is Romance philology not intrinsically interesting? Why should those agreeable ladies not find it fascinating?'

'Oh, of course, of course,' said the officer quickly. 'It's just that I have never seen so many of our passengers become so . . . how shall I put it? So *intrigued* by one of our lecturers.'

Von Igelfeld bade farewell to the officer and entered the cabin. He felt quite exhausted after the demanding question session and he looked forward to a short siesta before he ventured out onto the deck for a walk. But as he sat down on his easy chair, he noticed that there were several parcels on the table. He rose to his feet and crossed the cabin. He was puzzled: the steward must have delivered something while he was lecturing. But who would be sending him parcels?

There were three. One was a large box of chocolates, to which a card had been attached: *To one who is lonely, from one who knows what loneliness means. Else Martinhaus (Cabin 256).* The second parcel, which von Igelfeld opened with fumbling, rather alarmed hands, was a handsome edition of Rilke's poems, on the fly leaf of which had been inscribed: *A woman's soul is a huntress, forever in search of him who can quench the soul's fire. To dear Moritz-Maria, from*

Margarita Jens (second table from yours in the dining room).
And finally there was a framed picture of the ship, again a
purchase from the on-board shop, signed with the following motto: *I will go to the end of the seven seas for you.* The
signature on this present, regrettably, was illegible.

Von Igelfeld sat down weakly. This was extraordinary. Why
should three ladies whom he had never met take it upon
themselves to send him presents? And why, moreover, should
they make these protestations of affection when he had done
nothing to encourage them to do so? Was this the way that
respectable German widows behaved these days? If it was,
then Germany had changed utterly and profoundly from the
Germany he had once known. It was still necessary, however,
to observe the formalities and to thank the donors of the
gifts. He would write a note to Frau Jens and ask the steward to deliver it to her table. Frau Martinhaus had given him
the number of her cabin and so he could simply slip a note
under her door. And as for the donor of the picture, if she
could not identify herself properly on her gifts then she
should not be surprised to receive no acknowledgment.

Von Igelfeld sat at the Captain's desk and wrote out the
notes. He thanked the donors for their kind gifts and
expressed his pleasure that they had enjoyed his lecture so
much. He trusted that they would enjoy the remaining
lectures, and assured them that if he could help them at all
– on any point of philology or Portuguese grammar – they
had only to ask. The notes written, he had a long, luxuriant
bath in the Captain's bath, and then dressed for dinner.

In the dining room, there was a murmur of excitement
as von Igelfeld made his entry. This was the signal for five
determined ladies, including Frau Jens and Frau

Martinhaus, to rise to their feet simultaneously, all with the thought of intercepting von Igelfeld before he reached his table and inviting him to dine at theirs. Victory went to the fastest of these. Frau Jens's legs, unfortunately, were too short to carry her across the room with sufficient despatch, and the first person to reach von Igelfeld's side was Frau Magda Holtmann, the widow of a Bonn lawyer, whose previous skills as a member, some forty years ago, of the University of Gottingen's Women's Sprint Team gave her a distinct advantage over the other four.

Von Igelfeld had no wish to have dinner with anybody, but felt unable to turn down the invitation. So, under glares of barely concealed anger from other tables, the ladies of Frau Holtmann's table enjoyed his company over dinner, each of them thinking privately what a perfect match he would make for them individually and wondering whether fourteen days would be enough to accomplish the task of securing an offer of marriage. Each had gone over the advantages which she might have over her rivals – and rivals there undoubtedly were. In many cases it was fortune – perhaps the Professor had had enough of working in his Institute and would appreciate the life of a private scholar? In some cases it was social prowess – a small, but appreciative salon, perhaps, for the society of Wiesbaden? And in other cases, it was skill in culinary matters. How did a mere man *survive* without somebody to ensure that the table was always properly furnished with good German delicacies? Did the poor Herr Professor eat in restaurants all the time? Did he even get *enough to eat*? Men needed their food – it was well known. He was very thin; marriage would change all that.

By the end of dinner, von Igelfeld was exhausted. He had spent the entire meal dealing with the ladies' questions. What were his hobbies? Did he have relatives in Munster, by any chance? There had been a Professor Igelfold there, had there not, and the Igelfolds could be a branch of the same family, could they not? Did he enjoy walking? The hills above Freiburg were very suitable for that purpose! Was he ever in Freiburg? Did he know the von Kersell family? There had been a Professor von Kersell once, but something had happened to him. Did he know, by any chance, what that was?

After coffee had been served, von Igelfeld had looked very publicly at his watch and had excused himself.

'I always have to do an hour or so's reading before I go to bed,' he announced. 'And this sea air makes me so sleepy.'

The ladies had nodded their agreement. It was very important, they felt, to get a good night's sleep when at sea, and, indeed, on land as well.

Von Igelfeld rose to his feet, thanked his hostess, and made his way out of the dining room. Frau Jens, who had been waiting for her moment, reached the door just as he did.

'Why, Herr Professor!' she said. 'It's you!'

Von Igelfeld nodded weakly.

'I was just going for a stroll on the deck,' said Frau Jens. 'It would be a great pleasure if you were able to accompany me.'

Without waiting for an answer, she took him by the arm and led him away. Within the dining room there were sharp intakes of breath at several tables.

'Did you see that!' hissed Frau Martinhaus. 'That shameless woman!'

257

'Desperation knows no bounds,' agreed her table companion. '*Inter arma silent leges.*'

'Auf Englisch könnte Mann sagen: *Fat arms, tiny legs*,' said Frau Martinhaus, somewhat less than charitably.

Von Igelfeld walked round the deck with Frau Jens for five minutes. Then, wresting his arm from her grip, he excused himself and rushed back to his cabin. There were several ladies in the corridor, and these stopped him briefly, under the pretext of finding out details of tomorrow's lecture.

'We shall all be there!' said one of them brightly. 'Notebooks at the ready!'

Again, it took von Igelfeld several minutes to extricate himself, but eventually he succeeded in reaching the sanctuary of his cabin. Once inside, he locked the door firmly and collapsed into his chair. The day had been a nightmare from start to finish, and he wondered how he could possibly last out for two further weeks. It was all that journalist's fault. If she had not asked him about marriage, then all these ladies would not have had the idea placed in their heads that he was a suitable candidate for them. Perhaps he could ask her to publish a correction: to say that there had been a misunderstanding, and that he actually was married? The problems with that scheme were that she would presumably refuse – as it would make her look foolish – and that it was inherently very improbable that anybody could make so fundamental a mistake. There seemed to be no way out of it: he would have to brave it out for the remaining two weeks, taking as many meals as possible in his cabin and remaining locked up there for as much of the day as was consistent with remaining sane.

The next day, as it transpired, was even worse. Von Igelfeld was pestered from breakfast onwards, constantly being approached by ladies claiming to have an interest in Romance philology. When he retreated to his cabin there was no peace. Either the telephone rang, with an invitation from one of the ladies to join a bridge four or play table tennis, or there was a knock on the door from a caller with the same sort of invitation. The lecture, of course, was now even better attended, and the ladies attempted to outdo one another in donning their finest outfits and more extravagant jewellery. Hans-Dieter Dietermann's audience had now gone down to three, and the third lecturer, who was giving a short series of talks on the history of Gibraltar had nobody at all to listen to him.

After a further two days, they reached Naples. Von Igelfeld, who had now completed his lectures, received numerous offers to have dinner ashore, but politely turned them all down. The ship stood offshore, rather than docking, and the passengers were conveyed to land in large launches hired for the occasion. Von Igelfeld's launch was dangerously overloaded, as most of the ladies tried to secure a place on it once they knew he was on board, with the result that it almost overturned on the way in. For von Igelfeld, this was the final straw. When he got ashore, he rushed off, leaving the ladies, and hailed a taxi. This he instructed to take him to the railway station. Then, paying off the taxi driver, he gave him a substantial tip on the understanding that the driver would return to the harbour and leave word with the launch office to the effect that he had been called away on urgent business and was not returning on board for the rest of the cruise. It being Naples, however, where research has revealed that sixty eight per cent of the population is profoundly dishonest, the taxi driver merely pocketed the money and did not perform this commission. But von Igelfeld was not to know this; he merely purchased a single ticket to Siena, via Rome, and boarded the next available train. He did not care about his possessions on board ship. These could be sent on to him when the ship returned to Hamburg. He had simply had enough: the whole venture had been misconceived from start to finish.

The ship left Naples early the following morning. Von Igelfeld's absence was noticed at eleven o'clock, when they were five hours out to sea. Enquiries were made and the Captain concluded that the most likely explanation was that he had gone ashore in Naples and simply not returned. This was investigated, and it was at this point that the disturbing information surfaced that the launch tallies added up. Three hundred and eighteen people had gone ashore in Naples and three hundred and eighteen appeared to have returned. This was a miscount, in fact; only three hundred and seventeen had returned, but in these circumstances the Captain was obliged to reach a more sinister conclusion.

Man overboard procedures were begun. The ship stopped in its tracks and a thorough search was made of the entire vessel. There were announcements made on the public address system and the shocked passengers were asked if anybody had seen Professor von Igelfeld that morning. Unfortunately at this point another fatal error was made. Two elderly sisters, of failing eyesight, went to report that they had seen him on the deck that morning at eight o'clock. He had been leaning over the rails, they said, and they were, moreover, sure that it was him. They had been at all his lectures and they knew exactly who he was. They had, in fact, been looking at one of the stewards, who was not yet in uniform, and who was looking out for flying fish at the time.

The Captain ordered the ship about and a slow, melancholy search was made of the portion of sea which the ship had been traversing at roughly eight thirty that morning. Alas, nothing was found, and by the time light faded that evening the grim conclusion was reached that Professor von Igelfeld had been lost at sea. A signal was sent to the company in Hamburg and early the next morning a telephone call was made to the Institute of Romance Philology in Regensburg informing them of the tragedy.

Von Igelfeld had reached Siena on the same day as his sudden departure from the ship and had spent the evening in his usual hotel there. The next morning he had contacted his friend, Professor Roberto Guerini, who had immediately invited him to spend some time on his wine estate near Montalcino. This suited von Igelfeld very well, and the next few days there were many enjoyable walks through the woods and evenings spent in the company of his Italian friends. There was even a dinner party at the house of the Conte Vittorio Fantozzi, which was, as such occasions inevitably were, a noted success.

After the pleasant interlude in Montalcino, it was time to return home. Von Igelfeld, who had been provided by Guerini with clothing and a small suitcase, packed his bag and bade farewell to his friends. Then, thoroughly rested by the break, he caught an express train from Siena to Munich. When he arrived in Regensburg, he decided to go straight from the railway station to the Institute to deal with his mail. Then he would go home and answer the letters that had no doubt built up there in his absence.

Not having seen the German press while he was in Italy, he had of course failed to read the item which was carried by most of the nationals: GERMAN PROFESSOR LOST AT SEA! Nor had he read the fulsome tribute from Prinzel, quoted at length in the same newspapers, or the remarks of other members of the philological community, including Unterholzer, who had referred in most generous terms to *Portuguese Irregular Verbs* and had commented that it was a very great loss indeed that there would now be no successor volume. Even had he read these, he might not have expected to find, on his return to the Institute, that things had been changed, and that a new name had appeared on his door.

'Why are you in my room?' he asked, as he opened the door of his office, to find Unterholzer sitting at his desk.

Unterholzer looked up, and turned quite white. It was as if he had seen a ghost.

'But you're dead!' he blurted out after a few moments.

'I most certainly am not!' said von Igelfeld.

'Are you sure?' stammered Unterholzer. 'Don't be so ridiculous, Herr Unterholzer,' said von Igelfeld. 'There are very few things of which we can be sure in this life, but that, I should have thought, is one of them.'

'I see,' said Unterholzer, lamely. 'The only reason why I am here in this office is that the papers said that you had been lost at sea. I thought that you would like the thought of my having your office after you've gone.'

Von Igelfeld bristled. 'Whatever gave you that idea?' he

said sharply. 'I might well have quite different ideas.'

Unterholzer had risen to his feet. 'Oh, Moritz-Maria, I am so pleased that you are alive! I cannot tell you how sad I was . . .' He stopped as he realized his terrible solecism. He had addressed von Igelfeld by his first name, and they had only known one another for, what was it, fifteen years?'

'I'm so sorry,' he rapidly continued. 'I didn't mean to call you that. It was the emotion of the occasion . . .'

Von Igelfeld raised a hand to stop him. He was touched that Unterholzer, for all his faults, had been so upset at his death. One might even overlook his presumption in taking his room, or almost . . .

'Don't apologise,' he said, adding, 'Detlev.'

It was a terrible effort for von Igelfeld to utter Unterholzer's first name, but it had to be done.

'Yes, Detlev, we have known one another for many years now, and it might be appropriate to move to first name terms. So it will be *du* from now on.'

Unterholzer looked immensely relieved. 'Let us go down to the café and drink . . .'

'And drink a toast to *Brüderschaft*,' said von Igelfeld kindly. It was good to be alive, he thought. Life was so precious, so unexpected in its developments, and so very rich in possibilities.

They left the Institute and walked down to the café.

'To *Brüderschaft*!' said Unterholzer, raising his glass. 'To brotherhood.'

'To *Brüderschaft*!' said von Igelfeld.

They sipped at the wine. Outside in the streets, a passing band of students suddenly raised their voices in song, singing those wonderful haunting words of the *Gaudeamus*:

Gaudeamus igitur,
Juvenes dum sumus.
Post iucundum iuventutem
Post molestam senectutem
Nos habebit humus,
Nos habebit humus!*

Von Igelfeld smiled at Unterholzer. 'Aut Habebit mare!'† he joked. And Unterholtzer, who had not heard so good a joke for many years, laughed and laughed.

* Let us rejoice therefore / While we are young. / After a pleasant youth / After a troublesome old age / The earth will have us.

† Or the sea will have us!

AT THE VILLA OF
REDUCED CIRCUMSTANCES

Contents

On Being Light Blue

Professor Dr Moritz-Maria Von Igelfeld's birthday fell on the first of May. He would not always have remembered it had the anniversary not occurred on May Day itself; as a small boy he had been convinced that the newspaper photographs of parades in Red Square, those intimidating displays of missiles, and the grim-faced line-up of Politburo officials, all had something to do with the fact that he was turning six or seven, or whatever birthday it was. Such is the complete confidence of childhood that we are each of us at the centre of the world – a conviction out of which not all of us grow, and those who do grow out of it sometimes do so only with some difficulty. And this is so very understandable; as Auden remarked, how fascinating is that class of which I am the only member.

Nobody observed von Igelfeld's birthday now. It was true that he was not entirely alone in the world – there were cousins in Graz, but they were on the Austrian side of the family and the two branches of von Igelfelds, separated by both distance and nationality, had drifted apart. There was an elderly aunt in Munich, and another aged female relative in Baden Baden, but they had both forgotten more or less everything and it had been many years since they had sent him a birthday card. If he had married, as he had firmly intended to do, then he undoubtedly would now have been surrounded by a loving wife and children, who would have made much of his birthday; but his resolution to propose to a charming dentist, Dr Lisbetta von Brautheim, had been thwarted by his colleague, Professor Dr Detlev Amadeus Unterholzer. That was a humiliation which von Igelfeld had found hard to bear. That Unterholzer of all people – a man whose work on the orthography of Romance languages was barely mentioned these days; a man whose idea of art was coloured reproductions of views of the Rhine; a man whose nose was so large and obtrusive – vulgar even – the sort of nose one saw on head waiters; that Unterholzer should succeed in marrying Dr von Brautheim when he himself had planned to do so, was quite unacceptable. But the fact remained that there was nothing one could do about it; Unterholzer's birthday never went unmarked. Indeed, there were always cakes at coffee time in the Institute on Unterholzer's birthday, made by Frau Dr Unterholzer herself; as Unterholzer pointed out, she might be a dentist but she had a sweet tooth nonetheless and made wonderful, quite wonderful cakes and pastries. And then there were the cards prominently displayed on his desk, not only from Unterholzer's wife but from the receptionist and dental nurse in her practice. What did they care about Unterholzer? von Igelfeld asked himself. They could hardly *like* him, and so they must have sent the cards out of deference to their employer. That was not only wrong – a form of exploitation indeed – but it was also sickeningly sentimental, and if that was what happened on birthdays then he was best off without one, or at least best off without one to which anybody paid any attention.

On the first of May in question, von Igelfeld was in the Institute coffee room before anybody else. They normally all arrived at the same time, with a degree of punctuality which would have been admired by Immanuel Kant himself, but on that particular morning von Igelfeld would treat himself to an extra ten minutes' break. Besides, if he arrived early, he could sit in the chair which Unterholzer normally contrived to occupy, and which von Igelfeld believed was more comfortable than any other in the room. As the best chair in the room it should by rights have gone to him, as he was, after all, the senior scholar, but these things were difficult to articulate in a formal way and he had been obliged to tolerate Unterholzer's occupation of the chair. It would have been different, of course, if Professor Dr Dr Florianus Prinzel had taken that chair; von Igelfeld would have been delighted to let Prinzel have it, as he undoubtedly deserved it. He and Prinzel had been friends together at Heidelberg, in their youth, and he still thought of Prinzel as the scholar athlete, the noble youth, deserving of every consideration. Yes, there was little he would not have done for Prinzel, and it was a matter of secret regret to von Igelfeld that he had never actually been called upon to save Prinzel's life. That would have secured Prinzel's undying admiration and indebtedness, which von Igelfeld would have worn lightly. 'It was nothing,' he imagined himself saying. 'One's own personal safety is irrelevant in such circumstances. Believe me, I know that you would have done the same for me.'

In fact, the only time that Prinzel had been in danger von Igelfeld had either been responsible for creating the peril in the first place, or Prinzel had been able to handle the situation quite well without any assistance from him. In their student days in Heidelberg, von Igelfeld had unwisely persuaded Prinzel to engage in a duel with a shady member of some student Korps, and this, of course, had been disastrous. The very tip of Prinzel's nose had been sliced off by his opponent's sword, and although it had been sewn back on in hospital, the doctor, who had been slightly drunk, had sewn it on upside down. Prinzel had never said anything about this, being too gentlemanly to complain about such an affair (no true gentleman ever notices it if the tip of his nose is sliced off), and indeed it had occurred to von Igelfeld that he had not even been aware of what had happened. But it remained a reminder of an unfortunate incident, and von Igelfeld preferred not to think about it.

That was one incident. The other occasion on which Prinzel had been in danger was when von Igelfeld had accompanied him and his wife to Venice, at a time when the city was threatened by an insidious corruption. The corruption turned out not to be cholera, as so graphically portrayed by Thomas Mann, but radio-activity in the water, and Prinzel had become mildly radioactive as a result of swimming off the Lido. Again von Igelfeld was unable to come to the rescue, and Prinzel, quite calmly, had taken the situation in hand and returned to Germany for iodine treatment at the University of Mainz. There he had been decontaminated and pronounced safe, or as safe as one could be after ingesting small quantities of strontium-90.

Thoughts of radioactivity, however, were far from von Igelfeld's mind as he enjoyed his first cup of coffee in the Institute coffee room and glanced at the headlines in the *Frankfurter Allgemeine*. There was nothing of note, of course. Industrialists were sounding off about interest rates, as they always did, and there was a picture of an earnest finance minister pointing a finger at a chart. The chart could have been upside down, like Prinzel's nose, for all that von Igelfeld cared; matters of this sort left him unmoved. It was the job of politicians and bankers to run the economy and he could not understand why they often failed to do so in a competent way. It was, he assumed, something to do with their general venality and with the fact that quite the wrong type went into politics and finance. But it seemed as if there would never be any change in that, and so they would have to put up with these insolent people and with their persistent mismanagement. Far more interesting was the front-page item about a row which was developing over the appointment of a new director to a museum in Wiesbaden.

The new director, a man of modern tastes, had thrown out the old cases of fossils and rocks, and had replaced them with installations by contemporary artists. This had the effect of confusing those people who came to the museum hoping to see items of interest and found only empty galleries with a small pile of wooden boxes in a corner or a heap of old clothing, artistically arranged under a skylight and labelled: *The Garments of Identity*. These visitors peered into the wooden boxes, hoping to see fossils or rocks within, and found that they were empty, and that the boxes themselves were the exhibit. And as for the piles of clothing, what was the difference between them and the museum cloakroom, where people hung their overcoats? Were both not *Garments of Identity*, or would it be confusing to label the cloakroom *Garments of Identity*? Would people know that it was a cloakroom, or would they search in vain for a room labelled *Cloakroom*? Von Igelfeld frowned. This sort of thing was becoming far too common in Germany, and he had every sympathy with the friends of the fossils and rocks who were attempting to secure the new director's resignation. This was far more interesting than news of interest rates, and far more significant, too, von Igelfeld thought. What if the levers of power at universities were to fall into similar hands to the hands of this new director? Would he himself be considered a fossil or a rock, and thrown out, to be replaced, perhaps, by a wooden box? How would Romance philology survive in a world that honoured the works of Joseph Beuys and the like?

It was while von Igelfeld was thinking of these dire possibilities that he heard the door of the coffee room open. He looked up, to see his colleagues entering, deep in what appeared to be animated conversation. There was sudden silence when they saw von Igelfeld.

'Good morning,' said von Igelfeld, laying the newspaper to one side. 'It seems that I am here first today.'

For a moment nothing was said. Then the Librarian cleared his throat and spoke. 'That would appear to be so, Herr von Igelfeld. And seeing you here solves the mystery which I was discussing with Professor Dr Prinzel outside, in the corridor. "Where is Professor Dr von Igelfeld?" I asked. And Professor Dr Prinzel said that he did not know. Well, now we all know. You are here, in the coffee room, sitting in . . .' He tailed off, and moved quickly to the table where the coffee pot and cups stood in readiness.

They served themselves coffee in silence, and then came to join von Igelfeld around his table.

'How is your aunt?' von Igelfeld asked the Librarian. 'This spring weather will be cheering her up, no doubt.' The health of his demanding aunt was the Librarian's main topic of conversation, and it was rare for anybody to raise it, as they had all heard everything there was to be said about this aunt.

'That is very kind of you to ask,' said the Librarian. 'Very thoughtful. I shall tell my aunt that you asked after her. That will make her very happy. So few people care about people like her these days. It's good that at least somebody remembers.' He paused, throwing a sideways glance at Unterholzer and Prinzel. 'She will be very pleased indeed, I can assure you. And she does need some cheering up, now that they have changed her medicine and the new one takes some getting used to. It's Dutch, you know. I wasn't aware that the Dutch made medicines at all, but this one is said to be very good. The only problem is that it irritates her stomach and that makes her querulous at times. Not that she is always like that; it seems to be at its worst about twenty minutes after taking the pill in question. They come in peculiar yellow and white capsules, which are actually quite difficult to swallow. The last ones were white, and had the manufacturers' initials stamped into every capsule. Quite remarkable . . .'

It was Unterholzer who interrupted him. 'So,' he said. 'So this is a special day, is it not?'

Prinzel glanced nervously at Unterholzer. He had been hoping that he would not make an issue of the chair, but it seemed that he might. Really, this was most unwise.

Everybody knew that von Igelfeld could be difficult, and Unterholzer really had no *legal* claim on that chair. He might have a moral claim, as people undoubtedly did develop moral claims to chairs, but this was quite different from a claim which could be defended in the face of a direct challenge. It would be far better to pass over the whole incident and for Unterholzer simply to arrive slightly early the following morning and secure the chair for himself. He could surely count on their moral support in any such manoeuvre.

'Today, you see,' Unterholzer went on, 'today is special because it is the birthday of our dear colleague, Professor Dr von Igelfeld.'

'My!' exclaimed the Librarian. 'The same month as my aunt! Hers is on the twelfth. What a coincidence!'

'May Day,' said Prinzel. 'A distress signal at sea, but for you quite the opposite!'

They all laughed at the witticism. Prinzel was so amusing and could be counted upon to bring a welcome note of levity, particularly to a potentially difficult situation.

Von Igelfeld smiled. 'It is very kind of you to remember, Herr Unterholzer,' he said. 'I had not intended to celebrate it.'

Unterholzer looked thoughtful. 'I suppose not,' he said. 'A birthday can't be much fun when one has to celebrate it all by oneself. There's no point, really.'

Von Igelfeld stared at him. Unterholzer often took the opportunity to condescend to him, if he thought he could get away with it, and this was quite intolerable. If anybody deserved to be pitied, it was Unterholzer himself, with his wretched, out-of-date book on Portuguese subjunctives, and that nose. Who was he even to hint that von Igelfeld's

278

life might be incomplete in some way? It defied belief; it really did. He would tell Zimmermann himself about it, and Zimmermann, he knew, would laugh. He always laughed when Unterholzer's name was mentioned, even before anything else was said.

Prinzel intervened rapidly. 'I remember, Moritz-Maria, how we used to celebrate our birthdays, back in Heidelberg, when we were students. Do you remember when we went to that inn where the innkeeper gave us free steins of beer when he heard it was your birthday. He always used to call you the Baron! "Free beer for the Baron's birthday," he said. Those were his very words, were they not?'

Unterholzer listened closely, but with increasing impatience. This Heidelberg story had irritated him, and he was beginning to regret his act of generosity – supererogatory in the provocative circumstances – in drawing attention to von Igelfeld's birthday. He had not anticipated that Prinzel would launch into this embarrassing tribute to von Igelfeld. 'So why did he call Professor Dr von Igelfeld a baron, when he isn't one?' he asked. 'Why would anyone do that?'

Prinzel smiled. 'Because some people, even if they aren't barons in the *technical* sense have – how shall I put it?; this really is a bit embarrassing – some of the *qualities* that one normally associates with that position in life. That is why, for example, that my friend Charles von Klain is often addressed as *Capitano* by the proprietors of Italian restaurants. He has the appropriate bearing. He has no military rank, but he could have. Do you see what I mean?'

Unterholzer shook his head. 'I do not see why people should be called Baron or Count, or even *Capitano* for that matter, when they are not entitled to these titles.'

'It is not an important thing,' said von Igelfeld. 'It is really nothing.'

'But it is!' said the Librarian. 'These things are important. One of the doctors who visits my aunt's nursing home is a Polish count. Of course he doesn't use the title, but do you know, one of the other patients there, a charming lady from Berlin, could spot it. She said to my aunt: "That Dr Wlavoski is an aristocrat. I can tell." And do you know, when they asked the Director of the nursing home, he confirmed it! He explained that the Wlavoskis had been an important family of landowners in the East and they had been dispossessed – first by our own authorities when they invaded – and that was most unfortunate and regrettable – and then again by the Russians when they came in. They were a very scientifically distinguished family and they all became physicians or astronomers or the like, but the fact that they had been counts somehow shone through.'

They all looked at the Librarian. The conversation was intensely embarrassing to von Igelfeld. The von Igelfelds were certainly not from that extensive and ubiquitous class of people, the 'vegetable nobles' (for whom *von* was nothing more than an address). Of course he could be addressed as Baron by only the very smallest extension of the rules of entitlement; after all, his father's cousin had been the Freiherr von Igelfeld, the title having been granted to the family by the Emperor Francis II, and on his mother's side there were barons and baronesses aplenty, but this was not something that people like him liked to discuss.

'Perhaps we should change the subject,' said Prinzel, who could sense Unterholzer's hostility. The problem there was that Unterholzer would have liked to have been mistaken for a baron, but never could be. It was out of the question. And it was not just a question of physical appearance – which alone would have precluded it – it was something to do with manner. Unterholzer was just too . . . too clumsy to pass for anything but what he was, which was a man of very obscure origins from some dim and undistinguished town in a potato-growing area somewhere.

'Yes,' said Unterholzer. 'A good idea. We are, after all, meant to be serious people. Talk about barons and all such nonsense is suitable only for those silly magazines that you see at the railway station. Such silliness. It's surprising that it survives. So let us talk about your birthday, Herr von Igelfeld! How are you going to celebrate it?'

'I am not proposing to do anything in particular,' said von Igelfeld. 'I shall possibly go out for dinner somewhere. I don't know. I have not thought about it.'

'A birthday is a good time to review the past year,' said Prinzel. 'I always think over what I've done. It's useful to do that.'

'Or indeed to review one's entire life,' suggested Unterholzer. 'You might think with some satisfaction of all your achievements, Herr von Igelfeld.' This remark was quite sincere. In spite of his envy, Unterholzer admired von Igelfeld, and would have liked to have been more like him. He would have loved to have written *Portuguese Irregular Verbs* himself and to have enjoyed von Igelfeld's undoubted distinction. But of course he had not, and, in moments of real honesty, he acknowledged that he never would.

'Yes,' said Prinzel. 'You have done so much. You could even write your autobiography. And when you wrote it, the final chapter would be: Things Still Left to be Done. That would allow it to end on a positive note.'

'Such as?' interjected Unterholzer. 'What has Professor Dr von Igelfeld still to do?'

'I have no idea,' said Prinzel. 'He has done so much. We had better ask him.' He turned to von Igelfeld, who was taking a sip of his coffee. 'What would you really like to do, Herr von Igelfeld?'

Von Igelfeld put down his coffee cup and thought for a moment. They were right. He had done so much; he had been to so many conferences; he had delivered so many lectures; he had written so many learned papers. And yet, there were things undone, that he would like to do. He would like, for example, to have gone to Cambridge, as Zimmermann had done only a few years before. They had given Zimmermann a lodge for a year when he had been a visiting professor and von Igelfeld had visited him there. The day of his visit had been a perfect summer day, and after taking tea on the lawns of the lodge they had driven out to Grantchester in Zimmermann's car and had drunk more tea possibly under the very chestnut trees which Rupert Brooke had referred to in his poem. And von Igelfeld had felt so content, and so pleased with the scholarly atmosphere, that he had decided that one day he too would like to follow in Zimmermann's footsteps and visit this curious English city with its colleges and its lanes and its feeling of gentleness.

'I should like to go to Cambridge,' he announced. 'And indeed one day I shall go there.'

Unterholzer listened with interest. If von Igelfeld were to go to Cambridge for an appreciable length of time, then he might be able to get his office for the duration of his time away. It was a far better office than his own, and if he simply moved in while von Igelfeld was away nobody would wish to make a fuss. After all, what was the point of having empty space? He could give his own office over to one of the research assistants, who currently had to share with another. It was the logical thing to do. And so he decided, there and then, to contact his friend at the German Scholarly Exchange Programme and see whether he could fix an invitation for von Igelfeld to go to Cambridge for a period of six months or so. A year would be acceptable, of course, but one would not want to be too greedy.

'I hope your wish comes true,' said Unterholzer, raising his coffee cup in a toast to von Igelfeld. 'To Cambridge!'

They all raised their coffee cups and von Igelfeld smiled modestly. 'It would be most agreeable,' he said. 'But perhaps it will never happen.'

'My dear Professor von Igelfeld!' said the Master, as he received von Igelfeld in the drawing room of the Lodge. 'You really are most welcome to Cambridge. I take it that the journey from Regensburg went well. Of course it will have.'

Von Igelfeld smiled, and bowed slightly to the Master. He wondered why the Master should have made the Panglossian assumption that the journey went well. In his experience, journeys usually did not go well. They were full of humiliations and assaults on the senses; smells that one would rather not smell; people one would rather not meet; and incidents that one would rather had not happened. Perhaps the Master never went anywhere, or only went as far as London. If that were the case, then he might fondly imagine that travel was a comfortable experience.

'No,' said von Igelfeld. 'It was not a good journey. In fact, quite the opposite.'

The Master looked aghast. 'My dear Professor von Igelfeld! What on earth went wrong? What on earth happened?'

'My train kept stopping and starting,' said von Igelfeld. 'And then my travelling companions were far from ideal.'

'Ah!' said the Master. 'We cannot always choose the company we are obliged to keep. Even in heaven, I suspect, we shall have to put up with some people whom we might not have chosen to spend eternity with, were we given the chance. Hah!'

Von Igelfeld stared at the Master. Was this a serious remark, to which he was expected to respond? The English were very difficult to read; half the things they said were not meant to be taken seriously, but it was impossible, if you were German, to detect which half this was. It may be that the Master was making a serious observation about the nature of the afterlife, or it may be that he thought that the whole idea of heaven was absurd. If it were the former, then von Igelfeld might be expected to respond with some suitable observation of his own, whereas if it were the latter he might be expected to smile, or even to laugh.

'The afterlife must surely be as Dante described it,' said von Igelfeld, after a short silence. 'And one's position in the circle will determine the company one keeps.'

The Master's eyes sparkled. 'Or the other way round, surely. The company one keeps will determine where one goes later on. Bad company; bad fate.'

'That is if one is easily influenced,' said von Igelfeld. 'A good man may keep bad company and remain good. I have seen that happen.'

'Where?' said the Master.

'At school,' said von Igelfeld. 'At my Gymnasium there was a boy called Müller, who was very kind. He was always giving presents to the younger boys and putting his arm around them. He cared for them deeply. He was in a class in which most of the other boys were very low, bad types. Müller used to put his arm around these boys too. He never changed his ways. His goodness survived the bad company.'

The Master listened to this story with some interest. 'Do people read Freud these days in Germany?' he asked.

Von Igelfeld was rather taken aback by this remark. What had Freud to do with Müller? Again there was this difficult English obliqueness. Perhaps he would become accustomed to it after a few months, but for the moment it was very disconcerting. In Germany people said what they meant; they had the virtue of being literal, and that meant that everything was much clearer. This was evidently not the case in Cambridge. 'I believe that he has his following,' said von Igelfeld. 'There are always people who are prepared to find the base motive in human action. Professor Freud is a godsend to them.'

The Master smiled. 'Of course, you are right to censure me,' he said. 'We live in an age of such corrosive cynicism, do we not?'

Von Igelfeld raised a hand in protest. 'But I have not censured you! I would never dream of censuring you! You are my host!' He was appalled at the misunderstanding. What had he said which had caused the Master to conclude that he was censuring him? Was it something to do with Freud? Freudians could be very sensitive, and it was possible that the Master was a Freudian. In which case, perhaps his remark had been rather like telling a religious person that his religious views were absurd.

'I meant no offence,' said von Igelfeld. 'I had no idea that you were so loyal to Vienna.'

The Master gave a start. 'Vienna? I know nothing about Vienna.'

'I was speaking metaphorically,' said von Igelfeld hastily. 'Vienna. Rome. These are places that stand for something beyond the place itself.'

'You are referring to Wittgenstein, I take it,' said the Master. 'There used to be some of the older dons who remembered him. A most unusual figure, you know. He used to like going to the cinemas in Cambridge, where he would eat buttered toast. Very strange behaviour, but acceptable in a man of that ability.'

Von Igelfeld smiled. 'I have never eaten toast in a cinema,' he said.

'Nor I,' said the Master, somewhat wistfully. 'There is so much in this life that I haven't done. So much. And when I think of the years, and how they slip past. *Eheu! Eheu, fugaces!*'

The Master looked up at von Igelfeld, at this tall visitor, and, extracting a handkerchief from his trouser pocket, he suddenly began to cry.

'Please excuse me,' he said, between sobs. 'It's not easy being the Master of a Cambridge college. People think it is, but it really isn't. It's hard, damnably hard! And I get no thanks for it, none at all. All I get is criticism and opposition, and moans and complaints from the College Fellows. Their rooms are too cold. The college wine cellars are no what they used to be. Somebody has removed the latest *Times Literary Supplement* and so on. All day. Every day. Oh, I don't know. Please excuse me. I know it doesn't help to cry, but I just can't help it. If you knew what it was like, you'd cry too. They say such beastly things to me. Beastly. Behind my back and sometimes to my face. Right to my face. I bet they didn't do that to Wittgenstein when he was here. I bet they didn't. They just pick on me. That's all they do.'

Von Igelfeld leaned forward and put an arm round the Master's shoulders. Just like Müller, he reflected.

Von Igelfeld was shown to his rooms by the Porter, a gaunt man who walked in a curious, halting gait up the winding stone stairway that led to von Igelfeld's door.

'A very good set of rooms, this is,' said the Porter. 'We reserve these rooms for the Master's personal guests and for distinguished visitors, like yourself, Sir. You get a very fine view of the Court – probably the best view there is – and a passable view of the College Meadows.'

He unlocked a stout oak door on which von Igelfeld noticed that a painted name-plate bearing his name had already been fixed. This was a pleasant touch, and he made a mental note to make sure that they made a similar gesture in future to visitors to the Institute. Or at least they would do it for some of their visitors; some they wished to discourage – some of Unterholzer's guests, for example – and it would be unwise to affix their names to anything.

The Porter showed von Igelfeld round the rooms. 'You have a small kitchen here, Sir, but I expect that you'll want to eat in Hall with the other Fellows. The College keeps a good table, you know, and the Fellows like to take advantage of that. That's why we have so many fat academic gentlemen around the place, if you'll forgive the observation. Take Dr Hall out there, just for an example. You see him crossing the Court? He likes his food, does our Dr Hall. Always first in for lunch and always last out. Second helpings every time, the Steward tells me.'

Von Igelfeld moved to the window and peered out over the Court. A corpulent man with slicked down dark hair, parted in the middle, was walking slowly along a path.

'That is Dr Hall?' he asked.

'The very same,' said the Porter. 'He's a mathematician, and I believe that he is a very famous one. Cambridge is well known for its mathematicians. Professor Hawking, for example, who wrote that book, you know the one that everybody says they've read but haven't, he's a Fellow of that college over there, with the spire. You can just see it. There's him and there are plenty more like him.'

Von Igelfeld stared out of the window. He knew *A Brief History of Time*, although he had certainly not read it. It had brought great fame to its author, there was no doubt about that, but did it really deserve it? *Portuguese Irregular Verbs* was probably of equal importance, but very few people had read it; that is, very few people outside the circles of Romance philology and there were only about . . . He thought for a moment. There were only about two hundred people throughout the world who were interested in Romance philology, and that meant that *Portuguese Irregular Verbs* was known to no more than that. His reflection went further: one could place all the readers of *Portuguese Irregular Verbs* in the Court below and still only occupy a small part of it. Whereas if one were to try to assemble in one place all the purchasers of Professor Hawking's book it would be like those great crowds in Mecca or the banks of the Ganges during a religious festival. This was unquestionably unjust, and merely demonstrated, in his view, that the modern world was seriously lacking in important respects.

'I'm afraid these rooms lack a bathroom,' said the Porter, moving away from the window. 'That's the problem with these old buildings. They were built in the days before modern plumbing and it has been very difficult, indeed impossible, to make the necessary changes.'

Von Igelfeld was aghast. 'But if there is no bathroom, where am I to wash in the morning?'

'Oh, there is a bathroom,' said the Porter quickly. 'There's a shared bathroom on the landing. You share with Professor Waterfield. His rooms are on the other side of the landing from yours. There's a bathroom in the middle for both of you to use.'

Von Igelfeld frowned. 'But what if Professor Waterfield is in the bathroom when I need to use it? What then?'

'Well,' said the Porter, 'that can happen. I suppose you'll have to wait until he's finished. Then you can use it when he goes out. That's the way these things are normally done . . .' adding, almost under his breath, 'in this country at least.'

Von Igelfeld pursed his lips. He was not accustomed to discussing such matters with porters. In Germany the whole issue of bathrooms would be handled by somebody with responsibilities for such matters; it would never have been appropriate for a professor, and especially one in a full chair, to have to talk about an issue of this sort. The situation was clearly intolerable, and the only thing to do would be to arrange with this Professor Waterfield, whoever he was, that he should refrain from using the bathroom during those hours that von Igelfeld might need it. He could use it to his heart's content at other times, but the bathroom would otherwise be exclusively available to von Igelfeld. That, he thought, was the best solution, and he would make the suggestion to this Professor Waterfield when they met.

The Porter in the meantime had extracted a key from his keychain and handed this to von Igelfeld. 'I hope that you have a happy stay,' he said brightly. 'We are an unusual college, by and large, and it helps to have visitors.'

Von Igelfeld stared at the Porter. This was a very irregular remark, which would never have been made by a German porter. German porters acted as porters. They opened things and closed them. That was what they did. It seemed that in England things were rather different, and it was not surprising, then, that it was such a confused society. And here he was at the intellectual heart of this strange country, where porters commented on the girth of scholars, where bathrooms were shared by perfect strangers, and where masters of colleges, after making opaque remarks about Freud and Wittgenstein suddenly burst into tears. It would clearly require all one's wits to deal with such a society, and von Igelfeld was glad that he was a man of the world. It would be hopeless for somebody like Unterholzer, who would frankly lack the subtlety to cope with such circumstances; at least there was that to be thankful for – that it was he, and no

Unterholzer, who had come here as Visiting Professor of Romance Philology.

That evening the Master invited von Igelfeld to join him and several of the Fellows for a glass of sherry before dinner. The invitation had come in a note pushed under von Igelfeld's door and was waiting for him on his return from a brief visit to the College Library. He had not spent much time in the Library, but he was able to establish even on the basis of the hour or so that he was there that there was an extensive collection of early Renaissance Spanish and Portuguese manuscripts in something called the Hughes-Davitt Bequest, and that these, as far as he could ascertain, had hardly been catalogued, let alone subjected to full scholarly analysis. The discovery had excited him, and already he was imagining the paper which would appear in the *Zeitschrift*: *Lusocripta Nova: an Untapped Collection of Renaissance Manuscripts in the Hughes-Davitt Bequest at Cambridge*. Readers would wonder – and well they might – why it had taken a German visiting scholar to discover what had been sitting under the noses of Cambridge philologists for so long, but that was an issue which von Igelfeld would tactfully refrain from discussing. People were used to the Germans discovering all sorts of things; most of Mycenaean civilisation had been unearthed by Schliemann and other German scholars in the nineteenth century, and the only reason why the British discovered Minoa was because they more or less tripped up and fell into a hole, which happened to be filled with elaborate grave goods. There was not much credit in that, at least in von Igelfeld's view. The same could be said of Egyptology, although in that case one had to admit that there had been a minor British contribution, bumbling and amateurish though it was. Those eccentric English archaeologists who had stumbled into Egyptian tombs had more or less got what they deserved, in von Igelfeld's view, when they were struck down by mysterious curses (probably no more than long dormant microbes sealed into the pyramids). That would never have happened had it been German archaeology that made the discovery; the German professors would undoubtedly have sent their assistants in first, and it would have been they, not the professors themselves, who would have fallen victim. But it was no use thinking about English amateurism here in Cambridge, the very seat of the problem. If he did that, then everything would seem unsatisfactory, and that would be a profitless way of spending the next four months. So von Igelfeld decided to make no conscious comparisons with Germany, knowing what the inevitable conclusions would be.

He made his way to the Senior Common Room in good time, but when he arrived it seemed that everybody was already there, huddled around the Master, who was making a point with an animated gesture of his right hand.

'Ah, Professor von Igelfeld!' he said, detaching himself from his colleagues and striding across the room to meet his guest. 'So punctual! *Pünktlich* even. You'll find that we're a bit lax here. We allow ten minutes or so, sometimes fifteen.'

Von Igelfeld flushed. It was obvious that he had committed a solecism by arriving at the appointed time, but then, if they wanted him to arrive at six fifteen, why did they not ask him to do so?

'But I see that everybody else is here,' he said defensively, looking towards the group of Fellows. 'They must have arrived before six.'

The Master smiled. 'True, true,' he said. 'But of course most of them have little better to do. Anyway, please come and meet them. They are all so pleased that you took up the Visiting Professorship. The atmosphere is quite, how shall I put it? *electric* with anticipation.'

The Master took hold of von Igelfeld's elbow and steered him deftly across the room. There then followed introductions. Dr Marcus Poynton, Pure Mathematics; Dr Margaret Hodges, French Literature; Professor Hector MacQueen, Legal History (and history of cricket too), Mr Max Wilkinson, Applied Mathematics; and Dr C. A. D. Wood, Theoretical Physics.

'These are just a few of the Fellowship,' said the Master. 'You'll meet others over dinner. I thought I should invite a cross-section, so to speak.'

Von Igelfeld shook hands solemnly, and bowed slightly as each introduction was made. The Fellows smiled, and seemed welcoming, and while the Master went off to fetch a glass of sherry, von Igelfeld fell into easy conversation with the woman who had been introduced to him as Dr C. A. D. Wood.

'So you are a physicist,' said von Igelfeld. 'You are always up to something, you physicists. Looking for something or other. But once you find it, you just go off looking for something more microscopic. Your world is always getting smaller, is it not?'

She laughed. 'That's one way of putting it. In my case, I'm looking for Higgs's boson, a very elusive little particle that Professor Higgs says exists but which nobody has actually seen yet.'

'And will you find it?'

'If the mathematics are correct, it should be there,' she said.

'But can you not tell whether the mathematics are correct?' asked von Igelfeld. 'Can they not be checked for errors?'

Dr C. A. D. Wood took a sip of her sherry. 'It is not always that simple. There are disagreements in mathematics. There is not always one self-evident truth. Even here, in this college, there are mathematicians who . . . who . . .' She paused. The Master had now returned with a glass of sherry for von Igelfeld.

'This is our own sherry, Professor von Igelfeld,' he said, handing him the glass. 'The Senior Tutor goes out to Jerez every couple of years and replenishes our stocks. He has a very fine palate.' He turned to Dr C. A. D. Wood. 'You have become acquainted with our guest, I see, Wood. You will see what I mean when I say that he is a very fine choice for the Visiting Professorship. Very fine.'

'Absolutely,' said Dr C. A. D. Wood.

'You were saying something about disagreements amongst mathematicians,' said von Igelfeld pleasantly. 'Please explain.'

At this remark, the Master turned sharply to Dr C. A. D. Wood and glared at her. 'I cannot imagine that Professor von Igelfeld is interested in such matters,' he hissed at her. 'For heaven's sake! He only arrived today, poor man!'

'I am most interested,' said von Igelfeld. 'You see, there are disagreements amongst philologists. Different views are taken. It seems that this is the case in all disciplines, even something as hard and fast as mathematics.'

'Hard and fast!' burst out Dr C. A. D. Wood. 'My dear Professor von Igelfeld, if you believe that matters are har and fast in the world of mathematics, then you are sorely deluded.'

'I think Byzantine politics were harder and faster than mathematics,' sighed the Master. 'Or so it seems to me.'

'You know very little about it, Maestro,' said Dr C. A. D. Wood to the Master. 'You stick to whatever it is you do, old bean. Moral philosophy?'

Von Igelfeld felt uncomfortable. What had started as an innocent conversation – small talk really – had suddenly become charged with passion. It was difficult to make out what was going on – that problem with English obscurity again – and it was not clear to him why Dr C. A. D. Wood had addressed the Master as old bean. No doubt he would find out more about that, when Dr C. A. D. Wood had the opportunity to talk to him in private. In the meantime, he would have to concentrate on talking to the Master, who appeared to be becoming increasingly distressed. Dr C. A. D. Wood, he noticed, had drifted off to talk to Mr Wilkinson, who was looking steadfastly at his shoes while she addressed him.

'I am very comfortable in my rooms,' he said to the Master. 'I am very happy with that view of the Court. I shall be able to observe the comings and goings in the College, just by sitting at my window.'

'Oh,' said the Master. 'You will see everything then. The whole thing laid bare. Anaesthetised like a patient on the table, as Eliot so pithily said of the morning, or was it the evening, fussy pedant that he was. How awful. How frankly awful.'

'But why should it be awful?' asked von Igelfeld. 'What s awful about the life of the College?'

He realised immediately that he should not have asked the question, as the Master had seized his sleeve and was muttering, almost into his ear. 'They're the end, the utter end. All of them, or virtually all of them. That Dr C. A. D. Wood, for example, don't trust her for a moment. That's my only warning to you. Just don't trust her. And be very careful when they try to involve you in their scheming. Just be very careful.'

'I cannot imagine why they should wish to involve me in their scheming,' said von Igelfeld. 'I am merely a visitor.'

The Master gave a short chuckle. 'Visitors have a vote in this College,' he said. 'It's been in the statutes since 1465. Visiting Professors have a vote in the College Council. They'll want you to vote with them in whatever it is they're planning. And they're always planning something.'

'Who are *they*?' asked von Igelfeld. Was it the same *they* whom the Master had accused of persecuting him? Or was there more than one group of *theys*?

'You'll find out,' said the Master. 'Just you wait.'

Von Igelfeld looked into his sherry glass. There were those who said that the world of German academia was one of constant bickering. This, of course, was plainly not true, but if they could get a glimpse, just a glimpse, of Cambridge they would have something to talk about. And this was even before anybody had sat down for dinner. What would it be like once dinner was served or, and this was an even more alarming thing, over Stilton and coffee afterwards? And all the time he would have to be careful to navigate his way through these shoals of allusion and concealed meaning. Of course he would be able to do it – there could be no doubt about that – but it was not exactly what he had been looking forward to after a long and trying day. Oh to be back in Germany, with Prinzel and Frau Prinzel, sitting in their back garden drinking coffee and talking about the safe and utterly predictable affairs of the Institute. What a comfortable existence that had been, and to think that it would be four months, a full four months, before he could return to Regensburg and the proper, German way of doing things.

Shortly before they were due to go through for dinner, the Senior Common Room suddenly filled up with people, all wearing, as were von Igelfeld and the other Fellows, black academic gowns. At a signal from the Master, the entire company then processed through a narrow, panelled corridor and into the Great Hall which lay beyond. There, standing at their tables in the body of the Hall, were the undergraduates, all similarly gowned and respectfully waiting for the Master and Fellows to take their seats at the High Table.

The Hall was a magnificent room, dominated at the far end by an immense portrait of a man in back velvet pantaloons and with a bird of prey of some sort, a falcon perhaps, perched on his arm. Behind him, an idealised landscape was framed by coats of arms.

'Our founder,' explained the Master to von Igelfeld. 'William de Courcey. A splendid man who gave half of his fortune for the foundation of the College. He was later beheaded. So sad. I suspect that he was very charming company, when he still had his head. But then life in those days was so uncertain. One moment you were in favour and then the next you were de trop. His head, apparently, is buried in the Fellows' Garden. I have no idea where, but there is a particularly luxuriant wisteria bush which is said to be very old and I suspect that it might be under that. Possibly best not to know for certain.'

'You might erect a small plaque if you found the spot,' suggested von Igelfeld, as they took their seats at the High Table.

'Good heavens no!' said the Master, apparently shocked at the notion. 'Can you imagine how the Fellows would fight over the wording? Can't you just picture it? It's the last thing we'd do.'

Von Igelfeld was silent. It was impossible to discuss anything with the Master, he had decided; any attempt he made at conversation merely led to further diatribes against the Fellowship and, eventually, to tears. He would have to restrict himself to completely innocuous matters in any exchanges with the Master: the weather, perhaps; the English loved to talk about the weather, he had heard.

The Master, as was proper, sat at the head of the table, while von Igelfeld, as senior guest, occupied the place which had been reserved for such guests since the days of Charles II – the fourth seat down on the right, counting from the second seat after the Master's. On his left, again by im-memorial custom, sat the Senior Tutor, and on his right, a small, bright-eyed man with an unruly mop of dark hair, Professor Prentice. On the other side of the table, directly opposite von Igelfeld, was Dr C. A. D. Wood, who was smiling broadly and who seemed to have quite got over their earlier conversation. She was flanked by Mr Wilkinson and by a person whom von Igelfeld realised he had seen before. But where? Had he met him in the Court, or had he seen him in the Library on his visit early that afternoon? He puzzled over this for a moment, and then the person in question moved his head slightly and von Igelfeld gained a better view of his features. It was the Porter.

Von Igelfeld drew in his breath. Was the Porter entitled to have dinner at High Table? Such a thing would never have happened in Germany. Herr Bomberg, who acted as concierge and general factotum at the Institute, always knocked three times before he came into the coffee room with a message and would never have dreamed of so much as sitting down, even if he were to be invited to do so. And yet here was the College Porter, breaking his bread roll onto his plate and engaging in earnest conversation with Dr C. A. D. Wood.

Von Igelfeld turned discreetly to the Senior Tutor. 'That person on Dr C. A. D. Wood's right,' he said. 'I have seen him somewhere before, I believe. Could you refresh my memory and tell me who he is?'

The Senior Tutor peered myopically over the table and then turned back to von Igelfeld. 'That's Dr Porter,' he said. 'A considerable historian. He works mainly on early Greek communities in the Levant. He wrote a wonderful book on the subject. Never read it myself, but I shall one day.'

'Dr Porter?' said von Igelfeld, aghast. It occurred to him that he had completely misread the situation and now, with a terrible pang of embarrassment, he remembered that he had tipped Dr Porter for showing him his rooms. The money had been courteously received, but, oh, what a solecism on his part.

'I thought he was *the* Porter,' said von Igelfeld weakly. 'He showed me to my room. I thought . . .'

'Oh, he does that from time to time,' said the Senior Tutor, laughing. 'It's his idea of a joke. He gets terribly bored with his Greek communities and he pretends to be the College Porter. He shows tourists round sometimes and gives the tips to the poorer undergraduates to spend on beer. He never pockets them himself.'

This explanation relieved von Igelfeld of his embarrassment, but embarrassment was now replaced by astonishment and a certain measure of alarm. The English were obviously every bit as eccentric as they were reputed to be, and this meant that further surprises were undoubtedly in store. He would have to be doubly vigilant if he were to avoid either humiliation or, what would be even worse, the commission of some resounding social mistake.

There was not a great deal of conversation over dinner itself. The Senior Tutor made the occasional remark, and von Igelfeld answered him, but this was hardly a conversational flow. Professor Prentice said a little bit more, but he confined himself to questions about German politicians, of whom von Igelfeld was largely ignorant. Then, shortly after the second course was served, he made a remark about the wine.

'Disgusting wine,' he said, sniffing ostentatiously at his glass. 'Ghastly stuff. You don't have to drink it if you don't want to, Professor von Igelfeld.'

The Senior Tutor pretended not to hear this remark, but it was clear to von Igelfeld that he had. He bit his lip, almost imperceptibly, and then raised his own glass.

'Carefully chosen wine, you know, von Igelfeld,' he said, mainly for the benefit of Professor Prentice. 'Not a wine that would be appreciated by the ignorant – quite the opposite, in fact. When I chose it – and I chose it personally, you know

– I had in mind the slightly more *tutored* palate. Not a wine for undergraduates or *ouvriers*, you know. More for people who know what they're talking about, although, good heavens, there are precious few of those around these days.'

Von Igelfeld looked down at his glass, at a loss what to do.

'I am looking forward to drinking it,' he said at last, judging this to be the most tactful remark in the circumstances.

So the dinner continued, until at last the time came to return to the upstairs common room for coffee and port. There, with the Fellows and guests all seated in a circle, in ladder-backed chairs, the Junior Fellow circulated the port and conversation was resumed.

'Another visitor arrives tomorrow,' announced the Senior Tutor cheerfully. 'Our annual lecture on opera – an open lecture funded by the late Count Augusta, an immensely rich Italian who owned a helicopter factory. He studied here briefly as a young man and he left us a great deal of money, which he stipulated should be spent on opera matters. We've had some wonderful treats in the past.'

'Who is it this year, Senior Tutor?' asked one of the junior dons.

'Mr Matthew Gurewitsch,' announced the Senior Tutor. 'He is a well-known opera writer from New York and I am told that he is a very entertaining lecturer. He will be with us for one week exactly and then he goes on to interview Menotti. We are very lucky to have him.'

Von Igelfeld nodded approvingly. He knew little about opera, but was keen to learn more. It was possible that Mr Gurewitsch would talk about Wagner, or even Humperdinck, both of whom von Igelfeld approved of. But there were dangers; what if he chose to speak of Henze? For a moment he closed his eyes; to have to attend a lecture on Henze would be intolerable, the musical equivalent of attending a lecture on Beuys and his piles of clothes or his wooden boxes.

'And his subject?' asked another junior don.

'*Il Trovatore*,' said the Senior Tutor.

Von Igelfeld relaxed. He would attend the lecture, and attend with pleasure. Perhaps there would be indirect references to Wagner and to Humperdinck; one never knew what a lecturer was going to say until he started; or, should one say, until he finished.

Von Igelfeld spent the following morning in the Library. He made the acquaintance of the Librarian, who was delighted that somebody was prepared to work on the Hughes-Davitt Bequest.

'So few people seem to *care* about the Renaissance today,' said the Librarian. 'And yet, had it not happened, where would we be today?'

Von Igelfeld thought for a moment. Historical speculation of this sort was unprofitable, he thought. There was little point in thinking about that soldier who had prevented the spear from plunging into Alexander the Great and who had thus saved Western civilisation. But if he had not done so, and the Persians had conquered the Greeks, then . . . He stopped himself. It was unthinkable the Institute itself might not have existed and yet it was quite possible, had history been rather different. Ultimately, we were all at the mercy of chance. All our schemes and enterprises were dependent on the merest whim of fate; as had been the outcome of that decisive naval battle when England defeated the Spanish Armada, but would not have done so had the wind come from a slightly different direction. In which case, the University of Cambridge itself would today be *La Universidad de Cambridge*, or *Pontecam*, to be precise.

At lunchtime he returned to his rooms. He saw Dr Hall making his way purposefully towards the Refectory, and he remembered the uncharitable remarks of Dr Porter about stout dons. It was true, however, the dons at this college were very stout. Professor Waterfield, for example, whom he had met earlier that morning when they both arrived at the door of their shared bathroom at more or less the same time, was very stout indeed. There would certainly not be room for both of them in that bathroom should there be a struggle to see who would enter first.

There was, of course, no such struggle. Von Igelfeld politely asked Professor Waterfield whether he would care to return in twenty minutes, when the bathroom would again be vacant, and Professor Waterfield, although slightly surprised by von Igelfeld's suggestion, had mildly acquiesced.

'I should not wish to stand between you and cleanliness,' he remarked cheerfully as he returned to his room, and von Igelfeld, appreciating the quiet humour of this aside, responded: *'Mens sana in corpore abluto.'* Professor Waterfield did not appear to hear, or, if he did, chose not to say anything, which was a pity, thought von Igelfeld, as it was an aphorism that deserved a response. Perhaps he would have the opportunity to use it again when he next met his neighbour at the bathroom door; one never knew.

Now, beginning his ascent to his room, where he proposed to take his customary lunchtime siesta, he found himself face-to-face with a man whom he did not recognise from the previous evening's dinner. This person was carrying a suitcase and von Igelfeld, glancing down at it, saw the initials MG painted discreetly above the handle. This, he concluded, must be Mr Matthew Gurewitsch. He had noticed that the guest room on the floor below his, a distinctly inferior guest room, he had been led to believe, had been allocated to Mr Gurewitsch, and a small name card had been attached to the door in recognition of this arrangement. Feeling more confident of his surroundings, after he had introduced himself to Mr Gurewitsch, von Igelfeld showed him to his room, which was unlocked.

'A comfortable room,' said von Igelfeld, noting with pleasure that the furniture was distinctly more worn than his own. 'No bathroom, I'm afraid. But then these old buildings don't take too well to modern plumbing.'

'No bathroom!' exclaimed Mr Gurewitsch. 'Even the crypt on the set of *Aida* has hot and cold running water these days!'

'Well, that is opera,' said von Igelfeld. 'This is Cambridge. And it seems that there's no bathroom.'

'But what do I do?' asked Mr Gurewitsch.

'There's a bathroom over on the other side of the Court,' said von Igelfeld. 'It's attached to the Senior Common Room. I think that you will have to use that one.'

'You don't have one upstairs?' asked Matthew Gurewitsch hopefully.

Von Igelfeld was silent for a moment. If he told this new visitor about the bathroom that he shared with Professor Waterfield, then that would mean that there would be three people sharing, rather than two. Two was bad enough, of course – look what had happened that morning – but if there were three people using the one bathroom, that would be even worse. It did not matter that Mr Matthew Gurewitsch appeared to be an extremely agreeable man, it was purely a question of practicality. The bathroom issue was a problem which the College should face, and it was not up to visitors like von Igelfeld to have to shoulder the responsibility of everyone's bathroom needs. No, that would be to expect too much. He had no *locus standi* in bathroom matters in Cambridge and there was no moral obligation on his part to draw the attention of others to the existence of such bathroom facilities as there were.

At the same time, it was clear to von Igelfeld that he could not tell a lie. The motto of the von Igelfeld family was *Truth Always*, and he could not ignore this. It was true that he had deviated from it in that unfortunate encounter with Dr Max Augustus Hubertoffel, the psycho-analyst, but he had dealt with the moral sequelae of that lapse in as honourable a way as he could. But the incident had reminded him of the need for strict truthfulness. So his words would have to be chosen carefully, and here they were, forming themselves with no particular effort on his part: 'I do not have a bathroom in my rooms,' he said.

Although quite spontaneous, the words were well chosen. It was indeed true that von Igelfeld did not have a bathroom in his room. There was a bathroom in the vicinity – on the landing to be precise – but this did not belong to von Igelfeld and therefore the precise terms of Matthew Gurewitsch's question did not require it to be disclosed. He felt sorry for Matthew Gurewitsch, and for the many others like him in Cambridge who presumably had no bathroom, and this prompted him to invite the new visitor to join him for coffee in the Senior Common Room.

'I could introduce you to some of the Fellows,' he said expansively. 'Dr C. A. D. Wood, Mr Wilkinson . . .' He tailed off. Perhaps it was not a good idea. Poor Matthew Gurewitsch, no doubt exhausted after his journey, would hardly wish to be plunged into the unfathomable intrigues of mathematicians. 'Or we could talk just by ourselves,' he added. 'That might be better.'

Matthew Gurewitsch was happy to do either, and after he had found a place for his suitcase on a rather rickety table near the window, he and von Igelfeld made their way across the Court towards the Senior Common Room. Their conversation as they walked was easy, and von Igelfeld felt delighted that he should have made the acquaintance of this interesting man before people like Hall, Dr C. A. D. Wood and the Senior Tutor could buttonhole him and effectively put him off Cambridge forever. Here was a man who really knew about his subject, and von Igelfeld revelled in the snippets of information – inside information – which studded his conversation. Had von Igelfeld seen the la Scala production of *Il Trovatore* last season? No? Well, did he know that the conductor had caused an uproar by playing the tenor's showstopper in the original key of C, rather than down half a step (*anglice*, tone) as is usually done so that tenors can more safely interpolate a climactic high note that Verdi never wrote? 'Of course,' Matthew Gurewitsch added, 'the inauthentic high note was omitted, too. That's what Italian musicologists call philology.'

Von Igelfeld expressed surprise, and remarked that in future one would have to watch that roles of counter-tenors were not taken down for the convenience of basses. Or even the Queen of the Night could be transcribed for *basso profondo*, thus removing all those troublesome moments for sopranos. Would that not make it easier? Matthew Gurewitsch had laughed.

'Everything is possible in opera these days,' he said. 'That is what I wish to talk about in my lecture. I want to look at what has happened to *Trovatore* recently. I want to issue a warning.'

'That is very wise,' said von Igelfeld. 'People must be warned.'

They entered the Senior Common Room to find six or seven dons sitting in the various chairs which dotted the room. Dr C. A. D. Wood was present, and waved in a friendly fashion to von Igelfeld, and Dr Hall, who had decided against lunch in the refectory in favour of Stilton and biscuits in the Common Room, was sitting at a small table by himself, lost in quiet contentment.

Von Igelfeld took Matthew Gurewitsch over to Dr C. A. D. Wood and introduced them. She, in turn, made introductions to a rather mild-looking man who was sitting beside her, but who had stood up when the guests came to join them.

'This is Dr Plank,' she said.

Plank shook hands with von Igelfeld and then with Matthew Gurewitsch.

'I should warn you that you will not find Dr Plank's name in any college lists should you try to look for it,' remarked Dr C. A. D. Wood. 'And that is not because he is not a member of the College.'

This Delphic remark caused von Igelfeld to turn and

look at Dr Plank, who had now sat down and had folded his hands over his stomach in a relaxed way. If this man were in disgrace of some sort, and had been excluded from the lists, then it did not appear to distress him. This was very strange, and there was something in Dr C. A. D. Wood's voice, an edge perhaps, which gave von Igelfeld the impression that she did not like Plank and was only sitting next to him on sufferance.

For a few moments, nothing was said. Matthew Gurewitsch glanced at Plank and then at von Igelfeld. Then he looked at Dr C. A. D. Wood. Dr C. A. D. Wood looked at Matthew Gurewitsch, and then at von Igelfeld. She did not look at Plank. Plank looked down at his shoes, and then across the room at Dr Hall, who looked back at him for a moment and then transferred his gaze to his Stilton.

Then Plank spoke. 'The reason why there's no Plank in the lists is not because there's no Plank – there is – but because Plank is not spelled Plank. That is why.'

Von Igelfeld looked puzzled. This was another English idiosyncrasy. How many ways were there of spelling Plank? Planc? Planque?

Plank appeared to be enjoying the guests' confusion. 'You may be aware,' he said, 'that there are various English surnames which are spelled and pronounced in quite different ways. One of the best-known examples is Featherstonehaugh, which is pronounced Fanshawe. Then there is Cholmondley, which is simply pronounced Chumley, and of course anybody called Beauchamp is usually Beecham.'

Von Igelfeld nodded. 'I have noticed that,' he said. 'There was a Professor Chumley at a conference once and he pointed out that the spelling of his name was rather different. That would not happen in Germany.'

'No,' said Plank. 'I gather that German is spelled as you pronounce it. Curious, but there we are.'

'So how do you spell Plank?' asked Matthew Gurewitsch.

'Haughland,' said Plank.

Von Igelfeld could not conceal his astonishment. 'Haughland?'

'Indeed,' said Haughland (*voce*, Plank). 'It's an old family from the eastern fens somewhere. Virtually in the water.'

'But your humour remained dry,' observed Matthew Gurewitsch.

This remark brought silence, which was only broken when Dr C. A. D. Wood rose to her feet to leave.

'I have to go, Plank,' she said curtly. And then, more genially: 'Good afternoon, Professor von Igelfeld. Good afternoon, Mr Gurewitsch. I look forward to seeing you at dinner.'

That afternoon, von Igelfeld spent several very rewarding hours with the Hughes-Davitt Bequest before returning to his rooms to write a letter to Prinzel.

'This is an extraordinary place,' he wrote. 'Nothing is as it seems. However, I am immensely pleased with the Library and with the Hughes-Davitt Bequest, which has some first-rate material, wasted in this country, if you ask me; it would be far better looked after in Germany. However, at least I can put it into some sort of order and I shall eventually publish a paper on it. So my time here will be well spent.

'However, there is the issue of my colleagues. So far I have not met one, not one, who would survive in a proper German academic institution, apart from the other visitor at the moment, Mr Matthew Gurewitsch from New York.

He is very well informed and has a fund of information about operatic matters. I fear that he may not be properly appreciated here, but we shall see what sort of response he gets to his lecture at the beginning of next week. Poor man! The mathematicians and the like who live in the College are unlikely to understand what he has to say; for the most part their minds are taken up with mathematical disputes and with plotting against one another. This has made the Master a nervous wreck, and indeed he is close to tears most of the time.

'How I long to be back in Germany, where everything is so solid and dependable. How I long to be back in the Institute common room, exchanging views with my colleagues. I am even missing Unterholzer, although I cannot quite bring myself to write to him yet. Perhaps next week. Please make sure, by the way, that he does not try to take my room while I am away. I know that he would like to do this, as he has done it in the past. I am counting on you to see that it does not happen.

'In this pallid land, then, I remain, Your friend eternally, Moritz-Maria von Igelfeld.'

He posted the letter in the College post-box, and then, it being a pleasant evening, he went for a stroll through the Fellows' Garden and out along the river. The Fellows' Garden was peaceful, in a way that only an English garden can be peaceful, and even the thought of de Courcey's detached skull did not disturb the feeling of *rus in urbe* which the garden encouraged. He found the giant wisteria bush which the Master had mentioned, and he found, too, a magnificent fuchsia hedge which ran along the southern boundary of the garden. There were benches, too, carved stone benches on which weary Fellows might sit and enjoy the flowers and shrubs, and it was on one of these that von Igelfeld was seated when he heard footsteps on the gravel behind him. He turned round, jolted out of a pleasant reverie in which he was back in Italy, in Tuscany, with the smell of lavender and rosemary on the breeze. Dr C. A. D. Wood and Dr Hall were bearing down upon him along the small path that cut through the lavender beds.

'Ah, there you are Professor von Igelfeld,' said Dr C. A. D. Wood. 'Hall and I were hoping to find you. Dr Porter said that he had seen you through his binoculars –

he likes to watch the garden, you know. Nothing better to do, I suppose.'

The two Fellows joined him on his bench. As they sat down, the bench tilted slightly in the direction of Dr Hall, and von Igelfeld had to move over quickly towards Dr C. A. D. Wood in order to stop the entire party being tipped over.

'You have a beautiful garden,' said von Igelfeld conversationally.

'Yes,' said Dr Hall. 'And I find it best at this time of year – very early autumn, even if the colour is diminishing somewhat.'

'It's a good place to talk,' said Dr C. A. D. Wood. 'There's no chance of the Master interrupting one's conversation. He suffers from hay fever, and so this is the place where we go when we need to talk about anything important.'

'I would not wish to prevent you,' said von Igelfeld, beginning to rise to his feet.

Dr C. A. D. Wood pulled him back onto the bench. 'No,' she said. 'Please don't go. We actually wanted to talk to you, didn't we, Hall?'

Dr Hall nodded. 'That's why we came out here. We wanted to have a quiet word with you.'

Von Igelfeld said nothing. Was this the plotting which the Master had warned him about?

'It's about the Augusta lecture,' said Dr C. A. D. Wood. 'The opera lecture.'

'I am looking forward to it immensely,' said von Igelfeld. 'Mr Matthew Gurewitsch has some very interesting ideas. I suspect that he will be controversial.'

'Oh yes,' said Dr C. A. D. Wood quickly. 'He was a

313

good choice. That's why I hope that he has the chance to deliver his lecture.'

Von Igelfeld was confused. Why should there be any question about that? Mr Matthew Gurewitsch had arrived safely from New York and was all prepared to deliver the lecture, which he had already discussed with von Igelfeld. He could not see why any difficulties should arise.

Sensing his confusion, Dr C. A. D. Wood continued. 'The problem is that there are those who are keen to stop the lecture from taking place. There are those who are implacably opposed to opera on ideological grounds. They want the lecture to be more socially relevant. They want to use the money so kindly left by Count Augusta to be used for the advancement of knowledge in a quite different sphere – agricultural economics, for example. They seem to object in some way to the fact that the money was made from a helicopter factory near Bologna.'

She paused, watching von Igelfeld for his reaction.

'But that's outrageous,' burst out von Igelfeld. 'What possible difference does it make that Count Augusta had a helicopter factory? That is quite irrelevant, I would have thought.'

Dr Hall nodded vigorously. 'Somebody has to make helicopters,' he pointed out.

'Exactly,' said von Igelfeld. 'But quite apart from that, their objection disturbs the settled intention of Count Augusta, who surely had the right to decide what his money should be used for. That is a point of principle.'

'Principle,' echoed Dr Hall, tapping the edge of the stone bench with a slightly fleshy finger.

'It would also be discourteous, to say the least,'

continued von Igelfeld, 'for the invitation to Mr Matthew Gurewitsch to be withdrawn at this late stage, or indeed at any stage, once it had been issued.'

'Our thoughts precisely,' said Dr Hall unctuously, smoothing his hair as he did so. 'It's quite unacceptable behaviour, in our view.'

'But who can be behind it?' asked von Igelfeld. 'Who could possibly dream up something so base?'

'Plank,' said Dr C. A. D. Wood in a quiet voice.

'Haughland (Plank),' said Dr Hall. 'Haughland is Chairman of the Fellows' Committee. It's a very influential position, and if the Fellows' Committee decides to cancel Mr Matthew Gurewitsch's lecture, then there's nothing anybody can do about it.'

'But surely the Committee would never agree to that,' protested von Igelfeld. 'There must be other members who would vote against such a suggestion.'

Dr Hall nodded his agreement. 'Yes, there are other members, but they are weak. The Master, for instance, is on the Committee, but he always votes with Plank because Plank is in a position to blackmail him over something or other which happened years ago. So he would never stand up to him. Then there's Dr Porter, who lives in a world of his own imagination and who simply can't be predicted, either way. And Dr McGrew, who owes Plank money, and so on. So you see that even if the majority of the Fellows are against Plank, he happens to control that Committee.'

Von Igelfeld's face darkened as this perfidious story was unravelled. Such events would never have happened in Germany, but now nothing in England would surprise him. He was appalled at the prospect of Matthew Gurewitsch's invitation being withdrawn, and he blushed for the shame-lessness of his new colleagues. Although he was only a visiting professor, he felt that he would be tarnished to be associated with an institution that could behave in such a way. And yet what could he do?

'Something can be done, of course,' said Dr C. A. D. Wood. 'We could call an extraordinary meeting of the Fellowship and elect a new committee, replacing Haughland with somebody else. Perhaps myself even. I would be prepared, if pressed. For the sake of the College, of course.'

'But we would need every vote we could get,' inter-jected Hall. 'It would be that close. And I must say that, if similarly pressed, I would be prepared to take over responsibility for the College cellars. Nobody could argue that the Senior Tutor has done a decent job, even though he spends half his time in Bordeaux.'

'But we don't want to press you,' said Dr C. A. D. Wood. 'We just thought that we would mention the whole thing to you so that you would not be too disappointed if Mr Matthew Gurewitsch's lecture were to be cancelled. You obviously got on well with him. We saw you deep in conversation. We knew you'd be appalled to hear what Plank was up to.'

'I am,' said von Igelfeld. 'I am completely appalled. I can assure you that I shall vote in the way you suggest.'

'That's very good,' said Dr C. A. D. Wood, rising briskly from the bench. Dr Hall rose too, thus avoiding imbalance.

'The meeting will be tomorrow,' said Dr Hall. 'By our calculation, your vote clinches the matter. If you had said no, then it would have been an exact tie. That would have required the Master to exercise a casting vote, and that would have gone to Plank, because of the blackmail factor.'

'I am very glad you confided in me,' said von Igelfeld. 'It seems that I shall be able to help avert a dreadful situation.'

'Absolutely,' said Dr C. A. D. Wood. 'And here's another thing. Once we have the new Committee in place, we could put you in the Senior Tutor's quarters for the rest of your stay. He can move to his old rooms, near the kitchen. I wouldn't need the Senior Tutor's rooms myself, as I have perfectly good rooms of my own. But that would mean that you would be very comfortable up there, with your own bathroom.'

Von Igelfeld smiled with pleasure. 'And then perhaps Mr Matthew Gurewitsch could have my current rooms and consequently more immediate access to that shared bathroom.'

'That would be perfectly feasible,' said Dr Hall. 'All of this will become possible once we get rid of Plank.'

That evening there was a College Feast, it being the anniversary of the beheading of the Founder. Von Igelfeld found this information unsettling, as he had spent much of his time in the Fellows' Garden, prior to the arrival of Drs C. A. D. Wood and Hall, reflecting on the melancholy fate of William de Courcey and on the question of his head's current location. He had reached no conclusions on the matter, other than that mankind's moral progress was slow, and intermittent. People still lost their heads, here and there in the world, but not, thank God, in Western Europe any longer. That was no solution to the troubles of the rest of the world, which were enough, when one contemplated them, to make one weep, just as the Master wept. Perhaps the College was a microcosm of the world at large, and when the Master burst into tears of despair he was weeping for the whole world. That was possible, but the analogy would require a great deal of further thought and for the moment there was the smell of the lavender and the delicate branches of the wisteria.

Von Igelfeld was pleased to discover that at the Feast he was placed just two seats away from Mr Matthew Gurewitsch, and was able to join in the conversation that the opera writer was having with Mr Max Wilkinson, who had been seated between them. Mr Wilkinson, although a mere mathematician, proved to have a lively interest in opera and a knowledge that matched this interest. He quizzed Matthew Gurewitsch on the forthcoming production of the Ring Cycle, in miniature, at Glyndebourne, and Mr Gurewitsch expressed grave concern about miniaturisation of Wagner, a concern which von Igelfeld strongly endorsed.

'You have to be careful,' said Matthew Gurewitsch. 'You reduce the Rhine to a birdbath, and is there room, realistically speaking, for the Rhine Maidens, if that happens?'

'Exactly,' said von Igelfeld. 'And Valhalla too. What becomes of Valhalla?'

'It could become a sort of dentist's waiting room,' said Matthew Gurewitsch. 'No, you may laugh, but I have seen that happen. I saw a production once which made Valhalla just that. I shall spare the producer's blushes by not telling you who he was. But can you imagine it?'

'Why would the gods choose to live in a dentist's waiting room?' asked von Igelfeld.

There was a sudden silence at the table. This question had been asked during a lull in the conversation in other quarters, and it echoed loudly through the Great Hall. Even the undergraduates heard it, and paused, forks and spoons halfway to their mouths. Then, with no satisfactory answer forthcoming from the general company, the general hubbub of conversation resumed. Von Igelfeld noticed, however, that Dr C. A. D. Wood had shot a glance at Dr Hall, who had made a sign of some sort to her.

'They wouldn't,' said Matthew Gurewitsch, looking up at the intricate, hammer-beam ceiling. 'It's the desire for novel effect. But there should be limits.' He paused, before adding: 'There are other objections to miniaturisation. The size of some singers, for example.'

'They cannot be made any smaller,' observed Mr Wilkinson.

'No,' said Matthew Gurewitsch. 'And there are always problems with size in opera. Mimi, for example, is rarely small and delicate. She is often sung by a lady who is very large and who, quite frankly, *simply doesn't look consumptive*. But at least we can suspend disbelief in such cases – within the conventions. But we should not create new challenges to our disbelief.'

'Absolutely not,' said von Igelfeld.

The conversation continued in this pleasant vein. Matthew Gurewitsch alluded to the interferences with *Trovatore*, which he intended to expose in his lecture.

'Satires of *Trovatore* merely scratch the surface,' he said, 'leaving its mythic core untouched.'

'I would agree,' said von Igelfeld.

Matthew Gurewitsch smiled. 'Thank you. *Il Trovatore* is to opera nothing less than what *Oedipus Rex* is to spoken drama: the revelation of the soul of tragedy in its purest form. In both, ancient secrets unravel, devastating the innocent along with the guilty. But then, who is innocent?'

Von Igelfeld looked down the table towards Plank, who was sitting next to a woman who had been at dinner the previous evening, but to whom von Igelfeld had not been introduced. She was engaged in conversation with Plank, and had laid a hand briefly on his forearm, only to remove it almost immediately. Plank was smiling, and for a moment von Igelfeld was filled with a form of pure moral horror. How could he sit there, in full dissemblance, at the same table as the proposed victim of his plot? No Florentine painter could have captured the essence of Judas's table manners more clearly than flesh and blood that evening portrayed them in the form of Dr Plank, or so von Igelfeld reflected.

Matthew Gurewitsch, unaware of the peril which faced him, continued. 'In the tragic no-man's land between reason and unreason, the great crime is to have been born, would you not agree?'

'Yes,' said von Igelfeld. 'I would.'

'At that, a man may go to the grave never having known who he is,' continued Matthew Gurewitsch. 'Which is almost – almost, but not quite – what happened to Oedipus.'

There was more to be said on this subject, and it was said that evening. There were toasts as well, one to the Master – proposed by the Senior Tutor, who modestly praised the wine, his choice, before glasses were raised – and one to the Memory of the Founder. The Master then rose to give a short address.

'Dear guests of the College,' he began, 'dear Fellows, dear undergraduate members of this Foundation: William de Courcey was cruelly beheaded by those who could not understand that it is quite permissible for rational men to differ on important points of belief or doctrine. The world in which he lived had yet to develop those qualities of tolerance of difference of opinion which we take for granted, but which we must remind ourselves is of rather recent creation and is by no means assured of universal support. There are amongst us still those who would deny to others the right to hold a different understanding of the fundamental issues of our time. Thus, if we look about us, we see dogma still in conflict with rival dogma; we see people of one culture or belief still at odds with their human neighbours who are of a different culture or belief; and we see many who are prepared to act upon this difference to the extent of denying the humanity of those with whom they differ. They are prepared to kill them, and innocent others in the process, in order to strike at those whom they perceive to be their enemies, even if these so-called enemies are, like them, simple human beings, with families that love them, and with hopes and fears about their own individual futures.

'How might William de Courcey, by some thought experiment visiting the world today, recognise those self-same conflicts and sorrows which marred his own world and made it such a dangerous and, ultimately for him, such a fatal place? He would, I suspect, say that much has remained the same; that even if we have put some of the agents of division and intolerance to flight, there is still much evidence of their work among us.

'Here in this place of learning, let us remind ourselves of the possibility of combating, in whatever small way we can, those divisions that come between man and man, between woman and woman, so that we may recognise in each other that vulnerable humanity that informs our lives, and makes life so precious; so that each may find happiness in his or her life, and in the lives of others. For what else is there for us to hope for? What else, I ask you, what else?'

The Master sat down, and there was a complete silence. Nobody spoke, nor coughed nor murmured, nor otherwise disturbed the quiet which had fallen upon the room. At the end of the Hall, the portrait of William de Courcey was illuminated by the light of the many candles which had been placed upon the tables. His expression, fixed in oils, was a calm one, and his gaze went out, out beyond the High Table, and into that darkness that was both real, and metaphorical.

After a few minutes of silence, the Master rose to his feet, to lead the procession out of the Hall. Von Igelfeld noticed that there had been tears in his eyes, but that he had now wiped them away. They processed, still in silence, although now there was the sound of the scraping of chair legs on stone as the undergraduates rose to their feet to mark the departure of the High Table party. They too had been moved by the Master's words, and there were hearts there that had changed, and would never be the same again. In the Senior Common Room, the Fellows moved to their accustomed seats, around the flickering of the great log fire which de Courcey's will had stipulated should always be provided 'to warm the hearts of the Fellows and the poor scholars of the Foundation'. The poor scholars were excluded, of course, but the other part of the imprecation had been honoured.

Von Igelfeld found himself seated next to Dr C. A. D. Wood, who had Dr Hall at her other side. Plank was placed next to Matthew Gurewitsch and the Senior Tutor.

Sipping at his coffee, von Igelfeld glanced at Dr C. A. D.

Wood. She had no coffee cup in her hand, and was staring down at the floor, as if trying to read some message in the carpet. After a moment or two, she turned to Dr Hall, who had been staring miserably at the ceiling.

'I cannot proceed,' said Dr C. A. D. Wood suddenly, turning to von Igelfeld as she spoke. 'After those words of the Master's, I cannot continue with our plan. I am grievously sorry, Professor von Igelfeld. I misled you this afternoon. What I said about Plank was not true. There was no plan to cancel Mr Gurewitsch's lecture. He would never have done that. He is a good man, and I have been seduced, yes seduced, by my personal ambition, into misrepresenting his intentions. I can only ask your forgiveness.'

Von Igelfeld listened intently to this confession. He, too, had been greatly affected by the Master's address, but it had never occurred to him that Dr C. A. D. Wood and Dr Hall would have been the centre of such a perfidious plot.

Dr Hall now spoke, turning to von Igelfeld and fixing him with a mournful stare. 'What she says is correct,' he said. 'We have behaved very badly. Along with others, who I hope are feeling just as bad as we are. I am only sorry that it has taken a Road to Damascus to reveal to us just how wicked we have been.'

Von Igelfeld reached forward and placed his coffee cup on the table before him. 'And I have behaved badly too,' he said. 'I too have been obliged to consider my own actions.'

'Oh?' said Dr C. A. D. Wood. 'What did you do? Was it something to do with Plank?'

'No,' said von Igelfeld. 'But it was to do with Mr Gurewitsch too.' He paused, plucking up his courage. 'I told him that there was no bathroom on our stair. I told

323

him that he would have to cross the Court. And that was all because I didn't want another person sharing the bathroom with Professor Waterfield and myself. I did not actually lie, but I as good as lied.'

Dr Hall shook his head. 'That's the problem with these old buildings,' he said. 'There just aren't enough bathrooms.'

'Well, that may be so,' said von Igelfeld. 'But it doesn't excuse my action. I shall have to tell him immediately after coffee.'

'And we shall tell the others that there will be no emergency meeting called tomorrow,' said Dr C. A. D. Wood. 'And I shall say something decent to Plank.'

'Absolutely,' said Dr Hall. 'I propose to go straight over to him, right now, and tell him that I think that he's doing a very good job as Chairman of the Council.'

'That will please him,' said Dr C. A. D. Wood. 'Nobody's ever said anything like that to him before. Poor Haughland (*voce*, Plank).'

At the end of coffee, as the Fellows broke up for the evening, von Igelfeld made his way over to join Matthew Gurewitsch, who was examining one of the College portraits, a picture of a former Master, who had been beheaded under Cromwell.

'Mr Gurewitsch,' said von Igelfeld. 'I owe you an apology. I omitted to tell you that there was a bathroom at the top of the stairs and that you could use it.'

It was not an easy confession for von Igelfeld to make, but at least it was quick in the making.

'Oh that,' said Matthew Gurewitsch. 'Yes, don't worry.

I found it. I've been using it all along. Do you use it as well?' he paused. 'In fact, I must confess I've been feeling rather guilty about it. I wondered if I should be telling others about it.'

Von Igelfeld laughed. 'That makes it easier for me,' he said.

They walked across the Court together. The atmosphere in the College seemed lighter now, as if a cloud of some sort had been dispelled.

'You know,' said von Igelfeld. 'Walking in these marvellous surroundings puts one in mind of opera, does it not? This setting. These ancient buildings.'

'It certainly does,' said Matthew Gurewitsch. 'Perhaps I shall write a libretto about a Cambridge college. In fact, I seem quite inspired. The ideas are coming to me already.'

'Would it be possible for me to be in it?' asked von Igelfeld. 'I would not want a large role, but if it were just possible for . . .'

'Of course,' said Mathew Gurewitsch. 'And it will be a fine role too. Positively heroic.'

Von Igelfeld said nothing. The Master had been right; the world was a distressing place, but there were places of light within it, not tiny particles of light like the quarks and bosons which the physicists chased after, but great bursts of light, like healing suns.

At the Villa of
Reduced Circumstances

On his return from sabbatical in Cambridge – a period of considerable achievement in his scholarly career – Professor Dr Moritz-Maria von Igelfeld, author of that most exhaustive work of Romance philology, *Portuguese Irregular Verbs*, lost no time in resuming his duties at the Institute. Although von Igelfeld was delighted to be back in Germany, he had enjoyed Cambridge, especially after the Master's address had so effectively stopped all that divisive plotting. Mr Matthew Gurewitsch's lecture had been well attended and well received, with several Fellows describing it as the most brilliant exposition of an issue which they had heard for many years. Von Igelfeld had taken copious notes, and had later raised several points about the interpretation of *Il Trovatore* with Mr Matthew Gurewitsch, all of which had been satisfactorily answered. In the weeks that followed, he had struck up a number of close friendships, not only with those repentant schemers, Dr C. A. D. Wood and Dr Gervaise Hall, but also with their intended victim, Dr Plank.

Plank revealed himself to be both an agreeable man and a conscientious and competent Chairman of the College Committee. He invited von Igelfeld to tea in his rooms on several occasions, and even took him back to his house, to meet his wife, the well-known potter, Hermione Plank-Harwood. Professor Waterfield, too, proved to be a generous host, taking von Igelfeld for lunch at his London club, the Savile. Von Igelfeld was intrigued by this club, which appeared to have no purpose, as far as he could ascertain, and which could not be explained in any satisfactory terms by Professor Waterfield. Von Igelfeld asked him why he belonged, and Professor Waterfield simply shrugged. 'Because it's there, my dear chap,' he said lightly. 'Same reason as Mallory tried to climb Everest. Because it was there. And I wonder whether Sherpa Tensing climbed it because *Hillary* was there?'

'I find that impossible to answer,' said von Igelfeld. 'And the initial proposition is in every sense unconvincing. You don't climb mountains just because they're there.'

'I agree with you,' said Professor Waterfield. 'But that's exactly what Mallory said about Everest. *Ipse dixit*. I would never climb a mountain myself, whether or not it was there. Although I might be more tempted to climb one that wasn't there, if you see what I mean.'

'No,' said von Igelfeld. 'I do not. And I cannot imagine why one would join a club just because it is there. The club must do something.'

'Not necessarily,' said Professor Waterfield. 'And actually, old chap, would you mind terribly if we brought this line of conversation to a close? It's just that one of the rules of this place' – this was at lunch in the Savile – 'one of the rules is that you aren't allowed to discuss the club's *raison d'être* in the club itself. Curious rule, but there we are. Perhaps it's because it unsettles the members. London, by the way, is full of clubs that have no real reason to exist. Some more so than others. I've never been able to work out why Brooks's exists, quite frankly, and then there's the Athenaeum, which is for bishops and intellectual poseurs. I suppose they have to go somewhere. But that's hardly a reason to establish a club for them.'

Von Igelfeld was silent. There were aspects of England that he would never understand, and this, it seemed, was one of them. Perhaps the key was to consider it a tribal society and to understand it as would an anthropologist. In fact, the more he thought of that, the more apt the explanation became, and later, when he put it to Professor Waterfield himself, the Professor nodded enthusiastically.

'But of course that's the right way to look at this country,' he said. 'They should send anthropologists from New Guinea to live amongst us. They could then write their Harvard PhDs on places like this club, and the university too.' He paused. 'Could the same not be said of Germany?'

'Of course not,' said von Igelfeld sharply; the idea was absurd. Germany was an entirely rational society, and the suggestion that it might be analysed in anthropological terms was hardly a serious one. It was typical of Professor Waterfield's conversation, he thought, which in his view was a loosely held-together stream of non sequiturs and unsupported assertions. That's what came of being Anglo-Saxon, he assumed, instead of being German; the *Weltanschauung* of the former was, quite simply, wrong.

He arrived back in Germany on a Sunday afternoon, which gave him time to attend to one or two matters before getting back to work on the Monday morning. There was a long letter from Zimmermann which had to be answered – that was a priority – and von Igelfeld wrote a full reply that Sunday evening. Zimmermann was anxious to hear about Cambridge, and to get news of some of the friends whom he had made during his year there. How was Haughland (Plank)? Had Dr Mauve finished writing his riposte to the review article which Nenee-Franck had so unwisely published in the *Revue Comparative de Grammaire Contemporaine* the year before last? He should not leave it too late, said Zimmermann: false interpretations can enter the canon if not dealt with in a timely fashion, and then they could prove almost impossible to uproot. And what about the Hughes-Davitt Bequest? What were von Igelfeld's preliminary conclusions, and would they appear reasonably soon in the *Zeitschrift*? Von Igelfeld went through each of these queries carefully, and was able to give Zimmermann much of the information he sought.

He made an early start in the Institute the next morning, arriving even before the Librarian, who was usually the first to come in, well in advance of anybody else. The Librarian greeted him with warmth.

'Professor von Igelfeld!' he exclaimed. 'It is so wonderful to have you back. Do you know, only yesterday, my aunt asked after you! You will recall that some months before you went to Cambridge you had asked me to pass on to her your best regards. I did that, immediately, the very next time that I went to the nursing home. She was very touched that you had remembered her and she was very concerned when she heard that you had to go off to Cambridge. She said that she was worried that you would not be well looked after there, but I assured her that there was no danger of this. It's odd, isn't it, how that generation worries about things like that? You and I would have no hesitation about leaving Germany for foreign parts, but they don't like it. It's something to do with insecurity. I think that my aunt feels a certain degree of insecurity because she . . .'

'Yes, yes, Herr Huber,' von Igelfeld had interrupted. 'That is very true. Now, I was wondering whether anything of note had happened in the Institute during my absence.'

The Librarian looked thoughtful. 'It depends on what you mean by the expression "of note". If "of note" means "unusual", then the answer, I fear, is no. Nothing unusual has happened – in the strict sense of the word. If, however, "of note" is synonymous with "of importance", which is the meaning which I, speaking entirely personally, would be inclined to attribute to it, in the main, then one might conceivably come up with a different answer. Yes, that would probably be the case, although I could never really say *ex Germania semper aliquid novi*, if you will allow the little joke . . .'

'Very amusing,' said von Igelfeld quickly. 'Except for the fact that one should say *e Germania*, the *ex* form, as you know, being appropriate before a vowel, hence, *ex Africa* in the original. Be that as it may, certainly far more amusing than anything I heard in Cambridge. I'm afraid it's true, you know, that the British don't have a sense of humour.'

'I've heard that said,' agreed the Librarian. 'Very humourless people.'

'But if I may return to the situation here,' pressed von Igelfeld. '*Ex institutione aliquid novi?*'

The Librarian smiled. He knew exactly what von Igelfeld would be interested in, which would be whether anybody had requested a copy of *Portuguese Irregular Verbs* in his absence. Normally, the answer to this would be a disappointing negative, but this time there was better news to impart, and the Librarian was relishing the prospect of revealing it.

But he did not want to do it too quickly; with skilful manipulation of von Igelfeld's questions, he might be able to keep the information until coffee, when he could reveal it in the presence of everybody. They were always cutting him short when he had something interesting to say; well, if they tried that today, then they would have to do so in the face of very evident and strong interest on the part of von Igelfeld.

Oh yes, the world is unjust, thought the Librarian. They – Prinzel, Unterholzer, and von Igelfeld (Zimmermann, too, come to think of it) – had all the fun. They went off to conferences and meetings all over the place and he had to stay behind in the Library, all day, every day. All he had to look forward to each evening was the visit to the nursing home and the short chat with the nurses and with his aunt. It was always a pleasure to talk to his aunt, of course, who was so well informed and took such an interest in everything, but afterwards he had to go back to his empty apartment and have his dinner all by himself. He had been married, and happily so, he had imagined, until one day his wife walked out on him with absolutely no notice. She had met a man who rode a motorcycle on a Wall of Death at a funfair, and she had decided that she preferred him to the Librarian. He had tracked her down to a site outside Frankfurt – the sort of wasteland which funfairs like to occupy – and he had had a brief and impassioned conversation with her outside the Wall of Death while her motorcyclist lover raced round and round inside. He had implored her to come back, but his words were lost in the roar of the motorcycle engine and in the rattling of the brightly painted wooden planks that made up the outside of the Wall of Death.

Such was the Librarian's life. But at least von Igelfeld

was kind to him, and it would give him very great pleasure to tell him, when the moment was right, that a copy of *Portuguese Irregular Verbs* had been requested, and despatched, to none other than Señor Gabriel Marcales de Cinco Fermentaciones, cultural attaché at the Colombian Embassy. This was remarkable news, and although he could not say with certainty what it implied, it undoubtedly had interesting possibilities.

'Yes,' he said to von Igelfeld. 'I believe that there is something which will interest you. I shall obtain the details – I do not have them on me right now – and I shall tell you about it over coffee.'

During the hours before coffee, von Igelfeld busied himself in his room, going through the circulars and other correspondence that his secretary had not deemed sufficiently weighty to send on to Cambridge. Most of this was completely unimportant and required no response, but there were one or two matters which needed to be addressed. There was a request from a student in Berlin that he be allowed to work in the Institute for a couple of months over summer. Von Igelfeld was dubious; students had a way of creating a great deal of extra work and were, in general, the bane of a professor's life. That was why so few German professors saw any students; it was regrettable, but necessary if one's time was to be protected from unacceptable encroachments. On the other hand, this young man could be useful, and could, in the fullness of time, become an assistant. So von Igelfeld wrote a guarded reply, inviting the student for an interview. That task performed, he set himself to a far more important piece of business, which was to discover evidence of Unterholzer having been in his room during his absence.

Von Igelfeld knew that Unterholzer could be cunning, particularly when it came to issues of rooms and chairs. He would not have done anything so unwise as to have left a sign on the door with his name on it; nor would he have moved any of the furniture. Of course one could check the position of the chairs and possibly find that one or two had been shifted very slightly from their original position, but this was not proof of any significance, as the cleaners often moved things when they were cleaning the room. There were other potential clues: the number of paper clips in the paper container was a possibility, but then again Unterholzer would have been aware of this and would have made sure that he had replaced any such items.

Von Igelfeld looked closely at the large square of framed blotting paper on his desk. This was the surface on which he normally wrote, and if Unterholzer had done the same, then one might expect to find evidence in the form of the inked impression of Unterholzer's script. He picked up the blotter and examined it carefully. He had not had the fore-sight to insert a fresh sheet of paper before he left, and the existing sheet had numerous markings of his own. It was difficult to make out what was what, as everything was reversed. Von Igelfeld paused. If one held the blotter up to a mirror, then the ink marks would be reversed and everything would be easily readable.

He made his way quickly to the men's washroom, where there was a large mirror above a row of hand-basins. Switching on the light in the darkened room, he held the blotter up to the mirror and began to study it. There was his signature, or part of it, in the characteristic black ink which he used: M . . . M . . . von Ige . f . . d. And there was half a line of a letter which he recalled writing to Zimmermann almost six months ago. That was all legitimate, as were most of the other markings; most, but not all: what was this? It was clearly not in his handwriting and, if he was not mistaken, it was Unterholzer's well-known sprawling script. Moreover, and this suggested that no further proof would be needed, the blotting was in green ink, which was the colour which Unterholzer, and nobody else in the Institute, used.

'I have my proof,' muttered von Igelfeld under his breath. 'The sheer effrontery of it!'

It was at this point that the Librarian entered the washroom. He stood in the doorway, momentarily taken aback at the sight of von Igelfeld holding the blotter up to the mirror.

'Professor von Igelfeld!' he exclaimed. 'May I help you in some way?'

Confused and embarrassed, von Igelfeld rapidly dropped the blotter to his side. 'I have been looking at this blotter in the mirror,' he said.

'So I see,' said the Librarian.

For a few moments nothing further was said. Then von Igelfeld continued: 'I am in the habit of making notes to myself – memoranda, you understand – and I have unfortunately lost one. I am searching for some trace of it.'

'Ah!' said the Librarian. 'I understand. It must be very frustrating. And it would appear that poor Professor Dr Unterholzer must suffer from the very same difficulty. A few months ago I came across him in here doing exactly this, reading a blotter in the mirror!'

Von Igelfeld stared at the Librarian. This was information of the very greatest significance.

'This blotter?' he asked. 'Reading this very blotter?'

The Librarian glanced at the blotter which von Igelfeld now held out before him. 'I can't say whether it was that one exactly. But certainly something similar.'

Von Igelfeld narrowed his eyes. This made the situation even more serious; not only had Unterholzer used his room in his absence, but he had tried to read what he, the unwilling host, had written. This was an intolerable intrusion, and he would have to confront Unterholzer and ask him why he saw fit to pry into the correspondence of others. Of course Unterholzer would deny it, but he would know that von Igelfeld knew, and that would surely deprive him of any pleasure he had obtained from poking his nose into von Igelfeld's affairs.

Von Igelfeld returned to his room in a state of some indignation. He replaced the blotter on his desk and looked carefully around his room. What would be required now was a thorough search, just in case there was any other evidence of Unterholzer's presence. One never knew; if he had been so indiscreet as to read the blotter in the washroom, knowing that anybody might walk in on him, then he may well have left some other piece of damning evidence.

Von Igelfeld examined his bookshelves closely. All his books, as far as he could ascertain, were correctly shelved. He looked in the drawer which held his supply of paper and ink; again, everything seemed to be in order. Then, as he closed the drawer, his eye fell on a small object on the carpet – a button.

Von Igelfeld stooped down and picked up the button. He examined it closely: it was brown, small, and gave no indication of its provenance. But his mind was already made up: here was the proof he needed. This button was a very similar shade to the unpleasant brown suits which Unterholzer wore. This was undoubtedly an Unterholzer button, shed by Unterholzer during his clandestine tenancy of von Igelfeld's room. Von Igelfeld slipped the button into his pocket. He would produce it at coffee so that everybody could notice – and share – Unterholzer's discomfort.

When von Igelfeld arrived in the coffee room, the others were already seated around the table, listening to a story which Prinzel was telling.

'When I was a young boy,' Prinzel said, 'we played an enchanting game – Greeks and Turks. It was taught us by our own nursemaid, a Greek girl, who came to work for the family when she was sixteen. I believe that she had played the game on her native Corfu. The rules were such that the Greeks always won, and therefore we all wanted to be Greeks. It was not so much fun being a Turk, but somebody had to be one, and so we took it in turns.' He paused, thinking for a moment.

'What a charming game,' said the Librarian. 'My aunt tells me that when she was a girl they used to play with metal hoops. You would roll the hoop along the ground with a stick and run after it. Girls would tie ribbons to their stick. Boys usually didn't. If your hoop started down a slope you might have to run very fast indeed! She said that one day a small boy who lived opposite them, a boy by the name of Hans, rolled his hoop into a tramline and the hoop began to roll towards an oncoming tram. My aunt told me that . . .'

'One of Professor Freud's patients was called Hans,' interjected Prinzel. 'He was called Little Hans. He was always worried that the dray-horses would bite him. His father consulted Professor Freud about this and Professor Freud wrote a full account of the case.'

The Librarian looked aggrieved. 'I do not think it can be the same boy. I was merely recounting . . .'

'My wife reads Freud for the sheer pleasure of the prose,' said Unterholzer. 'She received some training in psychology during her studies. I myself have not read Freud, but it's perfectly possible that I shall read him in the future. I have not ruled that out.'

'This boy with his hoop,' said the Librarian. 'It was stuck in the line and was rolling directly towards the tram. I think that this must have been in Munich, although it could have been in Stuttgart, because my aunt's father, my great-uncle, removed from Munich to Stuttgart when my aunt was eight, or was it seven? Eight, I think, but don't quote me on that. I might be wrong. But the point is that when a hoop gets into a tramline, then there is only one way for it to go. That's the problem. You can imagine if you were that boy's father and you saw the hoop stuck in the tramline. Well, the father was there, as it happened, and he ran . . .'

He stopped, not because he had been interrupted, but because von Igelfeld had arrived. Immediately they all stood, Prinzel reaching forward to shake von Igelfeld's hand, followed by Unterholzer, who smiled with pleasure as he did so. Von Igelfeld watched Unterholzer; such hypocrisy, he thought, but so well concealed. Well, the button would put an end to that.

They settled down to enjoy their coffee.

'It's wonderful to have you back,' said Prinzel. 'The Institute doesn't seem to be the same place when you're away.'

No, thought von Igelfeld, it wouldn't be, would it? There would be a different person in my room. But he did not give voice to such churlish doubts, instead he remarked brightly: 'I cannot tell you how happy I am to be back in Germany. Cambridge is a fine place, but you know the problem.'

They all nodded sympathetically. 'Four months in an inferior institution must be very difficult,' said Unterholzer. 'I expect you had a battle to get anything done.'

'Yes,' said von Igelfeld. 'Everything is so irrational in that country. And the people, quite frankly, are utterly eccentric. You have to analyse their smallest pronouncements to work out what they mean. If it is bad weather they will say things like "Charming weather we're having!"'

'And yet the weather isn't charming,' said Unterholzer. 'Why then do they say that it's charming?'

'Why indeed?' agreed von Igelfeld. 'They often say the direct opposite of what they mean.'

'That's extremely strange,' said the Librarian. 'In fact, one might even describe that as pathological.'

'And then they consistently understate a position,' went on von Igelfeld. 'If they are very ill, or dying, they will say something like "I'm feeling very slightly below par." It's very odd. You may recall Captain Oates going out of his tent into the Antarctic wastes. He knew that he would never come back. So what did he say? "I may be some time." This actually meant that he would never come back.'

'Then why didn't he say that?' asked Unterholzer.

Von Igelfeld shrugged his shoulders. 'It is something which I shall never understand,' he said. 'It is quite beyond reason.'

Prinzel smiled. 'It was just as well that you understood how to deal with these people, Captain Oates and his like,' he said. 'I should have been terribly confused.'

'Thank you,' said von Igelfeld. 'But in spite of all this, I did enjoy the experience.' He paused, and they waited. This was the moment. 'And of course it was a great reassurance to know that I had my room at the Institute to come back to.'

The silence was complete. Von Igelfeld did not look at Unterholzer, but he knew that his words had found their target. He would wait a few more seconds before he continued; if he waited too long, the Librarian might start talking about hoops or whatever and he did not want the dramatic impact of his find to be diminished.

He took a deep breath. 'Speaking of rooms, I found something in my room this morning. It was very puzzling.' He put his hand into his pocket, watched by all eyes, and extracted the button, holding it up for all to see. 'This.'

'A button,' said the Librarian. 'You found a button.'

'Precisely,' said von Igelfeld. 'A button on the carpet.'

They all stared at the button.

'This button,' said Prinzel. 'Is it an important button, or just . . . just a button?'

'You would have to ask that question of the person who dropped it,' said von Igelfeld slowly, each word chosen and delivered with care, so as to have maximum effect. 'That person – whoever it might be – would be able to answer your question. I cannot.'

Von Igelfeld still did not look directly at Unterholzer. He gazed, rather, out of the windows, at the bare branches of the trees, ready for the onset of spring. Those who deceived would always be found out, he reflected. We reap what we sow, or, in this case, what we drop. That, he thought, was quite amusing, but he should not laugh now, nor should he even smile. Perhaps he could express the thought later, in confidence, to Prinzel, or he could write to Zimmermann and put it in as an aside, as a freshly minted aphorism. Zimmermann had a highly developed sense of humour and always appreciated such remarks.

Unterholzer put down his cup. 'Could you pass me the button, Herr von Igelfeld?' he said.

This tactic took von Igelfeld by surprise. Usually the accused does not ask to see the prosecution's principal exhibit, as he feels too embarrassed to handle it, fearing, perhaps, that he would not be able to conceal his familiarity with the object. But he could hardly refuse, and so he passed the button to its putative owner.

'Yes,' said Unterholzer, taking the button. 'Just as I thought. It's your own button, Herr von Igelfeld. If you look at the left sleeve of your jacket, you will see that there are only two buttons sewn on behind the cuff. On your right sleeve there are three. This button matches the others. What good fortune that it fell off in your office and not outside. It could have fallen into a tramline and rolled away.'

At this last remark, Prinzel and Unterholzer burst into laughter, although the Librarian, inexplicably, did not. Von Igelfeld, humiliated, said nothing. He did not understand what tramlines had to do with it, and it was outrageous that Unterholzer should have wriggled out of his difficulties in this way. His one consolation was that Nemesis would take note, would stalk Unterholzer, and would trip him up one of these days. It was only a matter of time.

The Librarian realised that von Igelfeld was somehow put out by the way in which the button incident had been concluded, and decided that this would be the right time to mention the Colombian request. He did not like to see von Igelfeld humiliated, particularly when it was at the hands of his colleagues. They were so rude, sometimes; always interrupting him as if they were the only ones who had any right to speak. Well, now he would speak, and they would have to listen this time.

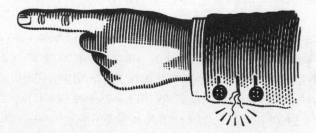

'Herr von Igelfeld,' he began, 'Putting buttons to one side – and who amongst us has not at some time shed a button, Herr Unterholzer? There is no shame in doing so, in my view. But be that as it may, there was a development while you were away. I thought I might mention it to you.'

Everybody looked at the Librarian, who for a few precious moments relished their evident anticipation. They could not interrupt him now.

'I had a request a month or so ago from a foreign embassy,' he said. 'A very particular request.'

The silence deepened. Unterholzer's lips were pursed, and von Igelfeld noticed that his hands were trembling slightly.

'Oh yes?' said von Igelfeld encouragingly. 'You alluded to something earlier on, Herr Huber. You have the details to hand now, I take it?'

The Librarian nodded. 'Yes, I do.' He paused, but only for a moment. 'The request came from the Colombian Embassy, in fact. They asked me for a copy of *Portuguese Irregular Verbs*, and I dispatched one to them immediately. And . . .' Now the tension was almost unbearable. 'And they asked me to provide a brief biographical note about yourself, *including any honours already received*, and to confirm the correct spelling of your name.'

The effect of these words was every bit as dramatic as the Librarian had anticipated. The information took a few moments to sink in, but when it had, all thoughts of buttons and such matters were replaced by a real and quite tangible sense of excitement. When all was said and done, what really mattered was the reputation of the Institute, and good news for one was good news for all. There may have been minor

344

jealousies – and these were inevitable in philology – but when there was a whiff, even the merest whiff of an honour from a foreign institution, then all such matters were swept aside. Now, in the face of this quite extraordinarily exciting news, the only thing that mattered was that they should find out, as soon as possible, what this development meant.

Prinzel was the first to suggest an explanation. 'I should imagine that it is an honorary degree from a Colombian university,' he said. 'There are some very prestigious institutions in Bogotá. The Rosario, for example, is very highly regarded in South America. It is a private university in Bogotá. I should think that is what it is. May I be the first to offer my congratulations, Herr von Igelfeld!'

Von Igelfeld raised a hand in a gesture of modesty. 'That could be quite premature, Herr Prinzel,' he protested. 'I cannot imagine that it will be an honour of any sort. I imagine that it is just for some small article in a government journal or newspaper. It will be no more than that.'

'Nonsense,' said the Librarian. 'They could get that sort of information from a press cuttings agency. They would not need a copy of the book for that.'

'Herr Huber has a very good point,' said Unterholzer. 'There is more to this than meets the eye.'

'Please!' protested von Igelfeld. 'I would not wish to tempt Providence. You are all most generous in your assumptions, but I think it would be a grave error to think any more of this. Please let us talk about other matters. The *Zeitschrift*, for example. How is work progressing on the next issue? Have we sent everything off to the printer yet?'

His suggestion that they should think no more of this mysterious approach from the Colombian Embassy was, of course, not advice that he could himself follow. Over the next week, he thought of nothing else, flicking through each delivery of post to see whether there was a letter from Colombia or something that looked as if it came from the Colombian Embassy. And as for Prinzel and Unterholzer, they had several private meetings in which they discussed the situation at length, speculating as to whether they had missed any possible interpretations of the Embassy's request. They thought they had not. They had covered every possibility, and all of them looked good.

Eight days after the Librarian's announcement, the letter arrived. It was postmarked Bogotá, and von Igelfeld stared at it for a full ten minutes before he slit it open with his letter-knife and unfolded the heavy sheet of cotton-weave paper within. It was written in Spanish, a language of which he had a near perfect command, and it began by addressing him in that rather flowery way of South American institutions. The President of the Colombian Academy of Letters presented his compliments to the most distinguished Professor Dr von Igelfeld. From time to time, it went on, the Academy recognised the contribution of a foreign scholar, to whom it extended the privilege of Distinguished Corresponding Fellowship. This award was the highest honour which they could bestow and this year, 'in anticipation and in the strongest hope of a favourable response from your distinguished self the Academy had decided to bestow this honour on von Igelfeld. There would be a ceremony in Bogotá which they hoped he would be able to attend.

He read the letter through twice, and then he stood up at his desk. He walked around the room, twice, allowing

his elation to settle. Colombia! This was no mere Belgian honour, handed out indiscriminately to virtually anybody who bothered to visit Belgium; this came from the Academy of an influential South American state. He looked at his watch. Coffee time was at least an hour away and he had to tell somebody. He would write to Zimmermann, of course, but in the meantime he could start by telling the Librarian, who had played such an important role in all this. He found him alone in the Library, a sheaf of old-fashioned catalogue cards before him. After he had broken the news, he informed the Librarian that he was the first person to know of what had happened.

'Do you mean you haven't told the others?' asked the Librarian. 'You haven't even told Professor Dr Dr Prinzel yet?'

'No,' said von Igelfeld. 'I am telling you first.'

For a moment the Librarian said nothing. He stood there, at his card catalogue, looking down at the floor. There were few moments in his daily life which achieved any salience, but this, most surely, was one. Nobody told him anything. Nobody ever wrote to him or made him party to any confidence. Even his wife had not bothered to tell him that she was running away; if the building were to go on fire, he was sure that nobody would bother to advise him to leave. And now here was Professor Dr von Igelfeld, author of *Portuguese Irregular Verbs*, telling him, and telling him first, of a private letter he had received from the Colombian Academy of Letters.

'I am so proud, Herr von Igelfeld,' he said. 'I am so . . .' He did not finish; there were no words strong enough to express his emotion.

'It is a joint triumph,' said von Igelfeld kindly. 'I would not have achieved this, Herr Huber, were it not for the constant support which I have received in my work from yourself. I am sure of that fact. I really am.'

'You are too kind, Herr von Igelfeld,' stuttered the Librarian. 'You are too kind to me.'

'It is no more than you deserve,' said von Igelfeld. A Corresponding Fellow of the Colombian Academy of Letters can always afford to be generous, and von Igelfeld was.

Not surprisingly, the arrangements for the bestowal of the honour proved to be immensely complicated. The cultural attaché was extremely helpful, but even with his help, the formalities were time-consuming. At last, after several months during which letters were exchanged on an almost weekly basis, the date of the ceremony was settled, and von Igelfeld's flight to Bogotá was booked. Señor Gabriel Marcales de Cinco Fermentaciones, the cultural attaché, proposed to travel out with von Igelfeld, as he was being recalled to Bogotá anyway, and he thought that it would be convenient to accompany him and ensure a smooth reception at the other end.

Von Igelfeld was doubtful whether this was really necessary, but was pleased with the arrangement on two accounts. Cinco Fermentaciones, it transpired, was most agreeable company, being very well informed on South American literary affairs. This alone would have made travelling together worthwhile, but there was more. When they arrived in Bogotá, there was no question of waiting at the airport for formalities; all of these were disposed of in the face of the diplomatic passport which the cultural attaché produced and with a letter which he folded and unfolded in the face of any official and which immediately seemed to open all doors. Von Igelfeld hesitated to ask what was in this letter, but Cinco Fermentaciones, seeing him looking at it with curiosity, offered an explanation at his own instance.

'I wrote it and signed it myself,' he said, with a smile. 'It says that I am to receive every assistance and consideration, and any request of mine is to be attended to with the utmost despatch. Then I stamped it with the Ambassador's stamp that he keeps on his desk and which seems to have quite magical properties. Hola! It works.'

Von Igelfeld was impressed, and wondered whether he might try the same tactic himself in future.

'Another example of South American magical realism,' said Señor Gabriel Marcales de Cinco Fermentaciones, with a laugh. 'Magical, but realistic at the same time.'

They travelled to von Igelfeld's hotel and Cinco

Fermentaciones made sure that his guest was settled in before he left him. The letter was unfolded and displayed to the manager of the hotel, who nodded deferentially and gave von Igelfeld a quick salute in response. Then Cinco Fermentaciones promised to pick up von Igelfeld for the ceremony, which would take place at noon the following day.

'In the meantime, you can recover from the trip,' he said. 'This city is at a very great altitude, and you must take things easily.'

'Perhaps I shall take a look around later this afternoon,' said von Igelfeld, looking out of the window at the interesting Spanish colonial architecture of the surrounding streets.

Cinco Fermentaciones frowned. 'No,' he said. 'I wouldn't do that. Definitely not.'

Von Igelfeld was puzzled. 'But those buildings? May one not inspect them, even just from the outside?'

Cinco Fermentaciones shook his head. 'No,' he said. 'You must not leave the hotel. It is for your own safety.'

Von Igelfeld looked at the manager, who nodded his agreement with Cinco Fermentaciones and made a quick, but eloquent, throat-slitting gesture.

'Outside is extremely dangerous,' the manager said quietly. 'The whole country is extremely dangerous.'

'Surely not in the middle of the city,' protested von Igelfeld. 'Look, there are plenty of people outside in the streets.'

'Yes,' said Cinco Fermentaciones. 'And most of them are extremely dangerous. Believe me, I know my own country. Even this letter' – and he held up his potent document – 'even this wouldn't help you out there.'

'But who are these dangerous people?' asked von Igelfeld.

'Brigands, desperadoes, *narcotraficantes*, guerrillas,' began Cinco Fermentaciones. 'Extortionists, murderers, anti-Government factions, pro-Government factions, disaffected soldiers, corrupt policemen, revolutionary students, conservative students, students in general, cocaine producers, hostile small farmers, dispossessed peasants . . . And there are others.'

'Disaffected waiters as well,' interjected the hotel manager. 'We regularly receive bomb threats from a movement of disaffected waiters who attack hotels. It is very troublesome.'

Von Igelfeld said nothing. He had heard that Colombia was a troubled society, but he had imagined that the trouble was confined to lawless areas in the south. The way that Cinco Fermentaciones and the hotel manager were talking gave a very different impression. Was anybody safe in this country? Was the Academy of Letters itself safe, or were there disaffected writers who needed to be added to Cinco Fermentaciones's intimidating list? For a moment he wondered whether he should pose this question, but he decided, on balance, to leave it unasked.

In the face of this unambiguous advice, von Igelfeld remained within the confines of the hotel, venturing out only into the walled garden, where he sat for an hour, admiring a colourful display of red and blue bougainvillea. That evening, after a light supper in the hotel dining room – a meal which he took in isolation, as there appeared to be no other guests – he slept fitfully, waking frequently through the night and anxiously checking that the door was still locked. There were strange noises in the corridor outside – a cough, the sound of footsteps, and at one point a muttered conversation, seemingly directly outside his door. In the morning, with the sun streaming through his window, the fears of the night receded, and he prepared himself with pleasurable anticipation for the day's events.

Cinco Fermentaciones called for him on time, dressed in a smart morning coat and sporting a carnation in his buttonhole.

'I hope that the night passed peacefully,' he said to von Igelfeld.

'Extremely peacefully,' replied von Igelfeld. This reply seemed to disappoint Cinco Fermentaciones, who made a gesture towards the door behind him.

'This country is unpredictable,' he said. 'One night is peaceful and then the next . . . Well, everything comes to a head.'

Von Igelfeld decided that he would not allow this pessimistic view to colour his experience of Colombia. Everyone in the hotel had been charming; the sun was shining benevolently; the air was crisp and clear. Cinco Fermentaciones could brood on political and social conflict if he wished; von Igelfeld, by contrast, was prepared to be more sanguine.

They set off for the premises of the Academy and ten minutes later arrived in front of a comfortable, colonial-style building in the old centre of Bogotá. There they were met by the President of the Academy, who came to the door to greet them. He was a distinguished-looking man in his late sixties, with a large moustache and round, unframed glasses. He led them into the Hall, where a group of about forty Members of the Academy, all formally dressed for the occasion, were seated in rows, every face turned towards the new Corresponding Fellow, every expression one of welcome.

'Most distinguished Academicians,' began the President, as he faced the membership. 'We have in our midst this morning one whose contribution to Romance philology has been exceeded by no other in the last one hundred years. When Professor von Igelfeld set aside his pen after writing the final sentence of that great work *Portuguese Irregular Verbs*, he may not have reflected on the fact that he had given the world a treasure of scholarship; a beacon to light the way of Romance philology in the years ahead. But that is what *Portuguese Irregular Verbs* has been, and that is what it has done. All of us in this room are in his debt, and it is in recognition of this, that, by virtue of my powers as President of the Academy I now confer Corresponding Fellowship on Professor Dr Moritz-Maria von Igelfeld, of the University of Heidelberg, *Magister Artium*; of the University of Göttingen; Doctor of Letters, of the Free University of Berlin; Member (third class) of the Order of Leopold of the Kingdom of Belgium.'

Von Igelfeld listened attentively as the roll of his honours and achievements was sonorously recited. It was a matter of regret, he felt, that the President felt that he had to mention the Order of Leopold; he had accepted that before he realised that it was the third class (a fact which he only discovered at the installation ceremony) and he had tended therefore not to mention it. Herr Huber, as a librarian, was not one to allow a detail to escape his attention, and so he could not be blamed if he had listed it in the biographical information he had provided. After all, Herr Huber himself had nothing, and even a third class award from the Belgians would have seemed worthwhile to him.

Von Igelfeld had little time for Belgium. In the first place, he was not at all sure that the country was even necessary, in the way in which France and Germany were obviously necessary. It would have been more convenient all round if part of Belgium had remained with France, as Napoleon had so wisely intended, and the Flemish part could then have been tacked onto the Netherlands, on linguistic grounds. And then there was the question of the Belgian monarchs, and in particular, Leopold, whose unapologetic behaviour in the Belgian Congo left a great deal to be desired. All in all, then, the Belgian order was something which was better not mentioned, although it was likely, on balance, to impress the Colombians.

The inauguration was simple; a medal was pinned to von Igelfeld's lapel, the President embraced him and kissed him on both cheeks, the large moustache tickling von Igelfeld's face, and then the Members of the Academy pressed forward to shake the hand of their new Corresponding Fellow. Thereafter, a light lunch was served, at which there was more hand-shaking, and the Members then dispersed. Von Igelfeld had prepared a lecture, just in case he should be asked to deliver one, but no opportunity presented itself. Nor did the President or any of the Members suggest that anything else should be done; the President, indeed, disappeared before von Igelfeld had the chance to thank him properly, and von Igelfeld found himself outside the Academy building, in the clear Andean sunshine, in the company only of Señor Gabriel Marcales de Cinco Fermentaciones.

'A moving ceremony,' said his host. 'I am not a Member of the Academy myself, although I feel that it would be very appropriate to be one.'

'I am sorry to hear that,' said von Igelfeld soothingly. 'But I am sure that somebody will propose you for membership one of these days.'

'I hope so,' said Cinco Fermentaciones. He paused, and looked at von Igelfeld. 'You wouldn't care to do that, would you?'

Von Igelfeld gave a start. 'I?' he said. 'I am only a Corresponding Fellow, and a new one at that. Surely it would be improper for me to propose a new member.'

'Not in the slightest,' said Cinco Fermentaciones. 'Indeed, it would be virtually impossible for them to turn me down if you proposed me. It would imply a lack of confidence in your judgment.' He reached into his pocket as he spoke and extracted a piece of paper. 'As it happens,' he went on, 'I have the proposal form with me here, already filled in. All that you would need to do is to sign it. Thank you so much for doing this.'

Von Igelfeld looked about him. Señor Gabriel Marcales de Cinco Fermentaciones had placed him in an acutely embarrassing position. If he turned him down, it would be an act of gross ingratitude to the man who, presumably, had arranged his own nomination as Corresponding Fellow. And yet, if he proposed him, the President and Members could be placed in a situation where they would be obliged to elect somebody whom, for all von Igelfeld knew, they may not have wished to elect in the first place.

'This is where you sign,' said Cinco Fermentaciones, placing the paper, and a pen, in von Igelfeld's hands.

There was really no alternative, and so von Igelfeld signed, handing the paper back to Cinco Fermentaciones with an angry glance. This glance either went unnoticed, or was ignored.

'You are very kind,' said Cinco Fermentaciones. 'Now I am in,' adding, 'at last.' He leant forward and embraced von Igelfeld, muttering further words of gratitude as he did so.

Von Igelfeld bore the embrace and the words of thanks with fortitude. He had walked right into a South American trap, and perhaps he should have realised it earlier. But the important thing was that whatever the motive of Cinco Fermentaciones had been in proposing him, the fact remained that he was now a Corresponding Fellow of the Academy of Letters of Colombia, an honour which had eluded even Zimmermann. And even if the President of the Academy were to be annoyed with him for proposing Cinco Fermentaciones, he would probably never encounter the President in the future and thus there would be few occasions for awkwardness.

Cinco Fermentaciones beamed with satisfaction. 'Now,' he said, 'we – or, rather I, have planned a few days for you in the country, as a reward, so to speak, for your having come all this way. A very well-known lady, who has perhaps the finest literary salon in all South America, has specially invited us to her villa in the hills. It will be a real treat.'

'I am most grateful,' said von Igelfeld. A few days in the country, being well looked after, would suit him very well. He was not due back in Germany for over a week, and what could be more enjoyable than sitting on a shady verandah, listening to the sounds of flocks of tropical birds, and knowing that at the end of the day a fine meal awaited one.

They returned to the hotel, where von Igelfeld packed his bags and had them carried to the car which Cinco Fermentaciones provided. Then, after a fortifying cup of coffee, they set off down a pot-holed road, through sprawling crowded suburbs, into the countryside. The warmth of the car and the drone of the engine made von Igelfeld feel drowsy, and by the time he woke up, they were driving down what appeared to be a private road, through plantations of fruit trees, towards a large, ochre-coloured house on the lower slopes of a mountain.

'The home of Señora Dolores Quinta Barranquilla,' said Cinco Fermentaciones. 'Our journey is at an end. We have arrived at the Villa of Reduced Circumstances.'

A servant met them at the large front door of the villa. He was a small man in an ill-fitting black jacket and wearing grubby white gloves. He took the suitcases from the back of the car and gestured for Cinco Fermentaciones and von Igelfeld to follow him. They went inside, into a house of high-ceilinged cool rooms, furnished with dark mahogany chairs and tables in the Spanish colonial style, with painted cupboards on which fruits, Virgins and hunting dogs contested for space with pink-faced cherubs. Then they passed through a portico into a courtyard, around the sides of which were arranged the doors which gave onto their respective bedrooms.

Left by himself in his bedroom, von Igelfeld unpacked his suitcase and noticed, with satisfaction, a spacious writing desk on which supplies of paper, along with bottles of

ink and a stick pen, had been laid. To the right of the desk was a bookcase housing several shelves of books. He glanced at the titles; there were collected essays, novels, works of philosophy, and several volumes of the poems of Pablo Neruda. He picked up one of the Neruda volumes, noting an inscription on the flyleaf: *Quinta Baranquilla, from his life-long friend, Pablo Neruda: I am not worthy of your friendship, but I have it nonetheless, and am content.* Von Igelfeld was intrigued; the salon run by Dolores Quinta Barranquilla was clearly every bit as distinguished as Cinco Fermentaciones had implied. He replaced the book and picked up the volume next to it, a Spanish translation of Hemingway. Von Igelfeld was not impressed by Hemingway, whom he had never read and whom he had no intention of reading. In his view, those who practised hunting and fighting in wars should not write books, as there was nothing of any interest to literature in those pursuits. Hemingway was a fine example of this. No German writer would have gone bull-fighting in Spain or deep-sea fishing off Cuba, and this showed in the almost total absence of these themes in German literature. He placed the Hemingway back on the shelf with distaste and looked out of the window. In the middle of the courtyard there was a small fountain, out of which water played gently. On a stone bench beside the fountain sat Cinco Fermentaciones, and at his side, engaged in earnest conversation with him, was a middle-aged woman in a red skirt and white blouse. This, von Igelfeld assumed, was Dolores Quinta Barranquilla. He moved closer to the window and stared at her, struck by her peaceful expression. It was a Madonna-like face of the sort that is not all that unusual in the Latin world; a face which Botticelli or Mantegna might have painted. He gazed at her, and as he did so, she suddenly looked up and met his eyes. Von Igelfeld froze, unable to move away from the window, but mortified to be caught in the act of spying upon his hostess. Then the spell broke, and he withdrew from the window, back into the shadows of his room.

A few minutes later, when he heard the knock on the door, he imagined that it was Dolores Quinta Barranquilla, and that she was coming to ask him to explain himself. He answered with some trepidation, but found that it was only the manservant in his ill-fitting jacket, who announced that drinks would be served in the salon at seven o'clock that evening and that the Señora would be honoured by Professor von Igelfeld's presence at that time. Von Igelfeld thanked him and the manservant nodded. If His Excellency was in need of anything, he was only to ring the bell which he would find in his room; they were short-staffed, alas! as things were not quite what they were in the past, but they would do their best.

'We are deeply honoured, Professor von Igelfeld,' said Dolores Quinta Barranquilla. 'Is that not so, Gabriel?'

'Indeed it is,' said Cinco Fermentaciones.

'To have a Fellow of the Academy of Letters in the house is always rewarding,' went on Dolores Quinta Barranquilla, 'but to have a Corresponding Fellow, why, that's a very particular distinction! Indeed, I cannot remember when last that happened.'

'Five years ago,' offered Cinco Fermentaciones.

Dolores Quinta Barranquilla thanked him for the information. 'Five long years!' she said. 'Five arid years now ended!'

Cinco Fermentaciones smiled. 'Indeed, this evening is almost like a meeting of the Academy.'

Dolores Quinta Barranquilla looked at him blankly, and he continued: 'You see, my dear Señora Dolores, we almost have two Members of the Academy in the room. I myself . . .'

Dolores Quinta Barranquilla clasped her hands together in delight. '. . . have been elected! I am thrilled, Gabriel. At last those provincial fools have begun to understand . . .'

'Not quite,' said Cinco Fermentaciones quickly. 'Please note that I said *almost* two Members. I have been nominated. Indeed, my nomination is quite recent, but I have every reason to believe that it will lead to my election to the Academy.'

Dolores Quinta Barranquilla turned to von Igelfeld and fixed him with a warm smile. 'I suspect that we might have you to thank for this,' she said. 'Our dear friend Gabriel has not been given the recognition that he deserves, I'm afraid. It comes from being out of Colombia.'

Cinco Fermentaciones held up a hand to protest. 'You are too kind, Señora Dolores. My contribution is small.'

'It was an honour to be able to propose Señor Gabriel

360

Marcales de Cinco Fermentaciones,' contributed von Igelfeld. 'His work in . . .' he paused, and there was an awkward silence as they both turned to look at him. Von Igelfeld was quite unaware of his candidate's work. Had Cinco Fermentaciones written a book? Possibly, but if he had, then he had no means of telling what it was and whether it was good or bad. Of course, one did not become a cultural attaché for nothing, and he must have done something, possibly more than enough to deserve membership of the Academy of Letters. He took a deep breath. 'His work in all respects is well known.'

Dolores Quinta Barranquilla raised an eyebrow. 'There are those who say that he bought the job,' she said, going on quickly. 'But I hasten to say that I am most certainly not one of those! There are so many people in this country who are consumed by envy. They are even some who say that I bought this villa, would you believe it?'

'And you did not?' asked von Igelfeld.

'Certainly not,' replied Dolores Quinta Barranquilla. 'Everything you see about you belonged to my paternal grandfather, Don Alfonso Quinta Baranquilla. I have bought nothing – nothing at all.'

'The Señora is modest,' said Cinco Fermentaciones unctuously. 'Even in her grandfather's day, the villa was the centre of intellectual life in Colombia. Everybody of any note came out from the capital at weekends and participated in the discussion that took place in this very room. Everybody. And then, more recently, in the days of her father, Neruda began to call when he was in this country. He would spend weeks here. He wrote many poems in this very room.'

'I am a great admirer of his work,' said von Igelfeld. 'His Spanish is very fine.'

'He is still with us, I feel,' said Dolores Quinta Barranquilla dreamily. 'Do you not feel that, Gabriel? Do you not feel Pablo's presence?'

'I do,' said Cinco Fermentaciones. 'I feel that he is with us here at the moment.'

'As are all the others,' went on Dolores Quinta Barranquilla. 'Marquez. Valderrama. Pessoa. Yes, Pessoa, dear Professor von Igelfeld. He travelled up from Brazil and spent several weeks in this house, in the time of my father. They talked and talked, he told me. My father, like you, was fluent in Portuguese. He and Pessoa sat here, in this very room, and talked the night away.'

Von Igelfeld looked about the room. He could imagine Pessoa sitting here, with his large hat on the table by the window, or on his knee perhaps; really, these were most agreeable surroundings, and the hostess, too, was utterly charming, with her mellifluous voice and her sympathetic understanding of literature. He could talk the night away, he felt, and perhaps they would.

The conversation continued in this pleasant way for an hour or so before they moved through for dinner. This was served in an adjoining room, by a middle-aged cook in an apron. Von Igelfeld had expected generous fare, but the portions were small and the wine was thin. The conversation, of course, more than made up for this, but he found himself reflecting on the name of the villa and the parsimony of the table. These thoughts distressed him: there was something inexpressibly sad about faded grandeur. There may well have been a salon in this house, and it may well have been a distinguished one, but what was left now? Only memories, it would seem.

Von Igelfeld slept soundly. It had been an exhilarating evening, and he had listened attentively to his hostess's observations on a wide range of topics. All of these observations had struck him as being both perceptive and sound, which made the evening one of rare agreement. Now, standing at his window the following morning, he looked out onto the courtyard with its small fountain, its stone bench, and its display of brilliant flowering shrubs. It was a magnificent morning and von Igelfeld decided that he would take a brief walk about the fruit groves before breakfast was served.

Donning his newly acquired Panama hat, he walked through the courtyard and made his way towards the front door. It was at this point, as he walked through one of the salons, that he noticed a number of rather ill-kempt men standing about. They looked at him suspiciously and did not respond when von Igelfeld politely said, '*Buenos Dias.*' Perhaps they were the estate workers, thought von Igelfeld, and they were simply taciturn. When he reached the font door, however, a man moved out in front of him and blocked his way.

'Who are you?' the man asked roughly.

Von Igelfeld looked at the man before him. He was wearing dark breeches, a red shirt, and was unshaven. His manner could only be described as insolent, and von Igelfeld decided that much as one did not like to complain to one's hostess, this was a case which might merit a complaint. Who was he indeed! He was the author of *Portuguese Irregular Verbs*, that's who he was, and he was minded to tell this man just that. But instead he merely said: 'I am Professor Dr Moritz-Maria von Igelfeld. That's who I am. And who are you?'

The man, who had been leaning against the jamb of the door, now straightened up and approached von Igelfeld threateningly. 'I? I?' he said, his tone unambiguously hostile. 'I am Pedro. That's who I am. Pedro, leader of Movimiento Veintitrés.'

'Movimiento Veintitrés?' said von Igelfeld, trying to sound confident, but suddenly feeling somewhat concerned. He remembered the warnings uttered by Cinco Fermentaciones in the hotel in Bogotá. Had Movimiento Veintitrés featured in the list of those who were dangerous? He could not remember, but as he looked at Pedro, standing there with his hands in the pockets of his black breeches and his eyes glinting dangerously, he thought that perhaps it had.

Von Igelfeld swallowed. 'How do you do, Señor Pedro,' he said.

Pedro did not respond to the greeting. After a while, however, he turned his head to one side and spat on the floor.

'Oh,' said von Igelfeld. 'I hope that you are in good health.'

Pedro spat again. 'We have taken over this house and this land,' said Pedro. 'You are now a captive of the people of Colombia, as are the so-called Señora Barranquilla and Señor Gabriel. You will all be subject to the revolutionary justice of Movimiento Veintitrés.'

Von Igelfeld stood stock still. 'I am a prisoner?' he stuttered. 'I?'

Pedro nodded. 'You are under arrest. But you will be

given a fair trial before you are shot. I can give you my word as to that.'

Von Igelfeld stared at Pedro. Perhaps he had misheard. Perhaps this was an elaborate practical joke; in which case it was in extremely poor taste. 'Hah!' he said, trying to smile. 'That is very amusing. Very amusing.'

'No, it isn't,' said Pedro. 'It is not amusing at all. It is very sad . . . for you, that is.'

'But I am a visitor,' said von Igelfeld. 'I have nothing to do with whatever is going on. I don't even know what you are talking about.'

'Then you'll find out soon enough,' said Pedro. 'In the meantime, you must join the others. They are in that room over there. They will explain the situation to you.'

Von Igelfeld moved over towards the door pointed out by Pedro.

'Go on,' said Pedro, taunting him. 'They are in there. You go and join them, Señor German. Your pampered friends are in there. They are expecting you.'

Von Igelfeld looked into the room. Sitting on a sofa in the middle of the room were Señora Dolores Quinta Barranquilla and Cinco Fermentaciones. As he opened the door, they looked up expectantly.

'Señor Gabriel Marcales de Cinco Fermentaciones,' said von Igelfeld. 'What is the meaning of all this, may I ask you? Will you kindly explain?'

Cinco Fermentaciones sighed. 'We have fallen into the hands of guerrillas,' he said. 'That is what's happened.'

'It's the end for us,' added Dolores Quinta Barranquilla, shaking her head miserably. 'Movimiento Veintitrés! The very worst.'

'The worst of the worst,' said Cinco Fermentaciones. 'I'm afraid that there is no hope. No hope at all.'

Von Igelfeld stood quite still. He had taken in what his friends had said, but he found it difficult to believe what he was hearing. This sort of thing – falling into the hands of guerrillas – was not something that happened to professors of philology, and yet Pedro was real enough, as was the fear that he appeared to have engendered in his hosts. Oh, if only he had been wise enough not to come! This is what happened to one when one went off in pursuit of honours; Nemesis, ever vigilant, was looking out for hubris, and he had given her a fine target indeed. Now it was too late. They would all be shot – or so Pedro seemed to assume – and that would be the end of everything. For a moment he imagined the others at coffee on the day on which the news came through. The Librarian would be tearful, Prinzel would be silenced with grief, and Unterholzer . . . Unterholzer would regret him, no doubt, but would even then be planning to move into his room on a permanent basis. Was that not exactly what had happened when he had been thought to have been lost at sea?

Von Igelfeld's thoughts were interrupted by Dolores Quinta Barranquilla. 'I am truly sorry, Professor von Igelfeld,' she said. 'This is no way for a country to treat a distinguished visitor. Shooting a visitor is the height, the absolute height, of impoliteness.'

'Certainly it is,' agreed Cinco Fermentaciones. 'This is a matter of the greatest possible regret to me too.'

Von Igelfeld thanked them for their concern. 'Perhaps they will change their minds,' he said. 'We might even be rescued.'

'No chance of that,' said Cinco Fermentaciones. 'The Army is pretty useless and, anyway, they probably have no idea that the place has been taken by these . . . these desperadoes.' He looked up as he uttered this last phrase. Pedro had appeared at the door and was looking in, relishing the discomfort of his prisoners.

'You may move around if you wish,' he said. 'You may enjoy the open air. The sky. The sound of the birds singing. Enjoy them and reflect on them while you may.' He laughed, and moved away.

'What a cruel and unpleasant man,' said von Igelfeld.

'They are all like that,' sighed Cinco Fermentaciones. 'They have no heart.'

Dolores Quinta Barranquilla seemed lost in thought. 'Not everyone can be entirely bad,' she said. 'Even the entirely bad.'

Von Igelfeld and Cinco Fermentaciones stared at her uncomprehendingly, but she seemed in no mood to explain her puzzling utterance. Rising to her feet, she announced that she would go for a walk, would do some sketching, and looked forward to seeing them both at dinner.

Von Igelfeld was aware of a great deal of coming and going among the guerrillas during the course of the day, but paid them little attention. He went for a brief walk in the late morning, but found the constant tailing presence of a young guerrilla disconcerting and he returned to the villa after ten minutes or so. It seemed that although Pedro was prepared to allow them to wander about the villa, he was determined that they should not escape.

After an afternoon of reading in his room, von Igelfeld

dressed carefully for dinner. Whatever the uncertain future held, and however truncated that future might be, he was not prepared to allow his personal standards to slip. Dressed in the smart white suit which he had brought on the trip he crossed the courtyard and made his way into the salon where Cinco Fermentaciones and Dolores Quinta Barranquilla were already sipping glasses of wine. They were not the only ones present, however: Pedro, dressed now in a black jacket, a pair of smartly pressed red trousers, and a pair of highly polished knee length boots was standing with them, glass of wine in hand, engaged in conversation.

'That's very interesting,' he said, referring to a point which Dolores Quinta Barranquilla had made just before von Igelfeld's entry into the room. 'Do you mean to say that Adolfo Bioy Casares himself was here. In this very room?'

'Absolutely,' replied Dolores Quinta Barranquilla. 'He spent many hours talking to my father. I was a young girl, of course, but I remember him well. He wrote us long letters from Buenos Aires. I used to write to him and ask him about his first novel, *Iris y Margarita.*'

'Remarkable,' said Pedro.

'I remember telling Che about that,' Dolores Quinta Barranquilla went on. 'He was very intrigued.'

Pedro gave a start. 'Che?'

'Guevara,' Dolores Quinta Barranquilla said smoothly. 'Che Guevara. He called on a number of occasions. Discreetly, of course. But my father and I always got on so well with him. I miss him terribly.'

'He was in this house?' said Pedro.

'Of course,' said Dolores Quinta Barranquilla. 'Such a nice man.'

Pedro nodded. 'He is sorely missed.'

'But now we have you!' said Dolores Quinta Barranquilla. 'Perhaps one day you'll be as well known as dear Che. Who knows.'

Pedro smiled modestly and took a sip of his wine. 'I don't think so.'

'You're too modest,' said von Igelfeld. 'You never know. I used to be unknown. Now I am a bit better known.'

'That is true,' said Cinco Fermentaciones. 'And now Professor von Igelfeld has become a Corresponding Fellow of the Academy of Letters.'

'Really?' exclaimed Pedro. 'Well, my congratulations on that.' He looked at von Igelfeld, as if with new eyes. 'You don't think . . .' he began. 'Might it be possible . . .'

Von Igelfeld did not require any more pressing. 'I would be honoured to propose you as a Member of the Academy. I should be delighted, in fact.'

'And I would support your nomination,' chipped in Cinco Fermentaciones. 'I am virtually a member myself and could expect to become a full Member provided . . . provided I survive.'

'But of course you'll survive,' laughed Pedro. 'Whatever made you think to the contrary?'

'Something you said,' muttered Cinco Fermentaciones. 'I thought that . . .'

'Oh that,' said Pedro nonchalantly. 'I'm always threatening to shoot people. Pay no attention to that.'

'You mean you never carry out your threats?' asked von Igelfeld.

Pedro looked slightly uncomfortable. 'Sometimes,' he said. 'It depends on whether it's historically necessary to shoot somebody. In your case, it is no longer historically necessary to shoot you.'

'I am pleased to hear that,' said von Igelfeld.

'Good,' said Dolores Quinta Barranquilla. 'Well, that's settled then. Let's go through for dinner. After you, Pedrissimo!'

Pedro laughed. 'That is a good name. My men would respect me more if I were called Pedrissimo. That is an excellent suggestion on your part.'

'I am always pleased to help Movimiento Veintidós,' said Dolores Quinta Barranquilla.

'Movimiento Veintitrés,' corrected Pedro, almost pedantically, thought von Igelfeld; or certainly with a greater degree of pedantry than one would expect of a guerrilla leader.

'Precisely,' said Dolores Quinta Barranquilla, taking her place at the head of the table. 'Now, Professor von Igelfeld, you sit there, and Gabriel, you sit over there. And this seat here, on my right, is reserved for you, dear Pedrissimo.'

Dolores Quinta Barranquilla had instructed the kitchen to make a special effort, and they had risen to the challenge. The depths of the cellar had been plumbed for the few remaining great wines (laid down some twenty years earlier by Don Quinta Barranquilla, who might not have imagined the company which would eventually consume them). These were served directly from the bottle, as decanting would have caused such vintages to fade. They were particularly appreciated by Pedro, who became more and more agreeable as the evening wore on. It might be impossible for him to travel to Bogotá in the near future to receive his Academy Membership, owing to the fact that the Government had put a price on his head ('Such provincial dolts,' Dolores Quinta Barranquilla had observed); however, he would be able to do so he hoped in the future, under a more equitable constitution.

They ended the evening with toasts. Pedro toasted von Igelfeld, and expressed the hope that the rest of his stay in Colombia would be a pleasant one. Dolores Quinta Barranquilla proposed a toast to Pedro, and hoped that he would shortly be received into the Academy; and Cinco Fermentaciones proposed a toast to the imminent success of Movimiento Veintidós, rapidly correcting this to Veintitrés on a glance from Dolores Quinta Barranquilla. Finally, von Igelfeld gave a brief recital of *Auf ein altes Bild* by Mörike, which Pedro asked him to write down and translate into Spanish when he had the time to do so.

Replete after the excellent meal, they all retired to bed and slept soundly until the next morning, when, to von Igelfeld's alarm, they were awakened by the sound of gunfire. Von Igelfeld tumbled out of bed, donned his dressing gown, and peered out of the window. A group of thirty or forty of Pedro's men were marshalled in the courtyard, breaking open a crate of weapons and handing them round. Dolores Quinta Barranquilla was there too, helping to pass guns to the guerrillas. Von Igelfeld gasped. They had got on extremely well with Pedro the previous evening, and both sides had obviously reassessed their view of one another, but he had not imagined that it would lead to their all effectively joining Pedro in his struggle. And yet there was Dolores Quinta Barranquilla, rolling up her sleeves and organising the guerrillas, and was that not Cinco Fermentaciones himself perched on the roof, rifle at the ready?

Von Igelfeld dressed and waited in his room. A few minutes later, there was a knock on his door and he opened it to find Dolores Quinta Barranquilla standing there, a rifle in her right hand and another in her left.

'Here's yours,' she said, handing him the rifle. 'The ammunition is over there.'

Von Igelfeld could not conceal his astonishment. 'I don't want this,' he said, thrusting the rifle back at her.

Dolores Quinta Barranquilla looked over her shoulder. 'You have to take it,' she whispered. 'If you don't, he'll shoot you. And if he doesn't shoot you, then the Army will shoot you if they take this place from the guerrillas. The local Army commander has a terrible reputation for not taking prisoners. So you effectively have no choice.' She pushed the rifle back into von Igelfeld's hands and gestured for him to follow her.

'I'll find a position where you won't be in danger,' she said. 'You can go to my study window. It's very small and it gives a good view of the driveway. If the Army comes up the driveway, you'll have plenty of time to pick them off without being too exposed yourself. It's the best place to defend the villa without too much personal risk.'

Mutely, von Igelfeld followed her to his allotted position and crouched down beside her window.

'You see,' said Dolores Quinta Barranquilla. 'That gives you a clear field of fire. Have you ever fired a rifle before?'

'Certainly not,' said von Igelfeld. 'The very idea.'

'Oh dear,' said Dolores Quinta Barranquilla. 'Well, you just look down those sights there and try to line them up against an Army target. Then you pull that thing there – that's a trigger. That's the way it works.'

Von Igelfeld nodded miserably. The pleasure at last night's reprieve was now completely destroyed. He couldn't possibly fire at the Army if they came down the driveway, but then what should he do? There was always the possibility of surrender, once the Army approached the house. Perhaps he could tie a piece of white cloth to the end of his rifle and stick that out of the window, but then that would hardly be effective if Pedro's men continued to fire from their positions. It was all very vexing.

Dolores Quinta Barranquilla left him in her study and went off to busy herself with passing ammunition to the guerrillas in their various positions about the house. Von Igelfeld drew a chair up to the window and sat down. He looked out down the driveway, along the line of trees that formed an avenue approaching the villa, to the countryside beyond. It all looked so peaceful, and yet even as he contemplated the scene there would be soldiers scuttling about in the undergrowth, edging their way into firing positions, ready to storm the villa. The sound of firing which he had heard earlier on had now died away, and there was a strange, almost preternatural quiet, as if Nature itself were holding her breath.

Von Igelfeld thought about his life and what he had done with it. He had done his best, he reflected, even if there was much that he still wished to accomplish. If the day turned out in the way in which he thought it might, then at least he had left something behind him. He had left *Portuguese Irregular Verbs*, all twelve hundred pages of it, and that was an achievement. It was certainly more than Unterholzer had done . . . but, no, he checked himself. That was not an appropriate line of thought to pursue. He should not leave this world with uncharitable thoughts in his mind; rather, he should spend his last few hours – or even minutes – thinking thoughts which were worthy of the author of *Portuguese Irregular Verbs*. These were . . . Now that he tried to identify them, no worthy thoughts came.

A shot rang out, and von Igelfeld grabbed his rifle, which had been resting against Dolores Quinta Barranquilla's desk. He looked out of the window. There was a small cloud of smoke over the orchard, and then, quite loud enough to rattle the glass in the study windows, there came the sound of an explosion. A man shouted – something unintelligible – and then the quiet returned.

Very slowly, von Igelfeld edged up the sash window and began to stick the end of the rifle outside. He paused. This brave gesture had produced no result. He was still there, alive, and nothing outside seemed to stir. This is war, he thought; this is the confusion of the battlefield. It is all so peaceful.

He looked down the avenue of trees. Was that a movement? He strained his eyes to see, trying to decide whether a shape underneath an orange tree was a person, a sack, or a mound of earth. He pointed the gun at it and looked down the sights. There was a V and a small protuberance of metal at the end of the barrel. Dolores Quinta Barranquilla had told him how to fire the weapon, but now that he was faced with the need to do so, he could not remember exactly what it was that he was meant to do. His finger reached for the trigger, fumbled slightly with the guard that surrounded it, and then found its position.

Von Igelfeld pulled the trigger. There was a loud report, which made him reel backwards, away from the window, and from the outside there came a shout. He closed his eyes, and then opened them again, his heart thudding within his chest. He had apparently fired the rifle and something had happened outside. Had he shot somebody? The thought appalled him. He had not the slightest desire to harm anybody, even the Colombian Army. It was a terrible thing to do; to come to a country to receive the Corresponding Fellowship of its Academy of Letters and then to open fire on the Army. Mind you, he reflected, he had not asked to come to the Villa of Reduced Circumstances; he had not asked to be kidnapped by guerrillas; and he had certainly not asked to be placed at this window with this rifle in his hands.

There was more shouting outside, and this was greeted by shouts from the villa itself. After a moment, there was silence, and then another shout. And then, to von Igelfeld's astonishment, a man emerged from behind a tree, a mere two hundred yards from the villa, and put his hands up. He turned round and shouted something, and suddenly a whole crowd appeared from the orchard and the surrounding trees, all of them shouting, lighting cigarettes, and, in some cases, throwing weapons to the ground. The man who had come out first continued to shout at them and was now approaching the villa. As he did so, Pedro came out of the front door and walked briskly across to meet him. The two shook hands, and then Pedro slapped the other man on the back and they began to walk back towards the front of the house. As he neared the door, Pedro turned in the direction of von Igelfeld's window and gave him a cheerful wave, accompanied by an encouraging gesture of some sort.

* * *

'Comrades!' shouted Pedro to the large group of guerrillas who had gathered in the courtyard, drinking red wine from paper cups. 'We have secured a great victory. The Provincial Army Headquarters this morning surrendered the entire province to our control. You saw it happen. You saw the Colonel here get up and surrender. Wise man! Now he is with us, fighting alongside us, and brings all his armoured cars and helicopters with him.'

These words were greeted with a loud cheering, and several paper cups were tossed into the air in celebration. Pedro, standing on a chair, smiled at his men.

'And there is one man who brought this about,' he declaimed. 'There is one man who – myself excepted, of course – deserves more credit than anybody else for this great victory. This is the man who fired the shot that tipped the balance and brought the Army to its senses. That man, comrades in arms, is standing right over there in the shadows. That man is Professor el Coronel von Igelfeld!'

For a moment von Igelfeld was too stunned to do or say anything. But he did not need to, as the guerrillas had turned round and were looking at him as he stood on the

small verandah outside Dolores Quinta Barranquilla's study.

'Well,' he said at last. 'I'm not sure . . . I was sitting there and I suppose that . . .'

His words were heard by nobody, as the guerrillas, now joined by another fifty or sixty men in the uniform of the Colombian Army, began to roar their approval.

'*Viva!*' they shouted. '*Viva el Coronel von Igelfeld*! *Viva!*'

Von Igelfeld blushed. This was most extraordinary behaviour on their part, but then they were Colombians, after all, and South Americans had a tendency to be excitable. As the cries of *Viva*! echoed about the courtyard, he raised a hand hesitantly and waved at the men. This brought further cheers and cries.

'*Viva Pedrissimo*!' shouted von Igelfeld at last. '*Viva el Movimiento*! *Viva el pueblo Colombiano*!'

These were very appropriate sentiments, and the words were well chosen. The guerrillas, who had now consumed more wine, were encouraged to shout out further complimentary remarks, and von Igelfeld waved again, more confidently this time. Then he returned to the study, the cries of *Viva*! ringing in his ears. He had noticed a very interesting book on Dolores Quinta Barranquilla's shelves, and he intended to read it while Pedro and his new-found friends got on with the business of the revolution. Really, it was all very tedious and he had had quite enough of military action. It had been very satisfactory being applauded by the guerrillas in that way, but the satisfaction was a hollow one, he thought, and was certainly much less rewarding than being elected a Corresponding Fellow of the Academy.

Von Igelfeld sat in the study until lunchtime, reading the book he had discovered. There was a great deal of

bustle about the villa, and several armoured cars and trucks arrived outside during the course of the morning. He thought of complaining to Pedro about the noise, as it was very difficult to read while all this was going on, but he eventually decided that he was a guest at this particular revolution and it would be rude to complain about the noise which his hosts were making. He would not have hesitated to do so in comparable circumstances in Germany, but in Colombia one had to make allowances.

Shortly before lunch was served, a helicopter arrived. Von Igelfeld watched it in annoyance from his window. Was it an Italian helicopter, he wondered, made in Count Augusta's helicopter factory near Bologna? He would ask at lunch, not that he expected to find anybody who knew anything about it, but he could ask. Several men in uniform stepped out of the helicopter and there were further cries of *Viva*! and even more bustle. Von Igelfeld returned to his book.

He was called to lunch by Dolores Quinta Barranquilla. He had not seen much of her during the morning, and she now appeared in a fresh outfit, a fetching red bandana tied about her neck and secured with a large emerald pin.

'I do hope that you're not too bored,' she said airily. 'Pedro and I have been very busy indeed. That was a general arriving in that helicopter. He says that the capital is falling – useless provincials – and that the Government is on the point of capitulation to the Movimiento. It's all happened before, of course, and it doesn't make much difference in the long run.'

'But I thought you said they were ruthless guerrillas,' said von Igelfeld, inserting a bookmark in the book. 'You implied that they were worse than anybody else. I heard you. You said that. You did.'

Dolores Quinta Barranquilla shrugged. 'Circumstances change. Look at Pedro himself. He's really rather well educated. He knows how to behave. I see no reason why he shouldn't be in the Government. Nobody can run this country, so it may as well be Pedro and his friends who don't run it.'

Von Igelfeld thought about this for a moment. 'I was wondering about leaving, Señora Dolores Quinta Barranquilla,' he said. 'I must say that I've enjoyed being at the villa, but I do have to return home, you know.'

'But of course,' said Dolores Quinta Barranquilla. 'There will be no problem over that. Of course we shall miss you, dear Professor von Igelfeld. I'll speak to Pedro. Perhaps you can go back to Bogotá in the helicopter, once the city has finally fallen. I don't expect you'll have to wait all that long.'

'That would be very satisfactory,' said von Igelfeld. 'I think I have had enough history for one day.'

'I shall talk to dear Pedro about it,' said Dolores Quinta Barranquilla. 'He's very reasonable, you know. All he wants to do is to help. There *are* men like that, you know. Not many, of course. But they do exist.'

The kitchen, which had excelled itself the previous night, again rose to the occasion. Further dusty bottles of wine were located in the cellar, and the cook, who was the elder brother of the manservant, retrieved his finest ingredients from the larder, including porcini mushrooms that had been preserved since the days of Dolores Quinta Barranquilla's father and were approaching their peak of flavour, pickled beans, and dried fish from Cartagena. Von Igelfeld was hungry from the morning's exertions, and thoroughly agreed with the observation made by Cinco Fermentaciones that battle sharpened the appetite. He made a mental note to mention this in a letter to Zimmermann, who would not be in a position to contradict the proposition and would undoubtedly be very impressed. Indeed there were few people in von Igelfeld's circle who would be able to make such a comment, a thought which gave von Igelfeld some satisfaction.

There were two extra guests at the lunch table. Von Igelfeld sat next to the Colonel who had surrendered, a charming man, he thought, who had a strong interest in the history of the Jesuits in South America. Then, on the other side of the table, was the General who had arrived by helicopter. He was a large man in a bottle-green uniform on which numerous military decorations had been pinned. He appeared distrustful of Pedro at first, but after the first course they became involved in a protracted political debate which seemed to bring them closer together. The General drank more wine than was necessary, thought von Igelfeld, and he hoped that he would not be at the controls of the helicopter if they were to go back to Bogotá that afternoon.

The Colonel had been informed of von Igelfeld's central role in that morning's encounter, and was full of praise for his courage and accuracy with a rifle.

'I realised immediately that the odds were unequal,' he said. 'That shot you fired went straight through the peak of my cap, just like that. I knew that if you could place a bullet so accurately, we would have little chance.'

'I am glad that we avoided bloodshed,' said von Igelfeld modestly.

'I only wish that our own professors were so brave,' remarked the Colonel. 'I cannot imagine that they would be much good. But then, I suppose you haven't met many of them.'

'Oh, I have met them,' said von Igelfeld. 'There were a number at a meeting of the Academy of Letters which I recently attended.'

The Colonel put down his knife and fork and turned towards von Igelfeld. 'The Academy? In Bogotá? You're a Member?'

'I am a Corresponding Fellow,' said von Igelfeld. 'I have only been to one meeting so far.'

The Colonel looked thoughtful. 'As a Corresponding Fellow,' he began, 'would you be entitled to propose new members, I wonder? Would you be entitled, do you think?'

Von Igelfeld looked down at his plate. He was becoming used to South American ways and perhaps there was no point in protesting. If this was the way in which the country worked, then he should perhaps accept it. No one person can change the *mores* of an entire nation.

'I should be pleased to propose you, Colonel,' he said. 'I am sure that your scholarship merits it.'

'Oh, thank you! Thank you!' enthused the Colonel. 'The Academy! Thank you so much.'

'Not at all,' said von Igelfeld. 'We can pick up the

proposal papers when we get back to Bogotá. Then I shall sign them immediately.'

'You're an excellent man,' said the Colonel. 'Now would you like a further glass of wine? I must say that the Señora keeps a wonderful cellar, doesn't she?'

Their conversation was interrupted by Pedro, who rose to his feet, glass in hand. One of his men had slipped into the room and had whispered a message. Pedro, having dismissed him, made a sign to the General, who nodded.

'Señora, Gentlemen,' began Pedro in formal tones. 'I have this minute heard from my intelligence officer. The Government in Bogotá is no more. The President of the Republic has decamped to Miami and the instruments of Government have been placed in the hands of our Movement. The way is clear for us to return to the capital and assume our rightful place in government. I now ask you to join me in drinking to the health of the new Government!'

They all rose. 'To the Government!' said the General in a loud voice. 'To the Government and *la Patria*!'

'And to our dear Pedrissimo!' added Dolores Quinta Barranquilla. 'How fortunate that day – only yesterday, I believe – that you joined us at the Villa of Reduced Circumstances!'

'Thank you,' said Pedro, 'my dear friends. We have great works ahead of us, believe me. But we shall accomplish these with alacrity and take the country forward into a new age of prosperity and achievement. That is what I believe. That is the policy of the new Government.'

'A very fine philosophy,' whispered the Colonel to von Igelfeld. 'Exactly the same philosophy as that professed by the last Government, and the Government before it.'

'And did they achieve what they set out to achieve?' asked von Igelfeld.

'Good heavens, no,' said the Colonel. 'But then governments don't run this country. This country is run by *narcotraficantes* and the like. Governments are window-dressing in this part of the world.'

'I find that very hard to believe,' said von Igelfeld. 'Surely you could not have a country run by criminals. Surely that is impossible.'

'*Au contraire*,' said the Colonel, reaching for a tooth-pick. 'That is exactly what happens. And our friend Pedro and his cronies know it full well. Just wait and see. Just you wait and see.'

They were told at the end of lunch to prepare them-selves for departure to Bogotá. Dolores Quinta Barranquilla had decided to stay behind, in spite of being invited to go to Bogotá and join the new Government. She had a respon-sibility for the villa, she explained, but she would like to have them all out for a literary weekend – the entire Cabinet – as soon as possible. Pedro thought this a good idea and got out his diary to check dates. So with Dolores Quinta Barranquilla staying behind, Cinco Fermentaciones, von Igelfeld, Pedro, the General and the Colonel, would all fly down to Bogotá in the General's helicopter.

Von Igelfeld packed his suitcase and made his way out to the helicopter. Climbing in, he noticed, to his relief, that the General was not proposing to pilot the aircraft, but that a moustachioed pilot in dark glasses was seated at the controls. Soon they were all strapped into their seats and with a great whirring of blades the helicopter pulled itself up into the mid-afternoon air. Down below, holding onto her hat in the breeze from the rotors, Dolores Quinta Barranquilla looked up and waved. Von Igelfeld waved back. She had been a fine hostess, and a brave one too. They would meet again, he hoped, perhaps in the not-too-distant future. And it was then that the thought occurred. *You should marry her.* He smiled. Impossible. *No, it would not be.*

They hovered over the villa for a moment, as if acknowledging the cheers of the guerrillas and soldiers down below. Then, swooping off, away from the mountainside behind the villa, they set off for Bogotá and for the political destiny that awaited them. Von Igelfeld closed his eyes. Soon he would be back in Germany, back in the Institute. He would be talking to Herr Huber over coffee. He would be inspecting his room for signs of intrusion by Unterholzer. He would be passing on *Zeitschrift* articles to Prinzel for checking. South America, and its revolutions, would be many miles away, a dim memory of a life which he had glimpsed and which had embraced him so wholeheartedly in its contortions. On balance he was glad that all this had happened, though, that he had been a man of action and come through it, alive. Now there was even less reason to read Hemingway. It would all seem too tame, too unrealistic.

Von Igelfeld spent that night in Cinco Fermentaciones's house in the centre of Bogotá. It was a noisy evening, as the population was out in full strength to celebrate the new Government. Fireworks were exploded and there was singing, but von Igelfeld succeeded nonetheless in sleeping well. The following morning, over breakfast, he announced to Cinco Fermentaciones that he would need to consult a travel agent about his return flight.

'I don't think that would be wise,' said his host.

Von Igelfeld raised an eyebrow. 'And why not?'

'Because Pedro expects you to stay,' said Cinco Fermentaciones. 'He telephoned me last night, after you had gone to bed. We are both to be in the Government.'

'That is quite unacceptable,' said von Igelfeld sharply. 'I have many other things to do.'

'It won't be for all that long,' said Cinco Fermentaciones. 'These governments don't last all that long. Eight, nine months perhaps. A year at the outside.'

'I still do not want to do it,' said von Igelfeld.

Cinco Fermentaciones sighed. 'In that case, I have no future.'

'I don't see what you mean,' said von Igelfeld. 'What's it got to do with your future?'

'If you're not in, then I'm not in,' said Cinco Fermentaciones. 'And if I'm not in the Government, then my enemies will kill me. By saying that you won't join, you're signing my death warrant. I shall have to make a will.'

Von Igelfeld was alarmed. 'But, please,' he said. 'I would not wish that to happen.' He paused. Perhaps he could serve in the Government for a short time and then resign. That might save Cinco Fermentaciones from his fate. He proposed this to Cinco Fermentaciones, who agreed that it would be a good compromise.

'Give it a month or so,' said Cinco Fermentaciones. 'Then you can resign. I'll be safely entrenched by then. Even better, I shall have myself appointed Ambassador to Paris or somewhere agreeable like that.'

Von Igelfeld agreed, reluctantly, of course, and his agreement cheered Cinco Fermentaciones, who had been looking rather despondent. Then, once they had finished their breakfast, they stepped out of the house into the large black limousine which Pedro had despatched to collect them. This took them through the streets of the Old Town to the Government Palace where Pedro, now wearing a handsome bottle-green uniform, very similar to the General's but distinguished by the addition of several extra gold stripes, met them on the steps.

That morning the Cabinet was sworn in and had its first session. Von Igelfeld did not say much, but he noticed that many members seemed to defer to him on difficult points; and he nodded or shook his head, almost at random, but nonetheless with a firmness of purpose which seemed to impress his fellow Ministers. Then they adjourned for lunch, at which large quantities of the country's finest wines were served. The company at the table was congenial, and members of the Cabinet moved from chair to chair between courses, so that everybody could have the chance to talk to one another. It was after one of these changes that he found himself sitting next to Pedro.

'I can't tell you how grateful I am to you, Professor von Igelfeld,' he said. 'If it weren't for you, there might have been a terrible battle, which we might not have won.'

Von Igelfeld waved a hand in an airy fashion. 'It was really nothing,' he said. 'Just one shot.'

'One shot,' echoed Pedro. 'But one shot was enough to bring down a rotten government.'

'Well . . .'

'And because of that,' went on Pedro, 'I have decided that the right thing to do is to ask you to perform a special duty. It will not be too onerous, I hope, but it will be special.'

'I am at your service,' said von Igelfeld. Presumably this would be something to do with the Academy of Letters. Perhaps the General wanted to be proposed for membership now, or Pedro's cousin perhaps.

Pedro laid a hand on von Igelfeld's shoulder. 'I should like you – we would all like you to become President of the Republic.'

Von Igelfeld stared at him in complete astonishment. 'President?'

'Yes,' said Pedro. 'And I can see from your expression that you accept! Thank you! Thank you!'

Turning from von Igelfeld, Pedro jumped onto a chair, glass in hand. 'Fellow Ministers!' he shouted. 'Silence for a moment! I ask you now to rise to your feet and toast the new President of the Republic of Colombia, President Coronel Professor von Igelfeld! *Viva! Viva! Viva!*'

Von Igelfeld did not know what to do. He heard shouts of *Viva!* about his ears and his back was slapped by several enthusiastic Ministers. Then somebody slipped a broad red sash over his shoulder, and a band struck up somewhere in the background. He looked down at his plate. What time would it be in Germany now, he wondered? What time would it be out in the rational world?

The following two weeks were very tedious for von Igelfeld. Installed in the presidential Palace, he had been given a comfortable office and a team of adjutants and secretaries. But there was really very little to do, apart from signing decrees, which were placed, ready-drafted in front of him on his desk. Occasionally people came to see him, but he found that they did not expect him to say anything, and so he merely sat there behind his desk and struggled with boredom and irritation while they spoke their piece. Occasionally he read the decrees that were placed before him, and once or twice he had to refuse to sign and sent them back to the officials with a stern note.

One such occasion was when a large elaborate document was placed before him and a pen put in his hand. He brushed aside the anxious official for a moment and began to read the text. As he did so, he became more and more alarmed.

'What is this?' he said at last. 'This document purports to be a declaration of war with Ecuador! What is the meaning of this?'

The official laughed nervously. 'It is not important, Señor Presidente. I suggest that you sign it. It is not important.'

'A declaration of war is not important?' snorted von Igelfeld. 'Is that what you're telling me?'

'Well, it's not a *serious* declaration of war,' said the official. 'Declarations of war don't mean quite the same thing in South America as they do elsewhere. They're more of a *statement*, really.'

'So this document does not create a state of war between us and Ecuador?' asked von Igelfeld. 'Is that what you're telling me?'

'Well, not exactly,' said the official unctuously. 'Technically we shall be at war with Ecuador, on the side of Peru. You may recall that they have had a long-standing dispute over the ownership of the Amazon Basin. Nothing really serious, of course, but they do go to war with one another every so often. If we join in, we will make a few incursions into Ecuador and perhaps blow up a few bridges. Not much more than that.'

'But,' said von Igelfeld, 'why on earth should we get involved in the first place? What's the point?'

The official smiled. '*El Presidente* will be aware of the fact that our air force is a little under strength. In fact, none of our planes works. Not one. Peru has offered us four new MIG fighters – four! – if we'll join them in a war against Ecuador. It's an absolute bargain.'

Von Igelfeld pursed his lips. 'I shall not countenance this,' he said crossly. 'Take this document away.'

The official nodded. He had not been too hopeful of getting the declaration of war approved, but it had still been worth a try. But he was angry, and he felt spiteful towards von Igelfeld.

'I shall have to ask the next President,' he said. 'He will be in office soon, I imagine.'

'Oh?' said von Igelfeld. 'When?'

'Two or three weeks,' said the official. 'After the *narcotraficantes* have disposed of Your Excellency.'

Von Igelfeld looked at the official. 'Disposed of me?'

The official looked sympathetic. 'Your Excellency is a brave man,' he said quietly. 'But then perhaps nobody has told Your Excellency why you were chosen for this office by Señor Pedro. He's the one who's running the country back there – Your Excellency is merely, how shall I put it delicately? – the figurehead. Señor Pedro knows that the *narcotraficantes* will assassinate whoever is President, and that's why they put Your Excellency in this position.' He paused, studying the effect of his words on von Igelfeld. 'I thought that Your Excellency would have known.'

'Of course I knew,' said von Igelfeld sharply. 'Any fool

could work that out. Now please leave me alone. I have to telephone the German Ambassador to arrange to pay a State Visit next week.'

It was a very curious feeling arriving back in Germany as the President of Colombia. The German Ambassador had been most supportive, and had stressed to the German Foreign Ministry that the President did not wish to be greeted with excessive pomp, but nonetheless there were certain niceties to be observed and von Igelfeld was obliged to inspect a guard of honour and stand at attention for several minutes while the national anthems of the two countries were played. Then, after a brief talk with a German Minister, who seemed to be particularly interested in selling him a nuclear reactor, von Igelfeld insisted on being driven to the Institute. They had been notified, of course, and everybody was lining the steps when he arrived. They never did this when I was not a president, he thought bitterly, but that was human nature, he supposed.

Surrounded by his Colombian diplomatic officials and his aide-de-camp, von Igelfeld drank a cup of coffee in the coffee room with his old colleagues.

'My aunt will simply not believe this,' said the Librarian. 'I told her that you had become President of Colombia and she became slightly confused, I'm sorry to say. In fact, the doctor was a little bit cross with me for telling her this as he said that she should not be subjected to excessive excitement.'

'Yes, yes,' said von Igelfeld. 'That is very true.' But he sounded as if his mind was not on the Librarian's tale, and indeed it was not. He had made his decision, and now he would implement it. The moment had come.

'I wish to make a speech,' said von Igelfeld to his Colombian staff. 'Make sure that somebody writes down what I have to say.'

'Certainly, Señor Presidente,' said his private secretary. 'We shall do as you order.'

'Good,' said von Igelfeld, clearing his throat. 'Dear colleagues, dear civil servants, diplomats, colonels, military attachés et cetera et cetera. In recognition of the close ties of friendship between the Republic of Germany and the Republic of Colombia, it is my pleasure today to invest our dear German hosts with well-deserved honours of the Colombian state.'

'Professor Florianus Prinzel, I hereby confer on you the Order of the Andes, First Class. This is in recognition of your contribution to scholarship, and its first-class nature.'

Prinzel smiled, and bowed to von Igelfeld, who nodded in acknowledgment and then continued: 'And on the Librarian, Herr Huber, I have great pleasure in conferring the title of Honorary Corresponding Librarian of the Colombian Academy of Letters.'

Herr Huber was too overcome to do anything, but his gratitude was palpable, and so von Igelfeld proceeded to the third task.

'And now, on Professor Detlev Amadeus Unterholzer, in recognition of his contribution to scholarship, I now confer the Order of the Andes . . .' There was a moment of complete silence, a moment in which von Igelfeld confronted one of the greatest temptations of his moral life, far greater than any quandary which had confronted him in the heat of the Colombian revolution. It would have been easy, oh so easy, to say, *Third Class*, as the Belgians had said to him. That would have taught Unterholzer. That would have paid him back for using his room without his permission; but no, he said instead, with a flourish, *First Class*, and Unterholzer, weak with emotion, stepped forward and took his hand and shook it.

All that remained for von Igelfeld to do was to resign as President of Colombia, which he did immediately after carrying out these last generous acts of liberality. His resignation speech was short, and dignified.

'I have served Colombia to the best of my ability,' he said, 'but now the torch must be handed to another. I therefore appoint dear Señor Pedro as my successor, with all the powers and privileges of the office. May he discharge the duties in an honest and decent way, remembering that in a bad country – and, please, I am not for a moment suggesting that Colombia is a bad country – there are many ordinary people who will be counting on those in high office to remember their suffering and their aspirations. My place is here. This is where I have been called to serve. *Viva el Presidente Pedro*! *Viva la Patria*!'

And with that he sat down. There was, of course, a certain amount of confusion amongst the Colombian officials, but they soon recovered their composure and went off to lunch in a restaurant which Herr Huber was able to recommend to them. Then von Igelfeld went to his room and began to attend to his mail. There was so much

to read, and he would be busy writing letters all that afternoon and well into the following day.

He looked about him. Were there signs of Unterholzer
having been in his room? He thought that some of the
books had been moved, although he could not be sure.
He stopped himself. He remembered being at a window,
looking down an avenue of trees, and waiting for an army
to advance. He remembered Dolores Quinta Barranquilla
standing beneath the rising helicopter and waving to
them as the blades of the aircraft cut into the thin Andean
air. And he heard again the cries of *Viva*! and the
expression of sheer relief on the faces of the guerrillas
and the soldiers as they realised that nobody was going
to ask them to die after all. And he realised then that

there were more important things to worry about, and
that we must love those with whom we live and work,
and love them for all their failings, manifest and manifold though they be.